OTHER WORKS BY JOHN RECHY
PUBLISHED BY GROVE WEIDENFELD

Numbers

Rushes

The Vampires

The Sexual Outlaw: A Documentary

CITY OF NIGHT

BY
John Rechy

GROVE WEIDENFELD
New York

Published by Grove Weidenfeld
A division of Wheatland Corporation
841 Broadway
New York, NY 10003-4793

The publisher wishes to express his thanks to the following
sources for permission to quote extracts from copyrighted
songs: "Children, Go Where I Send You," special permission
through arrangement with Unicorn Music Company, New York
City; "Heartbeak Hotel," written by Mae Axton, Tommy
Durden, and Elvis Presley, copyright 1956, Tree Publishing
Company, Inc., Nashville, Tennessee; "Way Down Yonder in
New Orleans," copyright MCMXXII by Shapiro, Bernstein
and Co., Inc., 666 Fifth Avenue, New York, NY 10019, used
by permission of the publisher.

Library of Congress Cataloging-in-Publication Data
Rechy, John.
   City of Night.
   I. Title.
PS3568.E28C5   1984   813'.54   83-49451
ISBN 0-8021-3083-6 (pbk.)

Manufactured in the United States of America

Printed on acid-free paper

First Grove Press Edition 1963

First Evergreen Edition 1988

10   9   8   7   6   5   4   3   2

for My Mother
and the Memory
of My Father

"The City is of Night: perchance of Death,
But certainly of Night. . . ."

—James Thomson, *The City of Dreadful Night*

Introduction

City of Night began as a letter to a friend in Evanston, Illinois. It was written in El Paso the day following my return to my hometown in Texas after an eternity in New Orleans. That "eternity"—a few weeks—ended on Ash Wednesday, the day after Mardi Gras. The letter began:

> "Do you realize that a year ago in December I left New York and came to El Paso and went to Los Angeles and Pershing Square then went to San Diego and La Jolla in the sun and returned to Los Angeles and went to Laguna Beach to a bar on the sand and San Francisco and came back to Los Angeles and went back to the Orange Gate and returned to Los Angeles and Pershing Square and went to El Paso . . . and stopped in Phoenix one night and went back to Pershing Square and on to San Francisco again, and Monterey and the shadow of James Dean because of the movie, and Carmel where there's a house like a bird, and back to Los Angeles and on to El Paso where I was born, then Dallas with Culture and Houston with A Million Population—and on to New Orleans where the world collapsed, and back, now, to El Paso grasping for God knows what?"

The letter went on to evoke crowded memories of that Mardi Gras season, a culmination of the years I had spent traveling back and forth across the country—carrying all my belongings in an army duffel bag; moving in and out of lives, sometimes glimpsed briefly but always felt intensely. In that Carnival city of old cemeteries and tolling church bells, I slept only when fatigue demanded, carried along by "bennies" and on dissonant waves of voices, music, sad and happy laughter. The sudden quiet of Ash Wednesday, the mourning of Lent, jarred me as if a shout to which I had become accustomed had been throttled. I was awakened by *silence*, a questioning silence I had to flee.

I walked into the Delta Airlines office and told a pretty young-woman there that I *had* to return to El Paso immediately. Though I had left money with my belongings scattered about the city in the several places where I had been "living," I didn't have enough with me for the fare, and a plane would depart within an hour or so. Out of her purse, the youngwoman gave me the money I lacked, and added more, for the cab. I thanked her and asked her name so I might return the money. "Miss Wingfield," she said in a moment of poetry not included in this novel because it is too "unreal" for fiction.

I thought I had ripped up the letter I had written about that Carnival season; I knew I had not mailed it. A week later I found it, crumpled. I rewrote it, trying to shape its disorder. I titled it "Mardi Gras" and sent it out as a short story to the literary quarterly *Evergreen Review*.

From childhood, I had wanted to be a writer. My mother was Mexican, a beloved, beautiful woman with truly green eyes and flawless fair skin; my father was Scottish, a confusing, passionate, angry man with blue eyes, which, in my memories, seem always about to shed tears. I learned Spanish first and spoke only it until I entered school. At the age of eight I began writing stories, all titled "Long Ago." At about thirteen, I started a novel called *Time on Wings*—about the French Revolution, which I researched diligently. The great enlightenment that comes only in midteens led me to "deeper" subjects, and I began an autobiographical novel titled—oh, yes—*The Bitter Roots*. It was about a half-Mexican, half-Scottish boy, doubly exiled in many ways: by his "mixed" blood (especially significant in Texas), by his present poverty contrasted to his parents' memories of wealth and gentility; he was "popular" only during school hours, after which he rushed home to secret poverty.

At sixteen, my "works" included many poems, among them two "epics" about angels at war in Heaven, more than 500 pages of *Time on Wings*, about 200 pages of *The Bitter Roots*, both started in pencil, continued on a portable typewriter my father, in one of his many moods of kindness within anger, bought me. I abandoned both books and went on to finish a short, strange novel titled *Pablo!*. Set in contemporary Mexico and the jungles of the Yucatán, it was framed about the Mayan legend of doomed love between the moon and the sun, who saw each other at the dawn of time. The main character in this "realistic fantasy"—in which animals talk, witches incite grave violence—is a youngman who tells the story of a "beautiful woman who died."

On scholarship given by the newspaper I worked for as copyboy, I went to college in El Paso. After classes, I often climbed the nearby Cristo Rey Mountains, bordered by the Rio Grande, usually waterless here. I read a lot, eclectically; my favorite writers included Euripides, Faulkner, Poe, Margaret Mitchell, Lorca, Melville, Jeffers, Hawthorne, Camus, Milton, Ben Ames Williams, Dickens, Emily Brontë, Nietzsche, Dostoyevsky, Chekhov, Donne, Gide, Henry Ballamann, Giraudoux, Pope, Djuna Barnes, Tennessee Williams, Proust, Joyce, Frank Yerby, Dos Passos, Thomas Wolfe, Capote, Mailer, James Jones, Henry James, Gertrude Stein, Beckett, Farrell, Nabokov, Kathleen Winsor, Swift. I saw many, many movies.

An English teacher offered to recommend me for a scholarship to Harvard, his school. But I went into the army. I didn't tell anyone except my immediate family—and I burned most of what I had written, except for *Pablo!*. I had been gone only a few weeks when my father died and I returned to El Paso.

The rest of that time of my life in the army is as "unreal" as an attached memory, with the exception of "leave time" in Paris. I went in a private and came out a private. Released, I went to New York to enroll in Columbia University. Instead, I discovered the world of Times Square.

My life assumed this pattern: I would invade the streets and live within their world eagerly; then I would flee, get a job, walk out of it—and return to the waiting streets like a repentant lover eager to make up, with added intensity, for lost moments. At the New School for Social Research, I began another novel, unfinished, *The Witch of El Paso*, about my dear great-aunt, *Tía* Ana, who had "deer eyes" and magical powers. Soon I extended my "streetworld" across the country.

In El Paso, a letter arrived from Don Allen, one of the editors of *Evergreen Review*, in response to my story-letter, "Mardi Gras"; he admired it and indicated it was being strongly considered for publication. Was it, perhaps, a part of a novel? he asked.

I had never intended to write about the world I had found first on Times Square. "Mardi Gras" for me remained a letter. But thinking this might assure publication of the story, I answered, oh, yes, indeed, it was part of a novel and "close to half" finished.

By then, I was back in Los Angeles under the warm colorless sun over ubiquitous palmtrees. But the epiphany of questioning silence which had occurred in New Orleans made me experience the streetworld with a clarity the fierceness of the first journey had not allowed. I could "see"—face—its unique turbulence, unique beauty, and, yes, unique "ugliness."

"Mardi Gras" appeared in Issue No. 6 of the famous quarterly that was publishing Beckett, Sartre, Kerouac, Camus, Robbe-Grillet, Ionesco, Artaud. Don Allen wrote that he would be in Los Angeles on business and looked forward to seeing the finished part of my book.

Instead, I showed him part of the setting of the novel I still had no intention of writing. I took this elegantly attired slender New York editor into one of the most "dangerous" bars of the time ("Ji-Ji's" in this book). Pushers hovered outside like tattered paparazzi greeting the queens. Inside the bar, the toughest "male-hustlers" asserted tough poses among the men who sought them or the queens. Don Allen said he thought perhaps the bar was a bit too crowded. As we drove away, the police raided it.

Later, Don—he became Don—would confess that he suspected there was no book. So he encouraged me to write other short pieces, which appeared in *Evergreen Review*; a lyrical evocation of El Paso and a Technicolor portrait of Los Angeles. Then Carey McWilliams, editor of *The Nation*, asked me to write for the magazine. For *Evergreen Review* and *The Texas Quarterly*, I translated into English short works by some young Mexican authors. The writing was yanking me from the streetworld, the "streets" pulled as powerfully. To connect both—and with sudden urgency—I wrote a story about Miss Destiny—a rebellious drag-queen who longed for "a fabulous wedding"—and about others in "our" world of bars, Pershing Square, streets. The story was very "literal"; I felt that to deliberately alter a "real" detail would violate the lives in that world. I sent the story to Don. He admired it a lot, but some in the growing staff of Grove Press, publishers of *Evergreen Review*, did not, and the story was turned down. That day, when I saw the people I had written about, Chuck the Cowboy, Skipper, Darling Dolly Dane, Miss Destiny, it seemed that not only my story but their lives and mine among them had been rejected: exiled exiles.

Alone smoking grass on the roof of the building where I rented a room, I looked in the direction of Pershing Square just blocks away. Nearby church bells tolled their last for the night. Everything seemed frozen in darkness. As children, we had played a game called "statues": Someone swung us round and round, released us unexpectedly, and we had to "freeze" in the position we fell (always—and this would assume importance for me later—adjusting for effect). Now the image occurred of a treacherous entrapping angel as the "spinner" in a life-game of "statues." It was that imagery which was needed—and had been there behind the reality—to convey Miss Destiny's crushed romanticism. I rewrote "The Fabulous Wedding of Miss Destiny," imbuing it with a discovered "meaning." I had begun my "ordering" of the chaotic reality I was experiencing and witnessing.

I had been asked by one of its editors to contribute to an adventurous short-lived quarterly, *Big Table*, which had broken away from *The Chicago Review* in a dispute over censorship. Soon, Miss Destiny debuted there, among Creeley, Mailer, Burroughs.

As sections from the growing book continued to appear in *Evergreen Review*, I began getting encouraging letters from readers, agents, and other writers, including Norman Mailer and

James Baldwin. When several editors—at Dial, Random House, others—expressed interest in the book, and there were two offers of an advance, I telephoned Don; I could not conceive of this book's appearing other than through Grove Press. Not only was Barney Rosset, its president, publishing the best of the modern authors—and battling literary censorship—but *Evergreen Review* had created the interest in my writing that others were responding to. As my now-editor, Don came to Los Angeles with a contract and an advance for the book I had begun to call "Storm Heaven and Protest."

But I still didn't write it.

I plunged back into my "streetworld." Hitchhiking I met a man who would become instrumental in my finishing this book. I saw him regularly, but I kept my "literary" identity secret; I had learned early—but not entirely correctly—that being smart on the streets included pretending not to be. Not knowing that I had graduated from college and had already published sections from a novel I had a contract for—but concerned that I might be trapped in one of the many possible deadends of the streets—he offered (we were having breakfast in Malibu, the ocean was azure) to send me to school. I was touched by his unique concern, and when he drove me back to my rented room on Hope Street, I asked him to wait. I went inside and autographed a copy of "The Fabulous Wedding of Miss Destiny" and gave it to him. He looked at it, and then at me, a stranger.

Then I needed to flee the closeness increased, perhaps, by the fusion of my two "identities." Consistent with another pattern, a letter arrived from a man who had read my writing: he would be happy to have me visit him on an island near Chicago. A plane ticket followed. Painfully trying to explain to my good friend who had picked me up hitchhiking that I *had* to leave Los Angeles, I left and spent the summer on a private island. When summer was ending, I migrated to Chicago, quickly finding its own Times Square.

But I was pulled back to Los Angeles. Extending the understanding that makes him, always, deeply cherished and special in my life, my friend who had wanted to put me through school—and whose "voice" is heard in part in the character of Jeremy in this book—now offered to help me out while I went to El Paso to finish—where it had begun—the book I again longed to write.

I returned to my mother's small house and wrote every day on a rented Underwood typewriter. My mother kept the house quiet while I worked. After dinner, I would translate into Spanish and read to her (she never learned English) certain passages I considered appropriate. "You're writing a beautiful book, my son." she told me.

It was difficult to write that book. Guilt recurred as I evoked those haunting lives. Oh, *was* I betraying that anarchic world by writing about it—or even more deeply so if I kept to myself those exiled lives? I increasingly found "meaning" in structure: In "Between Two Lions," I wanted to create out of the reality of Times Square a modern jungle in which two of its powerful denizens connect momentarily, but because of their very natures inevitably wound each other. The story of Miss Destiny found fuller meaning in the childhood game of "statues." I attempted to tell the story of Lance O'Hara as a Greek tragedy, the chorus of bar-voices warning of the imminent fall of the demi-god, the almost-moviestar on the brink of aging, the whispering Furies conspiring to assure the fall. From my early fascination with mathematics, I "plotted" the chapter on Jeremy as an algebraic equation drawn on a graph, the point of intersecting lines revealing the "unknown factor"—here, the unmasking of the narrator. Memory itself, being selective, provides form; each portrait-chapter found its own "frame." (The most difficult chapter to write was Sylvia's.) My rejected Catholicism was bringing to the narrator's journey a sense of ritual—and the bright colors of garish Catholic churches are splashed in descriptions throughout this book. As I wrote, stirred memories rushed the "stilled" present, and to convey that fusion I shifted verb tenses within sentences. The irregularly capitalized words I hoped would bring a visual emphasis that italics could not.

Before writing, I often listened to music: Presley, Chuck Berry, Fats Domino, Beethoven, Tchaikovsky, Richard Strauss, Stravinsky, Bartok—to absorb the dark, moody sexuality of rock, the formal structure of classical music, the "ordered" dissonance of modern composers.

Each chapter went through about twelve drafts, some passages through more than that—often, paradoxically, to create a sense of "spontaneity." The first four paragraphs that open this book were compressed from about twenty pages. The first chapter was written last, the last one came first. Although four years elapsed between the time I began this book—with the unsent letter—and the time it was finished, most of it was written during one intense year in El Paso.

Three titles had been announced with published excerpts: *Storm Heaven and Protest, Hey, World!* and *It Begins in the Wind.* The intertwining chapters that connect the portraits were called "City of Night" from the start. But I did not conceive of that as the book's title. I did consider: *Ash Wednesday, Shrove Tuesday, The Fabulous Wedding of Miss Destiny, Masquerade.* Finally, I decided: *Storm Heaven and Protest.* Then Don Allen—always a superb editor—suggested the obvious: *City of Night.*

The book was finished. That night—and this is one of the most cherished memories of my life—my mother, my oldest brother, Robert, and I were weaving about my mother's living room, bumping into each other, each with great stacks of the almost–700-page typescript, collating it—I had made three or four carbon copies.

The manuscript was mailed. I went to return the rented type-writer, but I couldn't part with it. I bought it; I still have the elegant old Underwood, now comfortably "retired."

Proofs came. As I read, I panicked. In print, it was all "dif-ferent"—wrong! About a third of the way through, I began changing a word here and there, a phrase, a sentence, a para-graph; then I started back at the beginning. By the time I had gone through the galley proofs, the book was virtually rewritten on the margins and on pasted typewritten inserts. But *now*—I knew—it was "right." I called Don, then in San Francisco, to "prepare" him. He was startled but agreed with the alterations. Despite Don's preparation, others at Grove reacted in surprise at the rewritten galleys. Knowing how expensive the resetting would be, I had offered out of my royalties to pay for it—a contractual provision. But Barney Rosset made no objection to changes, and he refused to charge me. Publication was rescheduled, and the book was reset.

I had no doubt that *City of Night* would be an enormous suc-cess. I was right. In a reversed way. I had thought it would sell modestly and that the book would be greeted with critical raves. The opposite occurred, dramatically.

Before the official publication date, my book appeared in the No. 8 slot of *Time*'s national bestseller list. Also before publi-cation, I saw my first review. Even for the dark ages of the early 1960's the title of the review in *The New York Review of Books* was vicious in its overt bigotry. What followed matched its headline. The book climbed quickly to the No. 1 spot on best-seller lists in New York, California. Nationally on all lists it reached third place. In a review featured on its cover, *The New Republic* attempted to surpass the attack of *The New York Review of Books*; it was a draw. The book went into a second, third, fourth, fifth, sixth, seventh printing and remained on the best-seller lists for almost seven months. In its assault of about eight lines, *The New Yorker* made one factual mistake and one gram-matical error.

Only the book's subject seemed to be receiving outraged at-tention; its careful structure, whether successful or not, was vir-tually ignored. I was being viewed and written about as a hustler who had somehow managed to write, rather than as a writer who was writing intimately about hustling—and many other subjects. That persisting view would affect the critical reception of every one of my following books, and still does, to this day.

I remained in El Paso. Once again, a letter came with a plane ticket, to New York. A man who had read my book and was outraged by its treatment in *The New York Review of Books* invited me to attend the American premiere of Benjamin Britten's *War Requiem* in Tanglewood. But I was waiting for an answer to a request I had made of Grove; and it arrived, a further advance on royalties so I could make the down-payment on a house for my mother.

I flew to New York to meet another major figure in my life, the man who had invited me to Tanglewood; and I spent the following months with him in a fourteen-storey apartment overlooking the Hudson River (an enormous eagle appeared on the balcony one day and peered in through a glass wall), then in Tanglewood; and then we went to Puerto Rico, the Caribbean Islands. On a beach I read in a New York gossip column that I was a guest of Mr. So-and-so on Fire Island, a place I have never visited. That was the first I would learn of several men claiming to be me, impostures made possible by the fact that I had decided not to promote this book, to retain my private life; only my publishers knew I was in New York, in Riverdale.

In late September I returned to El Paso, to another of the most cherished memories of all my life, of my mother joyfully showing me the house I had bought for her, her new furnishings. She had a dinner-reception for me, with my brothers and sisters and my special great-aunt.

Strangers appeared at my house, creating ruses to be let in. One youngwoman came to the door, claiming to be the "Barbara" of this book. In school, in the army, and on the streets, I had been what is called a loner—very much so. These incidents increased my isolation. But it seemed appropriate to me, this period of "austerity": I did not want my life to change radically while the lives of the people I had written about remained the same. In El Paso I began the transition from "youngman" to "man." I created my own gym in my mother's new home, and I began working out fiercely with weights.

Some excellent reviews began appearing, and eventually the book would be translated into about a dozen languages. Letters arrived daily—moving letters, from men, women, young ones, older ones, homosexual, heterosexual. I answered every one. When I went out, it was usually to drive into the Texas desert. I had only two or three friends. With the exception of brief trips to Los Angeles and one to New York, I remained in El Paso in relative isolation until my mother died and I left the city perhaps forever.

More than twenty years and seven books later, how do I feel about *City of Night*? It thrills me—not only for myself but for the many lives it contains, those always remembered faces and voices—that within my lifetime this book, so excoriated when it first appeared, has come to be referred to frequently as a "modern classic." And I no longer feel the guilt I battled so long, about the "real people" I thought I would "leave behind." No—they are a permanent part of my life, of that part of me—the writer— who tells of his journey as a "youngman."

John Rechy
Los Angeles, 1984

Part One

CITY OF NIGHT

LATER I WOULD THINK OF AMERICA as one vast City of Night stretching gaudily from Times Square to Hollywood Boulevard —jukebox-winking, rock-n-roll-moaning: America at night fusing its darkcities into the unmistakable shape of loneliness.

Remember Pershing Square and the apathetic palmtrees. Central Park and the frantic shadows. Movie theaters in the angry morning-hours. And wounded Chicago streets. . . . Horrormovie courtyards in the French Quarter—tawdry Mardi Gras floats with clowns tossing out glass beads, passing dumbly like life itself. . . . Remember rock-n-roll sexmusic blasting from jukeboxes leering obscenely, blinking manycolored along the streets of America strung like a cheap necklace from 42nd Street to Market Street, San Francisco. . . .

One-night sex and cigarette smoke and rooms squashed in by loneliness. . . .

And I would remember lives lived out darkly in that vast City of Night, from all-night movies to Beverly Hills mansions.

But it should begin in El Paso, that journey through the cities of night. Should begin in El Paso, in Texas. And it begins in the Wind. . . . In a Southwest windstorm with the gray clouds like steel doors locking you in the world from Heaven.

I cant remember now how long that windstorm lasted—it might have been days—but perhaps it was only hours—because it was in that timeless time of my boyhood, ages six through eight.

My dog Winnie was dying. I would bring her water and food and place them near her, stand watching intently—but she doesnt move. The saliva kept coming from the edges of her mouth. She had always been fat, and she had a crazy crooked grin—but she was usually sick: Once her eyes turned over, so that they were almost completely white and she couldnt see—just lay down, and didnt try to get up for a day.

9

Then she was well, briefly, smiling· again, wobbling lopsidedly.

Now she was lying out there dying.

At first the day was beautiful, with the sky blue as it gets only in memories of Texas childhood. Nowhere else in the world, I will think later, is there a sky as clear, as blue, as Deep as that. I will remember other skies: like inverted cups, this shade of blue or gray or black, with limits, like painted rooms. But in the Southwest, the sky was millions and millions of miles deep of blue—clear, magic, electric blue. (I would stare at it sometimes, inexplicably racked with excitement, thinking: If I get a stick miles long and stand on a mountain, I'll puncture Heaven—which I thought of then as an island somewhere in the vast sky—and then Heaven will come tumbling down to earth. . . .) Then, that day, standing watching Winnie, I see the gray clouds massing and rolling in the horizon, sweeping suddenly terrifyingly across the sky as if to battle, giant mushrooms exploding, blending into that steely blanket. *Now youre locked down here so Lonesome suddenly youre cold.* The wind sweeps up the dust, tumbleweeds claw their way across the dirt. . . .

I moved Winnie against the wall of the house, to shelter her from the needlepointed dust. The clouds have shut out the sky completely, the wind is howling violently, and it is Awesomely dark. My mother keeps calling me to come in. . . . From the porch, I look back at my dog. The water in the bowl beside her has turned into mud. . . . Inside now, I rushed to the window. And the wind is shrieking into the house—the curtains thrashing at the furniture like giant lost birds, flapping against the walls, and my two brothers and two sisters are running about the beat-up house closing the windows, removing the sticks we propped them open with. I hear my father banging on the frames with a hammer, patching the broken panes with cardboard.

Inside, the house was suddenly serene, safe from the wind; but staring out the window in cold terror, I see boxes and weeds crashing against the walls outside, almost tumbling over my sick dog. I long for something miraculous to draw across the sky to stop the wind. . . . I squeezed against the pane as close as I could get to Winnie: *If I keep looking at her, she cant possibly die!* A tumbleweed rolled over her.

I ran out. I stood over Winnie, shielding my eyes from the slashing wind, knelt over her to see if her stomach was still moving, breathing. And her eyes open looking at me. I listen to her heart (as I used to listen to my mother's heart when she was sick so often and I would think she had died, leaving me Alone—because my father for me then existed only as someone who was around somehow; taking furious shape later, fiercely).

Winnie is dead.

It seemed the windstorm lasted for days, weeks. But it must have been over, as usual, the next day, when Im standing next to my mother in the kitchen. (Strangely, I loved to sit and look at her as she fixed the food—or did the laundry: She washed our clothes outside in an aluminum tub, and I would watch her hanging up the clean sheets flapping in the wind. Later I would empty the water for her, and I stared intrigued as it made unpredictable patterns on the dirt. . . .) I said: "If Winnie dies—" (She had of course already died, but I didnt want to say it; her body was still outside, and I kept going to see if miraculously she is breathing again.) "—if she dies, I wont be sad because she'll go to Heaven and I'll see her there." My mother said: "Dogs dont go to Heaven, they havent got souls." She didnt say that brutally. There is nothing brutal about my mother: only a crushing tenderness, as powerful as the hatred I would discover later in my father. "What will happen to Winnie, then?" I asked. "Shes dead, thats all," my mother answers, "the body just disappears, becomes dirt."

I stand by the window, thinking: It isn't fair. . . .

Then my brother, the younger of the two—I am the youngest in the family—had to bury Winnie.

I was very religious then. I went to Mass regularly, to Confession. I prayed nightly. And I prayed now for my dead dog: God would make an exception. He would let her into Heaven.

I stand watching my brother dig that hole in the backyard. He put the dead dog in and covered it. I made a cross and brought flowers. Knelt. Made the sign of the cross: "Let her into Heaven. . . ."

In the days that followed—I dont know exactly how much later—we could smell the body rotting. . . . The day was a ferocious Texas summerday with the threat of rain: thunder—but no rain. The sky lit up through the cracked clouds, and lightning snapped at the world like a whip. My older brother said we hadnt buried Winnie deep enough.

So he dug up the body, and I stand by him as he shovels the dirt in our backyard (littered with papers and bottles covering the weeds which occasionally we pulled, trying several times to grow grass—but it never grew). Finally the body appeared. I turned away quickly. I had seen the decaying face of death. My mother was right. Soon Winnie will blend into the dirt. There was no soul, the body would rot, and there would be Nothing left of Winnie.

That is the incident of my early childhood that I remember most often. And that is why I say it begins in the wind. Because somewhere in that plain of childhood time must have been planted the seeds of the restlessness.

Before the death of Winnie, there are other memories of loss.

We were going to plant flowers in the front yard of the house we lived in before we moved to the house where Winnie died. I was digging a ledge along the sidewalk, and my mother was at the store getting the seeds. A man came and asked for my father, but my father isnt home. "Youre going to have to move very soon," he tells me. I had heard the house was being sold, and we couldnt buy it, but it hadnt meant much to me. I continue shoveling the dirt. After my mother came and spoke to the man, she told me to stop making the holes. Almost snatching the seeds from her—and understanding now —I began burying them frantically as if that way we will have to stay to see them grow.

And so we moved. We moved from that clean house with the white walls and into the house where Winnie will die.

I stand looking at the house in child panic. It was the other half of a duplex, the wooden porch decayed, almost on the verge of toppling down; it slanted like a slide. A dried-up vine, dead from lack of water, still clung to the base of the porch like a skeleton, and the bricks were disintegrating in places into thin streaks of orangy powder. The sun was brazenly bright; it elongates each splinter on the wood, each broken twig on the skeleton vine. . . . I rushed inside. Huge brown cockroaches scurried into the crevices. One fell from the wall, spreading its wings—almost two inches wide—as if to lunge at me—and it splashes like a miniature plane on the floor— *splut!* The paper was peeling off the walls over at least four more layers, all different graycolors. (We would put up the sixth, or begin to—and then stop, leaving the house even more patched as that layer peeled too: an unfinished jigsaw puzzle which would fascinate me at night: its ragged patterns making angryfaces, angry animalshapes—but I could quickly alter them into less angry figures by ripping off the jagged edges. . . .) Where the ceiling had leaked, there are spidery brown outlines.

I flick the cockroaches off the walls, stamping angrily on them.

The house smells of Rot. I went to the bathroom. The tub was full of dirty water, and it had stagnated. It was brown, bubbly. In wild dreadful panic, I thrust my hand into the rancid water, found the stopper, pulled it out holding my breath, and looked at my arm, which is covered with the filthy brown crud.

Winters in El Paso for me later would never again seem as bitter cold as they were then. Then I thought of El Paso as the coldest place in the world. We had an old iron stove with a round belly which heated up the whole house; and when we opened the small door to feed it more coal or wood, the glowing pieces inside created a miniature of Hell: the cinders crushed against the edges, smoking. . . . The metal flues that carried the smoke from the stove to the chimney collapsed occasionally and filled the house with soot. This happened especially during the windy days, and the wind would whoosh grimespecked down the chimney. At night my mother piled coats on us to keep us warm.

Later, I would be sent out to ask one of our neighbors for a dime—"until my father comes home from work." Being the youngest and most soulful looking in the family, then, I was the one who went. . . .

Around that time my father plunged into my life with a vengeance.

To expiate some guilt now for what I'll tell you about him later, I'll say that that strange, moody, angry man—my father—had once experienced a flashy grandeur in music. At the age of eight he had played a piano concert before the President of Mexico. Years later, still a youngman, he directed a symphony orchestra. Unaccountably, since I never really knew that man, he sank quickly lower and lower, and when I came along, when he was almost 50 years old, he found himself Trapped in the memories of that grandeur and in the reality of a series of jobs teaching music to sadly untalented children; selling pianos, sheet music—and soon even that bastard relationship to the world of music he loved was gone, and he became a caretaker for public parks. Then he worked in a hospital cleaning out trash. (*I remember him, already a defeated old man, getting up before dawn to face the unmusical reality of soiled bloody dressings.*) He would cling to stacks and stacks of symphonic music which he had played,

orchestrated—still working on them at night, drumming his
fingers on the table feverishly: stacks of music now piled in
the narrow hallway in that house, completely unwanted by anyone but himself, gathering dust which annoyed us, so that we
wanted to put them outside in the leaky aluminum garage: but
he clung to those precious dust-piling manuscripts—and to
newspaper clippings of his once-glory—clung to them like a
dream, now a nightmare. . . . And somehow I became the reluctant inheritor of his hatred for the world that had coldly
knocked him down without even glancing back.

Once, yes, there had been a warmth toward that strange
red-faced man—and there were still the sudden flashes of
tenderness which I will tell you about later: that man who
alternately claimed French, English, Scottish descent—depending on his imaginative moods—that strange man who had
traveled from Mexico to California spreading his seed—that
turbulent man, married and divorced, who then married my
Mother, a beautiful Mexican woman who loves me fiercely
and never once understood about the terror between me and
my father.

Even now in my mother's living room there is a glasscase
which has been with us as long as I can remember. It is full
of glass objects: figurines of angels, Virgins of Guadalupe,
dolls; tissuethin imitation flowers, swans; and a small glass,
reverently covered with a rotting piece of silk, tied tightly
with a fadedpink ribbon, containing some mysterious memento
of one of my father's dead children. . . . When I think of that
glasscase, I think of my Mother . . . a ghost image that will
haunt me—Always.

When I was about eight years old, my father taught me this:

He would say to me: "Give me a thousand," and I knew
this meant I should hop on his lap and then he would fondle
me—intimately—and he'd give me a penny, sometimes a
nickel. At times when his friends—old gray men—came to
our house, they would ask for "a thousand." And I would jump
on their laps too. And I would get nickel after nickel, going
around the table.

And later, a gift from my father would become a token of
a truce from the soon-to-blaze hatred between us.

I loathed Christmas.

Each year, my father put up a Nacimiento—an elaborate
Christmas scene, with houses, the wisemen on their way to the

manger, angels on angelhair clouds. (On Christmas Eve, after my mother said a rosary while we knelt before the Nacimiento, we placed the Christchild in the crib.) Weeks before Christmas my father began constructing it, and each day, when I came home from school, he would have me stand by him while he worked building the boxlike structure, the miniature houses, the artificial lake; hanging the angels from the elaborate simulated sky, replete with moon, clouds, stars. Sometimes hours passed before he would ask me to help him, but I had to remain there, not talking. Sometimes my mother would have to stand there too, sometimes my younger sister. When anything went wrong—if anything fell—he was in a rage, hurling hammers, cursing.

My father's violence erupted unpredictably over anything. In an instant he overturns the table—food and plates thrust to the floor. He would smash bottles, menacing us with the sharpfanged edges. He had an old sword which he kept hidden threateningly about the house.

And even so there were those moments of tenderness—even more brutal because they didnt last: times in which, when he got paid, he would fill the house with presents—flowers for my mother (incongruous in that patched-up house, until they withered and blended with the drabness), toys for us. Even during the poorest Christmas we went through when we were kids—and after the fearful times of putting up the Nacimiento —he would make sure we all had presents—not clothes, which we needed but didnt want, but toys, which we wanted but didnt need. And Sundays he would take us to Juarez to dinner, leaving an exorbitant tip for the suddenly attentive waiter. . . . But in the ocean of his hatred, those times of kindness were mere islands. He burned with an anger at life, which had chewed him up callously: an anger which blazed more fiercely as he sank further beneath the surface of his once almost-realized dream of musical glory.

One of the last touches on the Nacimiento was two pieces of craggy wood, which looked very heavy, like rocks (very much like the piece of petrified wood which my father kept on his desk, to warn us that once it had been the hand of a child who had struck his father, and God had turned the child's hand into stone). The pieces of rocklike wood were located on either side of the manger, like hills. On top of one, my father placed a small statue of a red-tailed, horned Devil, drinking out of a bottle.

Around that time I had a dream which still recurs (and later, in New Orleans, I will experience it awake). We would get colds often in that drafty house, and fever, and during such times I dreamt this: Those pieces of rocklike wood on the sides of the manger are descending on me, to crush me. When I brace for the smashing terrible impact, they become soft, and instead of crushing me they envelop me like melted wax. Sometimes I will dream theyre draped with something like cheesecloth, a tenebrous, thin tissue touching my face like spiderwebs, gluing itself to me although I struggle to tear it away. . . .

When my brothers and sisters all got married and left home —to Escape, I would think—I remained, and my father's anger was aimed even more savagely at me.

He sat playing solitaire for hours. He calls me over, begins to talk in a very low, deceptively friendly tone. When my mother and I fell asleep, he told me, he would set fire to the house and we would burn inside while he looked on. Then he would change that story: Instead of setting fire to the house, he will kill my mother in bed, and in the morning, when I go wake her, she'll be dead, and I'll be left alone with him.

Some nights I would change beds with my mother after he went to sleep—they didnt sleep in the same room—and I surrounded the bed with sticks, chairs. The slightest noise, and I would reach for a stick to beat him away. In the early morning, before he woke, my mother would change beds with me again.

Once—without him, because he was working on his music —we were going to take a trip to Carlsbad Caverns, in New Mexico: my mother, my sister and her husband my older brother and his wife, and I. My mother prepared food that night.

In the morning, before dawn, I woke my mother and went to my sister's house to wake her. When I returned, I saw my mother in our backyard (under the paradoxically serene star-splashed sky). "Dont go in!" she yells at me. I ran inside, and my father is standing menacingly over the table where the food we were taking is. Swiftly I reached for the food, and he lunges at me with a knife, slicing past me only inches short of my stomach. By then, my sister's husband was there holding him back. . . .

There was a wine-red ring my father wore. As a tie-pin, before being set into the gold ring-frame, it had belonged to his father, and before that to his father's father—and it was a ruby, my father told me—a ruby so precious that it was his

most treasured possession, which he clung to. As he sat
moodily staring at his music one particularly poor day, he
called me over. Quickly, he gave me the ring. The red stone in
the gold frame glowed for me more brilliantly than anything
has ever since. A few days later he took it back.

During one of those rare, rare times when there was a kind
of determined truce between us—an unspoken, smoldering
hatred—I was crossing the street with him. He was quite old
then, and he carried a cane. As we crossed, he stumbled on
the cane, fell to the street. Without waiting an instant, I run
to the opposite side, and I stand hoping for some miraculous
avenging car to plunge over him.

But it didnt come.

I went back to him, helped him up, and we walked the rest
of the way in thundering silence.

And then, when I was older, possibly 13 or 14, I was
sitting one afternoon on the porch loathing him. My hatred
for him by then had become a thing which overwhelmed me,
which obsessed me the length of the day. He stood behind me,
and he put his hand on me, softly, and said—gently: "Youre
my son, and I love you." But those longed-for words, delayed
until the waves of my hatred for him had smothered their
meaning, made me pull away from him: "I hate you!—youre
a failure—as a man, as a father!" And later those words would
ring painfully in my mind when I remembered him as a
slouched old man getting up before dawn to face the hospital
trash. . . .

Soon, I stopped going to Mass. I stopped praying. The God
that would allow this vast unhappiness was a God I would
rebel against. The seeds of that rebellion—planted that ugly
afternoon when I saw my dog's body beginning to decay, the
soul shut out by Heaven—were beginning to germinate.

When my brother was a kid and I wasnt even born (but
I'll hear the story often), he would stand moodily looking out
the window; and when, once, my grandmother asked him,
"Little boy, what are you doing by the window staring at so
hard?"—he answered, "I am occupied with life." Im convinced
that if my brother hadnt said that—or if I hadnt been told
about it—I would have said it.

I liked to sit inside the house and look out the hall-window
—beyond the cactus garden in the vacant lot next door. I
would sit by that window looking at the people that passed. I
felt miraculously separated from the world outside: separated

by the pane, the screen, through which, nevertheless—uninvolved—I could see that world.

I read many books, I saw many, many movies.

I watched other lives, only through a window.

Sundays during summer especially I would hike outside the city, along the usually waterless strait of sand called the Rio Grande, up the mountain of Cristo Rey, dominated at the top by the coarse, weed-surrounded statue of a primitive-faced Christ. I would lie on the dirt of that mountain staring at the breathtaking Texas sky.

I was usually alone. I had only one friend: a wild-eyed girl who sometimes would climb the mountain with me. We were both 17, and I felt in her the same wordless unhappiness I felt within myself. We would walk and climb for hours without speaking. For a brief time I liked her intensely—without ever telling her. Yet I was beginning to feel, too, a remoteness toward people—more and more a craving for attention which I could not reciprocate: one-sided, as if the need in me was so hungry that it couldnt share or give back in kind. Perhaps sensing this—one afternoon in a boarded-up cabin at the base of the mountain—she maneuvered, successfully, to make me. But the discovery of sex with her, releasing as it had been merely turned me strangely further within myself.

Mutually, we withdrew from each other.

And it was somewhere about that time that the narcissistic pattern of my life began.

From my father's inexplicable hatred of me and my mother's blind carnivorous love, I fled to the Mirror. I would stand before it, thinking: I have only Me! . . . I became obsessed with age. At 17, I dreaded growing old. Old age is something that must never happen to me. The image of myself in the mirror must never fade into someone I cant look at.

And even after a series of after-school jobs, my feeling of isolation from others only increased.

Then the army came, and for months I hadnt spoken to my father. (We would sit at the table eating silently, ignoring each other.) And when I left, that terrible morning, I kissed my mother. And briefly I looked at my father. His eyes were watering. Mutely he held out the ruby-ring which once, long ago, he had given me and then taken back. And I took it wordlessly. And in that instant I wanted to hold him—*because he was crying*, because he did feel something for me, because,

I was sure, he was overwhelmed at that moment by the Loss I felt too. I wanted to hold him then as I had wanted to so many, many times as a child, and if I could have spoken, I know I would have said at last: "I love you." But that sense of loss choked me—and I walked out without speaking to him. . . . Only a few weeks later, in Camp Breckenridge, Kentucky, I received a telegram that he was very sick.

And I came back to El Paso.

I felt certain that this time it would be different.

I reached our house, in the government projects we had moved into from that house with the winged cockroaches, and I got in with the key I had kept. There is no one home. I called my brother. My father was dead.

I hang up the telephone and I know that now Forever I will have no father, that he had been unfound, that as long as he had been alive there was a chance, and that we would be, Always now, strangers, and that is when I knew what Death really is—not in the physical discovery of the Nothingness which the death of my dog Winnie had brought me (in the decayed body which would turn into dirt, rejected by Heaven) but in the knowledge that *my Father* was gone, *for me*—that there was no way to reach him now—that his Death would exist only for me, who am living.

And throughout the days that followed—and will follow forever—I will discover him in my memories, and hopelessly—through the infinite miles that separate life from death—try to understand his torture: in searching out the shape of my own.

The army passed like something unreal, and I returned to my Mother and her hungry love. And left her, standing that morning by the kitchen door crying, as she always would be in my mind, and I was on my way now to Chicago, briefly— from where I would go to freedom: New York!—embarking on that journey through nightcities and nightlives—looking for I dont know what—perhaps some substitute for salvation.

MR. KING: Between Two Lions

1

34TH STREET IN New York City hurries urgently from river
to river, and on that street, east, is the soul-squashing building
where a few days later (not yet) I will add to the shadows in
that cavern of halls, rooms, community kitchens, yellow-
mirrored bathrooms *(and whatever light entered the maze from
outside squeezed in reluctantly through grimecoated windows
at the ends of each hall)*, and at one corner was the Armory
like an Errol Flynn movie, and on the next Lexington Avenue
rushes determinedly past bars and stores and checkertabled
Italian restaurants; and everywhere, gray steel buildings stab
the sky—and beyond the Armory, past technicolor Kress's,
is the goodbye Greyhound station, where I arrived from
Chicago one weepy day in September, welcomed by banner
headlines warning of a female hurricane—and I think suddenly for the first time:
My God! Im on an island!

From El Paso, I had gone to Evanston outside Chicago—a
serene green campus city—where I saw a friend I had met in
El Paso when he was in the army. Sensing the anarchic restlessness in me, he tried to persuade me not to go to New York
yet. (And through him—because I had given most of my
separation money to my mother and what I had was running
out—I got a job cleaning autumn yards.) In the afternoons,
in that quiet city—especially quiet now that summer was over
for the University students and the fall term hadnt yet begun
—my friend and I would walk through the campus, along the
lake. . . . And at the same time that I felt myself being lulled
by the serenity of the lake and the soon-to-fade green of the
scenery, the craving for a certain life drew me away from
them. Because even before I got there, New York had become
a symbol of my liberated self, and I knew that it was in a
kind of turbulence that that self must attempt to find itself.

After my separation from the army, I had come into my first contact with the alluring anarchic world which promised such turbulence. On my way to El Paso, I had stopped in Dallas for about a week, to postpone facing my mother with my decision to leave El Paso. In Dallas—*suddenly!*—with the excitement of someone exploring a new country I discovered that world. As abruptly as that, it happened; that sudden, that immediate: One day, nothing, and the next it was there . . . as if a trapdoor had Opened.

Those days in Dallas, without entering it then, I explored the surface of that seething world; and from the isolation of my early years and the equally isolated time in the army—purposely apart from everyone—I resolved to free myself swiftly, to leave my place by the Window, uninvolved with life, and hurl myself into its boiling midst. But it had to be after I had faced my mother again.

I couldnt tell why I was determinedly taking that journey. Perhaps in part it was because of the obsessive ravenous narcissism craving attention. Whatever it was, it was a compulsion for which I didnt have clear-cut reasons. I only knew that in the world I had discovered and not yet entered there was a desperation which somehow matched—and justified—my own. . . . And although, now, to you, this sounds unclear, I'll clarify it very soon. This is only by way of saying that when I reached New York, that world was waiting for me. I required no slow initiation.

2

Times Square, New York, is an electric island floating on a larger island of lonesome parks and lonesome apartment houses and knifepointed buildings stretching Up. (I will think dazedly one night: Someday this city will tear its wharf-lined fringes from the ocean and soar in desperation to the Sky. . . .)

Times Square is the magnet for all the lonesome exiles jammed into this city. . . . And this is how I found that world of Times Square.

In the incessantly running showers of the Sloane House YMCA the day I arrived in New York, the big hairy man made conversation with me; where am I from and what am I doing and am I working yet ("No? Good. I mean good that you dont have to be anywhere at a set time."), and will I come to his room and he'll buy hamburgers. Hes a merchant

marine, tanned from a recent Voyage to somefarwhere—on
his way now to Boston with I imagine a roll of money big
enough to make me greedy. Unfairly, Im almost broke—
$20.00 when I left Chicago, and one phone number what said
nervously we must have lunch sometime. And no prospect of
a job which will pay me before the money runs out.

In the tiny cubicle-room facing the courtyard across which a
lonesome youngman, also undoubtedly just arrived in the City,
played a doleful guitar by his window, we sit eating oniony
greaseburgers and ignoring the persistent sound of the running
showers. For a moment, I think it's the hurricane.

Outside, in the hallway, doors open and close. The sound
of feet walking up and down never stops. A hurried conversation outside, a door closes.

Even before this man speaks it, I know that something of
what Ive come to find in this city will soon be revealed in
this room.

"They dont call this Y the French Embassy for nothing,"
the merchant marine laughs. He has sized me up slyly: broke
and green in the big city—and he said: "You wouldnt be
broke if youd been at Mary's last night—thats a place in the
Village and everything goes." He watches me evenly for some
reaction, determining, Im sure, how far he can go how
quickly. "So I spot this cute kid there—" Hes still studying
me carefully, and when I dont say anything, he continues with
more assurance: "So I spot him and I want him—yeah, sure,
Im queer—whatya expect?" he challenges. He pauses longer
this time, watching me still calculatingly. He goes on: "And
the kid's looking for maybe a pad to flop in and breakfast—
hes not queer himself, I dont like em queer: If I did, Id go
with a woman—why fuck around with substitutes? . . . So
this kid goes with me—Im feeling Good, just off the ship,
flush—I lay 50 bucks on him."

A strange new excitement wells inside me.

He adds slyly, confident now that hes got me interested: "If
youda been there I woulda preferred you. . . ." He places his
hairy hand on my leg. "Unfortunately, Im almost broke now,"
he says, "but I got some more pay coming soon."

I stand up quickly; pause only for a moment at the door.
He calls after me:

"Hell, if you decide to make that scene later, try Times
Square—always good for a score. . . . And play it dumb—
they dig that."

I stand on 42nd Street and Broadway looking at the sign
flashing the news from the Times Tower like a scoreboard:
The World is losing. The hurricane still menaces—the sky
ashen with night rainclouds, and looking at it, which is
suddenly like a shroud, I panic, I think about this wailing concrete island, and I cant even swim: an island—and the
shrouded sky makes it a Cage.

Along this street, I see the young masculine men milling idly.
Sometimes they walk up to older men and stand talking in
soft tones—going off together, or, if not, moving to talk to
someone else.

The subway crowds surged in periodic waves, blank newyork faces, as if, for air, they had just crawled out of the little
boxes in the automat for say a quarter and two nickels.

I feel explosively excited to be on this street—at the sight
of the people and the lights, sensing the anarchy. . . . The
merchant marine's story about the youngman he had picked up
—and the implied offer of sexmoney to me—have acted on
me like a narcotic that makes me crave it.

Predictably (and the life I have come to find is unfolding
swiftly before me) the newyork cop comes by, to Welcome me,
I will think later. He was shaped appropriately like a zero.
Watching his approach, the other aimless youngmen leave
their stands along the street. Stopping before me, the cop says
to me in a bored, automatic, knowing tone: "Why dont you
go to the movies, kid? . . . I aint seen you before—so I dont
feel like running you in."

I take his advice. Two Sexy foreign movies at the Apollo
theater: I surrender to the giant cavernous mouth with decaying brown seats for teeth—gobble!—Where you'll see me often
later, in the balcony. But I kept thinking about the hurricane.
Im nervous.

Outside, the rain is coming furiously. I stand under the
marquee wondering where to go. Im reacting instinctively to
this world, studying the stances of other obviously drifting
youngmen.

Then he walks by me, hat slouched to one side, dont-give-
a-damn walk: a grayhaired middle-aged man—and says—
exactly how he came on: verbatim: "I'll give you ten, and I
dont give a damn for you." I follow the man, who has paused
a few feet from me.

"What did you say?" I asked.

He looks at me steadily: "Was I wrong?" he asks me, but
hes looking at me smiling confidently.

"I just asked what you said."

"You heard me," he says, without looking at me now, completely sure now. . . . "Well, for chrissake, you wanna come or not?"

"Yes."

"Then come on, we're getting wet."

That world has opened its door, and I walk in.

In the taxi he asked me have I eaten—and I have but I say no because I might as well make up for the greaseburgers earlier—you would too, as a citizen of the grubby world. "All right, we'll go eat," he said. This reminded him of A Funny Story. "I was in this Swank place once," he says, "and at the table next to me is this old woman, see, and shes with this great big beautiful blond boy, probably she picked him off the docks, hes uncomfortable as hell in a tie—he says to the waiter, 'I want wiver and onions.' The woman's embarrassed, see, she says in a low voice, 'Dear, why dont we have some Chateaubriand?—it's wonderful here.' 'Wiver and onions,' he insists. 'Some lobster?' she say. 'Wiver and onions! Wiver and onions!' he kept repeating. It broke me up."

At the restaurant he isnt sure theyll let me in dressed in levis. "But it aint so swank," he says, "and they know me here." Inside, I ask for the most expensive steak, still remembering the greaseburgers. . . . He peers at me, half-smiling: "No wiver and onions for you, huh?"

Later, in his apartment, he said, "Why are you so nervous, aint you been with a cocksucker before?—thats what I am, pal and I aint ashamed of it." He got into a purple robe, and I lay back and fix my eyes on a picture on the wall: rainclouds, a sad tree draped in something like moss—a skeleton vine, I think. If I squint, the tree looks like a shawled Mexican woman. I stop looking at the picture immediately. I try to stop thinking. . . . I feel him touch my body—hesitantly at first, despite his bravado; then more freely, intimately. For one wild instant I want to run out. . . . Then I heard his voice; indignant: "Why are you holding it, for chrissake?"

"So you wont bite." I wish instantly I hadnt said that.

He laughs, and Im relieved strangely. "Jesus!" he said. "You *are* green! . . . Where are you from?—the backward South somewhere?"

I purposely didnt answer, trying to forget El Paso. I listen to the rain, to the Wind lashing at the windows. And I feel a mixture of panic and excitement—one moment as if some-

how Im being liberated, at last; another moment as if Ive
entered a world for which Im not really prepared.

I move away from him.

"Christ, what now?" he says, and he sat up abruptly. He
wrapped the purple robe modestly about himself. "Hell," he
says, "you dont have to look at me." He handed me a cigarette. "Whats your name, pal?"

I told him my first name.

Hes annoyed. "My name is Ed King," he said precisely.
"K-i-n-g. What the hell are people afraid of giving their last
names for? . . ." Then almost gently: "Was that your first time
on 42nd Street?"

I told him yes.

"It aint good," I heard him say through the sound of the
rain. (It reminds me of the showers at the YMCA earlier—
except that eventually the rain would stop, but the showers
will go on Forever. . . . Crazily Im remembering a Mexican
kid song: "Let it rain, let it rain, Virgin of the Cave. . . .")
He moves away, sits on a chair a few feet from me, looking
at me. "No," he repeats, "it aint no good—whattaya wanna
hang around the streets for? Youre a nicelooking kid," he
goes on, "not what I would call Handsome," he says indifferently, "but—umm—youll do—"

He lost points.

"—but kinda Sexy, maybe, if you like your type—"

He gained the lost points, plus a few.

"—maybe a little new—but Available—" He hurled the
last word at me.

And he lost the points hopelessly.

"—so, cummon, whattaya wanna hang around the streets
for?" he went on. "Go on back Home and marry your girlfriend—you gotta girlfriend?—and raise lots of snottynosed
little bastards, and I'll tell you what: Keepem away from New
York—all those fuckin cities—are you from L.A.? No?
Keepem away from there too—you look like you could be—
I was there once, L.A.—too many creeps for me, though: like
a nuthouse. . . . That Pershing Square!—it's a loony asylum!
. . . 42nd Street, thats the lowest, though. All those lights, sure
you think theyre Pretty—Im tellinya, listena-me, they aint:
It's bullshit—got the same fuckin lights in New Orleans—are
you really from the South? New Orleans maybe—no, you
wouldnt be so nervous if you were—12 years old there and
youd know Everything: hell, I know a 12-year-old boy there,
hustles. But all this shit aint worth knowing, like I say. It

was Chicago for me," he said. He squashes the cigarette into a butt-crammed ashtray; the butts squirm like gutted white worms.

"You still wanna make the ten bucks?" he asked me abruptly.

I panic. I think hes lost interest; and I realize uncomfortably how important it is, to me, that he still want me. "Yeah, sure," I said, trying to sound casual.

"Yeah!—say yes *sir*, punk!—aint you got Respect for your elders?—hell, Im twice as old as you are, dont forget that. . . . Greedy bastards—allasame. . . . Well, then, for chrissake, I aint even got a quarter's worth from you," he says, coming back to the bed. "Now stop squirming and dont hold it—relax, if youre gonna go along with it—at least pretend you enjoy it—what the hell, I should pay and you act like you dont give a damn?—punks, allasame. I was like you once—you believe it?" he says, "and now look at me, playing the other side of this goddam game. What the hell, pal, people change, remember that, dont forget it for a moment, remember that and dont be so fuckin cocky. Now lay back, close your goddam eyes and stop staring at me like Im a goddam creep— hell, I aint ashamed of nothing. Pretend Im some milkfed chick back in—wherever the hell youre from. . . . Thats it, thats better. . . . Relax. . . . Thats it. . . ."

Later, he adjusted his robe modestly again, reached for his pants, handed me a $10.00 bill. "Thats what you came for, aint it?—so take it," he said looking at me very long.

I take the bill, crush it quickly into my pocket. Suddenly the room is explodingly hot. I want to leave quickly.

"And say thankyou, cantcha?" he adds, looking away now.

The roles we have just played for each other seem to materialize harshly now that it's over.

"And heres three more bucks for cabfare," he said. "It's always goodluck to give cabfare," he added. "You-wanna-come-back-sometime? . . . Hell, I dont care. I can pick up a different punk any night, see—and no skinny wiseass punk pulls any shit on me, pal, I know judo like the best of em. . . . But youre kinda new, I like that. Available, but kinda new. . . . Take my advice, I know what Im tellinya, go Home and get Married," he says guiltily, "that streetll swallow you so deep you wont know where you got sucked in, and it wont even throw you up like bad beer, itll digestya—" He gnashed his teeth harshly. "Hell, youll become a part of the 42nd Street army of punks—sleeping in movies, cant make it;

everybodys had you: the dayll come nobody wants you—then
what? . . . Bad scene, bad scene. . . . So you wanna see me
again or not? Tellyawot, we'll have dinner again, wanna have
dinner?—how about Friday?"

"All right—Friday," I say quickly, I want to get out. Im
sure I wont be there.

"You know where the public library is?" he asked me. "Fifth
Avenue and 42nd—here, I'll write it down so you wont forget.
I'll meet you there on the steps, between the two statues, the
two lions—Friday, seven oclock, if you want to—and dont
go fuckin around 42nd Street, you got ten bucks—dont be
greedy. Is it a date? If you dont show, hell, I'll know you took
my advice: went Home, got married—put down this fuckin
life. I'd prefer that, for your sake, pal—but if you dont take
that advice, be there, punk. . . . Shit, I might as well take
advantage of you if youre gonna stick anyway—someone else
will. . . ."

The hurricane hadnt come, and it was a cool night, like
those Texas winternights when my mother piled coats on us
to keep us warm and the heating stove glowed orange at the
stomach like a grotesque ironman. . . .

I did show up. I stand between the statues of the two lions
on the steps of the public library.

Hes disappointed that I didnt dress up. Im wearing a black
turtleneck sweater thinking cornily he'll like it. He didnt. "I
wanted to show you the nightclubs, pal," he said. "Cant go in
that circus outfit—now we'll have to go where theyll let you
in." Himself, hes carefully dressed, youll notice. He just got
a haircut, he smells of cologne. . . . "You shoulda worn a suit,"
he said. "Whats the matter?—dont you have any other clothes?"

Again in his apartment—later (after dinner and an expensive movie during which, at least five times, he asked me if
I wanted popcorn)—it was much easier than before. "Youre
learning," he said, "now youll never go back home—" and
adds cautiously, "Can I take your picture like that?" I said
no. "Suit yourself," he said aloofly, "no difference to me, Ive
had better, you believe it— and bigger." Then he asked me,
coughing between words, if I wanted to move in with him.
Not now, I said, maybe later. "Thanks, Ed," I said.

"*Ed!*" he shouted indignantly, although I had called him
that all night. "*Mister* King to you, punk!—respect me a little,
cantcha? . . . Hell, if you dont wanna move in, suit yourself
But think about it," he said, "better than the all-night movies,

and thats where youll end up—hell, you can sleep on another
bed, I'll get one for you, I wont bother you—expect sometimes, maybe—when I feel like it— I aint no wolf, pal."

We agreed to meet again, again between the two lions.

"I—uh—kinda—like you," he said hesitantly as Im leaving.
"But dont get no ideas," he added quickly, "theres dozens just
like you—all of you even get to look alike—pictures in a
fuckedup album. What the hell, I dont give a damn for you or
all the others like you, like I toldya: dime a fuckin dozen, no
fuckin good. . . . If youre there to meet me, okay. If not,
theres someone else around the corner—just as good, maybe
better. . . . But be there, punk—between the two lions."

3

In the morning of the day I was to meet him again, I moved
out of the Y—away from the never-stopping showers and the
fixed looks along the hallways; the doors opening and closing
all night.

And I moved into that building on 34th Street known as The
Casbah for its menagerie of Twilight people, and I added to
the shadows in one of those thousands of hallways in New
York City in immense apartment houses erected in the large
American cities before buildings grew tall and skinny rather
than short and fat. They squat self-consciously in the midst
of slick skyscrapers waiting sullenly to be bought, torn down,
replaced: And this one has four cagelike elevators corres-
ponding to each of the building's wings; moving up and down
grudgingly like tired old ladies constantly grumbling about
their present, unmerited station of life. . . .

As I stand in the hallway opening the door to the room I
had rented, a woman with burningly demented eyes just
seems to appear. "Im Gene de Lancey, sweetie," she said. I
live down the hall with my husband—his name's Steve. And
I want you to consider us your Best Friends." Then she disappeared, leaving behind her the odor of strong perfume and
wine. . . .

At night, on my way to meet Mr. King, I walk through
Times Square. And along that street—outside the Italian
restaurant featuring squirming spaghetti for 40¢ a plate; before
the racks of magazines with photographs of almost-naked
youngmen like an advertisement for this street; along the
moviehouses, the subway entrances; along that fourth-of-july

colored street: I saw the army of youngmen he knew so well
—like photographs in a strange exhibition: slouched invitingly,
or moving back and forth restlessly; pretending to be reading
the headlines flashing across the Tower—but oblivious, really,
of the world those headlines represent (but an integral part
of it); concerned only with the frantic needs of Inside—*Now!!*

I move on, that cold, autumnal newyork night, and this time
the sky was dotted with sad cold stars—and I walk through
Bryant Park behind the library, the fallen leaves crunching
beneath my feet like spilled popcorn—I walk past the shadows
of staring lonesome men along the ledges, suddenly astonishingly real in the instant flickering light of a struck match—
then shadows again, faceless—*and I get the feeling in the park
now that silence is a person listening to Me, watching. . . . I*
walked into the library, from 42nd Street, through the echoing
halls, toward the Fifth Avenue entrance.

Through the door, I see him standing on the steps, between
the two lions, waiting for me. He is even more neatly dressed
than before. Smoking. He looks at his watch, looks toward
either side of the street. I can almost smell the sweet cologne.
Carefully dressed and talcumed, clothes freshly pressed, his
grayish hair combed neatly. . . .

Frantically trying to look good for me!

Suddenly I turned back, away from him, down the hall and
the stairs, out the 42nd Street entrance, through the park
waiting somehow like a Trap—through the popcorn-crunch-
ing leaves, the shadows of the trees grotesque in the faint
autumn moon like in a witchstory . . . the stars hugely unconcerned.

And I take the subway back to 34th Street, to that giant
spider building I had moved into. . . .

And days later I saw him again, on Times Square, as he
crossed the street cockily with a hoodylooking black-haired
boy to get into a cab. He glanced at me, turned away quickly.

His hat still slouched defiantly to one side.

CITY OF NIGHT

FROM THE THUNDERING UNDERGROUND—THE MAZE of the New
York subways—the world pours into Times Square. Like lost
souls emerging from the purgatory of the trains (dark rattling
tunnels, smelly pornographic toilets, newsstands futilely splashing the subterranean graydepths with unreal magazine colors),
the newyork faces push into the air: spilling into 42nd Street
and Broadway—a scattered defeated army. And the world of
that street bursts like a rocket into a shattered phosphorescent
world. Giant signs—Bigger! Than! Life!—blink off and on.
And a great hungry sign groping luridly at the darkness
screams:

F * A * S * C * I * N * A * T * I * O * N

I had been in the islandcity several weeks now, and already
I had had two jobs, briefly: each time thinking now I would
put down Times Square. But like a possessive lover—or like
a powerful drug—it lured me. FASCINATION! I stopped
working. . . . And I returned, dazzled, to this street. The giant
sign winked its welcome: FASCINATION!

I surrendered to the world of Times Square, and like a
hype who needs more and more junk to keep going, I haunted
that world not only at night now but in the mornings, the
afternoons. . . .

That world of Times Square that I inhabited extends from
42nd Street to about 45th Street, from grimy Eighth Avenue to
Bryant Park—where, nightly, shadows cling to the ledges:
malehungry looks hidden by the darkness of the night; and
occasionally, shadowy figures, first speaking briefly, disappear
in pairs behind the statue with its back to the library and come
out after a few frantic moments, from opposite directions:
intimate nameless strangers joined for one gasping brief space
of time. Periodically the newyork cop comes by meanly swing-

ing his stick superiorly, sometimes flashing his light toward the bushes—and the shadows scatter from the ledges, the benches, the trees—walking away aimlessly.

But that world exists not only along the streets; it extends into the movie theaters. And the moviehouse toilets on 42nd Street and the toilets in the subways—with the pleading scrawled messages—form the boiling subterranean world of Times Square. Steps lead down from the moviehouse lobbies as if into a dungeon—and in the toilet, the purpose may be realized, and you walk up the steps—aware of the danger after the danger is over—you and he complete strangers again after the cold intimacy. You may move from the dungeon into the cavern of the moviebalconies and try to score again: swallowed instantly by that giant wolfmouth of dark at the opening of which the dreamworld of a certain movie is being projected: the actors like ghosts from an altogether Different world. . . .

By now winter was approaching in New York. Hurricanes and threats of hurricanes had stopped, and the air was clear. Daily the leaves turned browner, the orange disappeared. Along the walks in the parks, leaves fell like rejected brown stars.

As the weather had changed, from hurricane warnings to cool, I had stood along 42nd Street and Bryant Park waiting to be picked up, and with the changing season I felt a change within me too: a frantic lonesomeness that sometimes took me, paradoxically, to the height of elation, then flung me into depression. The figure of my Mother standing by the kitchen door crying, watching me leave, hovered ghostlike over me, but in the absence of that overwhelming tearing love—away from it if only physically—I felt a violent craving for something indefinable.

Throughout those weeks, on 42nd Street, the park, the moviehouses, I had learned to sift the different types that haunted those places: The queens swished by in superficial gayety—giggling males acting like teenage girls; eyeing the youngmen coquettishly: but seldom offering more than a place to stay for the night. And I could spot the scores easily —the men who paid other men sexmoney, anywhere from $5.00—usually more—but sometimes even less (for some, meals and drinks and a place to stay); the amount determined by the time of the day, the day of the week, the place of execution of the sexscene(their apartment, a rented room, a public toilet; their franticness, your franticness; their manner of dress, indicating affluence or otherwise; the competition on the street—the other youngmen stationed along the block like tattered guards for that defeated army which, Somehow, life had spewed out, Rejected.

I found that you cant always tell a score by his age or appearance: There are the young and the goodlooking ones— the ones about whom you wonder why they prefer to pay someone (who will most likely at least not indicate desiring them back) when there exists—much, much vaster than the hustling world—the world of unpaid, mutually desiring males —the easy pickups. . . . But often the scores are near-middle-aged or older men. And they are mostly uneffeminate. And so you learn to identify them by their method of approaching you (a means of identification which becomes instinctively surer and easier as you hang around longer). They will make one of the standard oriented remarks; they will offer a cigarette, a cup of coffee, a drink in a bar: anything to give them time in which to decide whether to trust you during those interludes in which there is always a suggestion of violence (although, for some, I would learn later, this is one of the proclaimed appeals—that steady hint of violence); time in which to find out if you'll fit their particular sexfantasy.

I learned that there are a variety of roles to play if you're hustling: youngmanoutofajob butlooking; dontgiveadamn-youngman drifting; perrenialhustler easytomakeout; young-manlostinthebigcity pleasehelpmesir. There was, too, the pose learned quickly from the others along the street: the stance, the jivetalk—a mixture of jazz, joint, junk sounds—the almost-disdainful, disinterested, but, at the same time, inviting look; the casual way of dress.

And I learned too that to hustle the streets you had to play it almost-illiterate.

The merchant marine at the Y had been the first to tell me that. With Mr. King I had merely acted instinctively. But I was to learn it graphically from a man I had met on Times Square. As he sat in his apartment studying me, I leafed through a novel by Colette. The man rose, visibly angered. "Do you read books?" he asked me sharply. "Yes," I answered. "Then Im sorry, I dont want you anymore," he said; "really masculine men dont read!" Hurriedly, his sexfantasy evaporated, he gave me a few bucks. Minutes later I saw him again on Times Square talking to another youngman. . . .

And so I determined that from now on I would play it dumb. And I would discover that to many of the street people a hustler became more attractive in direct relation to his seeming insensitivity—his "toughness." I would wear that mask.

By now, of course, I have met several of the shadows along Times Square.

There was Carlo, an actor, whom I met coming out of the subway head, who took me home and for a week came on strong—"helping me out": How sad that I should hang around the streets. If I move in with him, he'll give me Everything I Need. And when I was almost conned, he got a job in Hollywood, and, with apologies, split, giving me $5.00 that night— and a smiling! triumphant! goodbye! . . .

And Raub—a bastard—whose frog-shape and inclinations make me remember him as a "fraggot"—the fraggot with the enormous black-velvetdraped bed on Park Avenue: I was swiftly succeeded by, as I had very briefly succeeded, a string of others. . . . And there was Lenny from New Jersey, whom I saw twice a week, until one night he didn't show; and I learned later he'd been arrested for selling pornographic pictures.

There was, too, Im perversely glad to tell you, a cop met in an extension of the same world of 42nd Street. After midnight walking from the west to the east side, I crossed Central Park, and he was out rousting the bums sleeping in the park —the wagon parked a distance away. When he stopped me, I came on I was square: Just Now Came To The Big City. And he goes through the identification scene. Well, you havent really seen New York then," he said. "Maybe I can meet you somewhere on my day off and I'll show you around." I saw him a couple of times, but My Pride won out: To be with a cop—even for scoring—humiliated me, and that stopped.

Feeling that recurrent guilt which will come on me unexpectedly in that life, I placed an ad in the Sunday paper for a job: "YOUNGMAN desires gainful employment"—and the number of the telephone in the hallway where I lived.

"Can you come up now?" the faintly-British-accented male voice on the telephone said. It was Sunday evening. I took down an address on Sutton Place. "Take a cab," the voice said, "and I'll reimburse you when you get here."

In a fashionable apartment overlooking the East River, I face an elegant silver-haired man. At the door he had started, looked at me in surprise.

"What kind of a job are you looking for?" he asked me after offering me a drink.

"Anything that I like and that pays."

"Oh?" he said. "That must cover a lot of territory. . . . I have an opening," he said.

"What kind of work?"

"Oh, thats such a boring subject, isnt it?" he said. "Why not lets just get to know each other first." He sits very close to me. "Youre nervous," he said. "Maybe it's the suit youre wearing. You dont seem to be used to it," he said slyly. "You neednt have worn it, you know. Oh, Im terribly informal myself!" Yet he wore a cuff-linked shirt, vest, tie, coat. "Are you desperate for money?" he asked in an amused tone, as if he were reading a line out of a familiar play.

"I need it," I said.

He gave me a $10 bill. "For the cab," he winked.

"This job—" I started.

"I like you," he said, touching my arm.

"I have another appointment—with someone else," I lied, suddenly bewildered, realizing that hes obviously taken for granted that Im available.

"You know, youngman, I have to make a confession," he said, like someone exhibiting a trump card, "Ive seen you before. On Times Square. . . . When I called you, of course, I had no way of knowing it would be you. No idea in the world. But when you turned up, well, I was delighted. . . . I never speak to anyone on the streets. . . . And, incidentally, Im glad to see youve graduated out of Times Square and into the want-ads of the newspapers!" He went on with amused sureness: "Anyway, about the . . uh . . . job. Ive got . . . an opening."

"Doing what?" I asked him, trying for some strange reason to make him believe I am not the same person he has seen on Times Square—hoping very much to watch him retreat. But he didnt.

"Cawnt you guess?" he asked coquettishly. "Now dont tell me you go to Times Square just to see the pretty Fascination lights!" He made an attempt to mime the word "pretty" with a frivolous flutter of his hands. . . . "Why dont you give being in my . . . employ . . . a spin, youngman? We'll try it for, say, a week—or a few days. Youll move in of course. And if were both satisfied, well, we'll make it permanent. And if it doesnt work out," he shrugged, "I have many, many friends. . . . I can easily place you."

I feel a sharp resentment. I got up.

"If you let me 'employ' you," he persists cunningly, "you

wont have to be on the streets—or advertise in the papers."

At the door as I left, he snapped: "Oh, yes *do* keep the change for the cabfare. . . ."

The door slammed.

Outside, I quickly removed the tie I had been wearing.

I walked along the river—the sad horns from the boats mourning. Several obvious homosexuals sat on the benches under the pale lights.

"You got a light?" one asked me lonesomely. I gave it to him, and walked on.

Behind me, this islandcity glittered like an electric, magnetic animal. . . .

With that silver-haired man just now, I had realized this: It would not be in one apartment, with one person, that I would explore the world which had brought me to this city.

The streets . . . the movie theaters . . . the parks . . . the many, many different rooms: That was the world I would live in.

I walked back. The man who had asked me for a light still sat there.

PETE: A Quarter Ahead

1

THERE WAS A YOUNGMAN I HAD seen often around Times Square. Like me, he was there almost every night; and like me, too, he was, I knew, hustling. I would learn later his name is Pete. Although each of us had noticed the other—and it was obvious—we avoided pointedly more than glancing at each other whenever we met: He was very cocky, a wiseass; and, I figured, I struck him much the same way.

One night I saw him by the subway entrance on 42nd Street talking to an older man dressed in black. It was a warm night. After a series of wintry ones, the warmth returned miraculously and the street is crowded tonight, each person clutching for one last taste of a springlike night. . . . Theyre glancing at me, Pete and the older man. They talk some more, the older man nods yes, and Pete swaggers up to me. He said: "That score digs you, spote—" (He said sport like that: "spote.") "—he'll lay ten bucks on you—and itll be like cuhrazy," rolling his eyes. Pete's in his early 20s, not tall, very well built, dark; knowing eyes, sometimes moody, dreamy. Hes wearing an army fatigue cap rakishly almost over his eyes, so that he has to hold his chin up to look at you. . . . I turned and looked at the black-dressed man, and he smiled broadly at me, walked toward us. If he had worn a white collar, he would have looked like a priest. Pete says to me: "This is Al," indicating the older man, pats my shoulder—"Later, spote"—and disappears jauntily into the street, almost bouncing into the crowd.

"I havent seen you before—youre new?" the man in black was saying. He didnt wait for an answer: If he asks too many questions, he exposes himself to the possibility that he will get an entirely different answer from the one he wants to hear and it will shatter his sexdream.

I went around the corner with the black-dressed Al, down from 42nd Street—wordlessly—to a large room in an apartment house. "I dont live here," he explained as he opened the door into an almost-bare room: a bed, a table, two chairs. "I just keep this place—well—as a Convenience." He asked me

36

to take my clothes off, but, "Not the pants, theyll do," he tells me. He went to a large closet, and brought out some clothes. Theres a black leather jacket with stars like a general, eagled motorcycle cap, engineer boots with gleaming polished buckles. He left the closet door open, and I could see, hanging neatly, other similar clothes—different sizes, I knew. On the floor were at least seven pairs of engineer boots, all different sizes. "Ive reached the point," Al said. "where I can tell the exact size by just glancing at the person, on the street. . . . Here, put these on." I did, and they fitted. "Fine!" he said. "Now lets go." Im startled. "Where?" I asked him. "Outside," the man says, then noticing me hesitating suspiciously: "I just want us to take a little walk. Dont worry—I'll pay you."

That night, for about an hour, I walked with him through Times Square, from block to block in that area, into the park, silently—just walked. A couple of times I was tempted to leave, walk away with his clothes—but Im curious and I need the money. At the end of the hour we returned to the room, I removed the clothes. He didnt touch me once. He hands me $10.00. I looked at him surprised. I thought somehow I had disappointed him, and I felt grossly rejected. "Thats all," he said; he smiles. "You were fine, just fine," he says, sensing whats troubling me. "But, you see," he said, rather wistfully, "thats *all* I want; to be seen along Times Square with a young-man in those clothes."

A few minutes later, I was back on 42nd Street, and Pete was still there, slouched outside the spaghetti place. He smiled at me. "Some scene, huh?" he said.

"Did he give you anything for it?" I ask him.

"What do *you* think, spote? He gives me five bucks for everyone I get him. I meet him once every two, three weeks. He spots someone he digs, I introduce him. Hes too shy to talk to anyone, so I do it for him, and he lays some bread on me—and I dont have to do nothing," he says smartly.

"Did you ever go with him—*spote?*" I said.

"Oh, sure!" He laughed. "And thats all he digs, spote. He dresses everyone he goes with in that motorcycle drag—and it bugs him for me to call it that. Then he walks around with them. Hardly anybody ever walks away with his clothes— theyre too curious. Hes hung up on that drag, thats how he gets his Kicks. . . . Oh, sure, I been with him." Then proudly —his gaze shifting back and forth from me to the street, pegging people—he adds. "Im the only cat he walked around with *two* nights—*in a row!*"

2

Pete was a familiar figure in that world of Times Square. With his slouched army fatigue cap and his thick shaggy army jacket which he had dyed brown, his bouncing walk—it was easy to spot him in any crowd.

After that first night, I would meet him often, never by arrangement, but always at about the same time, around the same place. We would hang around together for a while, and then, compulsively, we'd split. Often, minutes later, we would meet again standing in the same place.

Although he wasn't much older than I—but because, as he told me, he'd been hustling the streets since he was 16—Pete liked to play the jaded, all-knowing street hustler, explaining to me how to make out. He had a series of rules: Walk up to people, dont wait to be asked; if you do, you may wait all day. Forget about the vice squad, and you'll never get caught. A quick score in a toilet for a few bucks can be worth more than a big one that takes all day. Stand at the urinal long after youre through pissing. At the slightest indication of interest from someone in one of the cubicles, go up to him quickly before he gets any free ideas and say. "I'll make it with you for twenty." But go for much less if you have to.

As we sat in Bickford's in the cold light, he told me without embarrassment that once he'd gone for 75¢. "It was a slow day, he explained, "and I had only four bits, just enough to make the flix. I thought, Do I buy a Hotdog or make the flix and try to score? It was raining—no one on the streets. So I made the flix. No scores. Then someone wants to give me 75¢, and Im in the balcony anyway, so I let him. Hell, man," he adds pragmatically, "I was a quarter ahead—I could still have that Hotdog." And he goes on: "Youll learn; sometimes youll stand around all day and wait for a 15-buck score, a 10-buck score, even a deuce—all day—so, hell, take what comes, spote —so long as it dont louse up all your time—but always ask for the highest. Ask for Twenty. That way they think they got a Bargain."

Part of Pete's technique as a hustler was to tell the men he'd been with that he knew other youngmen like himself, and if they wanted, he would fix them up. Like a social secretary, he kept mental dates when he'd meet certain people. If he still didnt have someone for the score, they would walk around Times Square until the man spotted someone he wanted. Pete

would make the introductions—as he had that night with me
and the black-dressed Al—and would get a few bucks for it.
. . . There was one problem, Pete explained: As the score got
to know more and more people, he'd dispense with Pete's
services.

Occasionally, we sat in the automat, talking for a long time,
Bragging, exaggerating last night's Big Score. Soon it would
turn bitter cold, he warned me (and, already, the wind raked
the streets savagely), and the hustling would become more
difficult; the competition on the streets keener. "You can
shack up with someone permanent, though," he told me, looking at me curiously as if he were trying to find out something
about me; "but me," he added hurriedly, "I dont dig that
scene—I guess Im too Restless."

He made it, instead, from place to place, week to week,
night to night. Or, he told me, he'd stay in one of the all-night
movies. Sometimes he would rent a room off Seventh Avenue
where they knew him. "And if you aint got a pad any time,
spote," he said, "you can pad there too." Then he changed the
subject quickly. "I dig feeling Free all the time," he said suddenly, stretching his arms.

And I could understand those feelings. Alone, I, too, felt
that Enormous freedom. Yet . . . there was always a persistent
sensation of guilt: a strong compulsion to spend immediately
whatever money I had scored.

I still lived in that building on 34th Street, its mirrored
lobby a ghost of its former elegance.

I paid $8.50 a week for the room. Opposite my window, in
another wing of the same building, lived an old man who
coughed all night. Sometimes he kept me awake. Sometimes it
was the old, old woman who staggered up and down the hallway whistling, checking to see that no one had left the water
running in the bathrooms or the gas burning in the community
kitchen. At times it was Gene de Lancey—the woman with
the demented eyes I had met the first day in the hallway—
who kept me up. Once she had been Beautiful—she had sighingly shown me pictures of herself, *then!*—now she was sadly
faded, and her eyes burned with the knowledge. She seldom
went out, although I did see her on the street one late afternoon, shielding her face with her hand. She'd knock on my
door sometimes early in the morning, often as I had just
walked in: I would wonder if she listened for me to come in.
I would open the door, and shes standing there in a Japanese
kimono. "Lambie-pie," she'd say in a childish whimper, "I

just couldnt sleep, I just gotta have a cigarette and talk—
Steve's asleep—" That was her present husband. "—and I
knew you wouldnt mind, sweetie." She would sit and talk into
the morning, with such passion, such lonesomeness, that I
couldnt bring myself to ask her to leave. She would tell me
about how everyone she had ever loved had left her: her
mother, dead—her father, constantly sending her to boarding
schools as a girl—her two previous husbands, Gone—her son,
disappeared. "Theres no love in this harsh world," she la-
mented. "Everybody's hunting for Something—but what?"
When, finally, she would get up, she would kiss me on the
cheek and leave quickly. . . .

I mentioned her to Pete, and he says: "Great, man, she
sounds like a swinging nympho—lets make it with her together
sometime!"

Like the rest of us on that street—who played the male role
with other men—Pete was touchy about one subject: his masculinity. In Bickford's one afternoon, a goodlooking masculine
youngman walked in, looked at us, walked out again hurriedly.
"That cat's queer," Pete says, glaring at him. "I used to see
him and I thought he was hustling, and one day he tried to
put the make on me in the flix. It bugged me, him thinking I
was queer or something. I told him fuck off, I wasnt gonna
make it for free." He was moodily silent for a long while, and
then he said almost belligerently. "Whatever a guy does with
other guys, if he does it for money, that dont make him queer.
Youre still straight. It's when you start doing it for free, with
other young guys, that you start growing wings.". . .

And because this is such a big thing in That life, youll hear
untrue stories from almost everyone whos paid someone about
the person hes paid. It's a kind of petty vindication, to put
down the hustler's masculinity—whether correctly or not—at
the same time that they seek it out.

Standing on the street, Pete would always come on about
the young girls that would breeze by like flowers, the wind
lapping at their skirts coyly. . . .

I found out Pete can be vengeful. I saw him in Bryant Park
and he was fuming. The manager of a moviehouse one block
away had refused to let him in. (I had seen the manager—a
skinny, tall, nervous, gaunt, pale-faced man. The theater is
one of the gayest in New York. Late at night men stand leaning along the stairways, waiting.) "Hes a queer," Pete said

angrily, "he dont give a fuck what goes on so long as it dont go on for money—thats why he wouldnt let me in." Later, Pete tells everyone the place is *crawling* with plainclothes vice squad, ready to raid it: Stay Away! And the theater balcony was almost empty for weeks.

He also told me that another hustler had taken a score from right under his nose in the park, and Pete went around telling people the other hustler had the clap. . . . "Make it anyway you can," he said when he finished telling me that, "and when you cant make it, get even."

He knew almost everyone on the street who paid. He would point them out to me. "See that blond pale kid? He pimps for this old guy: real swank pad, too. And, man, what a weirdo that old guy is. Dig: he pays by the hour, and talks, talks, talks!—hes a teacher or something—laid up in bed from an accident. I used to fall asleep—I'd wear sunglasses—and he never knew the difference, just kept on talking. . . ."

At least once I regretted not listening to Pete's advice.

"See that one over there?" he said, pointing to a harmless-looking middle-aged man in a raincoat. "Stay away from him, spote, hes psycho."

But remembering what he had told everyone about the theater whose manager wouldnt let him in, and remembering what he'd done to the hustler whod taken his score in the park, I figured this may be some kind of revenge on the man for whatever reason. The man looked entirely harmless, and I went with him.

After we had made a very ordinary scene—and I still hadnt got any money from him—his composure changed suddenly into savage rage. Before I knew it, he had pulled a knife on me. I dashed out, down the creaking steps. Like a demon—his shadow flung grotesquely down the stairs—he stands at the landing shouting:

"God! Damn! You! *God damn all of you!*"

3

I also learned not always to trust Pete.

One sharply cold windy Sunday afternoon—the clouds sweeping the newyork sky like sheets—I saw him coming toward me where I was standing. "You wanna score?" he says. "See that old cat over there?" He pointed to a small mousy man a few feet away. "He wants us both to come over to his house. Hes only good for five," he explained, adding quickly when he saw me hesitating: "but most of the time he'll lay more if he digs you. . . . Cummon, man," he coaxed me. "Lets go with him. It's a draggy day anyhow. And anyway, we get to eat there real good." He adds, smiling secretly. "And we dont have to do much. Oh, hes Special!" Remembering the man I had walked around Times Square with, wearing a jacket and cap, I began to laugh. "Not that," Pete says, "we wont be walking around Times Square in leather."

Without going to him, Pete motions yes to the man, who goes down the steps, into the subway. Pete and I follow. I was walking fast, to catch up with the man. "Cool it," Pete explains. "I know where we get off." Without glancing back, the man gets in one of the cars, and we got in another. "He doesnt want anyone to see him leaving with guys," Pete said. I had been through this before: Unlike the black-dressed Al, who walked you around for an hour through Times Square, some scores dont want to be seen leaving the street with a younger man. "He lives in—hold on—*Queens!*" Pete laughed. "And dig this, spote: I think he teaches at Queens College. They even got a school now," he says, shaking his head.

We got off at Queens Plaza, and followed the man to a large apartment house. We waited at the corner for a few minutes, and then we walked into the lobby. It's a moderate-priced apartment house, very quiet, softly lighted. We reached the second floor, and along the hallway, a door was open slightly. There stood the little man beaming at us sweetly. He had taken off his coat, and he was wearing a gayly colored apron now.

"Hello, hello, hello!" he chirped merrily. "Im so glad you boys could come. I was hardly expecting—"

Pete whispered to me (I couldnt see how the man could help but hear him, but possibly neither cared): "Play it Cool and go along with it." At times Pete seemed to have an enormous tolerance for the quirks of the people he knew: a tolerance which could instantly turn into intolerance when he felt he'd been had.

"Itll be just a few minutes, boys," the old man announced, "and then we'll have a Lovely dinner. You boys must be famished, and I just happen to have some Very Nice Steaks. Now," he says, and his voice trembles slightly, "you boys get —uh—Comfortable." He stood watching us intently. I glanced at Pete, and he had begun to unbutton his shirt.

"Do what I do," he told me, but I was strangely embarrassed suddenly, because by then Pete was taking off all his clothes.

"Come on, man," he says to me, annoyed. "You wanna score or dont you?" (Again, I knew the man, his gaze nailed on us, could hear him, and I realized conclusively this didnt matter.) "This cat's pretty swinging people if he digs you," Pete goes on, "and we can come back and have 'dinner.' " He laughed again. "Come on."

I finally did. Pete sat on the couch, glancing at a comic book. He was completely unembarrassed. I sat on a chair looking at a magazine. The man returned to the kitchen, humming gayly. "It'll be just a few more minutes, now boys—" He turned at the door and looks fondly at Pete. "Petey-boy," he said, "I do believe youve been gaining a few pounds—you should have more salads, less starches. . . . You boys dont know how to care for yourselves, but we'll fix that. . . . And you, my boy—" turning now to me like a doting mother "—you could stand a bit more weight—just a few more pounds, not much—and we'll fix that too." He disappeared into the kitchen, and I could hear dishes rattle.

I glanced up abruptly, and Pete is looking at me over the comic book. He smiles broadly.

Soon, the meal was served, on a small, carefully set table in the dining room. We were summoned by a tinkling little bell which the man jingled. I had never eaten like this before, and I start to put my pants on. Pete said no, emphatically, reminding me we're in the presence of "cool people" and I should play along. We sat at the table—just Pete and myself, facing each other. The man flutters in and out of the kitchen like a butterfly, returning, serving us lovingly, rearranging the silver, the glasses—standing back to see that they were Just Right. There was no place for him. He brought a chair and set it away from the table. He sat there, staring raptly as we ate. Completely unself-consciously Pete ate his food. I dropped my fork a couple of times, and the man rushed into the kitchen to get me a clean one. Finally we had finished, and the man places a cake before us, gives us a large portion. "And there's ice cream!" he announced joyously. "Vanilla?" he asked. Pete said, "Chocolate." I took vanilla. "All boys love cake and ice cream," the man said knowingly, and by then I was enjoying it. I even ate more cake.

"Now a nice rest," the man said. His voice shook slightly, as when he asked us to get "Comfortable." We went into the bedroom, where there were twin beds. Pete lay in one, I lay in the other. The man came in with a chair, which he stations between the two beds. "Now take a long rest," he said. Pete is looking at me steadily, as if to remind me to play along; winks—then pretends to fall asleep immediately. He even snored a couple of times. I lay in bed, my eyes supposedly closed, but I was glancing at the man: He sat on the chair, his chin propped on his hands: staring fixedly from one to the other; occasionally his face would brighten up benevolently like a mother watching over her adored children. . . .

After about 15 minutes, he "woke" us, and we sat in the bedroom, on one bed, Pete and I, and played checkers, while the man watched us with the fascinated attention of a child enjoying a cartoon. Pete couldnt play checkers, and we sat there merely moving them back and forth.

"We'll have to go now, Mom," Pete said finally. I looked at him startled. Had he called him "Mom"? Pete nods at me, indicating I must do the same. I couldnt bring myself to call him "Mom." The old man looked at me with a hurt look.

"We'll have to go now, Mom," Pete repeated. He gives me an exasperated look.

"Oh, must you?" the man said. "Im so sorry you cant stay longer." He removed the apron, rubbed his hands on it, folded it neatly, and he went into the kitchen. Pete follows him. I can hear voices. Then Pete returns, hands me $5.00. "You fucked up, spote," he told me, shaking his head. "You didnt call him Mom. Just five bucks. When hes real happy, he lays ten." He shook his head regretfully. "But we can come again, and if youre cool we'll score more. Why—didnya—call—him—Mom?"

A week later, alone, I ran into the same man. This time he knew me and he came and talked to me. "Do you have a young friend whod like to come up and have dinner with us?" he asked me. "I havent seen Petey-boy here today," he said, glancing around for him. "If you find another nice youngman, we'll have a lovely dinner, and youll each be $10.00 richer." "Ten?" I said. "Why, child," he said somewhat indignantly, "I *always* give ten." From my expression, he understood what had happened. "That Pete!" he said, and I thought he was going to stamp his foot. "Hes done it to me again. Why, I bet he only gave you five." I felt embarrassed to admit I'd been taken, and I said, no, he'd given me ten. "Well, Im relieved!" the man said. "Hes done that before, you know—gives his young friend only five, and keeps fifteen. But what can I do? It embarrasses me so, when Ive first met a youngman, to give him the money. Idont reallyknow whattodo." Then he smiles Tolerantly. "But Petey is a lovely youngman—only—only—"

He frowns slightly. "—only I wish he wouldnt call me Mom."

When I saw Pete again, one night in Bryant Park, I mentioned the money to him. He looked at his feet, pretending—I was sure he was pretending—embarrassment. "You gotta learn not to trust no one too much," he mumbled. Then he reached for his wallet, brought out three dollars. "Thats all I got now," he said, sighing ("What Am I Going To Do Now?!"). "Here, take em," he said. I did, and he stared at me in surprise. "Youre learning, spote," he said.

A few days later I got even with him.

I told him I knew a girl who wanted to be a stripper. I had met her not too long ago in the lobby of an apartment house I had just scored in. Her name was Flip, and she asked me to come up with her—just like that. She shows me sexy pictures of herself, turning me on. She was very pretty, very young. To the groaning sounds of "Night Train" she began to do a strip—then stopped coquettishly; tells me poutingly shes sorry, she cant go all the way: "You see, zoll—" (Thats how she said doll.) "—little Flip's got the mean rag on." Suddenly I realized without doubt that Flip was a man. She was the first dragqueen I had ever been with. I didnt let her know I had found out, and she went ahead and did what she told me she liked anyway. . . . When it was over, she says: "If you know any other cute zolls, tell them about me. Im always Ready, zoll."

When I told Pete about Flip (leaving out that she was actually a dragqueen), she too sounded like a nympho to him. "I gotta meet that chick," he told me—and later, I took him to her apartment. "We'll all three make it together," he said enthusiastically, "it's Sexier that way." And although he kept insisting as we stood outside Flip's door that I should stay, I said I had something else to do.

"Just ring the bell," I told him. "She wont even ask who you are. She'll just let you in."

I waited on the steps until I saw him ring the bell. The door opened. I heard Flip squeal: "Ooo, you are a zoll!"

That night I expected perversely to see an indignant Pete. But when I saw him, he said: "Man!—what a great Lay that chick is!" . . .

I felt very smug—and very surprised.

4

Then, one day—in the midst of that cold bitter winter, when the snow cut across the streets like an icy knife and the wind shrieked like something from Hell—one day, the memory of my Mother—accentuated by the long painfully written three-times-a-week letters without punctuation asking when I would be Back, asking me to promise not to get into trouble—that memory seized me with a racking violence—and I decided to put down Times Square again—a pattern of guilt which would recur periodically. I got a job, with a Foundation dedicated to Spreading The Greatness of The American Way of Life. And I kept away from The Streets. At night I would stay home or go to the movies—but not on 42nd Street or The Others. But —again—that job lasted only briefly, and impulsively, I quit. The cold air outside struck me like my lost freedom, regained. That very night I was back on Times Square.

"Where you been, spote?" Pete said. "I thought you got busted or something, I looked around for you. Dont split like that again, hear?" For the first time since I had known him, we shook hands.

After that, I saw him more and more often. Sometimes— having scored—we would meet afterwards and sit in the automat at 42nd and Park Avenue (this appealed to him as Classier). He told me he was staying in the room which the black-dressed Al rented to keep his motorcycle clothes in. "He dont dig anyone staying there," Pete told me, "but I finally conned him into letting me."

Yet, although I saw Pete at least once a day now, there was still the urgency, on both our parts, to split abruptly—to get away from each other.

Occasionally, we would go see "Mom." And the initial embarrassment I had felt was completely gone: It was always the same scene, the man never touched either of us, he merely sat staring. Once he even took a picture of us at the table.

By now Pete had learned how to play checkers. And one afternoon, strangely—as Pete and I sat on the bed playing checkers for much longer than we ever had before, as if there had been no third party, no "performance," actually enjoying it—with startling suddenness "Mom" abandoned his role as watcher, as doting mother, and nervously, claiming A Huge Headache, he asked us to leave. He folded the board hurriedly and abruptly dumped the checkers into their box.

As we left, he almost slammed the door.

"What bugged him?" Pete asked; then, shrugging, dismissing it, "I guess he did have a bad headache—shes kinda weird, anyway. . . . Fuck-im."

We didnt go back.

5

Now the nights began to warm up. It's that magnificent interlude in New York between winter and spring, when you feel the warmth stirring, and you remember that the dreadful naked trees will inevitably sprout tiny green buds, soon. Everyone rushes into the parks, the streets—and you even forget that, very soon, summer will come scorchingly, dropping from the sky like a blanket of steam. . . .

"I dont feel like fuckin around today," Pete told me one afternoon. He seemed pensive. "Lets just make the flix, spote—and forget all about trying to score."

We saw a double feature—one, a French movie about Lesbians in a girls' school. When we got outside, it was dark, the sky beaded wondrously with spring stars. "You really believe two chicks could dig each other that tough?" Pete asked me. I answer, "Sure." I was wondering what had prompted such amazing, for him, naïveté. "It sure seems strange," he went on. "Dig: I can see guys making it with each other—sure—for money—but— . . . Well, it sure seems strange, just digging each other like that—and those two chicks, man, they were both beautiful." We were standing outside. Even the lights on the signs seemed livelier in the warm air.

I didnt have any place to go, but I said, "Later," to Pete. This is how it had always been before. "No, wait," he says, "dont split—unless you got something to do." "Nothing," I said. "Lets stick together," he said. "I just dont feel like fuckin around tonight," he said moodily.

We went to a cafeteria on the same block and ate. The drifting youngmen were in there, sitting at the tables sipping coffee, staring at the older men who walked in. "Sometimes this whole scene bugs me," Pete said. "I guess maybe I should split—leave New York—go somewhere else: L.A., maybe. You wanna know something? I been in the East all my life—New Jersey—New York. . . ." He stared dreamily out the window. "Lets go to Washington Square!" he said abruptly.

In a few minutes, by subway, we were there.

In Washington Square there were many people. In the

center, around the fountain, the young painters and their girl-friends clustered; some had baby carriages. They seemed very happy. And I felt the same. I was sure it was the approaching warm weather. . . . One youngman with a beard played a guitar and sang softly in Spanish. Pete and I sat by the fountain, listening. Soon, we got up, walked around the west side—toward the "meat rack"—the gay part of the park. There, it was as if someone had hung a line of marionettes on the railing: the lonesome young homosexuals, legs dangling, look-ing, waiting for that one-night's sexual connection. . . . "This wouldnt be a good place for scoring tonight anyway," Pete says, "theres too many out for free fun." But we sit there too, silently.

Next to us, a Negro queen has nervously stationed herself—a screamingly effeminate youngman in a candy-striped shirt: twisting her neck haughtily, looking around her in pre-tended disdain. Soon a couple of her white "sisters" swish by, two equally effeminate youngmen. They stand talking to the Negro queen, gossiping breathlessly. Now theyre talking about gowns. "It was Fabulous!" said the Negro queen, "I dressed like the Queen of Sheba, and honey, I Mean To Tell You, I looked *Real!*"

"Wasnt thuh Queen of Shayba white?" says one of the white queens, a fiercely blond one, affecting a thick Southern accent.

The Negro queen's eyes open Wide. "Are you trying to dish me, Mary?" she says angrily.

"Honey," said the blond one, "all Ah asked was a simple question. Wasnt thuh Queen of Shayba White? For all Ah know, you *painted* youhself White. "

"Mary," says the Negro queen, ready to spring from the railing, "I may not be the Queen of Sheba, *exactly,* but I am The Queen of This Meat Rack—and I'll prove it to any nelly-assed queen that wants to try me."

"Youretoomuch," says the blond one airily. "Why! who-evuh heard of a nigguh *Queen?*"

In one instant, the Negro queen jumps off the railing, grabs the blond one by her thin shoulders and shakes her back and forth until she begins to sob, trying tearfully to tear herself away from the Negro queen. Finally, the Negro queen lets go, and the blond one rushes off wailing:

"Mothuh-fuckuh, if we wuz in The South, Ahd show you whos Queen of thuh Meat Rack!". . .

Pete said moodily: "She shoudnuh called her a nigger."

A fat zero-policeman comes by swinging his stick like a baton: "Move on, move on," he says. "Yes, sir, officer, sir," Pete says, raising his middle finger up at the cop as he passes by. . . . We move on, and it was beginning to get cool—the hint of spring withdrawing teasingly. We walk again through Washington Square. The guitarist with the beard has left, and we sit on a bench.

Sitting there with Pete, a great Loneliness overwhelmed me. Was it the sky? So like a Texas sky at night—the stars flung prodigiously in the expansive blackness. Or the sudden breathtaking memory of my Mother miles away? Her love radiates that great distance toward me stifling me. . . . Or was it the sudden change in the park?

The youngmen and girls had left—the older people were gone from the benches too. Now there remain only the hunting young homosexuals looking for a partner. They sit momentarily on benches, move away, stand restlessly. One sat near us. "You figure he thinks we're queer?" Pete asked me indignantly—and then he stared him away. . . . I wondered if the franticness of their search was overwhelming Pete as it was me; he was strangely silent. . . . Two youngmen walked by. Previously I had seen them standing a few feet apart, on the walk, moving slowly closer to each other. Then they had talked briefly—now they walked away together, speaking softly. They were both young, both goodlooking. I saw them smile at each other: For them, this night's search was over—not for money —but for a mutual, if fleeting, sharing. Staring after them, Pete says: "They coulda fooled me, even. They look like hustlers, dont they? And I bet theyre gonna make it with each other."

We move along Fifth Avenue, past a dimlit bar in a hotel. Through the windows we see a woman playing the piano. A man is leaning over her, her lips move in a song, she slides closer to him. . . . We pause for a while, and then we continue walking—into Union Square now, were we stand listening to a man in a tight suit heatedly hollering about what a blight Union Square is. "Perverts and tramps!" he yells. And a little old tramp staggers up to him, he reeks of wine, his nose like a red lightbulb—and he shakes his old finger unsteadily at the man yelling out damnation and says: clearly: "Listenere, you —you jes listenere: Theres gonna be hobos! homos! and momos! in Our Park long after youve grown deaf and dumb!"

"Hey, spote," says Pete to me, "whats a momo?"

"I dont know, I guess he just made it up."

"Thats cute," says Pete. "Homos, hobos and—and—what?"

"Momos," I said.

"Yeah: Momos. Hey! Maybe *we're* momos!" he laughs.

Weve reached the 34th Street, the corner of the Armory on Park Avenue.

"Heres where I live," I told Pete now.

"Can I come up and talk a while?" he asked me, rushing the words together.

"Im tired," I said quickly.

"Cummon," he insisted, "it's early yet—or you can come up with me Im still staying at Al's with all the motorcycle jackets. Come up there, I got a pint of juice, we'll kill it."

"It's too far," I told him.

He looked hurt.

"Okay. Lets go to my place," I said hurriedly.

There is still a doorman in the building where I lived: a Negro from Jamaica: a clinging relic, like the mirrored lobby, of its sadly gone elegance: Beyond the lobby and the doorman—who sits in a little room, nodding asleep through the night—the building is seedy two-room apartments and gray rooms—layers of wallpaper make the walls soft like quilts; the plumbing rattles; steam gives out on the coldest days. . . . We went up in the complaining elevator, into the apartment, broken up, in turn, into smaller apartments, tiny rooms. I turned on the light.

"This is nice," Pete said, looking at the dingy room. One thing was colorful: a Mexican blanket which my mother had sent me. . . . "I wish I had a place of my own," Pete says. "You know, I actually been thinking of getting a small apartment—with someone, maybe—you know, split the rent—it wouldnt be much that way. . . . You like living alone, spote?"

I pretended I hadnt heard him. . . . But long before that night when I had resolved to explore this world not with one person but with many, I had become aware that there was something about someone getting too close to me which suffocated me. . . .

"Maybe," Pete says, going on, "maybe—you know—I was just thinking—shacking up with another guy for a while—we could hustle together, really make the scores. It wouldnt be hard: I know lots of scores. Theyd stop digging me; dig you; so on—I mean, whoever it was, we would keep going like that. . . . I was even thinking—Christ—well—that fuckin street—it bugs me—sometimes I get nightmares about those toilets—I mean, all those fags—and—well, if I got a job, even—and split the rent with someone—well—"

"It's past midnight," I said interrupting him.

For a long while there seems to be nothing to say. Im aware of a smothering self-consciousness between us. I wanted him to leave. It was the first time anyone other than the curious men and women in the other rooms had been in this room with me.

"Can I stay here tonight?" I heard him ask clearly.

In a kind of panic, I want to say no. "Yes," I answered.

The lights are out now. The darkness seems very real, like a third person waiting. I lay on the very edge of one side of the bed, and he lay on the very edge of the other. A long time passed. Hours.

"Are you asleep?" he asked me.

"No—I cant sleep."

"Me neither," he says. "Maybe I should go." But he didnt move.

More silence.

And then I felt his hand, lightly, on mine.

Neither of us moved. Moments passed like that. And now his hand closes over mine, tightly.

And that was all that happened.

The man in the other wing of the building, on the other side of my window, began to cough very early, and I got up hurriedly and dressed. "I have to go out," I told Pete.

"Me, too," he said. "I have to see someone."

We avoided looking at each other. "I'll see you around The Street," he said at the door. "Man," he says—but his voice was forced, as mine was, "I got a real tough score lined up today—hes worth Twenty."

"Later," I said.

"Later—spote," he said.

I saw him again, many times—in the movie theaters, in Bryant Park, on Times Square. We would say hello to each other, stop, talk casually: He would exaggerate his scores, I would exaggerate mine. But we were never together for long any more. "I have to score," one of us would say, and we'd split.

Soon we wouldnt stop to talk to each other when we met. We would say hello, rush on. . . . And then one day, one stifling summer day, I saw him bouncing along the street in my direction. I turned sharply, pretended to be looking at some movie posters; and glancing back once, briefly, I notice that he—for the same reason I had turned away, to avoid meeting —had crossed to the other side of the street.

CITY OF NIGHT

THE WORLD OF TIMES SQUARE was a world which I was certain I had sought out willingly—not a world which had summoned me. And because I believed that, its lure, for me, was much more powerful.

I flung myself into it.

Summer had come angrily into New York with the impact of a panting animal. Relentless hot nights follow scorching afternoons. Trains grinding along the purgatorial subway tunnels (compressing the heat ferociously, while at times, on the lurching cars, a crew of Negro urchins dance appropriately to the jungle-rhythmed bongoes) expel the crowds—From All Points—at the Times Square stop. . . . And the streets are jammed with sweating faces.

The chilled hustling of winter now becomes the easy hustling of summer.

At the beginning of the warm days, the corps of newyork cops feels the impending surge of street-activity, and for a few days the newspapers are full of reports of raids: UNDESIRABLES NABBED. The cops scour Times Square. But as the summerdays proceed in sweltering intensity, the cops relent, as if themselves bogged down by the heat. Then they merely walk up and down the streets telling you to move on, move on.

Inevitably youre back in the same spot.

For me, a pattern which would guide my life on the streets had already emerged clearly.

I would never talk to anyone first. I would merely wait at the pick-up places for someone to talk to me—while, about me, I would see squads of other youngmen aggressively approaching the obvious street-scores. My inability to talk first was an aspect of that same hunger for attention whose effects I had felt even in El Paso—the motive which had sent me away from that girl who had climbed Cristo Rey, long ago, with me: I had sensed her yet-unspoken demands for the very attention which I needed, and she had sensed them in me too, I am certain. . . . And so, in the world of males, on the streets, it was *I* who would be the desired in those furtive relationships, without desiring back.

Sex for me became the mechanical reaction of This on one side, That on the other. And the boundary must not be crossed. Of course there were times when a score would indicate he expected more of me. Those times, inordinately depressed, I would walk out on him instantly. Immediately, I must find others who would accept me on my own terms.

From the beginning, I had become aware of overtones of defensive derision aimed by some scores at those youngmen they picked up for the very masculinity they would later disparage —as if convinced, or needfully proclaiming their conviction, that the more masculine a hustler, the more his masculinity is a subterfuge: "And when we got into bed, that tough butch number—*he* turned over on his stomach and *I*— . . ." a score had told me about a very masculine youngman I had seen on the streets. Later, I would hear that story more and more often. Whether that was true or not of the others, with me, there were things which categorically I would not—must not—do to score. To reciprocate in any way for the money would have violated the craving for the manifestation of desire toward me. It would have compromised my needs. . . . The money which I got in exchange for sex was a token indication of one-way desire: that I was wanted enough to be paid for, on my own terms.

Yet with that childhood-tampered ego poised flimsily on a structure as wavering and ephemeral as that of the streets (and a further irony: that it was only here that I could be surfeited, if anywhere), it needed more and more reassurance, in numbers: a search for reassurance which at times would backfire sharply—insidiously wounding that devouring narcissism.

a bar with two men from out of town who have come to explore, on vacation, this make-out world of Times Square, I ag..e to meet them later at their hotel room in the East 20s. When I got there that night—and after I had knocked loudly several times—the door opened cautiously on a dark room. One of the men peeked out, said, hurriedly in order to close the door quickly: "Im sorry but weve got someone else now; lets make it tomorrow."

But there were others to feed that quickly starved craving. In theater balconies; the act sometimes executed in the last rows, or along the dark stairways. . . . In movie heads—while someone watched out for an intruder; body fusing with mouth hurriedly—momentarily stifling that sense of crushing aloneness that the world manifests each desperate moment of the day—and which only the liberation of Orgasm seemed then to be able to vanquish, if only momentarily. . . . Behind the statue in Bryant park; figures silhouetted uncaringly in the unstoppable moments. . . .

Still, for me, there were those days of returning to what had once constituted periods of relative calmness, in my earlier years, when—to Escape!—I would read greedily. . . . Now, at that library on Fifth Avenue, I would try often to shut my ears to the echoes of that world roaring outside, immediately beyond these very walls. Again, I would read for hours. And this would be a part of the recurring pattern, when impulsively I would get a job, leave the streets, return to those books to which I had fled as a child. But because there would always be, too, that boiling excitement to be in that world which had brought me here—and, equally, the powerful childhood obsession with guilt which threatened at times to smother me—emotionally I was constantly on a seesaw.

And I began to sense that this journey away from a remote childhood window was a kind of rebellion against an innocence which nothing in the world justified.

In the library one night as I sit in the reading room surrounded by serene-masked people like relics from a distant world, a handsome youngman said hello to me. He sat at the same table. Noticing that he kept smiling and looking at me—at the same time that I felt his leg sliding against mine—I left. Sharply, I resented that youngman. His gesture had an implied attraction within the world of mutually interested men. While I could easily hang out with other youngmen hustling the same streets (although, since Pete, I seldom did for more than a few minutes, preferring to be alone), with them there was a knowledge—verbally proclaimed—that we were hunting scores, not each other. With this youngman just now, there had been the indication that he felt he could attract me to him as clearly as he had been attracted to me. . . .

The youngman followed me outside. As I cut across Bryant Park, I heard his steps quicken to approach me.

"I'd—like to meet you," he said, the last words hurried as if he had rehearsed the sentence in order to be able to speak it.

"Im going to go eat now," I said, avoiding even looking at him.

"All right if I sit with you and just talk?" he asked me. He was masculine in appearance, in actions. He could not have been over 20. But already there was a steady, revealing gaze in his eyes.

We went to a cafeteria. As we sat there, he told me he was a student at a college, he lived with his parents. On weekends he worked at the library. . . . Throughout his conversation, there were subtle references to the homosexual scene, which I didnt acknowledge. . . . Afterwards, for about an hour, talking easily, we walked along the river.

"I'd like to go to bed with you," he said bluntly. "We could rent a room somewhere."

Remembering Pete with a sense of utter helplessness, and surprising myself because of the gentleness with which I answered this youngman, I said:

"Youve got me all wrong."

In the following days (on this unfloating island with that life that never sleeps—in this city that seems to generate its energy from all the small, sleepy towns of America, sapped by this huge lodestone: the fugitives lured here by an emotional insomnia: gathered into like or complementary groups: in this dazzling disdainfully heaven-piercing city), in those following days, I discovered Third Avenue, the East 50s, in the early morning, where figures camped flagrantly in the streets in a parody stagline; the languid "Hi" floating into the dark, the feigned unconcern of the subsequent shrug when you dont stop. . . .

And there was Howard Thomson's restaurant on 8th Street in the near-dawn hours. They gathered then for the one last opportunity before the rising sun expelled them, bringing the Sunday families out for breakfast.

I discovered the bars: on the west side, the east side, in the Village; one in Queens—appropriately—where males danced with males, holding each other intimately, male leading, male following—and it was in that bar that I first saw flagrantly painted men congregate and where a queen boy-girl camped openly with a cop. . . . But because most of those bars attracted large numbers of youngmen who went there to meet others like themselves for a mutual, nightlong, unpaid, sexsharing— or for the prospect of an "affair"—the bars made me nervous, then; and, largely, I avoided them.

The restlessness welled insatiable inside me.

I discovered the jungle of Central Park—between the 60s and 70s, on the west side. In the afternoons, Sundays especially, a parade of hunters prowled that area—or they would sit or lie on the grass waiting for that day's contact. Even in the brilliant white blaze of newyork sun, it was possible to make it, right there, in the tree-secluded areas.

At night they sat along the benches, in the fringes of the park. Or they strolled with their leashed dogs along the walks. . . . The more courageous ones penetrated the park, around the lake, near a little hill: hoods, hobos, hustlers, homosexuals. Hunting. Young teenage gangs lurk threatening among the trees. Occasionally the cops come by, almost timidly, in pairs, flashing their lights; and the rustling of bushes precedes the quick scurrying of feet along the paths.

Unexpectedly at night you may come upon scenes of crushed intimacy along the dark twisting lanes. In the eery mottled light of a distant lamp, a shadow lies on his stomach on the grasspatched ground, another straddles him: ignoring the danger of detection in the last moments of exiled excitement. . . .

In Central Park—as a rainstorm approached (the dark clouds crashing in the black sky which seemed to be lowering, ripped occasionally by the lightning)—once, one night in that park, aware of an unbearable exploding excitement within me mixed with unexplainable sudden panic, I stood against a tree and in frantic succession—and without even coming—I let seven night figures go down on me. And when, finally, the rain came pouring, I walked in it, soaked, as if the water would wash away whatever had caused the desperate night-experience.

THE PROFESSOR:
The Flight of the Angels

1

THE MAN IN BED—STARING AT me appraisingly—was enormous. In one hand he held a pastel-blue cigarette—poised, daintily between two puffed fingers. He brings the cigarette studiedly to his mouth and blows out a shapeless cloud of uninhaled smoke. He looks crazily like a pink-faced genie emerging from the smoke. The other hand held a tapemeasure, which is partly wrapped about his sagging fat neck. . . . Hes somewhere in his 60s. His head is shaved completely. Huge dark eyes bulge behind thick glasses, like the crazy eyes painted on the glasses children wear on Halloween.

Beside me, in this well-furnished apartment, stands a young malenurse, who has brought me here from Times Square. He is perhaps 28, coldly blond, with a very pale face—a premature Oldness, a bitter knowingness. He acts like a haughty movie butler who feels superior to the guests. Even on the street when he approached me, he had looked at me with unconcealed contempt; lighting a cigarette as we walked here, not offering me one.

Scattered about the floor are manuscripts, books, magazines. The room is cluttered with statues, unhung paintings, vases with withered flowers. There was a large ugly German beer mug on a mantle.

Now the malenurse is looking at the old man—waiting, I knew, for some sign of approbation or displeasure from him.

After long moments of staring at me, unwinding the tapemeasure, winding it again, puffing elegantly on the pastel-blue cigarette, the old man, propped halfway up in the hospital bed, said finally:

"Well!" And his fleshy face shaped a smile—molded as if on pink clay. "Im not one bit disappointed," he announced grandly. "But then I never am—thanks to Larry here," ac-

58

knowledging the malenurse. "Larry knows my subtlest moods, my changing (oh, so changing!) tastes—and hes only been with me—how long, Larry?"

The malenurse answers quickly: "Four months, Professor."

"Ah, yes, of course, four months!" The man in bed goes on: "It's unfortunate that the world doesnt recognize talent like Larry's openly. Larry would be an Enormous Success. But then there are many things the world doesnt recognize. Yes. . . . Fine, Larry, now, if youll excuse us—" The malenurse walks out, almost brushing my shoulder, without looking at me.

"My dear youngman," the old man announces, "you are about to join the ranks of: My Angels!"

2

"Now, sit near me," he said. "Yes, do bring that chair over. Not that one: the other one, it's more comfortable, and I want you to be Comfortable. . . . Careful, now—my manuscripts. Push them aside, child—neatly, neatly—I was looking through some things before you came." Sighing deeply, he waves a chubby hand over the room, indicating the books and manuscripts littering the floor. "They are: Relics—from another life! . . . Now, first of all, let me explain some exterior situations: You see me here, now, in this hospital bed, where Ive been for months and months: Suffice it to say: an Eternity! An automobile struck me—and it would have been Poetic Justice, yes, if I could say I had been hit by a gigantic truck—driven by a young handsome truckdriver, who knelt to gather my shattered heap of flesh (you see: I say 'shattered heap of flesh' —I am frank with myself: Life wrecks all illusions—but you will find that out later), and to whom—had it been just such a handsome young truckdriver, though the very instrument of my infirmity—I would owe my life: There would have been something extravagantly Sexual—" He affected a slight tremor. "— about being struck by a truck—ummm— Well! . . . But, oh, the perversity of life: no such magnificent luck. It was no such earthangel who ran into me: but—ah, perversity, dear boy, keep it in mind: Perversity!—I was hit by a nervous, high-strung, skinny, homely, ineffectual, simpering oldmaid from Oklahoma, vainly trying to compete with our own glorious system of cabs! Not that I have anything against Oklahomans. As you will learn, I have some fond memories of— But that comes later. . . . And so it has taken all those months. This frail mechanism (if I may be allowed the indiscretion of referring to myself as 'frail'—ha, ha—but I speak only relatively) —this frail mechanism called the body has refused to heal. In other words, the hip bone is no longer connected to the— How does that song go? . . . Anyway, you see me now rigged up in a 20th-century torture—not entirely unlike those used by the Inquisitors of old. . . . But do bring your chair closer, youngman—I want to hear every word you say, every phrase. . . . You will notice I have a hearing aid—which at times I feel must indeed be connected to an electronic god, who whispers all kinds of naughty electronic gossip to me. And, sometimes, alas! falls deadly silent. . . . But you see, I am a bit of a poet, and you will understand—later, because I hope you will become my angel. (Robbie, forgive me, *forgive me!*)" He entreated Heaven. He draped the tape-measure loosely about his chest, released it momentarily, and let it lie limp along his body. I noticed a little red wire clamp marking a certain spot on the measure. "My dear boy," he explained, "Robbie is my Guardian Angel—about whom you must hear—but later— perhaps in another interview, a precious interview—because I am also a philosopher. The poet stands in awe of life, and the philosopher penetrates it—and I do both. And life, my dear, dear young angel, is a long series of Interviews. And so: On With The Terms, to plunge, as in epic poetry, *in medias res*. . . . Lets dispense with the—uh—matter of—funds. Larry, I can suppose—uh—met you on one of our numerous streets, and so I take it you are—uh—seeking—(how did one street angel put it to me not too long ago? Oh, yes:)—bread: a fitting designation for funds, reduced, in the manner of the streets, to The Essential: . . . bread. I will give you (this is always a rather touchy subject, and so I have established a fixed fee)— $7.50 an hour, and if a fraction of an hour, the full amount. All right? . . . Very good, thats Marvelous! And you will come to see me as often as—" His voice broke, he stares at the red mark on the tape-measure. "—as often," he finished sighingly, "as the interviews shall last. . . ." He reaches for a Kleenex, also pastel-colored, and touches his nose delicately. "Very well, then. . . . Im looking forward to knowing All About You my novice angel. Angel!" He puckered his lips and threw me a kiss. "I am all love, my dear boy—every inch (and there are, oh, so many!), every thought, every sigh—all Love: Love, dear child, which is, indeed, God! . . . Now do move closer. Yes. Now on with our First Interview!—the most important, really—in which we will get to know each other—in which we will turn a searchlight on the wonder of our mutual lives—ignoring momentarily the ugliness, of which—" he said sadly "—of which—there is—so much. . . . Ah, life—that vast plain of—what? . . . Like a cold card dealer, God deals out our destinies: It was mine to be born ugly. . . . But let me, now—by way of establishing an Important Contact with you—let me tell you, now, about The Angels. . . ."

He leaned back on the bed like a puffed-up balloon. I imagined him in a Macy Thanksgiving parade, wobbling from side to side with enormous eyes. . . . He reaches now for another cigarette—retrieves a lavender one, studies it, sets it back in the box. "That—the Lavender," he says, smiling slyly, "is for later: at the last of our interview. Now—lets see—" He finds a pink one, chooses it. "Pink—the color of a young flower. . . ."

I was staring fascinated at the enormous buttonround eyes in the incredibly childlike flesh of his face.

"I always like to know my angels—intimately," he went on. "It is so necessary. And I tell them about the others who have preceded them, so that, through them, they may learn to know me—and then, too, they form an angelic fraternity—a kind of angel-crown swirling about me, I like to think in my more poetic moments." The tape-measure hypnotized me. He kept winding it about his neck, his stomach, he tossed it toward his feet, brought it back, draped it about his shoulders, and he continued to talk, the bulging eyes staring—his voice tumbling on and on, piling words on words, as dishevelledly as the objects scattered about the room. "Now the rules," he says. "Yes, there are always rules: Let me tell you, first, what I—uh—Like —To—Do—and what we will do at the last of each interview." He giggled coyly, like a young embarrassed girl. "Come here, dear child. I must whisper it to you—not because Im ashamed but because it is so Dear to me that I must keep it close to me by whispering—" I got up from the chair and stood next to the bed. He whispered in my ear, his rubbery lips brushing it. "I like to—" He studied my expression as he said it. "And do you know why? Because—" He puckered his lips again. "—because it is: So Nice! . . . And so you see I ask for very little of My Angels."

I sat back down again.

"Now to get to know you," he went on. "Let me guess your birthplace. Im good at this. You dont talk like an Easterner.

Now where would it be likely you would have been raised? Your descent first?" he asked me. . . . "Oh, yes. . . . The Southwest! Thats it! . . . Texas!" And then he blurted the name of the city where I was born. I was tempted to say no, he was so smug, he had embarked on his game with such cocksureness. Lying there like an enormous doll, he almost appears to me like what God would look like. I nodded, yes. "You see," he went on with childish pride, "I told you I would guess. Now your age—" He guessed that too. "Your weight —" He was almost exactly right. "Your height—" He hit it. "Now the physical dimensions are over," he went on. "Except for one. Let me see your hand—no, the palm up. Now—bring the middle finger down as far as it will go. Mark it with another finger. Thats it. Now raise the middle finger and show me. . . . Fine. . . . A whore taught me that trick, and it is almost one hundred per cent accurate. . . . And now," he said, "I want to tell you about the angels. . . . But first a word about myself. I am a Professor, child—I am one of that fading breed that belongs to the school of thinking. (And let me add here, parenthetically, that for all I know you are a Brilliant Angel—I never take anything for granted when it comes to that—but then again you might be a—what?—a native angel," he said tactfully, "who knows only what he needs to know. And I have periods for all kinds, and during our interviews I shall discover what kind of angel you are.) But I was telling you about myself: Yes, I am a Professor— although I have had, variously, other appointments. I went to Yale. . . . And from there—where?—oh, yes, Mexico! I spent a great deal of time there. I met the most adorable people, and it was the famous painter Alfredo Sanchez who gave me the nickname that all my angels have called me in fondness at one time or another: The nickname is—" It sounded like "Tante Goulu." "It is the name of a fictional madam," he continues, "or, as you might say, the head whore of a House, ha, ha. And she was a bundle of love—like me. Ah, love. I have been in love many times—but let me tell you, without canceling out the possibility (oh, the infinite possibilities!) of something Magnificent between us (I am quite loyal), that throughout my life there has been but one Great Love: Robbie. . . . Robbie. My Robbie. My Angel. The Angel. (Oh, Robbie, Robbie! Forgive me: Your place is taken by the hundreds of angels who drift into my life." He invokes someone beyond the room.) "Anyway, child, I am a P-H-D—that is, a doctor, child—a Doctor of Learning: I dont cut up

people; I dig into their minds to find, perhaps, a latent jewel!
Like a deep-sea diver, I stand breathless before the unopened
oyster! . . . And Alfredo (you see, I spent some time in Mexico,
as I have told you, with the American embassy)—and, oh, yes,
I must tell you about the actress Lola del Rey: a Magnificent
woman—the most beautiful in the world— . . . . I must explain that although my preference is for youngmen—as you
may—have—gathered," he laughed, "I can still admire beauty
even in the other, less fair sex. I will tell you about Lola—
but later—and I must also tell you about the mistress of the
President, at the time—oh, it was a scandal!—she was a movie
actress, and then his wife—oh, later! . . . Now I must hear
all about you." He repeated the facts of my age, weight,
height. "And then, of course—" He indicated on his palm what
he had previously determined on mine. Then he went on:
"There are three chief categories of angels—though their
areas are sometimes not so well defined: earthbound, seafaring,
ethereal. . . . The first, child, are the truckdrivers, the marines.
One of my finest loves was an All-American. The day he
learned he'd been chosen, he came to me, he was my student,
and he said: 'Tante Goulu, I want you to be the first to know.'
He autographed a football for me. I detested football, but I
adored him, and he had such a simplicity, such a desire to be
on The Team—I helped him along, with his grades— Why,
had it not been for my fondness for him, the world might
have been deprived of one of its— What was he now? Oh, yes,
a tackle! The world would have been deprived of one of its
great tackles! . . . And the next category of angels is the seafaring: the sailors. I suppose perhaps they are the original
angels. I would watch them in San Diego—one summer I
spent at La Jolla—as they invaded our streets, descending, all
white, as if just arrived from Heaven, scattering themselves
among the rest of us, unworthy, mortals! . . . I knew one, once,
a young sailor who stayed with me. He was a very small boy,
like a golden child. Outside of his uniform, he would have
been an ethereal angel. He was the boyfriend of a very
famous writer—who later used one of the sailor's beautifully
naïve expressions as the title of a book. . . . Shall I amuse
you, child? (Our interviews must have comic relief: The
porter must come humorously to the castle door to admit the
murderer.) . . . Anyway, the writer asked the sailor: 'Where
would you like to go tomorrow?' It was here in New York,
on a weekend, and the charming golden angel answered: 'I
would like to see the sunrise on Wall Street.' And that became

the title of the writer's next book: *The Sunrise on Wall Street.*
Anyway, this sailor, this child, this golden angel, came to live
with me—he had an argument with the writer. I thought he
was on leave—but it turned out he was: Absent . . . Without
. . . Leave. And they came for him—two other angels with
arm bands: SPs—Storm Patrols—Shore Patrols—Something
Patrol. It broke my heart. And, later, Alfredo himself—who I
do not wish to imply, by mentioning his association with me,
is similarly inclined— . . . . Not that I am ashamed of my own
inclinations—not at all—but just as I would resent being
thought heterosexual, so I must assume he would resent the
opposite. . . . And I have had friends of *all* sexes! My life
has flung itself wide, Wide; like a windshield wiper I have
covered my allotted area, fully. . . . But perhaps that is a bad
allusion: the windshield wiper being so *slender!* . . . Alfredo
told me later: 'Tante Goulu, you let the emotions rule you.'
Yes, that is true. I can conceive of no more beautiful world
than one ruled by the emotions—what a lovely world! One
would not push through the subway, thinking one might crush
someone lovely. Oh, it would be a lovely world—ruled by the
positive emotions. But then, child, the world is All Wrong. You
see, it is backwards. How much more logical, for example, had
we been brought up on the idea that God is evil? Why, it
would make the world completely good. But, alas, they insist
God is good (and I am not talking about the God which is
Love—I am talking about the Other One, the one they *pray*
to!)—and all around us, cruelty, hunger, perversity—oh, perversity (like why was I run over by a weak old woman
when—? . . . but Ive already told you that story, and the time
of our interviews is too precious to retrace our footsteps).
Yes, all around us, evil—about which, perhaps, you might be
able to tell me something. Larry met you on Times Square;
that is a world of its own. . . . Now, Larry—he is *not* an angel."
He made a face. "He serves another function: he brings me
angels; he is *loyal.*" With a shrug. "But we were talking about
evil, and I had mentioned Times Square. Lately, I have been
intrigued by street angels. Larry brings them to me, I interview them. One, a lovely child, fell asleep during our interviews. He thought I wouldnt notice it behind the sunglasses he
wore—the dear child! And I pretended not to. I kept on nar-
rating my comments on life. It seemed fitting to lull him thus
to sleep. . . . And so you must tell me all about Times Square,
child, all, all. I want you to tell me all about yourself, too, I
want to know you, I want to hear you tell me about your life.

Was your childhood happy? You see, these interviews are
For You—and once I said this to a young Frenchman, who
believed it—as I would have you—and wanted him—to believe
it. But! He believed it differently. He robbed me! . . . You
wont rob me, will you, darling? No, I know you wont. Besides, we have a doorman—ha, ha—and—the—telephone—is
—within—my—reach. . . . Enough of that: It was merely a
feeble attempt at humor, child. . . . And thinking of a doorman—his uniform only—I remember Robbie. I met him at a
costume ball—it was a New Year, and Robbie was there: He
was dressed in an elegant uniform—I dont know what kind:
It was definitely military: sword, gloves, boots to his hips. . . .
Frankly, I dont think it was anything definite, really—he had
just improvised it, the dear child. But he looked Magnificent!
Like a prince! An Angel! . . . Gold brocade. Purple coat. White
tights. Ah! So slender! . . . The only other person I have ever
seen look quite as Elegant—in my long, long, spent life—is
Lola—Lola del Rey: She is like a queen of queens: a Beauty.
She had left Hollywood in exasperation: those insipid com-
edies, as if a goddess had been cast as a maid! It was
blasphemy. . . . An outrage against Beauty is the only blasphemy. . . . But to pick up the thread of my story: I asked a
friend of mine, 'Who is that magnificent youngman in the
white tights?' And he answered the magic name—Robbie!
My Angel!—my love—the first, really, of the Angels: The
Angel. Robbie. . . . And that child with the face of purity—
that child, I was to learn, was a call boy. . . . But I anticipate
my story. There is still another category of angels: The
Ethereal Angels—these are the artists, the poets, the dancers.
. . . Which will you be? Ah, but we'll find out later. . . . I knew
an ice-skater, who glided across my heart as if it were ice—at
first—at first, burying the blades of his ice-skates into my al-
ready-wounded heart— . . . I have a weak heart, child—at
times I stop and listen to it, listen to its beating, I cling to that
sound—can it be, I wonder at times, that it has stopped, and
am I now suspended between life and death?—but that would
be impossible because no such stage exists: Death is merely
the absence of life, and all philosophy that goes further goes
on superfluously. It must stop There. . . . So this ice-skater
warmed later, but then, as is the way of angels, he flew away—
skated away to someone he had met—through me—an investor
in a bigger show. . . . So you see, Life—my life—is the delving
into the mysteries of the heart: 'The heart is deceitful above
all things. . . . Who can know it?' We can *try!* Try, by sharing

our mutual space of time together, to fuse the secrets—to find an answer: Love. . . . And I must go on to explain why I think we should believe in an evil God. Why, the belief in a good God, child, is belied all around us, we dont understand, we turn *from* Him—and so turn toward the opposite: Evil. How much more logical if we were taught that God is evil? Life would not belie that. We would believe in Him, implicitly —and again, we would turn from Him—rebelling—but this time we would be turning toward Good, the opposite of the evil God, whose existence we couldnt possibly doubt. . . . Which leads me somehow to the conclusion," he chuckled, "that God, like Hamlet, is a woman: She changes Her makeup constantly, She primps, She flirts with us. In other words: She cant make up Her holy mind. . . . (A severely inelegant form, I must add, of unGodly High camp!). . . . And, good, my dear child, takes many forms: Take my earthangel—the All-American. For him, good was the football—and the wedding ring I bought for his sweetheart— Later! . . . For my Robbie—it was—but you shall learn about that in a subsequent Interview. . . . Oh, I am growing slightly tired, child." He snuffed out the cigarette he had been smoking, looked through the box by the bed, found the lavender one. Held it up toward me. "Now comes the time for the lavender," he said. He lit it, inhaled it deeply, deeply, this time, placed it on the ashtray; said: "Now, Angel, come here, stand near me—but first, lower the bed for Tante Goulu please. Thats it. Now come closer, you see I have great difficulty moving. There, thats nice, thats fine—stand a little this way—thats—just—fine. Youre a good boy, an angel. . . ."

When he had finished, he leaned back on the bed.

"Our first interview is over. . . . Larry!" he called, and instantly, the malenurse appeared. "Our young friend is leaving." Then to me: "Do you have a telephone where you can be reached?" There was one in the hallway, but I said no. "A permanent address, then?" he asked me. "Yes? Marvelous. Please leave it with me," he said, "and let me give you my number (we must observe the rules of Society). . . . I will see you tomorrow, then—tomorrow at this time. Please, please come—I will look forward to it. I shall listen to my heart until you come. And you must listen to yours and not deprive Tante Goulu of your company. . . . Larry—you will—please give—this youngman—a check."

The malenurse had a checkbook in his hand, he glanced at his watch, began to write. I looked at the check suspiciously.

The nurse flashed a look of huge contempt at me. "Dont worry," he snapped, "it's all right."

The man in bed turned his bulging eyes toward me and smiled, the flesh spreading as if he were getting larger by the moment, as if the balloon shape was being inflated. "Child— dont stand me up—I couldnt take it. Tomorrow—tomorrow— And remember—" He waved his fat hand in an airy benediction, his face rolling to one side like a stone, the tape-measure dropping toward the floor. He reached for it quickly, wound it securely about his hand. . . . "And remember," he finished, "remember: God Is Love. . . ."

3

I had been home only a few minutes that night when I received a telegram:

ABSOLUTELY NECESSARY THAT YOU COMMUNICATE WITH ME TOMORROW. I KNOW YOU WILL NOT DENY ME THIS HELP ASKED OF YOU IN ALL HUMILITY. I BANK UPON YOUR GOOD WILL AND THE SENSE OF SUPPORT THIS CONTACT NOW WILL MEAN TO ME. COME AS EARLY AS YOU CAN. REMEMBER G IS L.

"Who is it from, sweetie?" said Gene de Lancey, following me into the room. ("I cant sleep," she had explained in the hallway. "I just gotta have one little cigarette with you, lambie.") She peered at the telegram.

"It's from someone I just met," I told her. I knew it would be a very long time now before I got to sleep.

"Everyone's so Lonesome," Gene de Lancey sighed.

Early the next morning I went for my second "interview" with the Professor.

The malenurse opened the door. "The Professor is asleep right now," he said, eyeing me coldly. "He had a very bad night. . . . Youll have to wait out here," he said. I was about to sit down when I heard the Professor's voice from the half-opened door leading to his room. "Larry? Larry, who is there?" The malenurse eyes me with hatred, goes to the room. He returned: "Hes awake now; go in."

I had expected, because of the urgency of the telegram, to find the Professor in a state of desperation. He wasnt: He lay smiling on the bed. "Ah, child, child, you did come. . . . No, I wasnt asleep—I had just adjusted my hearing aid—I dont want to miss out on any of its fitful morning gossip! . . . I am

Delighted you came. Not that I didnt expect you to show up. I can tell sincerity just as I can guess weights, ages, heights—you see, I have not lived these sixty-odd years without learning something—and I must pass on to you some of the things I have learned of this ambiguous existence we call life. Now bring your chair and sit near me." He reaches for a pastel cigarette—feels with the other hand about his back, touching frantically. "Larry!" he calls desperately. "Larry!" And when the malenurse appeared, the Professor pleaded breathlessly: "Where is my tape-measure?"

I saw it lying on the floor, beside the bed. I picked it up and started to hand it to him. Before the Professor could take it, the malenurse snatched it from me, and gave it to him himself.

"Ah, thank you, child," the Professor says, to me, ignoring the malenurse, "you have saved— . . . My Life—and I will explain how—soon—during one of our future interviews—. . . You may go now, Larry, I have to interview this young—angel!" Now he drapes the tape-measure familiarly about himself, and I notice the chubby fingers searching out a certain place on it. His eyes are nailed to it momentarily—he moves the red marker. "Ah!" He held his fingers on the mark, as if he were praying a rosary. . . .

"Now during this interview," he announces, glancing at his jeweled watch, "we will hear all about you." Again, as if reciting a litany, he repeated the statistics he had determined yesterday—lovingly. "And there remains one important thing to determine: What kind of angel are you? That is the question. The anticipation of finding out is the thing, dear child. . . . The French actress, Odette, said to me once: 'Professor, you play at life as if it were a mystery novel, and you the detective.' And I answered, 'If so, my dear, you have provided the all-important clue.' . . . I am a student of life, my child, and my subjects are the angels who fly into my life. . . . *'Notre vie est un voyage, dans l'hiver et dans la nuit; nous cherchons notre passage dans le ciel, où rien ne luit,'*" he recites, glancing toward Heaven. "A *chanson suisse:* 'A dark voyage, through winter and night—seeking heavenward, where nothing shines.' . . . But let me contradict that: For me something does indeed shine: the wings of the angels—briefly, but clearly. Angels are all I see when I glance heavenward, and that is Enough. And I never know how I shall meet those angels—it was not always as it is now—when Larry chooses them for me. You see, I am bedridden. . . . Sometimes he brings me demiangels;

they last only one interview. But sometimes there are jewels
in the streets. . . . There was a lovely child, in Paris, a youngman who followed me out of the W.C.—and we played a
game, all through St-Germain-des-Prés. I would stop, he would
stop. He was almost barefoot, his shoes were badly ripped.
Each time I stopped, he would look at his shoes, wistfully,
glance at me, smile—oh, charming, charming. And when I
stopped at a café and sat down, he stood near me, and then a
waiter told him to move on: oh, the insolent arbitrariness! And
I protested, 'But that child is with me.' And I invited him to
sit with me. An earthangel. A streetangel. I bought him pairs
of shoes! And Paris, that magnificent city of statues, glowed
for me as if lighted by heaven itself. Alas, he was a robbing
angel," he sighed, feeling absently for his wristwatch. "But
what I had gotten from him! Ah!" He turned heavenward. "My
friend, the playwright—" He mentioned a French writer.
"—was fond of saying, 'We take when we must take, and we
give when we must give.' Oh, he was chic! . . . Now about
you. What is the appeal that the streets hold for you? What
do you look for? And, mainly, what do you find? The
streets: where one can find a glorious child without shoes
—or someone to buy them for him. In the streets where I
found, in Paris, another vivid angel: with his father and
mother. He was perhaps sixteen; he wore a tiny cross
around his neck, and it fell on his chest, the shirt open almost to his lovely navel. And the mother and father saw me
and said good day. They invited me to their drab home—
too drab to house such an angel as their child—and so,
understanding that, they let me have him: He lived with me
—for a space of time, a glorious space of time. And for that
glorious time, in gratitude, I saw that the father and mother
had glorious wine on their table—daily. . . . The mother
looked like a witch, Oh, yes! I believe in witches! There is
much in the occult, you know. How is it possible for our time
to believe in the fairytale of God and not in the other dark
powers? Which is more difficult to believe? I have seen witches,
I have seen them work, but I have not seen God. . . . I knew
a woman in California who practiced witchcraft: Her power
was Awesome. (She had a medium, a youngman . . . another
affair!) . . . And when she discovered—brutally—that people
came to her as one goes to see a clever fraud—not really believing in her Powers—when she discovered that, she *willed*
herself to death. Yes—she announced she would die, and she
did: trying futilely to prove by dying what she realized sud-

denly she had not proved by living: that she believed what she said. . . . People—people—" he started almost painfully: "people—die—when they see life— at last—without—Illusions— For some, it takes many, many years; for others, much less. And so each of us commits suicide: when we *will* our own deaths: That is the only Death. . . ." He paused, studying the tape-measure. "But enough about the dark powers of the heart—yes, deceitful above all things! . . . On to more pleasant things! . . . A friend of mine—a director—said: 'You are a talent scout, Professor.' And indeed, I always search out Talent, dear, dear, child—angel—uncategorized angel. (Am I being unfaithful to you, Robbie? Robbie! Guard me, watch over me!) . . . After I met Robbie, at that party, I learned he was a call boy. In other days he would have been referred to as a court favorite. But our unbudging standards of morality impose certain ugly names: The only immorality is 'morality' —which has restricted us, shoved into the dark the most beautiful things that should glow in the light, not be stifled by darkwords, darklights, darkwhispers. Why is what I do Immoral, when it hurts no one?—no one! an expression of: . . . Love. . . . Yet this unreasoning world ignores the true obscenities of our time: poverty, repression, the blindness to beauty and sensitivity—*vide,* the sneaky machinations of our own storm troopers—the vice squad!" He exhaled loudly after the impassioned asseveration; went on: "Another youngman, Smitty, a charming young angel himself, had brought Robbie along to that party. That night, I went to the restroom, as one does in the course of an evening—and happily, miraculously, who followed me in? It was Robbie. . . . That was during another one of my periods in New York. Things were not going too well— uh—financially. (I must explain: Im much better off now— much better—and whatever funds I have will be expended to finish my research into: The Lives of The Angels! . . . But, then, that time in New York, it was sadly different.) I was completing, on my own, a study on—of all things—the angels as they appear in literature: Blake, Milton, Dante. . . . And when I saw Robbie, I recognized The Archangel. . . . And what is there about angels that has so fascinated me? The fact, perhaps, that like birds they have wings: That, to paraphrase Pope: angels rush in where fools fear to tread. . . . They are the true rebels. . . . And am I exaggerating this world of winged fleeing creatures? Remember it was such a creature who brought about The Fall: But God, Who had given them wings, was a jealous God. . . . He denied them the existence He had created for them: The Flight. Out of spite, He created Adam and Eve—and voyeur-like, in His aged impotence, He watched them. . . . And it was that rebellious angel, now Satan, who won them over to his way—a rebellious life—who made them taste of the Tree of Truth, which God, in His petty omniscience, would deprive them of. . . . In each of my angels I find something different—but they all have one thing in common: they all have wings. It is their nature to fly away, leaving an emptiness—but a glowing emptiness!—in my heart. . . . At the house of Doña Mercedes, in Mexico (she was a grand Spanish woman, with a bosom which expanded yearly, to house, I told her, her gigantic Heart)—at her house, where I stayed briefly, there was a charming houseboy. Very beautiful: and the blades of his back were like sprouting wings when he crouched. Doña Mercedes said: 'He looks more like a featherless bird to me.' Of course she could not see with my Clarity. This was one of the fallen breed, who rebelled, but was caught, put in servitude. . . . My Robbie had established his own heaven in the admiring eyes of others. He was at the time one of Smitty's boys—that is, Smitty was Robbie's 'Madam'—or, should I call him, his 'Monsieur'?— is there no word? . . . And that night, when he walked into the restroom after me, Robbie groped me!—yes! *he* groped *me!* Dear child, I said naïvely to him, What Are You Doing? I would have suspected he was following Smitty's instructions had he not groped me so—so *Sincerely!* . . . Smitty, you might say, had risen from the ranks: from gas station attendant, in Los Angeles; thats where he began—right in the station restroom. Then he became a bartender, a famous call boy; acquired some other boys—five or six—which he sent out on assignments. Robbie was one of them. . . . I met Smitty when a friend gave him to me, for a night, for a long-ago birthday. Smitty could have been my guardian angel, if sex had been the only consideration. But he belonged to everyone at the same time. . . . I asked my host: How much do these boys get? He told me—$15.00. And that night I was with Robbie, sitting there for a long while, unable to do anything, dreamily prolonging, I suppose, the anticipation of what $15.00 would get me: a taste of Heaven—promised—for that small sum. Less than I paid in Munich for that beer mug you see there: That beer mug is me, it has no beauty, no wings—it is ugly, it can break. The shattered pieces will be remembered. . . . And Robbie made the first move—that enchanted night in bed. . . . We were together two brief hours (much longer, he assured me, than he had ever spent with his other clients)—$7.50 an hour: and that is how I have arrived at that figure: You see, I told you, I am Loyal! . . . I remember the American heiress stranded by her young lover at the train station in Frankfurt. And all she could say was: 'God damn!' A more fitting eulogy would have been: The angel has flown; on golden wings he is gone. And she should have remembered that wings that can take away can also bring—and so I said to her, as she looked one last frantic time about the station, 'Look around, this is a world of angels.' . . ."

Now the malenurse entered with a tray. "Youve fixed a tray for my guest, of course?" the Professor asked him.

"I didnt know he'd be here," said the malenurse. He left, returned with a tray for me.

"Larry is not an angel," the Professor said again. "There is even, wouldnt you say? something Uncomfortable about him. I distrust him sometimes. Do you suppose—" he asked, lowering his voice, "—that Larry is a misplaced agent for the FBI —in the *wrong* cell?" He laughed, pleased with himself. "Perhaps," he whispered in posed secrecy, "he is writing a book about me—but then, it wouldnt be the first time I have been between covers!" He proceeded to eat, talking between mouthfuls. When he had finished, he placed the tray on the table. "We have talked enough," he said. "Come over here, uncategorized angel. Stand next to me now. We have looked into the Soul long enough for today—now: Now let us look in the other, equally sacred, direction. . . ."

Later as I walked out the door of his bedroom, I heard him call after me: "God Is Love. . . ."

In the outside room, the malenurse sat reading a thick book. He rose, walking swiftly toward me as if I would escape. He thrust the book at me: "The Professor wrote this!" he said. "Hes written many great things!" I reached for the book; but before I could even read the title, he withdrew it from me, not allowing me to touch it. "Heres the check," he said.

4

The next day I received a more desperate telegram: VITAL UNTIL FURTHER NOTICE TO THE CONTRARY THAT YOU MAINTAIN DAILY CONTACT WITH ME. I NEED THIS CONTACT VERY BADLY NOW FOR THE REASSURANCE IT GIVES ME IN MOMENTS

OF VARIOUS CONFUSIONS AND DANGERS TO MY
PEACE OF MIND. CAN EXPLAIN ALL WHEN YOU
COME TO SEE ME. G IS L.

When I saw the Professor, again there was no mention of
the telegram. The tape-measure was on the bed. . . . The "interview" proceeded: the mountainous anarchy of the facts of
his life piling higher and higher. Occasionally, I stopped
listening, the drumming of his voice lulling me. There were
episodes begun, interrupted, picked up, sometimes not finished
—the story of Robbie winding through it like a wayward river.

"I spent that first delirious night with Robbie," the Professor
was saying, "and it was Glorious! He knew his calling—unlike—" he says, looking at me accusingly, "—unlike others
who merely play at this life. And I would say this to them," he
continued, staring fixedly at me, "yes, I would say: 'You sit
and listen to me, you stand and let me at the end of our interview—but you dont really Give.' . . . There are painters who
paint without heart, poets who write without compassion—
they are cold. There is too much coldness in this world: Alas!
the Ice Age of the heart has not left us. Here and there, a
flicker of compassion arises courageously to thaw out the icy
blanket—but it is just that: a valiant flicker, soon snuffed out
by the very ice it sought to melt! . . . Smitty gave his body, in
any fashion at all, without question, without terms: His pro-
fession was to please, and one got what one paid for. Robbie
gave his body *and* his soul. . . . He was like a saint who gives
himself completely for his cause. . . . That first night," he said,
the accusing gaze relenting, "that first night with Robbie, I
gave him the $15.00, and then, when he was already outside,
I called him back. I gave him $10.00 more—all I had. And my
friend, the author, Martin St Dennis—the Notorious American
writer, child: an *enfant*—if now an aging *enfant—terrible*—
. . . It got back to him that I had given Robbie $25.00, and
Martin told me indignantly: 'Absolutely not, Professor! You
will ruin those boys! Their fee is $15.00—not a cent more!'
He couldnt understand what I had received from Robbie, my
Robbie. But Martin is not a very perceptive person: His books
are searchlights on the facts of our world—but cold, too, like
searchlights. And where his heart should be, there is a novel.
. . . I wish that were original but it is not: A psychiatrist said
that to him once, who, incidently—how shall I say it and be
modest?—was intrigued by me. He—the psychiatrist—persuaded me to let him give me the Rorschach test—to test my
subconscious!—and I let him—on a lark. I looked at one of

the inkblots, and he said, 'What do you see?' I answered, 'I
see *you*, trying to see *me!*' . . . And that reminds me of a
young assistant to the good Dr. Kinsey. The assistant didnt
fool me a second; he was a professional voyeur. Do you know
what that is, my dear young angel? A watcher! Science—oh,
yes—truly—he was most dedicated to the science of Sexology.
. . . Countess von Braun was fond of saying: 'If Sex is a
science, its only laboratory is the Bedroom! . . . I introduced
the young assistant to two charming youngmen I knew (one
of them gained a certain notoriety by playing the naked sailor
in the musical *Island Paradise)*, and the assistant Expressed An
Interest in seeing one of their 'wild parties'—for The Research.
. . . Shall I amuse you? . . . Well! These boys werè not *that
kind*—they were very quiet lovers—and I do not mean any
trace of contempt when I say 'that kind'—it is a most extraordinary kind, that kind. Anyway, the assistant was so
insistent (The Insistent Assistant!) that they decided to 'stage'
a wild party for him. And they did. It was incredible! The
good assistant kept moving from room to room, watching—
and, child, it was more than the glimmer of scientific discovery
that shone in the good assistant's eyes! . . . He asked to interview me, for The Book, but I told him my affairs with the
angels are too precious to reduce them to lines on a graph!
For example, how could he have indicated on a graph what
Joe Jones (it was part of his distinction that he had such a
common name—at first)—what Joe Jones meant to me? He
was definitely an earthangel—and is there a graph for such a
breed? . . . He was an Oklahoma cowboy, discovered on the
range—who came to the newyork Rodeo (I am not referring
to the one in Madison Square Garden: Im referring to the
Rodeo of this city itself), and whom I was able—my lucky
star was shining—to corral in my own small patio—sadly not
large enough for him who was used to The Plains—but briefly,
briefly, I had that earthangel, but the bronco god called him,
and off he galloped: to the vaster plains of Broadway—and I
heard later he changed his name to Cam Rider—rather, the
agent who Sponsored him changed it; the agent was fond of
saying: 'He jes cam' ridin into my life.' . . . How could the
good assistant, with all his science, have indicated Cam Rider,
né Joe Jones, on his graph? Impossible! . . . And at the party
which these two youngmen gave to entertain the assistant (although he would not have called it 'entertainment'—it was always Material! Research! Study! Science!)—at that party, he
would ask for specific performances. I must say the boys in the

group had never had such a marvelous time—with no fear of
a raid, since the assistant was well protected: And thus, in the
future, you will see life imitating science! . . . It was after
Robbie had left that I went to that party. I saw Robbie after
that magic first night, at different places, but I could not
afford him. Once I had given him $25.00, I couldnt give him
less. I wasnt—let me again remind you—doing well—uh—
'breadwise,' then: It was a dry period: And I thought that
Heaven had allowed me only that brief time with Robbie. And
then one day he called me: My Robbie! 'Professor,' he said,
'can I come up?' My heart died to speak the next words:
'Angel-child,' I said, 'I cannot afford you at the moment—in
fact, the memory of you is so precious to me, that I cannot
even afford that—but it is one of those rare prizes of life that
memories have no price!' And then, after a brief wordless
interlude in which my heart refused to budge, my guardian
Angel sighed into the telephone: Professor, havent you ever
heard of *love?*' . . . I had never dared to hope—me, a mountain
of spent flesh—and that supple magnificent youngman. . . .
And yet there it was: The Word: The Magic Word: Love.
. . . I called up a friend of mine—for once, I was not too
proud. I needed money badly, I told him. That afternoon,
when Robbie came over, I gave him $100.00. He looked
hurt when I gave it to him. 'This was for love,' he told me.
'Child,' I told him, 'Robbie—Angel—the money is also an
inadequate expression of my Love.' And I pressed it into his
hand. . . . Ah! if indeed it were possible to shatter this sorry
scheme of things—I would begin by replacing that first sharp
slap which brings us howling into life—I would replace it . . .
with a Kiss. . . . I would breathe Love into each child. . . .
But my Robbie's wings began to feel for the breeze, wings
are meant for flying, and before I knew it he was Gone. He
wrote me, he was in Europe—stranded briefly. I sent him
funds. Then it was South America. By then things were much
better for me, and I sent him money—a long-distance bond
between us—but what I sent was but a meager expression of
my Love—but what else could I do? And always he would
write back, endearingly, endearingly!—the dear child—that
he should send it right back to me, but he needed it badly—
he would pay it back—because what he had from me was
Greater. But he knew it pleased me to give him things. . . .
And then, suddenly, no more letters—" He broke off abruptly,
reached for a Kleenex, touched his cheeks. "Can I accuse
him for the emptiness he left in my heart? No! It was his

nature—the very nature which made me love him—his nature, to occupy my heart forever and my life only fleetingly: He had wings; he had to fly away. . . . Or perhaps," he said cautiously, almost in a whisper, "could it be that Love had indeed touched him powerfully—Love for me—and that that Love, at war with his angel's love of flight—had—lost out? . . . I dont know." He went on dully now. "I have heard hes now in Los Angeles—Im not sure—Ive heard he works in a bar— . . . Its been so many years. . . . Maybe he has soared to Heaven to bring Beauty to that drab place. . . ."

He paused—a rare, long pause. Then, with a flourish of his cigarette, he continued more enthusiastically: "The Countess Sabrisky once asked me if I believed in Heaven, and I answered: 'Of course I believe—I have had it on earth!' . . . I was referring to the angels—my angels—why, even Milton, the poet, in his epic poem, was on the side of the rebellious angels. He makes us sympathize with *them* against God: They are as heroic as American colonists rebelling against extra taxation! . . . But listen to me, I have gone on and on, and I must interview you, my new angel. . . . And, child, there is a favor I have to ask you: I must have a photograph of you, to put in my Album. . . . I have pictures of most of my Angels. . . . Please—over there—on that shelf—that album—please bring it to me. . . ."

I rose from the chair, mesmerized by the words which came almost like an endless song. I saw an album. On top of the album was a book: a thick, important-looking volume—much like the one the malenurse had thrust at me that day, but a different color. I glanced at the author's name. It was the Professor's. I brought the album to him.

"Now move over here. No, you can bring your chair this time. The other is for the closing moments of our Interview— ha, ha—our momentary close farewell. First we establish emotional contact, by speaking to each other, by telling each other, as we have been doing, about each other's lives: And then: . . . sex," he said bluntly, strangely flatly.

He begins turning the pages of the album, holding it over so that both of us can look at it. From its black pages emerge various photographs of different youngmen: some are large, others almost frail—some goodlooking, some harsh. The Professor is saying: "This is my All-American angel. I still have his football—somewhere—" He glanced about the room. "I must get rid of that beer mug," he said absently; going on, showing me the picture of a squarefaced youngman: "When he got married," the Professor explains, "I gave him the money for the wedding ring. He insisted he would pay me back, but I refused: I said: 'Somehow this will be *our* wedding ring.' And he said to me, 'Tante Goul, thats why I asked *you* for the money—and not someone else.' " (I looked at the large blank bulldog face in the picture. I wondered how much the ring had cost.) . . . "And look here, this is the Oklahoma cowboy. If I had been able to, I would have bought him his own Rodeo. Ah, Cam Rider!" he sighed. (I saw a studiedly masculine face mounted on a long lean body—the smile on his face like a stamp.) "And this—this is the Mexican child with shoulderblades like sprouting wings: He had never been inside the Bellas Artes. His eyes were more brilliant than the theater! He wanted to come to America, he would speak about it to me glowingly, and I would describe it to him equally glowingly: It was his dream. Would I bring him here? Alas, he got into trouble with the police." (The face of the dark youngman had stared at the camera with an obviously forced anxiety to please.) "Here is the young French boy—and with him are his mother and father—they insisted on being photographed with the adorable child." (The picture showed a tall starkly pompous older man and a fat goodhumored-looking woman. Between them was a very young, handsome boy, his shirt open to the waist. One of the woman's arms was draped proudly about the boy's shoulders; the other hand held a bottle of wine toward the camera.) . . . "This is for the last," the Professor said, skipping a page, bringing the book to his chest momentarily; goes on: "And this is the most poetic of my poetic angels—he wrote the Most Divine, sensitive poems—crystals! —I helped him to get a grant—not through any foundation, mind you, but part of mine: My life's source at that time thus contributing to his." (The youngman in the picture wore his hair poetically over his forehead.) "He was a beautiful poet—" the Professor sighed, "and when I told him I would help him, he told me, passionately, that he would dedicate his first volume to me. Ive wondered if it came out. . . . Danny, the ice-skater: He glided across my not-so-icy heart. . . . And this one!—a Mr America candidate!" (The body in the photograph gleamed coldly as if chiseled out of ice.) . . . There were other photographs—youngmen in Spain, France, Italy, Germany, Mexico, America . . . several sailors, servicemen, various youngmen in trunks: all staring at the world with a look strangely in common: a look which at first I thought was a coldness behind the smile and then realized must be a kind of muted despair, a franticness to get what the world had offered others and not extended readily to them. . . .

And now the Professor turns back to the page he had skipped. I knew whom the picture would be of: "This—Is—Robbie," he announced. (I saw a handsome youngman sitting on a foreign car, squinting at the sun, smiling widely as if someday he would own the world; as if the world for him was a mirror. But even in the picture he seemed to resent the brightness of the sun, greater than his own.)

"I have here," the Professor sighed, hugging the album closely again, "the indefinable shape of love—to which, dear child, you must not deny my adding your photograph. . . ." I wondered suddenly if. I would photograph with the same hard look. . . . I remember Mr King: "Pictures in a fuckedup album.") "Yes, Love, indeed," the Professor said, "which has many forms. Who loved the most? I? They? Who was the taker, who the giver? Who can tell? Someday—at the last of my Research—I shall know. . . . Now," he said, "take the chair and come stand near me—please. . . ."

I placed the album under the heavy book with the Professor's name on the cover. I could feel the bulging eyes on me as I lifted the book, slipped the album under it on the shelf. I went and stood by the bed.

When I was ready to leave, the Professor waved as usual. Again he sighed after me: "God Is Love!"

Outside, the malenurse stared frozenly at me.

5

The next day I received a third telegram: "NECESSARY" had become "VITAL," and now "VITAL" was replaced by "URGENT." The implied desperation of the telegrams, by now, didnt surprise me, and when I saw the Professor the next day, I expected he would be as composed as I had left him. I was wrong.

Now he seemed very tired. During the "interview" he reached incessantly for a glass of water, swallowed pills. I noticed that the red mark on the tape-measure had been discarded, or it had fallen off. . . . The words still tumbled on anarchically: He strung a necklace on which the beads were his love affairs: describing them intimately.

Suddenly—at the end of the interview, as I stood by the bed, his huge arms hugged me to him.

The smooth rubbery flesh of his gigantic face brushed briefly against my cheek.

I pushed him away—moved back quickly.

From a distance of about two feet his great eyes stared at me, very long. Then, after many moments of such intense wordless relentless staring, he gasped at me: "Those papers! —under the album!—get them!"

Responding quickly to his sudden urgency, I brought the papers to him. He went through them feverishly, and then he brought out three closely printed sheets bound together. He flung them at me. "Read it if you can read!" he shouted viciously.

At the top of the sheet was his name—and then: "RESUMÉ," was printed beneath it: It listed his years at Yale, his many degrees—including honorary ones. "Read it all!" he shouted at me; he trembles. "Go on!" . . . The list continued: foreign service appointments, honorary titles, publications in scholarly reviews, foreign publications, books he had written, citations awarded him. . . .

I looked up from the list and saw the man who had accomplished all this:

And the balloon face, pitiably tilted like a sad dog's, is staring at me with something that could be only racking pain. . . .

"That is me too!" he shouts at me. "I am Respected, Admired, listened to, read!—but what do you care about that? You see only the ridiculous man who made you stand by the bed with your pants down. But do you know *the rest?*"

The transformation was sudden and incredible. His great head was thrust forward toward me, almost beseechingly, like that of a great wounded animal, the eyes almost popping from his face behind the glasses.

"The angels who drained my life!" he said contemptuously. I watch his eyes in fascination, wondering if the tears that may emerge will be giant tears coming from the giant eyes in the giant face.

"The angels! The voracious angels!" he shouts. "The ones who drained me—who never knew *Me!*—never respected Me. Love? Bought! Bought for the prospect of a trip to America, a wedding ring which I would never wear, pairs of shoes and bottles of wine—*bought!* Bought for $7.50 an hour! Bought! . . . for a hundred dollars . . . which was . . . cunningly . . . expected . . . when the word . . . Love . . . was spoken. . . ." There were no tears, the eyes had already run dry.

The malenurse rushes in. "Professor!" he calls urgently, reaching for pills, water. The Professor continues sobbing. The malenurse hugs him to him, closely, tenderly, sheltering him, rocking his head in his arms like a baby, soothing him—his lips kissing the shaved head. . . . The malenurse glares at me suddenly, eyes brimming with hatred. "What Did You Do To Him?" He shoots the words at me like bullets.

"Leave him alone," the Professor sighs, freeing himself from the youngman's sheltering embrace.

The malenurse marches out.

"Larry—" the Professor says, the sobs slowly subsiding, "—Larry is not—. . . an angel. . . ."

And now, spent, he leans back in the propped-up bed. He reaches for a cigarette, shuffling through the box; he finds a black gold-banded one, puts it into his mouth; sighs calmly now: "Forgive me, child. My nerves. It's lying here so long. I spoke rashly. We all do at times. I had no right to—. . . And actually," he said sadly, "actually I dont—really like—. . . to kiss. . . . And after all—the terms—were made—at the beginning—of the interviews. . . . They were, in fact, made long, long ago. . . . Now, child, stand near me again, please. . . . Let me—let me—express—" He stopped. And then with something of contempt aimed both at himself and me, he finishes: "Let me express—My Love. . . ."

When he was through, he said: "God bless you, darling angel. Yes—" he sighed wearily "—God Bless All of You—. . . And me. . . ." He waved his fat hand in the familiar airy benediction, his eyes drooping. For the first time since I had known him, I see him remove the glasses now. The eyes look at me intently. The huge eyes behind the glasses were actually tiny. . . .

"Now go—" he sighed "—yes—fly away—join that endless —endless!—flight of angels. . . ." The eyes closed. His hand moves to the very tip of the tape-measure.

I received no more telegrams. After a week, I telephoned the apartment, and the malenurse answered. "The Professor is dead," he said. His voice was shaken; controlling tears. "The interviews are over," he said, and I knew that in a moment he would be crying. But before I could hear the inevitable sobs, he had hung up.

CITY OF NIGHT

AND THEN THE DAY CAME IN NEW YORK *when, standing on a street or in a park, I would see someone and wonder whether I had been with him—or just talked . . . one night . . . somewhere.*

Briefly, I went to Southampton with someone I had just met. I lay on the beach all day turning brown, trying in idleness to squelch the recurring panic, longing for something still vastly undefined. And briefly, with the same person, I went to Vermont, to a cool, cool summer interlude in a house set in the midst of the green mountains.

As we drove back into the islandcity—into the jungle of knifegleaming buildings—I knew suddenly I wouldnt stay much longer in New York.

I would return to El Paso.

And once again I got a job—determined that the money I would go home with would not be street money.

I said goodbye to Gene de Lancey in the hallway where I had met her, as she had drifted out of the dark corridor of that enormous building. Of all the faces that I would remember from that time in New York—hers, branded with years-long loneliness, was the only one that was around to say to me:

"I hate to see you go. I'll miss you, lambie-pie—much, much more than I can say!"

I walked west to the Greyhound station on 34th Street. I would leave this city unmissed except by Gene de Lancey, even my absence undiscovered. New people would replace me on Times Square and in the park. . . . As I remembered those short, short, short interludes with the streetpeople (sometimes remembered with wryness, sometimes with huge sadness for something undiscovered within them), would they also remember me?—as someone of a long line who had expelled, with them, mementarily, the loneliness: yet, ironically, in-

81

creased it perhaps in the instants following the vagrant soon-to-recur contacts—with others?

I had an acute sense of the incompleteness intrinsic in sharing in another's life. You touch those other lives, barely —however intimately it may be sexually—you may sense things roiling in them. Yet the climax in your immediate relationship with them is merely an interlude. Their lives will continue, youll merely step out. A series of encounters multiplying geometrically. . . . A prismatic network of . . . (I remember the Professor, I see the tiny eyes behind the thick glasses) "interviews."

Like mechanical dolls, people around me along the blocks proceed doggedly to their various morning destinations; wait, mobbed, at the stoplights, restlessly pausing before rushing at each other, meeting in a melée in the middle of the street. They will brush shoulders, unaware, stumble, move on: each person enclosed by his own immediate world.

Suddenly, unexplainably, I wanted to laugh.

The grinding journey to— . . . Where?

In a few days, by the beginning of autumn, I was back in El Paso.

As I opened the door of my mother's house, I saw her standing there waiting for me. She hugged me fiercely to her, and I glanced beyond her at the fragile case with the glass angels. . . .

Now there were steps to retrace.

I called the girl I had climbed Cristo Rey with. Her father answered: She was gone; married; she had a baby. . . .

Alone, I returned to climb that mountain.

Here, on Holy days, I had seen long processions of people from El Paso, Ysleta, Canutillo, Smeltertown, Juarez, as they marched up chanting devout prayers—kneeling at intervals, shawled ladies gripping rosaries. The priests leading the procession; men carrying sadfaced saints. . . . Under the hot white sun, I had wanted to be . . . then . . . a part of that belief that transfixed those faces as they climbed.

And at the top of that mountain—now, years later—I wondered suddenly if emotionally I had really ever left this city.

Almost physically, as I walked down, I could feel those very mountains which awesomely rim the city crushing me as in that childhood dream. But of course it was something else: the memories of that childhood which I had tried to bandage by fleeing the spurious innocence. Returning here again, I felt how easily I could regress to those early attitudes. The memory of the guarded isolation of that window (in that house which we had vacated, that house where my dog had died) drew me again to a craving for a powerful symbolic window away from the world.

If I was to resist these lulling echoes, within this very city I had to usurp those memories. . . .

Once, years ago, El Paso had been a crossroads, between the Eastcoast and the Westcoast, for the stray fairies leaving other cities for whatever restless reason. As a young boy, crossing San Jacinto Plaza (sleepy crocodiles in a round pond, then, so tired and sleepy they wouldnt even wake up when little kids grabbed them by their tails and flipped them into the water), I had seen the giggling groups of birls camping with the soldiers. I had walked quickly past that park. . . . Now the inevitable smalltimecity roundup had come. The cops had swooped jealously on the fairies and to jail they went—and from jail: Away Again.

Still, in this plaza, stray hunters turn up.

But I couldnt remain there long.

I went to a movie theater in South El Paso—resolved, that night, to slaughter those seducing memories in this way:

The man followed me to the head, propositioned me there. I pretended I was a transient, reverting to the poses learned in New York. I told him I needed money. He agreed. In a parked car, in a dark section of this childhood city, I made it.

Crushing into my pocket the ten-dollar bill he had given me: rather than feeling liberated as I had expected, I felt a scorching horrendous guilt.

And I knew that no matter how long I would be in El Paso, I would never again allow that other life of New York to touch me here.

The next day, with my mother, I went to the cemetery where my father was buried. There was only a tiny weather-faded marker over his grave. Memories of his pride at having once been so widely recognized swarmed over me. (And when he had died, as if the world had chosen belatedly to nod once more to him, his picture had appeared with the notice of his death on the front page of the newspaper, and my mother had received telegrams from as far as Mexico City.) . . . But that tiny marker over his grave seemed to acknowledge what life had done to him. When we left the cemetery, we went across the street, and we chose a marble stone for his grave.

A few days later, I returned to the cemetery, alone. The tiny marker had been replaced by the marble stone. Within that ground, his body had decayed. He lived only in my thoughts of him. I looked at the childhood-coveted ring which he had given me the last time I had seen him alive. To a great extent, for me, it was all that was left of him.

Now I drove around the city in my brother's car, still retracing those early years.

I stopped before the house where Winnie had died, where I had grown up. The porch no longer slanted. The skeleton vine was gone. The walls had been painted white. A dark shade was pulled over the window where I had looked out at the cactus garden, the street . . . my dead dog in the wind. . . . I tried from the sidewalk to look into the backyard. . . . My mother's white sheets had hung on a line there, and I had watched her in unfocused fascination. Those remembered clean, clean sheets in the Texas wind. . . . Now a new fence blocked my view. But without seeing it, I knew the yard had changed too.

About that house there remained no trace of those angry years.

I listen for the wind.

But the air was completely calm.

The sun looks down blindly at me.

Part Two

"They've been so long on lonely street
They never will go back. . . ."

—*Heartbreak Hotel*

CITY OF NIGHT

SOUTHERN CALIFORNIA, WHICH IS SHAPED SOMEWHAT like a coffin, is a giant sanatorium with flowers where people come to be cured of life itself in whatever way. . . . This is the last stop before the sun gives up and sinks into the black, black ocean, and night—usually starless here—comes down.

And although youll soon discover youre still separated from the Sky, trapped down here now by the blanket of smog and haze locking you from Heaven, still theres the sun, even in winter, enough—importantly—to tan you healthy gold . . . and palmtrees drooping shrugging what-the-hell . . . green-grass . . . cool, cool blessed evenings even when the afternoons are fierce.

And flowers . . .

Roses, roses!

Orange and yellow poppies like just-lit matches sputtering in the breeze. Birds of paradise with long pointed tongues; blue and purple lupines; joshua trees with incredible bunches of flowers held high like torches—along long, long rows of phallic palm-trees with sunbleached pubic hair. . . .

Everywhere!

And carpets of flowers even at places bordering the frenetic freeways, where cars race madly in swirling semicircles—the Harbor Freeway crashes into the Santa Ana Freeway, into the Hollywood Freeway, and when the traffic is clear, cars in long rows in opposite lanes, like cold steel armies out for Blood, create a *whooooosh!* that repeating itself is like the sound of the restless windswept ocean, and the cars wind in and out dashing nowhere, somewhere. . . .

Anywhere!

Along the coast, beaches stretch indifferently.

You can rot here without feeling it.

All that, I would see and realize later.

Now it's the Greyhound station in the midst of the Westcoast Times Square, the area about Los Angeles Street, Main Street, Spring, Broadway, Hill—between about 4th and 7th streets.

(From El Paso—knowing that my journey had somehow just begun—I had returned to New York. Again to the sexual anarchy. . . . In a period of about a month, I lived on East 16th Street, then 70th Street, finally Riverside Drive, in a once-mansion converted now into rooms-for-rent: From a large window I could see the trees along the strip of park—the river gray beyond it—and as those trees turned bare, sighingly releasing their leaves, I knew New York for me had been exhausted. I must find another city.)

I walk along Main Street, Los Angeles, now. The juke-boxes blare their welcome. Dingy bars stretch along the blocks —three-feature moviehouses, burlesque joints, army and navy stores; gray rooming houses squeezed tightly hotly protesting against each other; colored lights along the street: arcades, magazine stores with hundreds of photographs for sale of chesty unattainable never-to-be-touched tempest-storm leggy women in black sheer underwear, hot shoeshine clipstands, counter restaurants . . . the air stagnant with the odor of onions and cheap greasy food.

Instantly, I recognize the vagrant youngmen dotting those places: the motorcyclists without bikes, the cowboys without horses, awol servicemen or on leave. . . . And I know that moments after arriving here, I have found an extension, in the warm if smoggy sun, of the world I had just left.

As I stand on the corner of 6th and Main, a girlish Negro youngman with round eyes swishes up: "Honey," she says— just like that and shrilly loudly, enormous gestures punctuating her words, "you look like you jest got into town. If you aint gotta-place, I got a real nice pad. . . ." I only stare at her. "Why, baby," she says, "dont you look so startled—*this* is L.A.! —and thank God for that! Even queens like me got certain rights! . . . Well," she sighs, "I guess you wanna look around first. So I'll jest give you my number." She handed me a card, with her name, telephone number, address: Elaborately Engraved. "Jest you call me—anytime!" she said.

And the spadequeen breezed away, turned back sharply catching sight of another youngman, with a small suitcase. I heard her say just as loudly and shrilly: "Dear, you look like you jest got into town, and I— . . ."

I turn the engraved card over, and on it there is written in ink: WELCOME TO LOS ANGELES!

I walk into a bar by the corner, next to the loan shop.
HARRY'S BAR. . . . It's a long bar with accusing mirrors
lining its back. A canvas hanging across the ceiling from wall
to wall makes the bar resemble an elongated circus tent. . . .
Although it is early afternoon, there are many people here. I
realize immediately that this is a malehustling bar. Behind the
counter a gay young waiter flutters back and forth, all airy
bird-gestures. The scores sit eyeing the drifters who are stationed idly about the bar, by the jukebox, leaning against the
booths.

I sit at the counter and ask for a draft beer. The fluttering
bartender winks. WELCOME! his eyes beam. . . . Now the
man next to me says: "You shouldnt be spending your money."
He slurs the words, hes very drunk. He pushes my money back
toward me, replaces it with a dollarbill of his own on the
counter. "Wottayadrinkin?" he asks me. I change from draft
to bourbon.

Hes a slender not-yet middle-aged man—well dressed—
although in his juiced-up state, his clothes are slightly disheveled. He is not effeminate, but from the way hes looking
at me calculatingly, I know hes a score. I sit there next to
him for long minutes, and he doesnt say anything. I begin
to think hes lost interest. I go to the head, through the
swinging door. The odor of urine and disinfectant chokes me.
There are puddles of dirty water on the floor. Over the streaky
urinal, crude obscene drawings, pleading messages jump at
you. Someone has described himself glowingly, as to age,
appearance, size. Beneath the self-glorifying description, another had added: "Yes, but are you of good family?" Another
scrawled note—a series: "Candy is a queen." "No she isnt."
"Yes I am. . . ." And in bold, shouting black letters across the
wall:

IN THE BEGINNING GOD CREATED
FAIRIES & THEY MADE MEN

The drunk man walks into the head. "You broke?" he asks
me abruptly. I wasnt; I said yes. "Wanna come with me?" he
said.

We leave the bar—the bartender calls after us: "Have a
good time!" . . . Outside, we turn left, past the burlesque
house with the fullblown tantalizing pictures of busty women.
We enter the hotel next door.

A ratty-looking man with a cigar barely glances at us, opens
a splotchy old register book, we scribble phony names. "Three

dollars," the man behind the counter says. The man Im with opens his wallet. Bills pop out. He counts out three. The man behind the desk says: "That rooms open, you can lock it from the inside." He doesnt give us a key. . . . We go up the long grumbling stairway. Along the hall a door is half-open, a youngish man sat alone on a bed, in shorts, rubbing the inside of his thighs. We move along the maze of . . . lost . . . rooms, until we reach ours. Inside, the room is almost bare. For an ashtray theres a tin can. No towels. The walls are greasy, sweaty plaster peeling in horrendous childhood-nightmare lepershapes snapping at you—no window-screens. Paper curtains with ripped edges like saws hang dismally over the window: a room crushed in by the brief recurring lonesomeness that inhabits it throughout the days, the nights. The bed is slightly rumpled—as if only a hurried attempt had been made to straighten it after its previous occupancy.

The man almost reels. "Heres money," he says, again opening his wallet; some bills flutter carelessly on the rumpled bed. I take them. He stuffs the other bills clumsily back into the wallet.

"You gonna rob me, boy?" he asks me suddenly.

Then he grins drunkenly. "Hell," he says, "Idon-givfuck—happens—happened—manytime. . . . Don-givfuck." His look sobered momentarily. His eyes, which are incredibly deep, incredibly sad, look at me pleadingly. "Gonna rob me?"

Im thinking: He wants to be robbed, thats why he came up here with me, hes asking me to rob him. . . . I feel a sudden surge of excitement—as if Im being tested. He pushes the wallet loosely into his back pocket.

After a few frantic moments during which I didnt even take off my clothes but merely lay in bed with him touching me, he sighed: "Whew!"—closed his eyes. He turned over on his stomach and seemed to pass out. His wallet is almost sliding out. With an excitement that was almost Sexual, I reach for it. It slips out easily. He didnt move. . . . I stand over the bed looking steadily at him, very long, fixing the scene in my mind, experiencing the same exploding fusion of guilt and liberation I had felt that first time, with Mr King. I hear the man almost-sob: "Gonna rob me?"

The monotonous beat from the jukebox outside invades the room persistently.

I replace the money I had just removed from his wallet. I lay the wallet—intact—beside him. And I walk out, past the unconcerned glance of the man at the desk.

Outside, in the rancid air, I stand looking at the carnival
street. Through the grayish haze of the smoggy afternoon, the
sun shines warmly but feebly—the great myopic eye of
Heaven. . . .

Somehow—I knew—in that room just now—I had failed the
world I had sought.

A few minutes later I was in Pershing Square.

I walk about the teeming park for the first time—past the
statues of soldiers, one on each corner of the Hill Street side—
past an ominous cannon on Olive, aimed defiantly at the slick
wide-gleamingwindowed buildings across the streets: the banks,
the travel agencies (representations of The Other World, to
which I will flee recurrently in guilt and feel just as guilty for
having abandoned, if never completely, the world of the parks,
the streets)—past the statue of Beethoven with a stick, turning
his back fiercely on the Pershing Square menagerie.

Throughout the park, preachers and prophets dash out *Damnation!* in a disharmony of sounds—like phonographs gone
mad: locked in a block-square sunny asylum among the
flowers and the palmtrees, fountains gushing gaily: Ollie, all
wiry white hair, punctuating his pronouncements with threats
of a citizen's arrest aimed at the hecklers . . . Holy Moses, his
hair Christlike to his shoulders, singing soulfully . . . the
bucktoothed spiritual-singing Jenny Lu howling she was a
jezebel-woman (woe-*uh!*) until she Seed The Light (praise the
Lord-*uh!*) on the frontporch to Hell (holy holy Halleluj-*uh!*),
grinding, bumping at each *uh!* in a frenzied kind of jazz; and
a Negro woman, sweating, quivers in coming-Lord-type ecs-
tasy: "Lawd, Ahs dribben out da Debil! Ah has cast him back
to Hell! Lawd, fill me wid Yuh Presence!" —*uh!*-ing in a long
religious orgasm. . . . Gone preachers wailing receiving God:
Saint Tex, who got The Word in Beaumont scorched one
wined-up morning on the white horizon: BRING THE WORD
TO SINNING CALIFORNIA! . . . And five young girls, all
in white, the oldest about 16, stand like white candles waxing
in the sun, all white satin (*forgive my uncommitted sins!*),
holding in turn a picture of Christ Crucified, and where the
blood was coming, it was wax, which caught the light and
shimmered like thick ketchup; and the five white angelsisters
stand while their old man preaches *Sinners! Sinners!! Sinners!!!*
—and the cutest of the angelsisters, with paradoxically Alive
freckles snapping orange in the sun, and alive red sparkling

hair, is giggling in the warm Los Angeles smog afternoon
among the palmtrees—but the oldest is quivering and wailing,
and one day, oh, I think, the little angelsister will see theres
nothing to giggle about, Truly—her old man having come
across with the rough Message, and of course she'll start to
quiver and wail where once she smiled, freckles popping in
the sun. . . . And an epileptic youngman thanks God for his
infirmity—his ponderous, beloved Cross To Bear. . . .

Among the roses.

And while the preachers dash out their damning messages,
the winos storm Heaven on cheap wine; hungry-eyed scores
with money (or merely with a place to offer the homeless
youngmen they desire) gather about the head hunting the
malehustlers and wondering will they get robbed if— . . . Pickpockets station themselves strategically among the crowds as
if listening in rapt attention to the Holy Messages. And malehustlers ("fruithustlers"/"studhustlers": the various names for
the masculine young vagrants) like flitting birds move restlessly about the park—fugitive hustlers looking for lonely fruits
to score from, anything from the legendary $20-up to a pad
at night and breakfast in the morning and whatever you can
clinch or clip. . . . And the heat in their holy cop uniforms,
holy because of the Almighty Stick and the Almightier Vagrancy Law; the scattered junkies, the smalltime pushers, the
teaheads, the sad panhandlers, the occasional lonely exiled
nymphos haunting the entrance to the men's head; more fruits
with hungry eyes—the young ones searching for a mutual,
unpaid-for partner; the tough teenage girls making it with the
lost hustlers. . . . And—but mostly later at night, youll find,
when the shadows will shelter them—queens in colorful shirt-
blouses—dressed as much like women as The Law allows that
particular moment—will dish each other like jealous bitchy
women, commenting on the desirability or otherwise of the
stray youngmen they may offer a place for the night. And they
giggle constantly in pretended happiness.

And on the benches along the inside ledges, the pensioned
old men and women sit serenely daily in the sun like retired
judges separated now stoically from the world they once
judged. . . .

All!—all amid the incongruous music of the Welkian-
Lombardian school of corn, piped periodically from somewhere along the ledges! All amid the flowers!—the twin
fountains which will gush rainbowcolored verypretty at night.

. . . The world of Lonely-Outcast America squeezed into Pershing Square, of the Cities of Terrible Night, downtown now trapped in the City of Lost Angels. . . .

And the trees hang over it all like some apathetic fate.

MISS DESTINY:
The Fabulous Wedding

1

THE FIRST TIME I SAW MISS DESTINY was of course in Pershing Square, on the cool, almost cold, moist evening of a warm smoggy day.

Im sitting in the park with Chuck the cowboy on the railing facing 5th Street. "Oh oh, here comes Miss Destinee," says Chuck, a cowboy youngman with widehat and boots, very slim of course, of course very slow, with sideburns of course almost to his chin, and a giant tattoo on his arm that says: DEATH BEFORE DISHONOR. "Destinee's last husband jes got busted pushing hard stuff, man," Chuck is going on, "an she is hot for a new one, so watch out, man—but if you ain got a pad, you can always make it at Destinee's—it's like a gone mission, man!"

Indeed, indeed! here comes Miss Destiny! fluttering out of the shadows into the dimlights along the ledges like a giant firefly—flirting, calling out to everyone: "Hello, darling, I love you—I love you too, dear—so very much—ummmm!" Kisses flung recklessly into the wind. . . . "What oh what did Chuck say to you, darling?" to me, coming on breathlessly rushing words. "You must understand right here and now that Chuck still loves me, like all my exhusbands (youre new in town, dear, or I would certainly have seen you before, and do you have a place to stay?—I live on Spring Street and there is a 'Welcome!' mat at the door)—oh, they *nevuh!* can forget me—of course I loved Chuck once too—" (sigh) "—such a butch cowboy, look at him—but havent I loved every new hustler in town?—but oh this restlessness in me!— and are you married, dear?—oh, the lady doth indeed protest Too Much—" (this last addressed to Jenny Lu, still bumping (woe-*uh*!). I *adore* Married men—as long as they are Faithful to me, you understand, of course—and I must warn you right here and now about Pauline, who is the most evil people in

94

this city and you must stay away from her when she tries to make out with all kinds of—Ah Beg To Tell You—" ("Whewoo!" sighed Chuck.) "—untrue promises as some—people—have—found—out—" looking coldly at Chuck, then rushing on: "Oh I am, as everyone will tell you, A Very Restless Woman—"

She—he (Miss Destiny is a man)—went on about her—his—restlessness, her husbands, asking me questions in between, figuring out how Bad I was ("Have you been 'interviewed' yet by Miss Lorelei?—I mean Officer Morgan, dear—we call her Miss Lorelei. And dont let her scare you, dear—and Im sure you wont—why, Miss Lorelei—I mean, Sergeant Morgan—is as much a lady as I am: I saw her in the mensroom one time, and she ran everybody out—except this cute young boy—and— . . .")—looking alternately coyly and coldly at Chuck then me seductively: all of which you will recognize as the queen's technique to make you feel like such an irresistible so masculine so sexual so swinging stud, and queens can do it better than most real girls, queens being Uninhibited.

Now Miss Destiny is a youngman possibly 20 but quite as possibly 18 and very probably 25, with false I.D. like everyone else if she is underage: a slim young queen with masses and masses of curly red hair (which she fondly calls her "rair"), oh, and it tumbles gaily over a pale skinny face almost smothering it at times. Unpredictably occasionally she comes on with crazy Southern sounds cultivated, you will learn, all the way from northern Pennsylvania.

"Oh my dear!" she exclaims now, fluffing out her "rair," "here I am talking all about my Sex life, and we have not been Properly Introduced! . . . Im Miss Destiny, dear—and let me hasten to tell you before you hear it wrong from othuh sources that I am famous even in Los gay Angeles—why, I went to this straight party in High Drag (and I mean *High*, honey—gown, stockings, ostrich plumes in my flaming rair), and—"

"An you know who she was dancing with?" Chuck interrupted.

"The Vice, my dear," Miss Destiny said flatly, glowering at Chuck.

"An she was busted, man—for ah mas—mask— . . ."

"Masquerading, dear. . . . But how was I to know the repressed queer was the vice squad—tell me? . . ." And she goes on breathlessly conjuring up the Extravagant Scene. . . .

(Oh shes dancing like Cinderella at the magic ball in this

Other World shes longingly invading, and her prince-charm-
ing turns out to be: the vice squad. And oh Miss Destiny
gathers her skirts and tries to run like in the fairytale, but the
vice grabs her roughly and off she goes in a very real coach
to the glasshouse, the feathers trembling now nervously. Miss
Destiny insists she is a real woman leave her alone. (But oh,
oh! how can she hide That Thing between his legs which
should belong there only when it is somebody else's?) . . . All
lonesome tears and Humiliation, Miss Destiny ends up in the
sex tank: a wayward Cinderella. . . .)

"Now, honey," she says with real indignation, "I can see
them bustin me for Impersonating a man—but a woman!—
really! . . ." And you will notice that Miss Destiny like all the
other swinging queens in the world considers herself every bit a
Lady. "But nevuh mind," she went on, "I learned things in
the countyfawm I didnt know before—like how to make eye-
shadow out of spit and bluejeans—and oh my dear the kites I
flew!—I mean to say, no one can say I didnt send my share
of invitations out! . . . Of course, I *do* have to go regularly to
the county psychiatrist (thats a mind doctor, dears)—to be
(would you believe it? this is what they actually told me:)
'cured'! Well! One more session with him, and I'll have *him*
on the couch!—but now—" turning her attention to me fullblast, because, you will understand, Miss Destiny scouts at
night among the drifting youngmen, and at the same time you
can tell shes out to bug Chuck: and when she asked me would
I go to the flix with her now ("across the street, where it is
Divine but you mustnt be seen there too often," she explains,
"because they will think youre free trade— . . ."), Chuck
said: "It would not do you no good, Destinee, they will not let
you in the men's head."

."Miss Destiny, *Mister* Chuck," she corrects him airily.

And went on: "Didnt I tell you all my exhusbands are
jealous of me? Chuck lived with me, dear," she explains, "as
just about every other studhustler has at one time or another,
I must add modestly. But, baby, it was a turbulent marriage
(that means very stormy, dear). Why, I just couldnt drag
Chuck from the window—he—"

"Oh, man," interrupts Chuck. "Next to Miss Destinee's pad
theres this real swell cunt an she walks aroun all day in her
brassiere—standin by the window, an she—"

"But I fixed that!" Miss Destiny says triumphantly. "I
nailed the damn windowshades so no one can look out at that
cunt anymore! . . . Oh!" she sighed, her hand at her forehead,

"those days were trying days. Chuck's a good hustler—but hes too lazy even to try to score sometimes. And, honey, my unemployment check went just so far: You see, I took a job just long enough to qualify for unemployment, and then I turned up all madeup and they let me go—and everytime they call me up for a job, why I turn up in drag and they wont have me! . . . But anyway— . . ."

Looking at Chuck and Miss Destiny—as she rushes on now about the Turbulent Times—I know the scene: Chuck the masculine cowboy and Miss Destiny the femme queen: making it from day to park to bar to day like all the others in that ratty world of downtown L.A. which I will make my own: the world of queens and malehustlers and what they thrive on, the queens being technically men but no one thinks of them that way—always "she"—their "husbands" being the masculine vagrants—fleetingly and often out of convenience sharing the queens' pads—never considering theyre involved with another man (the queen), and as long as the hustler goes only with queens—and with other men only for scoring (which is making or taking sexmoney, getting a meal, making a pad)—he is himself not considered "queer"—he remains, in the vocabulary of that world, "trade."

"Yes," Miss Destiny is going on, "those were stormy times with Chuck—and then, being from cowcountry, God bless him, Chuck believes every Big story: like when Pauline told him she'd really set him up—"

"Man," Chuck explained, laughing, "Pauline is this queen thats got more bull than Texas!"

"Can you imagine?" Miss Destiny says to me. "She offered him a Cadillac! Pauline! Who hasnt even got enough to keep her dragclothes in proper shape! . . . But nevuhmind, let him be gullible (thats someone who believes untrue stories). And, besides," she says with a toss of her head, "I flipped over Sandy, a bad new stud. . . . But Chuck's still jealous of me— he knows Im looking for a new husband—now that poor Sandy (my most recent ex, dear) got busted, and I know he didnt have any hard narcotics on him like they say he did— they planted them in his car— . . . Shake that moneymakuh, honey!—" (this to a spadequeen swishing by) "—and I still love my Sandy—did the best I could, tried to bail him out, hire a good attuhnee, but it was no good—they laughed when I said he was my husband. The quality of muhcee is mighty strained indeed—as the dear Portia said (from Shakespeare, my dears—a very Great writer who wrote ladies' roles for dragqueens in his time). And it breaks my heart to think of my poor Sandy in the joint away from women all that time, him so redhot he might turn queer, but oh no not my Sandy, hes all stud. If I know him, he'll come out of the joint rich, hustling the guards. . . . And I tried to be faithful—but the years will be so long—and what can a girl do, and restless the way I am?—restless and crying muhself to sleep night aftuh night, missing him—missing him. But my dears, I realize I Will Have To Go On—he would want it that way. Well, queens have died eaten by the ah worm of ah love, as the Lovely Cleopatra said—she was The Queen of Ancient Egypt —" (quoting, misquoting Shakespeare—saying it was a lovely he-roine who said it in the play—taking it for granted—a safe assumption in her world—that no one will understand her anyway). "Then Miss Thing said to me (Miss Thing is a fairy perched on my back like some people have a monkey or a conscience)," she explained, "well, Miss Thing said to me, 'Miss Destiny dear, dont be a fool, fix your lovey rair and find you a new husband—make it permanent this time by really getting Married—and even if you have to stretch your unemployment, dont allow him to push or hustle' (which breaks up a marriage)—and Miss Thing said, 'Miss Destiny dear, have a real wedding this time.' . . . A real wedding," Miss Destiny sighed wistfully. "Like every young girl should have at least once. . . . And when it happens oh it will be the most simpuhlee Fabulous wedding the Westcoast has evuh seen! with oh the most beautiful queens as bridesmaids! and the handsomest studs as ushers! (and you will absolutely have to remove those boots, Chuck)—and *Me!* . . . Me . . . in virgin-white . . . coming down a winding staircase . . . carrying a white bouquet! . . . and my family will be crying for joy. . . . And there will be champagne! cake! a real priest to puhfawm the Ceremony!—" She broke off abruptly, shutting her eyes deliriously as if to visualize the scene better. Then she opened them again, onto the frantic teeming world of Pershing Square. . . .

"They will bust you again for sure if you have that wedding, Miss Destinee," said Chuck gravely.

"It would be worth it," sighed Miss Destiny. "Oh, it would be worth it."

Then we noticed a welldressed man standing a few feet from us in the shadows, staring at us intently until he saw us looking back and he shifted his gaze, began to smoke, looked up furtively again.

Miss Destiny smiled brightly at him, but he didnt smile back at her, and Miss Destiny said obviously he is a queer and so he must want a man. "So darlings, I will leave you to him and him to whomevuh eenie-meenie-miney he wants. But let me tell you, my dear—" me—confidentially "—that when they dress that elegantly around here, why, they will make all kinds of promises and give you oh two bucks," and Chuck said oh no the score was worth at least twenty, and Miss Destiny laughs like Tallulah Bankhead, who is the Idol of all queens, and says in a husky voice, "Dalling, this is not your young inexperienced sistuh you are talkin to, this is your mothuh, who has been a-round. . . . Why, Miss Thing told me about this sweet stud kid going for a dollar!— . . . Ah, well, as my beloved sweet Juliet said, Parting is: such—sweet—sorrow— . . ." And she sighed now, being Juliet, then whispered to me loud enough for Chuck to hear, "There will be other times, my dear—when you are not Working."

And she moved away with peals of queenly laughter, flirting again, fluttering again, flamboyantly swishing, just as she had come on, saying hello to everyone: "Good evening, Miss Saint Moses, dear— . . ." spreading love, throwing kisses, bringing her delicate hands to her face, sighing, "Too Much!" after some goodlooking youngman she digs, glancing back at Chuck and me as the man moved out of the shadows, closer to us, jingling money.

So there goes Miss Destiny leaving Pershing Square, all gayety, all happiness, all laughter.

"I love you too, dear, ummmm, so much. . . ."

2

Those first days in Los Angeles, I was newly dazzled by the world into which my compulsive journey through submerged lives had led me—newly hypnotized by the life of the streets.

I had rented a room in a hotel on Hope Street—on the fringes of that world but still outside of it (in order always to have a place where I could be completely alone when I must be). Thus the daulity of my existence was marked by a definite boundary: Pershing Square: east of there when the desire to be with people churned within me; west of there to the hotel when I had to be alone. . . . At times, after having combed the bars, the streets, the park, I would flee as if for protection to that hotel room.

Yet other times I needed people fiercely—needed the anarchy of the streets. . . .

And Main Street in Los Angeles is such an anarchy.

This is clip street, hustle street—frenzied-nightactivity street: the moving back and forth against the walls; smoking, peering anxiously to spot the bulls before they spot you; the rushing in and out of Wally's and Harry's: long crowded malehustling bars.

And here too are the fairyqueens—the queens from Everywhere, America—the queenly exiles looking for new "husbands" restlessly among the vagrant hustlers with no place to stay, and the hustlers will often clip the queens (if there is anything to clip), and the queens will go on looking for their own legendary permanent "Daddies" among the older men who dig the queens' special brand of gone sexplay, seldom finding those permanent connections, and living in Main and Spring Street holes: sometimes making it (employed and unemployed, taking their daddies and being taken by the hustlers) —sometimes hardly, sometimes not at all.

And the malehustlers live with them off and on, making it from bar to lonesome room, bragging about the $50 score with the fruit from Bel Air who has two swimming pools, jack, and said he'd see you again (but if he didnt show, you dont say that), and youre clinching a dime and a nickel for draft beer at Wally's or Harry's or the 1-2-3 or Ji-Ji's so you can go inside and score early, and make it with one of the vagrant young girls to prove to yourself you're still All Right.

And so Main Street is an anarchy where the only rule is Make It! . . . And the only reminders of the world beyond its boundaries are the policewagons that cruise the streets— the cops that pick you at random out of Hooper's all-night coffee shop after 2:00 in the morning. . . . The free jammed ride to the glasshouse for fingerprints . . .

Rock-n-roll sounds fill the rancid air.

This was the world I joined.

A couple of blocks away from Main Street, on Spring— squashed on either side by gray apartment buildings *(walls greasy from days of cheap cooking, cobwebbed lightbulbs feebly hiding in opaque darkness, windowscreens if any smooth as velvet with grime—where queens and hustlers and other exiles hibernate)*—just beyond the hobo cafeteria where panhandlers hang dismally outside in the cruel neonlight *(fugitives from the owlfaces of the Salvation Army fighting Evil with no help from God or the cops; fugitives from Uplifting missionwords and lambstew)*—is the 1-2-3.

Outside, a cluster of pushers gather like nervous caged monkeys, openly offering pills and maryjane thrills, and you see them scurrying antlike to consult with Dad-o, the Negro king of downtown smalltime pushers—and Dad-o, sitting royally at the bar like a heap of very black shiny dough, says yes or no arbitrarily.

And that is the way it is.

I saw Miss Destiny again one Saturday night at the 1-2-3. And that is when it swings.

"Oooee . . ." she squealed. "I *wondered* where you were, baby, and I have thought about you—and thought, why hes gone already—*Escaped!*—and oh Im so glad youre not, and come here, I want you to meet my dear sistuhs and their boy-friends—" being, naturally, the downtown queens and hustlers who are Miss Destiny's friends.

And squeezing expertly through the thick crowd, Miss Destiny led me into a cavern of trapped exiles—of painted sallow-faced youngmen, artificial manikin faces like masks; of tough-looking masculine hustlers, young fugitives from every-where and everything, young lean faces already proclaiming Doom; of jaded old and middle-aged men seeking the former and all-aged homosexuals seeking the latter—all crowded into this long narrow, ugly bar, plaster crumbling in chunks as if it had gnawed its own way into the wall; long benches behind the tables, splintered, decaying; mirrors streaked yel-low—a bar without visible windows; cigarette smoke tinged occasionally with the unmistakable odor of maryjane hovering over us almost unmoving like an ominous hand. . . . And the faces emerge from the thick smoke like in those dark moody photographs which give you the feeling that the subjects have been imprisoned by the camera.

"This is Trudi," Miss Destiny was saying, and Trudi is probably the realest and sweetest-looking queen in L.A., and youd have to be completely queer not to dig her. Her hair is long enough for a woman, short enough for a man. Her eye-lashes were painted arched over round blue coquettish eyes, and of all the queens I will meet in L.A., Trudi has most ac-curately been able to duplicate the female stance so that, un-like most other queens, she has not become the mere parody of a woman. "Hi, baby," she says, pursing her lips cutely, "welcome to the snakepit." She indicates the scene about her as if she had been born to reign over it.

"And this is Skipper," Miss Destiny continues, and as if

presenting his credentials adds, in a lower tone for me only—
and I can barely hear her over the blasting music: "He used to
be a physique model, baby, and he became quite famous in
Hollywood once—hes even hustled Officer Morgan—and
that's the truth—but he'll tell you all about that, Im sure—"
And Skipper is restlessly scrutinizing the familiar scene; almost—it seems at times—in bewilderment—as if looking
around him each moment, he is newly aware of where he is.
Often he squinted as if to cloud the scene from his mind. He
is now—and it will turn out is usually—talking about a plan
to hit the Bigtime again. "Hi, jack!" he says, and his eyes rake
the bar. . . . And all at once he doesnt look nearly as young
as he first appeared.

"And my dear, Dear sistuh Lola—" Miss Destiny is saying
(queens calling each other sisters); and Lola is quite possibly
"dear, Dear" because undoubtedly shes the ugliest queen in
the world, with painted eyes like a silent moviestar, and a
black turtleneck sweater running into her coarse shiny black
hair so that it seems shes wearing a hood—and has a husky
meanman's voice and looks like nothing but an ugly man in
semidrag. "Always room for one more," she rasps, welcoming
me.

And you have of course already met Mistuh Chuck," Miss
Destiny says sighingly, and Chuck tipped his widehat in salutation: "Howdee."

"And this is Tiguh—" Miss Destiny went on. And Tiger
(names, you will notice, as obviously emphatically masculine
as the queens' are emphatically obviously feminine and for the
same reason: to emphasize the roles they will play) is a heavily
tattooed youngman who has precisely that quality you sense
in caged tigers glowering savgely through iron bars.

"And Darling Dolly—" Miss Destiny said.

And Darling Dolly corrects Miss Destiny: "Darling Dolly
Dane, Destiny dear."

And Destiny corrects her: "Miss Destiny, Darling Dolly
Dane, dear."

Truly, you will admit, Darling Dolly Dane is cute in the
dimlight and smokeshadows, with softlooking creamskin and
dancing eyes and a loose sweater tonight and slacks—acting
like a flirt teenage girl out to get laid.

"And Buddy—" Miss Destiny finishes with the introductions.

Buddy is a blond very young boy, I would say 19—at whom,
as Miss Destiny and I sit at the already-crowded table, Darling
Dolly Dane is glaring. Miss Destiny tells me confidentially, to

explain the cool looks between Darling Dolly and Buddy, that Buddy had been living with Darling Dolly Dane until last night when she found he hocked some of her drag clothes and she locked him out and he had to sleep in his brokendown Mercury, which may not even be his. . . .

Now a score at the bar is ostentatiously turning us on to free drinks—and cokes for Darling Dolly, who is making such a thing about her Not Drinking. On a small balcony over the head, the rock-n-roll spades are going, perched like a nest of restless blackbirds. A queen, obviously drunk, has climbed on it and has started to do an imitation strip, and Ada, who runs the bar and is a real woman—a mean, tough blonde like a movie madam—climbs after her dragging her roughly off the balcony just as the queen is unsnapping her imaginary brassiere, saying:

"Sssssssssssssufferrrrrrrrrrr. . . ."

At the table, everyone is talking, eyes constantly searching the bar. The beat of the music somehow matches the movements, the stares, the muted desperation all around; the smothered moans of the spade now blaring words from the balcony is like a composite moan, a wail emanating in unison from everyone crushed into this dirty bar. . . . Darling Dolly is breathlessly explaining the Severe Jolt she got when she got home and found her best drag clothes gone: "My lovely lace negligee—my studded shoes!" Buddy shakes his head and says to the table: "I needed the bread." Darling Dolly stabs him with a look. Chuck says hes heard of a malehouse in Hollywood where he can make hundreds of dollars a day: "But I don know where it is so I cain apply." Miss Destiny says, "Chuck, my dear, you are just too lazy to get ahead—remember the $15 score I got you and you fell asleep?" . . . Trudi is wondering wheres her daddy, and Miss Destiny explains to me that Trudi's "daddy" is an old man whos been "keeping Trudi for ages—and keeps Skipper, too, sometimes—but indirectly": Skipper living off and on with Trudi and hitting it big occasionally—"after being Really Big in Hollywood once"—and going away, coming back to Trudi's. . . . Nearby, an emaciated man with devouring deep-buried eyes is pretending to read the titles on the jukebox, but it's obvious that he is fascinatedly studying Tiger's tattoos—and Tiger, noticing this, glances at him with huge undisguised contempt, which sends the emaciated man into an ecstasy of sick smiles.

Now the queens at the table are wondering aloud who the score buying the juice is digging: the queens or otherwise, and which one. And which does it turn out hes digging? The queens. And which one? Darling Dolly Dane. And when this became known, by means of the "waitress," Darling Dolly skips over to him, perches on the stool next to him at the bar, and says, "Another tall cool Coca-Cola please, honey, and make it straight." Miss Destiny sighed, "Well, lordee, Tara is saved tonight."

Immediately Skipper had a plan to clip the score, and Trudi says philosophically, "Dont get nervous, youll shake the beads"—(the beads being life—fate—chance—anything)— "and besides, Darling Dolly saw him first." Miss Destiny says theyre all Too Much. Suddenly shes becoming depressed— and the obvious reason is that the score who it turned out dug queens didnt dig her.

"Oh, Im *really* depressed now!" Miss Destiny said. Someone had mentioned that Pauline had just walked in. I looked, and theres Pauline—a heavily painted queen who thinks she looks like Sophia Loren—with a collar like the wicked queen's in Snow White.

Miss Destiny said icily: "Pauline . . . is a lowlife . . . prostitute."

Trudi: "A cheap whore."

Lola, in her husky man's voice and glowering nearsightedly: "A slut."

Trudi: "A common streetwalker."

Lola: "A chippy."

Miss Destiny—conclusively, viciously: "A *cocksucker!*"

Chuck gagged on his beer. "She ain got nothin on you, Destinee!"

Then quickly, diverting attention from Pauline and putting Chuck down with a look, Miss Destiny asked me abruptly do I know anyone in Hollywood who has a beautiful home with a beautiful Winding Staircase where she can come down—"to marry," she explains, "my new husband and spend my life blissfully (thats very happily, dear) on unemployment with him forever."

Darling Dolly Dane returned suddenly very angrily lisping the man had offered her two bucks, after such a show of buying drinks. "And do you know what the sonuvabitch *wants* for two miserable goddam bucks?"

"To marry you," said Destiny aloofly.

Skipper had a plan to clip the score.

"I dont have my husband picked out yet," Miss Destiny went on as if there had been no interruption. "That part isnt too important yet—I'll wait until I fall in love again (dont look at Pauline, shes looking over here)—the important thing now is the Winding Staircase."

Darling Dolly Dane: "Two miserable bucks!"

Lola: Youve gone for less, dear."

Darling Dolly Dane, wiggling: "This aint no change-machine, Mae."

Chuck: "Hey, sweetie, you light up with a nickel?"

Skipper: "Darling Dolly, you go with the cholly, and I'll cool it by the parking lot—"

Tiger: "Stomp the shit out of him."

Trudi, sighing as if no one but she really understands: "My dears, I tell you it's the goddam beads."

Buddy: "Darling Dolly, tell him *ten* so you can get your drag clothes out of hock."

Miss Destiny sighs: "Oh! this! is! too! depressing!—really, my dears, you talk like common thieves and muggers—and what am I doing here? . . . Now as I was saying—what?—oh, yes— . . ."

Now the score—checking the looks and mean sounds—starts to leave, and Darling Dolly rushes after him, leaving Skipper plotting, and she whispers something to the score (on tiptoes; she is very short), and as they went out together, Buddy laughs and laughs: "Two bucks!" And Lola said, "Youve gone for less, dear."

I promised Destiny to tell her if I met anyone with a beautiful home and a winding staircase.

"Baby," she said abruptly, unexpectedly moodily, "dont you think I look *real?*" And before anyone can answer, possibly afraid of the answer, she went on hurriedly, "Oh, but you should have seen me when I first came out."

"Here it comes, dears, the goddam Miss Destiny beads," said Trudi, recognizing Miss Destiny's cue and looking over the crowd for her "daddy," who is to meet her here tonight and take her—she says—to Chasen's—Beverly Hills' exclusive restaurant.

And indeed, just like that, Miss Destiny—on—has begun to tell me about when she first came out and how she became Miss Destiny. Soon, Im the only one listening to her, the others moving away restlessly, having heard it or portions of it or a version of it: Trudi finds her "daddy"—a fat middle-aged man—and Chuck goes to the bar and is now talking to a flashily dressed fruit in a redcheckered vest. Skipper is playing the shuffleboard, ramming the disk vengefully into the pins. . . .

Wordlessly entranced, the emaciated man is standing next to Tiger where hes leaning against the peeling wall. Buddy has left the bar, probably going to Main Street or the park. And Lola is sitting alone at the bar, elbows propping her ugly face dejectedly. Looking at her from the distance, I realized how much she looks like a lesbian.

"Before I flipped," Miss Destiny was saying, rushing, as if the hurried flow of her words would keep me with her, "I was very Innocent," and I could sense the huge depression suddenly, perhaps that one rejection just now echoing into the very depths of her consciousness setting off a thousand other rejections. "Of course," she went on, "Miss Thing had told me, 'Why how ridiculous!—that petuh between your legs simpuhlee does not belong, dear.' And oh, once, when I was a kid, I asked my father for *paperdolls*, and he brought me some Superman *comicbooks* instead—and then, oh! I asked him for *Superman* paperdolls. . . . And they were always so ashamed of me when I wanted to dress up—and my father threw me out—on a cold night, too—and I took my doll with me that I slept with since I was little—and I had to quit college (where I studied Dramatics, dear, but not for long, because they wouldnt let me play the girl's part), and I went to Philadelphia. And the first thing I did, why, I bought myself a flaming-red dress and higheeled sequined shoes and everyone thought I was Real, and Miss Thing said, 'Hurray, honey! youve done it—stick to it,' and I met a rich daddy, who thought I was Real, and he flipped over me and took me to a straight cocktail party. . . ."

And so, with Eminent contradictions (I must warn you), the wayward saga of Miss Destiny unfolds—that night at the 1-2-3, in the ocean of searching faces:

"Naturally," she continued, "I got into the Finest circles. Philadelphia society and all that—and Im sippin muh cocktail at this party when in walks the most positively gorgeous youngman I have evuh seen. And he stares at me! Walked away from the hostess—who was a real lady (a society model, baby, and later she became a Moviestar and married that king—you know)—" muttering bitch after Pauline who just then passed brushing my shoulder purposely to bug Miss Destiny "—and this gorgeous youngman, why, he comes to me and says—just like that—'You Are My Destiny!' and I thought he said, 'You are *Miss* Destiny,' mistaking me you know for some other girl, and when the hostess says Im the most beautiful fish shes evuh seen, what is my name, Im terrified the gorgeous youngman will drop me if Im not who I think he thinks I am, so I say, 'I am *Miss* Destiny,' and *he* thinks I said, 'I am *his* destiny' (he told me later), and he says, 'Yes oh yes she is,' and from then on I am Miss Destiny—"

(Oh they go home that night and Miss Destiny must confess she is not a real woman, but, oh, oh, he doesnt care, having of course flipped over her, and he takes her to his country estate, his family naturally being Fabulously rich, and they simply Idolize Miss Destiny. . . .)

"His name was Duke," Miss Destiny sighed, "and when I met him, oh I remember, they were playing *La Varsouviana* (thats 'Put Your Little Foot,' dear)—you see, although it was a cocktail party, it was so Elegant that they had an orchestra —and how I loved him, and I know thats a strange name— Duke—but it was his real name, not a nickname—but he would be a wild rose by any other name and smell as sweet! . . . Being aristocrats, all his family had strange names: his mother's name was ah Alexandria, just like the ah queen of ah ancient Sparta who killed the ah emperor in Greek mythology (those are very old stories, dear)—"

Suddenly here is Darling Dolly Dane back gasping tugging at Miss Destiny, who of course resents the intrusion in the middle of her autobiography. "Destiny, Destiny, quick," Darling Dolly pleads, "Ive got to have the key to your pad right away quick hurry!" I notice Darling Dolly is carrying a small bundle that looks suspiciously like a pair of pants. All right, all right—and what does Darling Dolly want the key for? Darling Dolly Dane says she just clipped the score she went with who promised her the deuce, remember? She told him dont bother getting a room, give the extra bread to her, honey, and: "I know a swinging head in an apartment house right around here," Darling Dolly told the score, who was pretty juiced anyhow. So they go up to the head, and the score is thinking this is really getting Saturday-night kicks: gone sex! with a cute queen! in a head! And she took off his pants cooing and his shorts cooing and ran out with both pants and shorts—and wallet. "And look!" she said now, pulling out the wallet, which was green, green like a tree. "So Ive got to go to your pad in case he comes back looking for me.'" "Without pants?" Destiny asked, and adds: "And why my pad? why not yours?" Darling Dolly explains it's too far and too early. Miss Destiny tilted her head, consulting her gay fairy. "Miss Thing says dont give you the key," Miss Destiny said, "but then Miss Thing aint nevuh been busted—so here—" Darling Dolly dashed out with the key. Miss Destiny sighed Darling Dolly was positively Too Much, and I noticed Chuck going out, widehat over his eyes, with the flashy fruit. . . . Lola is still sitting very much alone glowering at her makeup face in the mirror behind the bar. . . .

And Miss Destiny continues typically as if nothing had interrupted her story:

"And then, before I knew it, Duke was dead. . . . He was a truckdriver, and sometimes we were so poor we couldnt even make it: I had to hustle in drag in order to keep us going—of course, he didnt know this—" And then remembering The Wealth and the country estate: "Well, you see his family disinherited him, they couldnt *stand* me." And then remembering the way his family Idolized her: "Well, you see they *loved* me at first, until they Found Out—"

(Now Duke the Aristocrat is Duke the Truckdriver, disinherited but oh so in love with Miss Destiny, and on a cold murky damp foggy day his truck turns over on the highway, the brakes screech shrilly, the wheels are turning round, round, round. . . . The sirens wail: Eeeeeeeeeeeeeeeeeeeeeeeeeeeeee-uh. And When They Came To Tell Miss Destiny, she senses it before they say anything and says: I Want To Be Alone . . . and there is no one to turn to. . . .)

"You see I was an orphan," and then remembering her father who threw her out: "I had lived with my aunt and uncle and called them my father and mother—and it was my uncle who threw me out, the same uncle who Raped me when I was eight years old and I screamed it hurt so and my aunt said forget it, it would go away (she was a degenerate). . . . And each time I close my eyes, I see those goddam wheels going round, round, round—and I hear that tune they were playing when I met him. ('Put your little foot')," she hummed. . . . "And it won't stop until I hear the *crash!* . . . Oh!"

(So Miss Destiny lones it to Washington D.C. where she makes it with men who think shes Real. And when they reach That Point in the cramped car she must insist on, she will say no honey not that, I have got the rag on—she will of course be welltaped. "But thats no reason why we cant have a swinging time anyway." And if not she will say shes underage and threaten to scream rape. (And dont ask how, Or If, she always got away with it.) But a jealous bartender, who Knows, tells three sailors who want to make it with her that shes not a fish, shes a fruit, and the sailorboys wait outside for her, mean, and start to tear off her beautiful dress and say, If youre

*a girl wow the world is yours honey, but if youre a goddam
queer start praying. . . . And oh Miss Destiny runs as you will
begin to think she is always doing, and they grab her roughly
as you will begin to think they are always doing, and she
rushes into the street and into a taxi passing by luckily and
the driver says have you been clipped or raped lady?—and:
I will take you to the heat station. She says oh no please forget
it . . . and goes back to Philadelphia to place a Wreath on
Duke's grave, and comes to Los Angeles with a Southern
Accent. . . .)*

"And I became what you see now: a wild restless woman
with countless of exhusbands," Miss Destiny said. "But do you
know, baby, that I have never been Really Married? I mean in
White, coming down a Winding Staircase. . . . And I *will!* I
will fall in love again soon—I can feel it—and when I do, I
will have my Fabulous Wedding, in a pearlwhite gown—" and
she went on delightedly until she caught sight of Pauline's reflection in the panel of mirrors behind the bar, and something
about the way Pauline was looking in our direction clearly
threatened she would come right over and introduce herself
and bug Miss Destiny.

"Goddam queer," Miss Destiny murmured, and she was
fiercely depressed.

3

I left the 1-2-3 and went to Ji-Ji's bar—another malehustling
and queen bar: but tougher. You walk under a small tattered
awning into a dark cavelike room. Beyond the dark, through a
tunnel-like opening, the bar leads into a small narrow lunch-
counter, where malehustlers and queens sit eating. And Ji-Ji,
the old, haggard queen who owns this bar, reigns over it
adoringly as if it were a wayward mission—a hidden underground sheltering those rebels from the life that spat her out.
. . . Dad-o, the Negro pusher, is here now, huddled at one end
of the bar, almost eaten up by the darkness, except where the
light from under the bar gleams in shiny eery highlights on
his sweaty skin; hes talking to a skinny boy next to him—
obviously a pusher.

It is much more quiet here than at the 1-2-3—the superficial
gayety is absent, there is a brooding silence: an undisguised
purposefulness to make it. Even the scores who haunt Ji-Ji's
are colder. They stand appraising the young malehustlers as if
they were up for auction.

As I walked in, a tall newyorkdressed man leans toward me and murmurs: "Lets get out of here and go to my place, boy —I got a bar there myself." His assurance bugs me strangely. The guilt seizes me powerfully. I feel an overwhelming shame suddenly for looking so easily available. "Youre taking a lot for granted," I said. He shrugs his shoulders. "It's Ji-Ji's, isnt it?" he says—but—not so sure of himself any more—he walks away hurriedly. . . . I leave the bar immediately, the sudden inexplicable shame scorching me inside. The youngman who had been with Dad-o is now outside. The night is brighter than the bar. . . . The youngman asks me furtively if I want to turn on. He opens his hand, tiny joints of marijuana squirm in his palm. He looks strangely like a biblical prophet—with a beard, infinitely sorrowful eyes. I say no.

When I came back to the 1-2-3, Chuck was back too. He asked me to go outside with him. "I got some sticks," he says, "you wanna blast?" (I remember the prophet-faced young-man only moments earlier.) . . . I walk with Chuck along Spring Street, left, across Broadway, then Hill, beyond the tunnel, around the area with all the trees. Chuck says: "I don really dig this stuff, man—too much of a hassle to hold any, an I don dig hasslin it noway—but somebody turned me on free—so might jes as well. . . ." We squatted there among the shadows, shut in by the trees, smoking like Indians—or maybe, like children forbiddenly in a garage.

We went to Main Street, and Im feeling an intensified sense of perception—as if suddenly I can see clearly. Now Main Street is writhing with the frantic nothing-activity in the late hours. We walked into Wally's, exploding with smoke. Then to Harry's bar and more smoke, more streaky mirrors, more hungry eyes and stares—and later, before the burlesque house with the winking lights and the pictures of nude women, we saw three girls, and Chuck went casually and talked to them and they said yes. They belonged obviously to that breed of young girls with whom the hustlers periodically prove their masculinity. Like the malehustlers, they live the best they can from day to day. . . . We went back to the 1-2-3 to look for Skipper or Buddy to come along with us. Miss Destiny was standing outside with Lola, and when she saw the girls with us, she stomped angrily inside the bar. We found Skipper, and we got into Buddy's car and Skipper made it run, and since no one had a place to go, we drove to Echo Park.

And the night was miraculously clear as it rarely is in Los Angeles, and the moon hung sadly in the sky as unconcerned

as the world, as we sexhuddled in the car with the three lost
girls. . . .

We left the girls at Silverlake and came back to the 1-2-3,
where Miss Destiny, skyhigh, rushed at us shrieking, "You
know whats the crazy matter with you, all of you? youre so
dam gone on your own damselves you have to hang around
queens to prove youre such fine dam studs, and the first dam
cunt that shows, you go lapping after her like hot dam dawgs!"
Then she cooled off right away and said drive her to Bixel
Street, where someone (shes playing it mysterious like someone is turning her on free because shes such a gone queen)
is laying all kinds of stuff on her. When we got to Bixel, it
turns out Trudi's daddy has paid for the stuff, including a tin
of maryjane and rolls of bees, and hes asked Miss Destiny to
take it to her place and Bring Everybody and theyll be up
later and we'll have a party. We rode back, and on Broadway
the cop-patrol is driving meanly. Skipper put on his dark
shades, Chuck lowered his widehat, I sank into the seat (the
junk: the roust), and goddamned Miss Destiny waves at the
cops—"Yoohoo, girls"—shes flying out of her gay head.
Luckily they didnt hear her and they already had someone in
back, so they went by with everyone-hating faces. Just as
Skipper parked, Trudi's daddy drives up in his tough stationwagon with Trudi behind him wrapped in—I swear—a fur
stole—"Like Mae West," she cooed.

And we all went up to Miss Destiny's.

4

Destiny's place is two ugly tight rooms with naileddown
windowshades and a head. You climb two narrow stairways
and then make your way through a maze of cramped halls
lighted just enough by greasy lightbulbs to reveal the cobwebs
and the dirt—long narrow corridors like in the movie-serial
when we were kids: *And the Dragon Lady put Terry and the
Pirates in a narrow hallway and she punched a button and the
walls kept coming closer . . . threatening to crrrrrush! everyone to . . . death!!*

Miss Destiny opened the door and turned on the light. The
light screamed in our pupiled eyes, transforming the cobwebs
on the ceiling into long nooselike shadows. Darling Dolly Dane
was curled up on a couch, and Lola and a seedy-looking soldier
were carrying on on another—this is the kitchen but it has
two bed-couches. Lola hollers in her ugly man's voice turn

the fucking lights off. "Put out thy own dam lights, as the stunning Desdemona said," Miss Destiny answered. Both the soldier and Lola started adjusting their clothes, and Miss Destiny says arent they Too Much?—everyone here has seen boys and girls, and besides, all the world is a swinging stage!

Now Lola goes into the other room, and in a few minutes, lo and behold! here she is back, in Japanese drag! posing at the door: kimono with beautiful colored butterflies—sandals —slanted eyes! and she is saying something like teeny-vosey which she says means kiss in Chinese—but the soldier (he playing the stud with her when we walked in) isnt paying her any more attention, and its obvious, the way hes looking, that hes a godown fruit serviceman—a not very attractive butch fruit whom Lola thought was a stud (and queens are fooled more often than they admit). Pissed off, Lola grabs the soldier's cap, pushes it over his head, and very much like a rough man shoves him through the door: "You gotta make reveille, dear!"

And while we're turning on juice and joints and pills— Trudi's fat daddy saying, "Come on boys, come on turn on" —palming all of us excitedly—the queens are changing into high drag in the other room—much more successfully than Lola. Now Trudi minces out in blacklace negligee, panties and brassiere (her chest taped to give her real-appearing cleavage under the falsies)—looking I have to say disturbingly real like one of those girls in the back pages of the scandal magazines that advertise those slinky gowns and underclothes with crazy names like tigerlily nightie and heaven-in-the boudoir panties and French-frivolity brassiere—and Darling Dolly Dane is all pink ruffles and queen-cuteness, and Miss Destiny (being more modest and more the regal type anyway) makes her entrance, last of course, in green satin eveningdress and fluffed out rair with golden sequins. . . .

Right after that, Buddy came in with a score. Miss Destiny says shes sorry but theyll have to use the head. The score is obviously disappointed. A few minutes later and we hear the score coughing spitting. Lola says acidly she despises amateurs and queers. Now they come out, and the score is not only disappointed but nervous, afraid of the scene. As he started toward the door, Trudi calls out, "Dont be nervous, dear— blame the beads!"—and Skipper is going to Talk to him— but Buddy said no he got all the bread himself—and: "Did you hear the square spitting, man? did you?—" indignantly "—Christ, and I only *pretended* to shoot!" Darling Dolly is doing an imitation strip, proud of her smooth girlskin and figure, and everytime she bumps (like the queen at the 1-2-3 earlier), she says, "Sssssssssssuferrrrrrrrr. . . ." Trudi's daddy is giggling almost hysterically now, opening drinks, passing pills, joints.

Suddenly theres a racket outside the window, like someone throwing a bottle, and Miss Destiny says, "It's that psycho bitch!" and pulls the shades from the nails and theres the sexhungry nympho in the next building hanging out the window in her halfslip and brassiere (and she isnt badlooking) saying whats going on we're disturbing the peace. *Her* piece, giggles Trudi, smothering herself cozily in her stole. And Miss Destiny coos, "Come on over, dear, come on over," to placate her, and the sexhungry woman almost jumps through the window—"I'll be right over, hear?" "Hoddawg!" said Chuck, and this puts Miss Destiny on. In just a few minutes heres the nympho and says it's so warm she'll take off her blouse if you dont mind, and I mean she wasted no time. Appalled at such uncouth effrontery, Darling Dolly Dane, smoking elegantly, inhaled accidentally and almost choked.

To top it all off for Miss Destiny, who was becoming Most Depressed, heres another queen at the door: Miss Bobbi, with a drunk who tries to sober up immediately, rejects the scene, turns to leave—but Skipper gets a chance to Talk to him. "Cool it, cholly," is all Skipper said, and the man reached for his wallet nervously, hands the money to Skipper, and stumbles out hurriedly.

Miss Bobbi says icily hand over the bread which rightly belongs to her. Skipper gave her a nofooling? look. Miss Bobbi says *she* brought the score here, *after all!* Skipper says who got it? Miss Bobbi says she was *going* to until Skipper came on so bigassedly. Skipper says the score would have clipped *her,* and you saw it, jack, the score *gave* the bread to him. Miss Bobbie swished out in a huff.

In absolute depression, Miss Destiny flung herself on the couch crying oh no, "Miss Thing, what are we doing here?" —clinging to a Poor Pitiful Pearl doll on the couch—a sadeyed orphan doll—but everyone was talking and moving and no one paid her any attention. So she freshened up her makeup peering into a tiny stonestudded compact saying shes a mess, and please, to me, sit beside her, *please!* Then she imagined she saw Darling Dolly in the mirror making sexeyes at me, and Miss Destiny says *Well That Is The Limit!* "Darling Dolly Dane is a common whore!" Miss Destiny almost-shouted at me and no one hears her but me, the radio turned on to one of those California night-stations with the smothered rock-n-roll sexmoans, "and all of you! especially you! are just bums! nogood lowlife hobos! who will end up! on Thunderbird! or worse than hobos: hypes! hopelessly hung up and cant get it!" and shes going on very unlike the gay Miss swinging Destiny. "And I! dont! know! what! Iamdoing! here! amongst all this: *tuh-rash!* I! Went!! To College!!! And Read Shakespeare!!!!"

I whispered dont tell anyone, but me too.

"Next youll be the Prince of Wales," she says bitchily, glowering at Chuck and Buddy making up to the nympho, who was fanning herself with her slip now.

And Miss Destiny goes on haughtily—sure of her ground: "Then—tell—me: if you read Shakespeare, Who Is Desdemona?" doubting it superiorly, giving me The Supreme Test: Shakespeare and his queenly he-roines who were first, remember, played by men.

I answered (and remember the pills, the liquor, the mary-jane): "Desdemona was a swinging queen in the French Quarter who married a spadestud who dug her until a jealous pusher turned him on that his queen was making it with a studsailor, and the spade smothered the queen Desdemona and the heat came for him and he killed himself. . . ."

Miss Destiny stared at me a long while—not speaking. And as she was staring at me like that, Lola—who had gone to the head outside, Destiny's being occupied—returned howling theres a man in the head outside and he aint got no pants! Miss Destiny sprang up, rushed at Darling Dolly Dane:

"You dizzy silly cunt! you brought him here didnt you?"

"Where else, Miss Destiny?" Darling Dolly Dane pleads helplessly, covering her face dramatically.

"Go give him his pants!"

"How can I, Destiny? I dont know where I *left* them!"

"*Miss* Destiny!" Miss Destiny screamed.

"*Miss* Destiny dammit!" Darling Dolly Dane shrieked back.

"Here!" Miss Destiny rushes into the other room, comes back with a pair of pants (which turn out later to be Buddy's, who is with the nympho in the other room), empties the pockets on the floor, tosses the pants at Darling Dolly Dane, shouting: "Throw them through the transom!"

Darling Dolly rushes out whimpering.

"Silly bitch," says Miss Destiny, glaring at her when she

returns giggling now the man must have thought the pants came from Heaven.

Now Miss Destiny sat on the floor next to me. "You *do* know who Desdemona is!"

Then again there was a long silence between us.

Suddenly!

Suddenly, and strangely—strangely then but not so now: now, inevitably and very clearly like this: Something was released inside Miss Destiny and something established between us in that moment by the simple fact of the mutual knowledge of Desdemona: that something released and that something established which she had yearned for with others from person to person in this locked world—and trying always futilely before, had given up. And of course too it was the liquor, and rejection earlier smashing at her stomach like a huge powerful fist—and the pills pushing-pulling in opposite directions, jarring her—the memory too of the Real girls with whom three of us had gone earlier—and this importantly: the loneliness churning beneath that gay façade desperately every awake moment shouting to be spoken, to be therefore shared: released by something as small as this, the common knowledge of the sad sad tale of Desdemona— or maybe more accurately than released: say, erupting out of the depths of her consciousness, aroused by the earlier rejection, resulting in that rare fleeting contact made rarely somehow like a match struck in the dark for a breathless sputtering instant. . . . And so now, because of Desdemona and all this meant to Miss Destiny, and all the things set off from the knowledge, Miss Destiny blurted suddenly frantically:

"*Oh, God!* . . . Sometimes when Im very high and sitting maybe at the 1-2-3, I imagine that an angel suddenly appears and stands on the balcony where the band is going—or maybe Im on Main Street or in Pershing Square—and the angel says, 'All right, boys and girls, this is it, the world is ending, and Heaven or Hell will be to spend eternity just as you are now, in the same place among the same people—*Forever!*' And hearing this, Im terrified and I know suddenly what that means—and I start to run but I cant run fast enough for the evil angel, he sees me and stops me and Im Caught. . . ."

(Like in the game of statues long ago and someone swung you round and round and you stayed frozen as you fell, and the angel is the swinger now. . . .)

And Miss Destiny went on desperately:

"And I know it sounds crazy but I came here believing—no, not really Believing—but hoping maybe, maybe somehow crazily *hoping!*—that some producer would see me, think I was Real—Discover me!—make me a Big Star! and I would go to the dazzling premieres and Louella Hopper would interview me and we would stand in the spotlights and no one would ever know I wasnt Real—"

(That impossible strange something that will never happen. . . .)

And Miss Destiny rushes on feverishly:

"And at night in bed drowning in the dark, I think tomorrow will be just like today—but I'll be older—or I come unexpectedly on myself in a mirror or a reflection in a window, and it takes my breath: *Me!!* . . . And I think about my wedding and how Fabulous I'll be—but I want to fly out of my skin! jump out! be someone else! so I can leave Miss Destiny far, far behind. . . ."

(And Miss Destiny wakes up at night terrified by the knowledge of that strange impossibility, and the darkness screams Loneliness! and impossibility, whirling around us —and soon youll have to face the morning and yourself— the same, again. . . .)

In the other room someone yelled, and it was the nympho. I heard Chuck shouting Whoooooooppeeeee!! . . . and Darling Dolly shrieked: "Chuck, get *off!*—thats Buddy!" And Lola came out rushing yelling at no one, "Leave me alone! Im ugly! Im ugly!"—her face smeared grotesquely with paint and enormous tears— "Im ugly, Im ugleeeeeeeee!" and Trudi trying to soothe her with her fur stole—momentarily leaving Skipper, who is passed out drunk. . . .

"All this is going on," Miss Destiny sighed, hugging the orphan doll, "and when tomorrow someone will maybe ask us, What did you do last night?—we'll answer, Nothing. . . . And, oh, do you believe in God?" she asks me abruptly, and I answered it's a cussword. "Oh, yes, my dear," Miss Destiny said, "there *is* a God, and He is one hell of a joker. Just— look—" and she indicates her lovely green satin dress and then waves her hand over the entire room. *"Trapped!* . . . But one day, in the most lavish drag youve evuh seen—heels! and gown! and beads! and spangled earrings!—Im going to storm heaven and protest! *Here I am!!!!!* I'll yell—and I'll shake my beads at Him. . . . And God will cringe!"

Now Miss Destiny leans toward me and I can smell the sweet liquor and the sweet . . . lost . . . perfume—and with a franticness that only abysmal loneliness can produce, she whispered.

"Marry me please, dear!"

5

I was out in the street with the jazzcat from New York wearing dark shades who had somehow turned up later at Destiny's. And Los Angeles was dreary in the earlyhours with the sidewalks wet where theyve just watered them and the purplish haze of the early morning. And he asked me which way I was going. That way, I said. Me too, he said. And we walked through the streets.

Then somewhere a bell began to sound, and I looked up instinctively at the sky. . . . *One day that bell will sound and Miss Destiny's evil angel will appear!* . . .

I left Los Angeles without seeing Miss Destiny after that night. And I went to San Diego, briefly.

And I returned to Los Angeles.

A few of the people I had known were gone—even in that short time—back to the Midwest or to Times Square, or had been busted, or moved to Coffee Andy's in Hollywood, or gone to Golden Miami. They had disappeared, one day: One day youre here and thats fine, and the next day your gone and thats fine too, and someone has that very day come in to take your place whatever it might have been.

Chuck was still here, boots and widehat. And Skipper . . . And Trudi still blaming it on the beads . . .

I asked Chuck about Miss Destiny, one night, when we were again at the 1-2-3, but this time it was quiet. Not even the jukebox was playing. Everyone was broke. Not a single score. Even the pushers hung dismally inside the bar.

Chuck said he hadnt seen Miss Destiny in a long time, she had just disappeared. Somewhere. "Man, she was a gone queen," he said, pushing his cowboy hat back in a kind of tribute to Miss Destiny.

I asked him did she have her Fabulous Wedding.

"Oh, sure, man, I did not go though—someone tole me about it, she had it out in Hollywood, man, in this real Fine pad, an I heard she akchoolly dressed like a bride, man —she married some studhustler from See-a-dal, and it musta been a real Fine bash, if I re-call Miss Destinee right. . . ."

Then he went on to tell me he had a job washing dishes for a few days but he quit and how some score has promised to put him in some malehouse in Hollywood where he'll make at least $50 a day.

Later I saw Pauline (and now the jukebox was playing the song which I will always think of as part of L.A.: *For Your Love*—and the sad throaty sounds of Ed Townsend meaning it), whom (Pauline) I had met before I left, having found Miss Destiny's warning that first night in the park was justified: Pauline coming on Big with how she would have her own beautyshop in a few weeks and whoever she dug would have it Made and Made Big.

"Let me *tell* you about *Destiny*—" Pauline said. "You *left* before she got *married*—well, she had her wedding all right, she didnt *invite* me, but I *heard,* and it was *Hor-ri-ble.* It was *A-tro-cee-ous.* She had her winding staircase all right, too, and she *stumbled* on her train and *ripped* her veil and came *face down!* Then the place was *raided.* And *thats* where Miss Destiny the college co-ed is now, *busted!*—in the *joint* —*again!*—for *masquerading*—and this is not the first time she gets knocked over so she will be cooling it there *for quite a while!* And can you imagine the *sight?* Miss Destiny in bridal drag sitting crying in the paddywagon this is her *wedding day? . . .*"

Trudi claims Miss Destiny is living in Beverly Hills with the man who sponsored the wedding (though Trudi didnt go either, afraid theyd raid it, but they didnt, and she says she wishes now she'd been a beautiful bridesmaid like Destiny asked her, and it broke Destiny's heart when Trudi said no but thats the beads). "And I hear the Destiny looked simply Fabulous in her gown and red hair," says Trudi, "and, honey, it just goes to show you some more about those goddam beads—here the Destiny meets this rich daddy who wants to see a queen get married in drag to a butch stud-hustler, and the Destiny says does he have a winding stair-case? and he does. . . ." Well, anyway, Trudi says, so far as she knows, Miss Destiny is still living in Beverly Hills (Skipper says oh no, Bel Air, if she really made it Big) with the rich daddy and her stud husband.

"The rich cholly," says Skipper knowingly, "I bet he digs Destiny's stud, not Destiny—but he gets kicks watching them make out, jack. You know, hes queer—" and Skipper goes on to tell me how hes tired of the small hustling and how hes ready to push back into the Bigtime—and Trudi says, "Don't be nervous. babe, youll shake the beads."

And so, of Miss Destiny's Wedding there are many versions.

No one seems to have gone to it.

But everyone has heard about it.

Only one thing is certain. Miss Destiny is no longer around.

And I wondered if somehow she had escaped her Evil Angel.

And again for a period I avoided the park and the bars—and when I came back, Chuck of course was still around. And now we're sitting in Pershing Square at the same place where I first met Miss Destiny. . . . (And Jenny Lu is in the park too, as if The Angel had got *her* number—woe-*uh!* . . . and Holy Moses . . . and Saint Tex, who outstayed The Word and was reConverted by Saint Thunderbird to California . . . and the five white angelsisters with Christ still bleeding wax. . . .)

Suddenly Chuck said:

"Oh, man, did you hear about Miss Destinee?—you remember her, that far-out queen with the redhair? Well, man, some queen was saying how she got this letter from Destinee. An remember this ah this ah head doctor she was going to, man?—the one she said she would have on the couch next time? Well, he finally cured Miss Destinee, man—Miss Destinee wrote she ain a queen no more, she has honest-to-jesus-gone-Christ turned *stud,* man!—an that ain all, man!" he goes on gleefully "—Miss Destinee wrote she is getting married, man!—*to a real woman! . . .*"

And Chuck pushed his widehat over his eyes as if to block his sudden vision of a world in which such crazy things can happen.

I imagine Miss Destiny sitting lonesomely in Somewhere, Big City, America—carefully applying her makeup—and I think:

Oh Destiny, Miss Destiny! I dont know whats become of you, nor where you are—but that story Chuck just told me, as you yourself should be the first one to admit, is oh Too Much to believe!

CITY OF NIGHT

FROM FACE TO FACE, FROM ROOM to room, from bed to bed, the shape of the world I had chosen emerged—clearly but without definable meaning. Each morning the pale sun rose in the imitation-blue sky of Los Angeles, and the endless resurrection of each new day began. Like the palmtrees that lined the streets of the city, the world seemed to be shrugging indifferently.

For me then there followed a period of untrammeled anarchy as I felt my life stretching toward some kind of symbolic night, as the number of people I went with multiplied daily. With those many people—only in those moments when I was desired—the moments before we became strangers again after the intimacy—I felt an electric happiness, as if the relentless flow of life had stopped, poised on the very pinpoint of youth; and for those moments, youth was suspended unmoving.

Now I began to feel that world demanding even further anarchy. Often I remembered the man I had met that first afternoon in Los Angeles, when, with his money already in my hands, I had suddenly found myself unable to steal from him. It was something that remained unfinished: a test prepared by that chosen world which I had failed. . . . The man's face dimly mysteriously haunted me.

There was still, too, the narcissistic obsession with myself —those racked interludes in the mirror—the desperate strange craving to be a world within myself. And I felt somehow, then, that only the mirror could really judge me for whatever I must be judged.

As the weeks passed, under that hazily smeared sky, I would stand often in the midst of the masked turbulence of Pershing Square, watching it fascinated. At the same time, I felt an overwhelming sadness as intense as if I were the only person in the world who had ever felt it for this life: awed by the terrifying spectacle of this outcast boiling world.

And so the park became the focal point of my life, those long, long afternoons.

Like a lord surveying his kingdom, Sergeant Morgan marches through the park in the afternoons, nodding condescendingly at the familiar faces of the perennial park pensioners pinned to the benches. . . . I see him stomping along the sidewalk now, imperiously flanked by two younger cops. They walk like soldiers, in perfect step, the two on each side like younger, if slimmer, imitations of the fat one in the middle, marching as if to the cadenced rhythm of a drum heard only by them. I had seen the fat cop often—but he hadnt stopped me. Now, watching the determined march, I think: Hes after someone. As they approached me—and they were looking straight ahead—the fat one turns sharply, toward me. "Come on, you!" he barked.
Boom!
Boom!
Boom!
Along the way they pick out two other youngmen: one a slim, sullenfaced boy of about 18; the other, squarefaced, older, smiling and composed, cocky even, as if this to him is routine.

Now down the escalator we go. Into the parking lot below the park, across the lot: The people getting their cars stare at us, wondering what weve done, hoping for the worst. . . . Up the steps again, into the other side of the park. Down more steps, through a door, into a room, where, ostensibly, they keep park tools—but hidden in typical sneak-cop fashion, it's a place for police interrogations, like a baby joint.

Inside, another policeman is sitting at a desk. There are two small rooms. On a board behind the desk are many photographs of hardened wanted faces: staring stonily into the room as they had stared into the camera and at the cop behind it—as they had stared defiantly at the world. On a small bench facing the desk, the three of us theyd picked up sit waiting now for the identification scene to begin.

They frisk us. They look through our wallets, our pockets, they ask how much money we have—what we're wanted for, sneering when all three of us answer: "Nothing." They check our arms for "tattoos"—hypo needle marks. . . . Then they run their hands slowly down our legs, between them—and I am amused at how lovingly, thoroughly, slowly they do that part. Now they glare at us disappointed when they

find nothing incriminating on us. The one at the desk calls
the police station. We hear our names, code numbers covering certain offenses. Again theyre disappointed: none of us
here is Wanted.

As the cop at the desk writes out spot-interrogation cards,
the fat cop stations himself before us, stands fat-legged, bull-
spread, the stick like a scepter before him. He reminds me
of an arbitrary general-sir. He has a round chubby face, like
a soft beachball, red; tiny mud-eyes. If he had a white beard
and wore a red cap, he would resemble a fierce Santa Claus.
He booms:

"I

Am

Sergeant Morgan!"

As If Announcing The Second Coming Of The Lord.

"Why I brought you down here," he says, "is I never
talked to none of you before—but I been keeping my eye on
you—I seen you hanging around the park." Eyes snap calculatingly from one of us to the other. "And I gotta know
everyone in this park. . . . Now I dont know what youre
after. But I suspect! . . . What Im saying is: Watch out! I
wont have no wise guys in My Park. . . . No pickpockets,
No hypes. No heads. . . . No hustlers! Understand?" He
studied each of us for a reaction. We look at him in deliberate
blankness. "Im getting a good look at you now" (and he
was) "and I got cards on allayou. If I keep seeingya in the
park, I can grabya on open charge. And I'll do it; and when
they let you out, I'll grabya again. This here aint no warning.
It Is A Threat. . . . Ever-one's hearda Pershing Square, and
I figure thats why youre here—cause you heard what goes
on. Well, it aint so easy as you think—and it aint gonna be,
not while Im around—no sir!" He swings his stick menacingly. I get the feeling one of the other cops is a rooky and the
fat one is trying to impress him. "Now lotta people in this
park knows me and likes me," he went on, "they tell me
things I wanna know—so I always know wot goes on. And
Im gonna let you innonna secret: We got plainclothesmen
all over, watchinya. You wont get away with nothin! Now
maybe I cain tell you stay outta the park cause it's public—
but I sure as hell can make it Rough for you." He stopped
abruptly, as if for applause.

"Go on now, get out!" he snaps like a tough cop in a movie. He turns his back on us—petulantly.

Outside, the sullenfaced boy walks a short distance into the park with me, says: "Im beginning to think this town is nowhere, man, I aint scored for nothing today—but I get stopped by the fuzz."

Then catching sight of an obviously intrigued man-in-a-suit, he goes and sits next to him.

Like all the others warned to stay out of the park, I continued to return and the fat cop didnt bother me. And this is how they do, unless youre wanted for something definite: They warn you to stay out, they leave you alone—and then when the heat is on (when some robbery supposedly involving a young Pershing Square vagrant has been headlined in the papers—or, as I had heard Trudi describe it once at the 1-2-3, "when Officer Morgan is going through her period"), they pick you up for vagrancy. And the papers gleefully announce:

RAID IN PERSHING SQUARE.

Now, as the anarchy welled inside me, I went through each day on pills and marijuana.

And then one afternoon, High, sitting in the park, hearing the convulsed chanting, the spiritual singing—in the midst of the lonesome hunting, the sexual hunger in the eyes all around—the franticness to fill each space of time with *something!*—I imagined—*Suddenly!* as if in a nightmare—as the crowds emerged from the depths of the subterranean garage, swarmed from across the streets—that all the world was pouring into Pershing Square in a tidal wave of faces—that frantically each person would shout his Loss—into Eternity —to an uncaring Heaven!

In panic, I returned to that rented room on Hope Street. I shut the windows, drew the shades, bolted the door.

Still, I could hear life shrieking at me. . . .

Now again there came a time when I stayed away from the streets. I took a job. . . . Again the guilt. At night I found relief from the strange terror in the joints of marijuana which I smoked on the roof of that hotel. As the false clarity of the weed seized me, I would look onto the city showered by the black of the Night—and imagine, as if in a dumb show in which all emotion is muted, that I was separated from the world: as I had felt as a boy watching out the window, separated from life.

The world was revealing its death to me by the process of slow discovery: the slowly gnawing loss of innocence; and I found myself longing for the God in Whom, unquestioningly, I had believed as a child. But this world of loneliness and desperation belied Him. The sky was now a black cave where once it had been limitless, stretching into that Heaven of childhood angels and peace.

As the doleful sounds of the bells from the church across the street mourned into the night, I looked from the roof in the direction of Pershing Square:

One day, in sorrow at His own creation, God plunged into Hell. . . . Now the world spun dizzily like a ferris wheel out of control.

CHUCK: Rope Heaven
by the Neck

1

"HEY, MAN!—HOW YOU MAKIN IT? . . . Cummon over—jine me." Chuck sat familiarly on the railing at Pershing Square under the statue of a World War I soldier valiantly facing the street. Wearing a new pair of cowboy boots—resplendently Bright (orange, brown, traces of yellow)—which hes showing off by rolling his levis an extra turn—Chuck sits there as if on his own frontporch. "Where you been?" he asks me.

(I didnt tell him this, but I'll tell you: After staying away from the park as compulsively as, always, I returned, I had gone to San Diego again: to the beach at La Jolla set like a jewel in a ring of gleaming sand. I would lie alone for hours on that still-cool beach, just staring at the sky, at the patterns of the hastily smeared clouds: as I had lain looking into the El Paso sky when I was a kid, when I had climbed that range of mountains called Cristo Rey, to get closer to that Sky; hugged by the jutting sandy hills: lying there—alone—looking up—at times at the sky itself, times at the clouds, times toward the giant statue of the peasant-faced Christ at the top of the mountain. . . . And years later I was lying on the sand at La Jolla, trying now perhaps to find in the shape of those California beach-clouds the lost patterns I had found as a kid. Vainly. . . . The idleness of the not-yet crowded beach hinting lazily of spring—and the keyed-up idleness of the streets in the city—San Diego!—at night swarming with aimless sailors—this only emphasized the formless terror and panic. . . . I returned to Los Angeles, to that same room on Hope Street, to that same roof at night—to the same maryjane daze whose miracles were slowly diminishing. . . . And I returned, soon, to Pershing Square, as, before, I had returned to Times Square. . . .)

125

I only told Chuck: "Ive been away."

"Ain that somethin now?" he said. "Me, too—I been away too. I had this gig justa while ago." He yawned as if even the memory of work tired him. "It was in this parking lot out in Hollywood. This score I met out here, he got me that job. But, hell, I figure: So I make a few bucks working, I blow them—jes like that! Shoot, I get along jes as good without. Why hassle moren you got to?" Then, squinting at the sun, he added philosophically: "Theres jes two kindsa people that don gotta work: Those that got all the money, an those that ain got none. . . . An me," he said happily, "I ain got nothin."

I sat next to him on the railing. In my mind, later, Chuck, like that statue, would become a part of my memory of Pershing Square: Chuck, sitting there complacently in the lazy afternoons, in the same spot, shoulders hunched, hands holding on to the railing, balancing himself—long, lanky legs locked loosely under the bar by booted toes as if on a fence, on a ranch; sandy hair jutting out from the widehat over long sideburns—as he looks at the passing scene of Pershing Square with what I would usually think was amusement—but wonder, occasionally, Is it more like bewilderment? . . . When something unusual—unusual in the sense of Pershing Square—happened within the area of his vision —or, rather, of his consciousness, since the two seemed at times to be completely separated—he would shout: "Yippee!" with more energy than he would muster for anything else— as he might have at a rodeo—or at the movies rooting in child-excitement for The Rangers.

Others in that restless, nervous world came and went, suddenly disappearing altogether. But Chuck seemed always to be here. And unlike the other youngmen hustling the park, he seldom even moved about hunting for scores. Not because of vanity or self-confidence, I am sure, but because he preferred to move as little as possible, he waits for someone to come to him. And, usually, they did: In that world of downtown Los Angeles, Chuck was one of its best-liked citizens—as much by the scores as by other hustlers—perhaps because, with him, everything always seemed to be going right. . . . He moved effortlessly from day to day as if taking a necessary journey which he must make as easily as possible.

"You know what I mean about hassling a gig, don you?" he asked me. "I mean, crazy if you dig what youre doing an thats what you want—but *jes* workin—! Hell, I would jes as soon hang aroun here. . . . Hell, I made a few bucks in that there parkin lot—an—dig—I bought me these here boots." He raises one gaudy-booted foot for inspection. "Tough, huh?" he asked. "I wanted some with Red on em—but they didn have none."

I nodded yes on both counts: I understood about working —and the boots were "tough."

"So: I hang aroun here an make it jes as good," he said.

It's that limbo-time in Los Angeles arbitrarily called "spring," merely because, technically, summer hasnt come. The weather inches toward summer, boundaryless, and the only difference you notice, in the park, is that the crowds become even thicker as the days become slowly warmer.

Now, in the park—and it is mid-afternoon—there are the familiar sights of mangled American outcasts of every breed. Under the drooping palmtrees, old men and women sit on benches; and outside the enclosed lawn, along the outer ledges, the vagrants of all ages—the younger ones out to score and the older ones out merely to fill the necessary space of time required of that day to qualify them as being "alive" —sit singly or in groups, always waiting: the masklike faces of people expecting anything or nothing. . . .

"When I got this gig, parking cars," Chuck was going on, "I figured theres got to be that malehouse somewhere in Hollywood I heard so much about, an someone'll spot me, sign me up for it." This was a familiar thing with him—said now half-jokingly. "This score, man, he says: 'Chuck, you jes work in my parkin lot an someone's bound to show that knows where it is an you can go there an apply.' But, hell, nothin happened, An I Got Tired." He shrugs his shoulders. His hat was pushed away from his face, turned toward the sun. "Gettin a tan," he explains, yawning lazily, very long, "an—uh—it makes me—unhhh—real—sleepy."

Directly behind us, the howling voice of the Negro woman who preaches there every day rises in a wail as she goes through a religious Revelation. She clutches her throat, gasping out choked obsessed mutterings; eyes shut deliriously, one hand dangling intimately between her slightly spread arched legs—like a burlesque queen. "Comin, Lawd!" she announces triumphantly. She gasped now as if shes seen Him, lurking among the California palmtrees. She greets Him with bumping hips. "Comin, Lawdee!" and her hands are stretched out in supplication or welcome.

And Chuck said happily: "Yippeee! Man-oh-man! She has made it!—I swear she has made it!" Then he yells to her: "Grab Him, lady! You jes grab-im while you got-im—an don let go!"

Now he turns to face me. He yawns again. "The best way to get there," he mused now, "is to take it slow."

"Get where?"

He shrugged. "Wherever. . . . I mean, wherever you *wanna* go. Like for her—" indicating the Negro woman "—her, see, she wants to make it to Heaven. . . . Or, I mean, like, if you wanna make it to New York or Denver— . . . Or Nowhere, like me. . . ."

And there it was.

There was what had intrigued me about Chuck from the very beginning: His easy, happy acceptance of Nothingness. It wasnt resignation—it was acceptance. I look at him as he smiles into the bright glare of the sun. . . . In the midst of all the turbulence, he was always enviably cool—almost as if some compassionate angel had whispered a secret to him (which must have been something like: "Rest"), and based on that secret, he seemed to live his life untouched by turmoil—yet the turmoil surrounded him constantly.

"Now you take Skip," Chuck is going on. "That stud, he is gonna bust wide open one of these days—I mean, he is gonna explode! Boom! It's like he has gotta firecracker with a long fuse up his ass—an that fuse gets shorter an shorter— an one day: *Baroom!!* . . . An take Buddy: he is gonna end up with his picture hangin in a postoffice. . . . An Tiger— one day he is gonna kill one of them guys he makes it with —he hates everyone, man. . . . An you too, man," he says to me now, "hell, you always ack like youre hyped up or comin off: Always movin. Where you think you gonna go so fast?—an what's gonna be there if you get there? . . . Me, I'll take it real slow, real cool—easy—I'll last longer."

And so how could I explain to him the frantic running that, for me, was Youth? With the stark realization that I could never outrun It, I became more and more anxious to find some kind of meaning in Youth itself. . . . And so how can I explain this to Chuck?—always smiling, always drifting happily, effortlessly. . . . He was right about the other young-men hustling Main Street and the park. Although they never spoke of their terror—and for that matter neither did I—it was stamped in every frantic gesture, in every empty pose of unconcern. . . . We worked at indolence from bar to park

to bar. . . . Not Chuck. His idleness had an aspect of purity.
Again: The world for him was a vast plain which he must
occupy for a space of time, easily. . . . And yet— . . . Yet
there was something incomplete about his easygoingness.

"Now there is one thing I wouldnt mind," he was going
on good-humoredly. "I wouldnt mind finding that male
whoorhouse I been hearing about. Out in Hollywood.
Wouldnt that be a gassy kick?—get signed up workin there?
Even hustle chicks for a change. Man, I will tell you somethin: Usually I don get no real good buzz outta guys swinging on my joint. Most of the time, I fall asleep. When I
fall asleep, I ain got no problem. I always sleep with a
Hardon. . . ."

With Chuck—and I knew this instinctively and without a
doubt—there was nothing ulterior in his making it with
males. It was merely easier in the world in which he found
himself. That sexually he liked only girls, I never doubted.
The other scene would have been too complicated for him
to hassle. . . . And I had never heard even the scores and
queens, who would often in bitchiness claim that "today's
trade is tomorrow's competition," say it about Chuck.

"Not that I got anything against anyone swinging on a
joint, dig?—if they wanna—" he was going on.

There was little he condemned, little he didnt accept—
even to being rousted by the cops. . . . Once, weeks before,
sitting with him at Hooper's coffee-and-donuts after two in
the morning, we had been picked up at random from the
other faces there by two cops. Chuck had remained lacka-
daisically cool, almost Philosophical. He told me: "Shoot,
unless they really want you for something, we will be back
here in jes a few minutes. On weekends, man, this late, they
got too many in the joint already. . . . But we are gonna
take a little trip to the glasshouse," he predicted—and he
was right—the glasshouse being where they interrogate you,
fingerprint you without booking you: an illegal L.A. cop-
tactic to scare you from hanging around . . . (I remember:
As we were being taken to be fingerprinted, along with five
others out of Hooper's—one of the night typists at the
station, a pretty roundfaced girl, said to the one next to her:
"Thats a cute bunch they got there." And Chuck called to
her: "What time you get off, honey?" She answered saucily:
"When do *you* get *out?*"—just as the cop, Meanly, stormed
back to squelch the Romance. . . .)

Along the walks in the park, the hunters and watchers

slowly thickened. I noticed three malehustlers standing a few feet from us. I can hear snatches of their conversation: "—I rolled him for a C, man— . . ." "Man, I didnt even let im touch me an I scored 20 bills . . ." The preaching has increased. The angelsisters are marching solemnly to Their Corner—led by the sinister deacon old man. . . . A man is now standing inches before the howling Negro woman, and as she bumps, he puts his hands behind his neck and thrusts his pelvis lewdly at her, shouting: "Go!"—while she continued howling: "Lawd! Don lure me wid da Debil! Lawd! Ah done seed Yuh in all Yuh Glory! Lawd!" as if playing hide-and-seek with God. . . . A tattered gray old man, drunk, passes by, mumbling: "Goddamn! God-Jesus-damn!" . . . Chuck is staring at all this. He shakes his head. I wait curiously for whatever comment hes about to make.

What he said was: "Man, dig those birds." Before us, two pigeons were cooing romantically at each other. "Now ain they something? They make it with each other in Broad Daylight, an nobody busts them for in-decent ex-posure. . . . What happened to that guy?" he said abruptly—and always he would speak out whatever had formed in his mind, as if expecting that others were following his thinking identically. One moment he could be consumed almost childishly with glee—and like a child dazzled by sights of spinning ferris wheels and rollercoasters, the next moment he could shift his interest easily to something else.

"Which guy?"

"Oh, you know, man—the score you was with that time— the one that wanted pod so bad."

Sometime ago, on Main Street, I had met a man from out of town who was almost breathlessly intrigued by what he called "the lowlife"—and particularly with what for him was its ultimate manifestation: smoking marijuana. I told him I could get the weed for him and we'd get high. He was so completely square that I figured—correctly—I could get him to pay as much as two bucks for each joint—which at that time was four bits a stick but which I could score for free from a queen from San Francisco. That night, I couldnt find her anywhere. I tried to pick up at Dora's—a junk bar—but the heat was on, and the twitching pusher who hung out there—talking to you in the sinister, evil-smelling mazelike head downstairs where he made all his transactions—told me he couldnt get anything that night—"not even a benny." At Ji-Ji's, Dad'o hadnt even shown up—nor the pusher with the prophet-like face. . . . Then we ran into Chuck in the park, and while the score stood wide-eyed digging the "low-life" scene, I told Chuck what I was looking for—and why. He conceived a plot: He would split, get some ordinary cigarettes, remove the tobacco, and re-roll them in brown paper. I'd meet him in a few minutes and he would give them to me, playing a real "lowlife" scene for the score. It worked. . . . Later, in a ratty rented room—which I was sure the score had chosen for "lowlife atmosphere"—the score gagged on the faked joints; said: "This is sure powerful stuff you got us, boy." After smoking about two of the ordinary cigarettes, he was convinced he was Heavenly High. . . . "You sure *are* getting high," I told him, "just look at your pupils, theyre about to explode!" "Is that how you can tell?" "Sure!" . . . "Yeah," he said, rushing to the mirror to look at his lowlife pupils, "I Sure Am High. Power-ful stuff, powerful!"

Now, I told Chuck how it had turned out.

"Great, man," he said. "An dig: No one got hurt—he got his kicks, same as if he had smoked the real stuff. . . . An what the hell, if it hadda been the real stuff, it wouldda been his luck to get busted or something. Maybe he'dda become a real strong head, even!" And now he smiles and said: "I even used some of that there men-tho-lated tobacco."

And so, for Chuck, the scene had been the Good Deed of a Boy Scout.

Enter Darling Dolly Dane!

"Im positively deadass tired," she says, rushing over to us. "Babies, there just aint no one at the 1-2-3—someone's been spreading rumors that theres so much junk being sold there that the cops are gonna knock it over any day!"

Queens usually avoid the park in the daytime, and when they do come in, they tone down their effeminateness—necessarily: they are too easily spotted by the cops. Even so, Darling Dolly is wearing a shirt that could easily have been a blouse.

Chuck: "Darlin Dolly, huccome you ain got no makeup on this afternoon?"

Darling Dolly sighing: "Sweetheart, the fuzz just aint as Tolerant as you are, God Bless You. . . . Have you seen Trudi? No? My God!—the poor girl's in a State of Nerves. Skipper has disappeared—Again!"

"That ain new," said Chuck, "he disappears all the time."

Darling Dolly Dane, adjusting her collar so it sticks up

higher. "Of course it aint new—but Trudi worries each time like it is—and the way Skipper's been drinking lately! . . . And this time she aint seen him for More Than Three Weeks. Now you know how he stays with her, and goes away, and comes back—but he dont stay away *that* long. And! Poor Trudi's even checked the joint, and those nasty bulls there and all! (And, babies, this is The Real Truth, I cross my heart: One of the bulls thought Trudi was real fish —she went in drag, and you know how Real she looks— and one of them, he tried to put the make on her, and Trudi said, 'Fuck off, fuzz!') . . . And Trudi says they told her, no, Skipper aint been busted. . . . Poor Trudi—my God! —youd have to look Far and Wide to find a more Loyal Woman! . . . Well, honeys," says Darling Dolly, "your baby sister's gonna be on her way now. . . . Honestly, if the fuzz dont stop bugging us, there just aint gonna be a Decent place where a Respectable Queen can go to in the afternoons. . . . Why, we'll just have to start cruising the tearooms, and then theyll call us a menace. . . . And By The Way!" planting her hands indignantly on her hips, "have you seen that Buddy?!"

"Whats he done to you this time?" said Chuck.

"Do You Know What He Done?" Shes dragging out the obvious for dramatic effect.

"Again?" asked Chuck.

"Yes."

"Well," said Chuck, "I bet he clipped your dragclothes an hocked em."

"Thats right! . . . Now I let him, Out of the Goodness of My Heart, stay with me—again! And! After he hocked all my very best drag!—for ten measly bucks, mind you! And then! He comes knocking on my door he aint got no pad to stay. And, honeys, I am a gentlewoman, and I let him stay in my pad. I-never-was-no-good-at-learning-my-lessons. And! That cunthungry sonuvabitch—he done it again—and some-one told me he *gave* one of my bracelets to some ugly cunt hes been after. . . . Oh, if I see him! Oh, if I just see him! I swear: Im gonna make the wildest scene ever, no matter where I find him! Right here in Pershing Square, even! . . . And if the cops come, why, I'll just let them know he stole my drag, and, honeys," she adds slyly, eyes twinkling with cop-bitchiness, "the cops got so many queens on the force themselves that theyll certainly understand what a girl feels like with all her drag clothes in hock! Why! She feels: Lost!

. . . And did I ever tell you who I saw at the Long Beach Drag Ball last Halloween?" she goes on gleefully-bitchily. "Sergeant Lorelei—thats who! And honey, he was the maddest drag youve even seen. She looked like Sophie Tucker—simply the maddest drag *I* ever laid eyes on! I guess he thought nobody would recognize him out of his uniform."

She looks furiously now about the park, remembering her stolen drag again. "That Buddy! . . . Now you know I aint opposed to clipping no one, especially scores that wanna pay you a couple of bucks for all kindsa kicks and tricks," she adds—and Im remembering the man whose pants she clipped and left him in the head. "But! When a thief! clips a thief!—well! That Is Too Much! The line has gotta be drawn somewhere—or we'll all be: Lost! And, for me, This Is The End. . . . And, babies, it's no secret: I got a weakness for Buddy —although—" she adds flirtatiously, pursing her lips as if in a kiss "—I love you two too. Still and all, I do got a weakness for Buddy. He may not have the world's biggest piece of meat—but never mind: I aint one to go around flipping over size. Still, he is just as cute as can be—and that sonuvabitch, he knows I am hung up on him. So He Does This—takes advantage of my gentle nature! . . . Anyway, cute or not, this is definitely The End!" She glanced about the park. "Oh, oh, here comes Miss Sergeant Morgan. I'd better split!" With a wave of her hand, she left us, weaving her way along the walk, peering into the park to see if she can spot Buddy.

And indeed! Sergeant Morgan is making his rounds of the park—flanked by two cops as usual. As he passes us, his giant ass swings like the stick he carries.

"You really think he went to that drag party like Darlin Dolly said?" Chuck asks me.

I imagined the fat body in drag as Darling Dolly Dane had described it, and I laughed. "Sure. Why not?"

And Chuck says: "Man, you gotta admire those dam queens like Darlin Dolly an them. . . . They sure have got guts. They live the way they gotta live. . . ."

2

The sun is shifting, shadows stretching. And the Pershing Square panorama, in preparation for the night, is exhibiting itself in all its flashy afternoon shreds. The dismal old tramps sit in wrecked heaps. New preachers have invaded the park.

New hustlers. New scores. Jenny Lu is at it again. And the angelsisters are hymning in the distance about how much Jesus loves them. A man in black preaching charity is saying: "Give!—instead of selling! Giving! is an act: of Righteousness!"

Chuck said: "You notice lately in the park how many guys want you to go with them for free?"

The preacher shouts:

"Idleness!"

Chuck: "Man, I am gettin tired jes sittin here."

"Ignorance!"

Chuck: "You know, I never could stay in school without cutting. Man, I used to look out that window an then jes run out—an that old teacher, man, she even throwed a rock at me once."

"Selfishness!"

Chuck: "Yeah, a lot of guys you think are scores—they wanna get you for free." He shook his head.

Now, in the increasing warmth, he rolled up his shirt sleeves, scratched his arm—lovingly—where the tattoo is, proclaiming, amid leaves and rosebuds: DEATH BEFORE DISHONOR. . . . "My old lady," he explained, "she akchoolly went with me when I had this here Tattoo put on me. Ma, she says: 'It's kinda sweet, having somethin like "Mom" on your arm'—but I guess, she figures—well—" . . . He smiled brightly, remembering the longago scene with apparent fondness. "Did I ever tell you that story?"

I shook my head. During the months I had been in Los Angeles, I had been with Chuck many times, sitting often on this very corner with him—but, before, he had never been this talkative. Something about the afternoon is making communication easier. And for me, in the midst of the turmoil of my own life, he seems like a kind of symbolic anchor. . . . Yet I constantly expected a contradiction to the easiness. But there had been none.

"See, when I got this Tattoo," he was saying, "it was back in Georgia where I was born. . . ."

"Georgia? I thought you were from Texas."

He smiled embarrassedly. "Well, see, I always tell people I am from Texas—cause I was hung up on being a Cowboy —an I akchoolly lived there, too. . . . See, when I was a kid, I used to go to these movies—Westerns— . . . Oh, no, man, it was not Texas. It was Georgia all right— . . ."

I smile now at the thought of his Texas and the Texas I

had known: the city, not the plains of which he had dreamily
conceived in Georgia, longing for Cowboy Country. The
cactusstrewn desert . . . not the cactus which for me had
grown in a feeble cluster outside that window, in that vacant
lot. . . . The Texas I knew. . . . Memories of the wind . . .
the dirt . . . tumbleweeds . . . my dead dog. . . . That wind
blowing not freely across the plains but threateningly sweeping the paved streets into that injured house . . . El Paso . . .
Texas . . . for me, not the great-stretching, wide-plained land
of the movies—but the crushing city where I had been raised
in stifling love and hatred.

Chuck said: "I was gonna tell you about Ma an this
Tattoo." He fixes his grayish eyes straight ahead, on nothing
immediate: on the past, maybe, remembering the scene. "See,
I was, oh, just a kid—an one day, Christ, when I was 15,
that little town in Georgia, well, I jes got tired of it. . . . I
mean, it wasnt bugging me or nothing—I jes knew it was
time to split. Like something calling you. My old man, he
died long ago. There was five of us— all brothers—an Ma.
She took care of us, on a kind of farm like, outside that
town, see? So I tole her one day, I am gonna split that town
—go somewhere else. Man, she was cool, my Ma. She did
not say: 'Dont go,' 'Wait'—or nothin. She jes looks at me an
nods, understanding like. Then she asks me when am I leaving. Tomorrow, I tells her. An, man, she says—dig this—she
says' 'Well, we are gonna go into town, you an me.' "

(I see my own mother standing before the glasscase with
the angel figurines: arms outstretched, waiting to reclaim
me. . . .)

"We had this old Ford," Chuck said. "I remember it real
good—an I remember her drivin it into that ole town like
she was on a hotrod! Yippee! . . ." He adjusted his hat firmly
on his head as if the wind, even remembered, were powerful
enough to blow it off.

"So we go to this bar," he went on, "an she orders beer.
'Beer,' she says to the bartender, 'for a boy that is gonna be
a man!' Hell, man, I wasnt even old enough to be in that
place. But everyone knowed Ma, an they did not care. She
says we are gonna have one good Drunk, because, she figures,
if my Old Man was aroun, he'dda taken me out, but he ain,
so it's up to her. . . . Shoot, I had juice before. Me an my
brothers, we used to really get juiced up." He sits up on
the railing now, enthusiastically remembering—looking far
beyond the park. "Once, man, we got so fuckin drunk—man

—me an my older brother—we jes started throwin rocks at the sky! Throwin rocks at the sky, man! Crazy! Not mad or nothing—you know—but jes like, you know, to make sure it's there. . . . Throwin rocks at the sky," he echoes himself slowly, shaking his head, as if somehow, in some way he has not discovered and maybe never will and knows it, this is greatly important to him. "But those rocks, man, they jes kep comin right back at us. Didnt reach the Sky. . . . I guess—" he laughed, the barest trace of a mood disappearing instantly, "I guess we wasnt throwin them hard enough."

(And I remember my own longing to watch Heaven, punctured, spilling down to earth. . . .)

Now Chuck catches sight of a man standing before us, looking in our direction. "That is a cool score, man—I know him. You wanna score off im (I am feelin too tired myself) —or you wanna hear the rest of the story?"

"The story," I said, feeling, suddenly, a great closeness to him—and at the same time a huge, undefined sadness.

And he seemed childishly pleased by the decision, as he continues: "An we're in that bar jes drinkin up that beer, an Ma keeps sayin, 'This is what your Pa wouldda done—an dammit to hell I aim to do it for him an do it right!' . . . We split that bar, an the sun was going down—all red an crazy an everything—like it gets in the South." He squinted at the hazy feeble Los Angeles sun—and again he seemed to be looking beyond it: to the memory perhaps of another— brighter—sun. "An then—get this—then Ma points to this house, an she says: 'Cat-house.' Thats what she said, an she says: 'Thats where you are gonna go next, youngman.' Hell, man, I'd been there before with my brother. In fack—but Ma didn know this—there was this real cute whoor there— she wasnt no young chick, exactly, but she looked real nice in bed—an man, she throwed a mean screw. She said she would not charge me nothin—cause I was bettern a truck- driver. An thats what she said, man—an that is the truth. She said, 'Them others, they are work; you are dayoff!' " He said this not with the vanity, the bragging of the male ex- hibiting his masculinity, but with the pride of a child who has gotten an A in school and can prove it with his report card. "So, when I come outta that house, Ma's waitin on me. She says: 'Okay?' I said: 'Fine, Ma, fine.' . . ." He looks down at the Tattoo. "Oh, yeah, The Tattoo," he remembers. "So we go get more juice. 'Im gonna teach you right,' she keeps tellin me. We're wobblin aroun the town like a couple of drunk buddies—but Ma, like I say, she knowed everyone, an everyone figures we're jes cuttin up some." He chuckled. "Ma fall in a ditch, starts cussin up a mammy-screwin storm!—" and now he throws back his head laughing "—an she says shes gonna sue the city, she sprained her ankle or somethin—says shes gotta rest till the pain goes. . . . But I knowed she is jes high, that is all."

The score in front of us moves away, toward a youngman in an army shirt who has just strayed into the park. The youngman, recognizing the man as a score, let his hand dangle suggestively between his legs to attract the score more quickly.

Chuck said: "So Ma spots this tattoo place, an she says lets go there an rest, plops down on a chair. Man, I can almost see her now—she is almost passed out: 'Whew!' she keeps sayin. An she keeps sayin how she is gonna sue the city! An all them tattoos starin her right in the bloodshot eye! . . . Well, for a while she falls asleep—dozes—an when she woke up, all them angels and flowers is starin her in the face, an she says: 'Hallelujah it's like Heaven!' Thats what she akchoolly said—God's Truth! . . . I said: 'Ma, Im gonna get me a tattoo an remember you with when Im gone.' An I have spotted this one of this chick with great big boobs, you know, nekkid—an Im lookin at that one. An Ma notice what I am lookin at—an she says: 'Youngman, you better not remember me when you look at that!' . . . Well, the man there says he can put 'Mom' right on my arm, an thatll do it. But Ma—dig this—she says: 'Sure, that will be real nice an everything, but I want something Prettier on my son's arm—something pretty to remember his Ma by— something like flowers an leaves—the works!—an it's gotta say something sweet, so it says it for me all the time when he is away.' She sees this real mean picture there of a tattoo —an it says DEATH BE-FORE DIS-HONOR." He reads it off his arm, exhibiting the tattoo proudly as if showing a medal. "This here one. . . ."

And he goes on: "So Ma choose this one—an that is how I got it. Ma said it is gonna keep me outta trouble. An it has. I ain never been busted— . . . Well—" he confesses almost sheepishly "—well, once—but jes once—for stealing a horse —get that, man!—stealing a horse!—but I been to the glass-house lots, I wouldnt shuck you about that. . . . Even Sergeant Morgan, you know what he said to me, man, after the first time he took me downstairs when I landed in this here park

—when he took me to that toolhut downstairs—you know—?
... Well, he says: 'Youre too lazy to do any bad in the park.'
An he don bug me since. . . . Hey! Did I tell you about this
queen from somewhere like Chicago?" he asks me, shifting
abruptly to something he just remembered. "Man, you know
what she does? She spots some stud she digs, an she says
she'll lay some bread on im if he'll make it with her. Well,
man, when she has gone down on the stud, she says nothin
doin, she ain payin cause the stud wasnt no dam good. So,
then, see? the stud, he gets real bugged like, an he starts
beatin on her ass—an, dig, that is what she really digs: she
digs getting beat on, an she is getting her real kicks free! . . .
She sure didnt get there with me, though," he says, shaking
his head. "Hell, beating on her, thats too much sweat. I jes
split. Then I find out about her scene. Isnt that a kick in the
pants—I mean, like ain it? . . . Some people sure like to do it
funny. . . . An that reminds me of something else—a real
funny story. . . . When I was in Frisco once, this guy gave
me a ride. You wouldnt believe it unless you saw it, man.
Man, that guy, he was dressed up in boots with silver chains
wrapped aroun them an a hat with these silver studs, an
black gloves—an, dig, he even carried a gunbelt with all
kindsa things danglin from it. An all those silver studpins
all over everything. Dig this: At his pad he gives me tea! An
I don mean pod, either; I mean real tea! Then he shows me
this collection hes got—all kindsa weird costumes. An boots!
—boots an costumes up the ass. You know what that guy
done then? He dresses me up in chaps, boots, everything, an
then he goes down on my boots, jes squirmin up a storm
on the floor, lickin them cowboy boots an leather chaps,
rubbin his face on em. Man, I . . . Hey! Theres Buddy."

Buddy is standing by the water faucet, looking cautiously
into the park. Next to him is a skinny, ugly, tough young girl,
and I notice a screamingly shiny bracelet on her wrist.

"Hes lookin out for ole Darlin Dolly," said Chuck.

"You seen Darling Dolly?" said Buddy, coming over. The
girl stayed by the faucet.

"Shes looking for you," I said, perversely amused at how
this put Buddy on.

He shakes his head regretfully. "I hocked her dam dragclothes again. Hell, I had to, I was busted real low. . . ." And
he adds, echoing Skipper—Im sure—trying to sound Tough:
"Im tired of these small fucking scores, Im gonna knock me
over a big one. A liquor store—or a bank!" It sounds almost

ludicrous; he looks like a little boy. . . . And yet others like
him would shoot into the frontpage unexpectedly: and one day
a picture of a familiar face—the lost-boy look coming through
the rehearsed tough-mug look—would greet you from the
stacks of newspapers at the corner.

"Not me," says Chuck. "Too much hassle."

"I sure would hate ole Darling Dolly making a scene right
here," said Buddy, "and she told me she would. She means it,
too. She said she'd start screaming at me wherever she saw me.
And that sure would embarrass me. . . . Hell, I aint gonna
hang around queens any more. . . . The only reason Im here
is: Im looking for this score that digs watching me make out
with a chick." He indicates the girl still standing by the faucet.
"Oh, oh," he said, moving away. "I think I see Darling Dolly
over there." With the girl, he dodged hurriedly through the
crowds.

"That chick hes with," said Chuck, "man, I got the crabs jes
standing next to her once."

3

A woman in her late 30s walks past us. I had seen her many
times before, usually about the men's head. She had a palewhite ghostface, her eyes outlined starkly in black. She
never smiled. She would stand before some youngman—the
rattiest looking and the youngest—then she'd whisper to him.
. . . She was the only female score I knew of in the park.

"She sure looks tired," Chuck said as she passed by.

Carried by the wave of the woman's apparent lonesomeness,
I asked Chuck abruptly: "Dont you ever get tired of this
scene?"

"Me? Uh—well— . . . Hell, yeah, man," he said, "I am
always tired." He had misunderstood me. "Thats huccome I
jes sit aroun. . . . But you wanna know somethin—? I sure
wouldda dug being a cowboy. . . . An I was—once."

"In Georgia?" I couldn't help saying.

"Oh, no, man—thats where I was *born*. . . . But I always
used to see those Western flix—an, man, those cowboys, they
seemed to be having a ball all the time. Thats for me, I
thought. Cause, see, I didnt wanna hassle it—I jes wanted to
let whatever's gonna come, come easy an jes the way it should.
I figure a ranch is the best place to let it happen. I would
imagine sitting there on a fence—an ridin on a horse, looking
out at the miles of sand an sky, an nothin is gonna fuck it

up. You jes wait—an that way nothin happens. Easy an slow. An then I figure: I'll get me a horse, when I wanna cut up, an jes ride away, man, like that—you know. . . . Like—yeah—like you got Heaven roped by the neck."

I wonder at his vision of Heaven. Not clouds. Not angels. No. . . . But the wide, wide plains, great hills, and uncomplicated plain cupped in the warm embrace of the golden sun. . . . An endless stretching beyond the great soft hills . . .

"See, I hitchhiked West the day after Ma an me went into town," Chuck is saying. "This guy who gives me a ride, he says: 'Where to, sonny?' I says, 'West!' . . . An thats where I went!" Again, his eyes search the park, as if wondering where the West of his imagination twisted into the West of Los Angeles. "This cat," he goes on, "he says hes gonna go to Houston or Dallas—some place like that, I forget. . . . An we jes drive along. An then there it is, jes like in the movies: Man, jes miles an miles of plains an sky an more sky. Then I see these horses out the window. I tell the man, 'Heres where I am goin.' He says, 'It's the middle of nowhere, sonny.' 'Nowhere,' I tole him, 'thats where I wanna go.' . . . An I got outta that car, an I jes started running like I was crazy, hooting and howling. . . . An this one horse, hes left the others an hes comin straight at me. Straight at *me!* An I climbed that fence, an there he is, that horse, jes starin me in the eye, an me starin back at him. An, man, I tell you; that horse, he *smiled* at me —crooked, you know—but smiling. An I figure he jes started roaming, like me—an somehow I knowed he was lookin for me. See, we're in the same spot—both beginning. An I smiled back. . . . An, man, that horse *understood!* He nods his head, saying yes. Yes! So I jumped on him, an I rode away. . . . Along them beautiful plains, those crazy clouds—*ooo-ee!*—man, I couldda been going to Heaven an I wouldnuh been any Happier. . . . But then these three mean studs ride up to me on horses—an they say Im stealing this here guy's horse. Stealing it, man! If anything, we stole each other. . . . So I figure, hell, they are gonna lynch me, like I seen in the flix. . . . But I was jes a kid an that man they took me to, the owner, he was kinda nice. He understands, an he offers me a gig. . . . But it was not like I figgered. I jes worked aroun the place, doing, you know, odd things. It was not that I minded it or nothin. It was jes this: I never got to be near that horse no more—except when I got drunk," he smiled. "Then I would go an find him—an he would be waiting there for me, his neck up straight, waiting. An we'd take off again. It happen over an over. I jes couldnt keep away from that Horse. . . . Then, one time, the owner, he says he hates to do it but hes gonna get me busted to teach me a lesson if I do it again. Well, it happen again. I got high, an I rode that horse into them hills —and this time I got busted, jes like the man said. The cop said I was a menace. . . . So I left that place. . . . An what bugs me: I never said goodbye to my Horse. . . . And when I left, I think: Well, hell, it ain like in the movies." . : . It was the only note—perhaps not even there—of bitterness I remember ever having detected in his voice. But now he laughed: "I figure then my saddle days is over—thumbing days beginning. Yahoo! . . . An this guy gives me a ride—an that was the first guy ever put the make on me. See—you wone believe it, but it is the truth—when we got to this motel, he says we will stay there overnight. An I was deadass tired, so I say sure. . . . In the morning, that man, hes comin on hes sorry—sorry for what happened; says it's the first time an everything—an hes sorry. I didnt know what he was talking about. But he keeps going on until I knowed what was buggin him: he'd swung on my joint—an, man, he didn know I been asleep all the time. . . . So he lays some bread on me—an I come on to L.A. an land in this here park. . . . Sergeant Morgan, hes the one that tole me what goes on. He took me downstairs, warns me about all the hustling goin on an everything. An while hes talking an Im saying to him: 'Nope, not for me'—Im figurin: Hell, I don know how to do nothin—an I ain never gonna have that Horse—so, hell, I'll stick aroun. . . . An here I am," he said. He stretches his legs—owning the railing: his home, this park. . . .

Now it was beginning to get cooler. In Los Angeles, night comes like a blessing, even after the warmest afternoons. Soon, long shadows will protect the exiles, shelter them soothingly before the concealing night. And as it becomes later and the loneliness and the determination become hungrier, the frenziedness will increase. And even now, it's beginning. Ollie, Holy Moses, preaching, shouting. . . . Shrieks of pain, muted pleas to God, going up unheeded or unheard. . . . The Negro woman has returned: Shes "Comin, Lawd!" again, as if He really gave a damn. . . . Jenny Lu strums her guitar to emphasize her scarlet past: "Sin!" (Plunk!) "The flesh!" (Plunk!) "Fornication!" (Plunk! *Plunk!!*) . . . Two obvious scores stare at the youngmen. They are of that calculating breed who look at you like merchandise: "How big is it? . . . How long can I have it? . . . Youre asking too much—I'll give you— . . ."

Youngmen along the ledges. . . . Lonesomeness is alive. . . .
The fixed eyes. . . . The youngman in the army shirt is still
here, still waiting. . . . An old harpy mutters to no one remembered fragments from the jungle of her spent mind. . . .
And the ghostpale woman is whispering to a ratty-looking
teenage boy who smiles incredulously at what shes saying.
. . . A couple of queens, in anticipation of the night, have now
bravely stationed themselves along the walk. Catching sight
of a cop coming around the corner, they shift their stances
quickly to those as masculine as they can muster—but still a
parody. But the cop stops short of them, talks gruffly to the
youngman in the army shirt. . . .

Chuck has been staring steadily into the park which is seething with all the live lonesomeness. . . . "An here I am," he
echoes himself.

"And afterwards?"

I realized, startled, that I had spoken—that the question
which had finally formed—the question which had been
bothering me about Chuck throughout all the time I had
known him, which had made his enviable easygoingness incomplete—had sprung involuntarily from my mouth. And
having spoken that question, I look at him, and I feel suddenly
sad. . . .

Chuck as an old man! . . .

With the others, even when they spoke about the Bigtime,
you could sense their stifling awareness of what their lives were
stretching toward: the bandaged streets, the nightly dingy
jails, the missions . . . the forgetfulness-inducing wine. . . .
Life had dealt out their destinies unfairly, and they knew it
even while they bragged. But with each frantic step, each
futile gesture of revolt, they prepared themselves. . . .

But Chuck?

Chuck, sitting on this railing, always smiling—easygoing,
easily the most likable. . . .Chuck. What of him? When he
became an old man, would he look as coolly at the world then,
still as if it were that wide-stretching uncomplicated plain?—
when it lengthened into mutilated scenes of Missions and hand-
outs? . . . He belongs on the range, I thought—on the frontier
which disappeared long ago—existing now, ironically, only on
those movie screens that had lured him as a child. . . . "And
afterwards?" I had asked him.

He was still staring into the park. "Huh?" he said. "Man—"
he starts. "Well, man—" And then, as he turned toward me
briefly, the hat pushed back to get whatever still lingered of

the smoggy sun, I saw the familiar smile gracing his face radiantly. . . . Had he even understood my question? I wondered, as, following his gaze, I realized why he is staring intently into the park. . . .

Alone, about 17 or 18 years old—buttocks firm and saucy sculptured by a tight black skirt—her face heavily painted but still that of a very young girl—coy, a flirt, aware of her attractiveness—a cute young girl is walking in our direction, through the park. . . . And as she passes us now, she smiles. She walks to the water faucet, bends over to drink, staying there very long, casting surreptitious glances in our direction—exhibiting her little butt, stuck out toward us. Now, shaking her hair, which is vibrantly red and long to her shoulders, she stands by the faucet, waiting in posed bewilderment as if wondering where she will go next.

"Hoddawg?" Chuck said, jumping off the railing in a sudden burst of energy. "Dig the smart little butt on that chick, man!" And pushing his widehat rakishly to one side of his head, he began to walk toward her, where she is now making her way slowly through the less-thick part of the park.

And afterwards—?

Suddenly the question I had asked made no difference.

A short distance away, Chuck turned back to look at me, pushed the hat momentarily back on his head, and his mouth formed the word again:

"Hoddawg!"

He winked broadly—and then in a genuine cowboy gait, he swaggered toward the girl, who, aware now that he was coming after her, wiggled her butt cutely.

CITY OF NIGHT

AMONG THE BANDS OF MALEHUSTLERS that hang out in downtown Los Angeles, there are often a few stray girls: They are quite young, usually prematurely hardened, toughlooking even when theyre pretty. They know all about the youngmen they make it with and sometimes live with: that those youngmen hustle and clip other males. And aware of this, they dont seem to care. Occasionally, one of those girls will go into the park with a malehustler, sitting there until he will maybe spot a score; and then, as if by tacit agreement, theyll split: the youngman going off with the score, the girl back to Hooper's coffee-and-donuts, where, in the afternoons at that time, they usually hung out.

One among them intrigued me especially. She was the prettiest—about 19, with long ashblonde hair and hypnotic eyes. She always looked at you with a half-smile that was somehow wistful, as if for her the world, though sad, still amused her. I knew from Buddy, who had been with her and who dug her ("But shes kinda strange," he said, "like she aint always there"), that she lived with three malehustlers in a small downtown apartment—one of them the squarefaced youngman I had been interrogated with that afternoon in Pershing Square. . . . She was very hip—she talked like all the rest, and very tough. But with her, somehow, it all seemed wrong, incongruous in a way I couldnt really understand. It wasnt only that she was so pretty; some of the others were too. It was something else, something altogether different about her from the others. . . . A kind of toughmasked lonesomeness.

One afternoon, at Hooper's, I sat near her at the counter. Outside, the cops had stopped a madeup queen. The girl next to me smiles and says: "Oh, oh, another queen busted—for 'jay-walking.' " I moved next to her, and for the next few minutes we spoke easily. Then I caught her looking at me very strangely. She says unexpectedly: "You know, man, theres something that bugs me about you. Ive seen you in the park

144

and around here, and you look like all the others—but theres something else." I was surprised to hear her say about me precisely what I thought about her. At the same time, I panicked: I don't like people to know me too well. . . . "I mean," she went on, "like you never really hang around too much with the others—and you dont talk to anyone too much." . . .

We left Hooper's and went into the park, sitting there briefly, listening to the afternoon preachers. It felt good to be sitting here with this girl, to be seen with her by some of the men I had scored from.

Abruptly, as if suddenly bugged by the park, she asked me to come up to her place. "I live with three guys," she said, "but they're always out here in the afternoon."

The door to the apartment is open. "It's always unlocked," she said. "If you ever need a pad, come up—we got lots of room."

The cramped apartment is completely disheveled—unwashed dishes piled in the sink, frozen-food trays and beer cans discarded on the floor—her clothes and those of the others strewn all over the rooms. There were two beds in the one bedroom, a couch, and a mattress on the floor.

Again I catch her looking at me in that strange way—and she said—just like this—just as abruptly and unexpectedly at this: "I bet you dig Bartok."

I told her yes.

"Me, too, man," she said. "See, I knew it. . . . Thats what I meant when I said something about you bugged me. I mean, you *look* like you belong but— . . . Why do you hang around this scene?" she asked me.

"I dont know," I answered her.

"I dont really know why I hang around either," she said.

From under one bed, she pulls out a cheap record-player, and there was a record already on the turntable. "It's the only one Ive got," she said. It begins to play: Bartok's *Music for Strings, Percussion and Celesta.* Scratchily on the cheap machine—but still beautifully—it plays the haunting, haunted music.

I lay beside her on the rumpled bed, and I hold her hand—which is very cold—while the music played; and she pressed herself suddenly against me with a huge lost franticness.

"Man," she said, "I know the scene: Youve got to pretend you dont give a damn and swing along with those that really dont—or you go under. . . ."

Startlingly, as I rolled over on her, she gets up suddenly.

Suddenly she looks mean. "Why dont you get out of that scene?" she snaps. "All of you keep telling yourselves youre straight—and you make it with chicks to prove it—and when you make it with other guys, you say it's only for the bread —and besides, with them, you dont do anything back in bed— if you dont! . . . Sure, maybe it's true—Now!" She turns the record off. "Why dont you split the scene, man—*if you really want to!*" she said. Then in a tone that was as much bitter as mean, she challenged: "I bet youve never even clipped a wallet from those guys you go with."

I remember the almost-time. . . . "No."

"Get out of it—now!" she said. "Get a job!"

"I've worked more than you think," I said, strangely defensive.

"But you always come back," she thrust at me quickly.

"Yes."

"Then why?"

"I dont know," I said again.

She returns to the bed. And now she begins to remove her clothes. . . . As we clung to each other in a kind of franticness, she said:

"My name is Barbara."

I would meet her at Hooper's after that, and later we'd go to her apartment. Always, she plays that one record. I would hold her while the music played. And yet, always, the meanness would recur. "Cool it," she said once, when I was coming on with her. She went into the bathroom, returned with a rubber. "You never know what the hell you guys have had your pricks in," she said brutally.

"What about you?" I came back at her just as brutally. "Every hustler in the park's had you—several times." I regretted it instantly.

"I know," she sighs almost sadly. . . .

Afterwards, for those times I was with her, she would lie like a lost child, huddled and small and warm now. And somehow terrified. . . .

Then for several days she didnt show at Hooper's. Buddy told me she'd asked the three malehustlers she had been living with to move out. "You getting hung up on that chick, or something?" he asked me. I told him no. But the next day, when she didnt turn up, I went to the apartment.

For the first time, the door is locked. I knocked very long before anyone answered. Now the door opens. She stood there in her slip—and she looks strangely prettier than I had ever seen her: those strange eyes staring at me, into me.

"Im sorry," she said hurriedly, breathlessly, "I cant see you now." She was about to close the door.

"Now or later," another voice said—a woman's voice. I looked beyond the door, and a tall, slender girl I had never seen before is standing there, dressed in black slacks. She looked at me with almost-hatred. "Shag, man," she said roughly, "I mean, split—Barbara dont need you guys any more. . . . Shes got me."

And she put her arm intimately about the other's bare shoulders.

Now, seized by a feeling of loss which had to do with Barbara—but also with something unrecognized which extended beyond her—I went to clean-aired San Francisco (where I would return—later—and stay much longer)—but soon I was back in Los Angeles.

The park, then, was hot with cops. Days earlier, a young vagrant had murdered a girl who had just arrived in town— and during the time that followed—vengefully—vengefully for not having spotted the psyched-up stud before the papers implicated them—the bulls stormed the park. And all the young drifters stayed away.

And Main Street, though also fuzzhot, is even more crowded now.

When the bars close on Main Street, their world spills into the streets. Malehustlers, queens, scores—all those who havent made it yet in one way or another—or have made it and are trying again—disperse into the night, squeezing every inch of nightlife from the streets.

They stand pretending to be looking into store windows— continue their searches into the all-night moviehouses—the burlesque-movie theaters, where along the dark rows, in the early jammed hours of the morning on weekends, men sit, fly open, pulling off. . . . Or the scattered army goes to Hooper's on Main Street—where periodically the cops come in, walk up and down the counter sullenly, picking you out at random—and youre suddenly intensely studying the cup of coffee before you.

Life is lived on the brink of panic on the streets, intensifying the immediate experience—the realness of Today, of This Moment—Now!—and panic is generated by the threat of the vicesquad (plainclothesmen sitting in the known heads licking their lips; sometimes roaming the streets, even offering you money before they bust you); by the copcar driving along the streets —a slowly moving hearse. Like a gang looking for a rumble from a rival gang, cops haunt this area, personally vindictive. . . .

And for the homeless drifters there is also the panic that one day youll wake up to the fact that youre through on the streets, in the bars—that everyone has had you, that those who havent have lost Interest—that youve been replaced by the fresher faces that come daily into the city in that shifting wave of vagrants—younger than you now (and Youth is at a premium), and now the interest you once felt is focused on someone else. One day someone will say about you: "I had him when he was young and pretty."

And as a reminder of this, beyond Los Angeles Street, in the same area of the world of Main Street but not really a part of it, is Skid Row—and you see prematurely old defeated men, flying on Thunderbird or Gallo wine, lost in this sunny rosy haven—hanging shaggily like zombies waiting for the Mission to open; folded over in a pool of their own urine where theyve passed out along the alleys. . . .

If youre young, you avoid that street, you concentrate on Today.

Tomorrow, like Death, is inevitable but not thought of. . . .

At night, the fat Negro woman sprawled like chocolate pudding between Harry's Bar and Wally's mumblingly coaxes you to take a copy from the slender stack of religious magazines falling from her lap to her fat tired feet. The magazine shouts: AWAKE!

And along that strip, the gray hotels welcome the scores and malehustlers: No Questions Asked. For a few minutes—unless you havent got another place and stay all night—you occupy the fleetingly rented room, where inevitably a neonlight outside will wink off and on feebly like exhausted but persistent lightning. . . . Throughout the night there are sounds of rapid footsteps running down the stairs.

In the morning, if you stay, you walk out into the harsh daylight. The sun bursts cruelly in your eyes. For one blinding instant you see yourself clearly.

The day begins again. . . . The same.

Today!

SKIPPER: A Very
Beautiful Boy

1

ALONG THE PANEL OF AMBER MIRRORS at Harry's bar, a panorama of searching eyes emerges out of the orangy twilight of cigarette smoke and dimlights: a stew of faces floating murkily in the smoky darkness.

In the mirror I see the fat man on the stool beside me as he extends money across the bar to buy my drink. I turn away from the image of myself sitting next to him. I face him directly.

Like pale dough, his pudgy face—coagulating into a tiny upturned nose—seems molded about a cigar which he munches lewdly, his puffy rounded lips caressing it intimately. He reeks of cologne and beer, cigar smoke.

With one fleshy hand he slides the drink in my direction—after counting his change ostentatiously and stuffing it into his wallet. "Drink up, sonny!—drink up and I'll buyyanother-one."

The skinny man standing beside us at the crowded bar slices the air with a cigarette holder. "Who are you playing tonight?" he asks the fatman. "Santa Claus?" Emaciatedly skinny, in his late 30s—his eyes gaunt with years of frustration—he stands there—body curved vampishly, one hand on his hips, the other balancing the black cigarette holder like a parody trumpet, lightly—lightly—between long manicured fingers.

"Dont pay attention to her, sonny," the fatman says to me. When he smiles, the flesh squeezes his tiny eyes, almost shutting them. "Shes just in from New York," he explains, indicating the skinny man, "and I told her she'd have to see Main Street." . . . And so the fatman has been playing the role of initiated Guide to the other's First-Trip-to-Main-Street-and-Vice amazement.

149

"Dont—call—me—'she,'" the skinny man said, stretching his lips across his face tightly in a straight pink line. . . . I can tell hes Gigantically intrigued with this bar; nevertheless hes affecting indifference. Crazily, I imagine him walking along Madison Avenue in New York, mincing in a tight olive-green suit as if his legs were tied at the knees; carrying a pencil-thin umbrella as affectedly as he carries—and he carried it—the cigarette holder; entertaining, in the evenings, his equally closeted friends—with Cocktails. Late at night, he will lonesomely pull off, looking at pictures of youngmen. . . . Sometime tonight, I felt certain—if I stuck around (twice I had started to leave, repelled by the fatman, and twice he had showily slapped a large bill on the bar for drinks: "Drink up; buyanother-one")—sometime tonight, I would hear the skinny one, in excited tones, claim surprise that "supposedly straight men" take money from homosexuals in exchange for sex. . . . Still, I felt strangely sorry for him for the mask which defensively he has to wear.

But I avoid looking at them now. I study this familiar bar: the exotic plants painted to suggest a jungle: a giant butterfly, trying futilely to *Escape!*—the canvas from wall to wall drooping heavily from the ceiling, shelteringly or oppressively. Pinpoints of colored lights dart into the darkness from the pinball machines . . . feeble childhood sparklers, expiring. . . . In the booths, figures huddle intimately—shadowy clustered vulture forms when you first walk into the smoky twilight, features swallowed by the darkness, emerging into the splashes of light like flotsam out of shallow water; then eyes become visible, incessantly finding a new object to focus on.

Like buyers in a market place, scores in groups, before scattering singly about the bar for the actual Hunt, may exchange remarks about the malehustlers: discuss them openly, weighing one against the other—as if, like inanimate objects, the hustlers cannot hear. . . . And like conspirators against a common enemy who must nevertheless be used, the malehustlers, also momentarily together, braggingly discuss how much a particular score is worth. . . . So the two armies—scores and hustlers—meet here nightly.

And nightly a game of charades is played at Harry's. Unlike the ones who haunt the streets, even the most masculine scores here usually—but not always—become effeminate in groups, their gestures progressively more airy as the night advances toward the desperation of after-midnight; as the liquor releases the feminine self. And the hustler emphasizes his masculinity in one of various poses—one leg propped against the wall; cigarette held between thumb and finger—eyes veiledly following a likely prospect: the rehearsed, inviting Tough Look. . . . Bodies sprawl on the benches along the booths. There is the swaggering unceasing exodus to the smelly toilet at the end of the long bar—a gaping toothless mouth. . . .

An air of determination is in every gesture here, in every look, every move. People come to Harry's primarily for one of two purposes: to buy or to be bought.

Occasionally the femmequeens from the 1-2-3 or Ji-Ji's breeze in like wilted flowers, carried on the currents of smoke: giggling, regally scanning the bar—making studied defiant exits with great airs, grand queenly shrieks of exiled laughter. And they indicate a kind of contempt for those other men in the bar who only desire other males, without posing, as far as the law allows them, as real women the way the queens do. . . .

The skinny man has been raking the bar, putting everyone down with a bitchy comment. Defensively, he must reject this alluring, disturbing world to which the fatman is connivingly exposing him. "My God!" the skinny man says, "look at that one—his pants are about to fall off his waist! . . . And there goes that one to the restroom again!" . . . Suddenly, his eyes abruptly stopping their swirl about the bar, he blurted unexpectedly, as if his thoughts had pushed the words out without his control: "I like *that* one!" He points with his cigarette holder at Skipper, who is standing by the jukebox while obviously avoiding buying his own drink. The fatman slapped his forehead in affected amazement, and in a highpitched, incongruous voice shrieked: "Oh, no, Mary, you cant mean *that* one!" His blubbery lips envelop the stub of the cigar, almost swallowing it. "You dont mean the one in the black T-shirt!"

"Yes, I do mean the blond one," said the skinny one, having gone this far. Then he said to the fatman: "And dont call me 'Mary.'"

Skipper, aware of the skinny man's interest, brings his hands together, fingers intertwined, and flexes his body slowly. The light from the jukebox weaves colors sinuously on him—and from the distance he looks like a very youngman, a boy. . . .

"Honey," the fatman was going on, addressing the skinny one, who still holds the cigarette aimed at Skipper as if it were a magic wand that would bring him over, "I could have had him when he was Young and Pretty!"

On the stools next to us, sit two middle-aged men. They have been talking in whispers, but now, as they glance surreptitiously but obviously at the fatman. one word emerges clearly from their sibilant sounds: "Fat."

The fatman drops the cigar butt suddenly on the floor, letting it fall from his mouth; brings his ovaled fatfoot heavily on it, squashing it angrily into the debris of cigarettes on the floor. The two middle-aged men, aware he has heard them, turn away nervously, making rushed incoherent conversation as they clutch at their beers as if for protection—as they move against the wall.

The fatman's eyes follow the two doggedly. With renewed venom now, he goes on about Skipper: "I'll bet hes over 30— hes been around longer than just about any of them."

"Maybe hes not as young as some of the delinquents around here," said the skinny one, "but I still feel rawthuh Intrigued."
... And then, in an uncontrolled burst, in which the Mask slid off shockingly, he said: "I think hes positively *Savage!*" He flung his eyes ecstatically toward the smoky Heaven. Quickly, realizing what hes just said, he composes himself, adjusting his pose consistent again with his earlier charade of Maiden. He sips his drink, shifts his skinny hips; says:

"This whole place is Positively Indecent; it should be razed!"

The fatman roars with laughter. "Why dont you go talk to him?"

"But what will I say to him?" the skinny man asks in renewed interest. He brought his hand to his chest in a gesture of uninitiated Helplessness.

"Nothing." The fatman contracted the mountains of flesh into a shrug.

"You mean *he'll* talk to me?"

The fatman says viciously: "No. I mean, Mary, that all you have to do is wave a few bills before him and he'll drop his pants for you—right here!"

Even in the orangy dark, I can see the skinny man blanch; he tightens his lips, sucks them in between his teeth, breathing deeply. His eyes hurl their hatred at the fatman. For a long time, the two men look at each other, resenting the common knowledge that binds them together. "I-dont-believe," the skinny man said pitifully, at last wresting his eyes in defeat from the embattled stare of the other, "that-men-take-money-from-other-men-for-sex."

"If you dont want to pay for him," the fatman said ruthlessly, driving his words into the skinny one like a pike, "I'll buy him for you. . . . Easy enough."

The skinny man flings a frantic look of Deep Hurt at him.

"Go on, honey," the fatman pursues mercilessly. "You got to learn. You aint pretty yourself, you know." He buries his fat elbow in the skinny man's ribs, almost knocking him off-balance. *"Go on!"*

"I—have—Never—paid—for—sex," the skinny man murmurs.

"I told you: I'll buy him for you—if you haven't got the guts to do it yourself," said the fatman pitilessly. "Go on, offer him a drink—bring him over and I'll fix it up for you. Leave it to me, honey. I mean, your blond 'savage' is certainly—uh—entertaining."

"If *you* want him." said the skinny one, "why dont' *you* go after him?"

"I like the one I have," the fatman said. In his voice, nevertheless, there is a tone of deep resentment. . . . If I make the scene with him, he will probably yawn after it's over; say something to put me down. He will give me the money contemptuously—but necessarily Bigly. He will adjust his expensive tie carefully, pointedly emphasizing what he would be trying to convince himself the real difference between our worlds is: trying to forget the previous one-sided desire—which will recur in him again and again for whomever. . . . "Good luck," he might even say, but I'll know that hes looking forward to the time when whatever of desirability he may have seen in me—as he has seen it in others, from night to night—will have evaporated. . . . Looking up, I see my own reflection now in the panel of mirrors; and reflected behind me, that life that has fascinated me greets me victoriously: All along this long closed-in bar, the composite face of this submerged world stares defiantly at me.

"Your blond in the T-shirt is really too much," the fatman is going on. "You just wont believe it!" he says to the skinny one. "He carries some clippings—and those photographs!"

"What Photographs?" said the skinny one.

"Shes interested all right," the fatman says, winking at me, trying to ally me with him against the skinny one.

"I—Told—You," said the skinny one firmly. "Don't Call Me 'she.' "

"Oh, Mary, get off it!" the fatman says impatiently with a fatwave of his hand, as if he were stripping off the skinny one's mask. "Who do you think youre fooling? Youve got the hot-pants—and youll pay for it—just like I do—*because you have to!*" he lashed. "So stop your goddam pretending—And Face It!" He turns his swollen round back to his skinny friend.

Mouth ovaled, a look of enormous indignation on his face, the skinny man moved away. He stood momentarily in the middle of the bar—then he marched rigidly toward the door. I watch him as he stands there undecided. And then, abruptly, he turns back.

"Did he leave?" the fatman asks me.

"No."

"I knew it!" he says triumphantly, transferring the pounds and pounds of his fleshy body on the stool to face the door. He stares at the skinny man, now standing only a few feet from the jukebox, glaring back at the fatman. I look at the fatman. In the pudgy pigfeatures there is something indefinably sinister.

About to speak to Skipper—almost hypnotized by him—the skinny man backed away quickly. He looked at the fatman —the fatman challenging him from the distance. Suddenly, abandoning in bewildered rashness the pose of virginal novice, the skinny man says something to Skipper, who turns slowly to face him, answers. The skinny man rushes to the bar. Avoiding looking in our direction, he returned with a drink, which he handed hurriedly to Skipper, as if he were giving away, at last, a treasured, guarded part of himself which he was nevertheless compelled to give. . . .

"Well!" the fatman sighs triumphantly. He seems somehow vindicated by the skinny man's submission, like a bullish sergeant justifying his own existence by enlisting recruits.

"Do you know him—the guy in the black T-shirt?" he asks me. Without the cigar, his face looks blank, incomplete, the dough-flesh smeared carelessly over his face.

"Sure—hes a great guy."

"Well, Christ, why doesnt he give up—hes been around for years!"

Since that first night, at the 1-2-3, when Miss Destiny had introduced him to me as a "model" who had been in the movies, I had of course seen Skipper often. That same night, I had been with him—with Chuck and the girls we picked up on Main Street. With compulsive determination—I remem-bered—he had crossed the wires to start Buddy's car; as if he were terrified of inertia. . . . Later, he had put one of the girls down for coming on that she wanted to get into The Movies. "Go home," he said curtly. . . . Often, I saw him in the bars, playing the pinball machine, struggling with it to get a high score, until inevitably the TILT would light up mockingly. Or I would see him playing the shuffleboard, smashing the pins angrily, the disk spinning back dizzily toward him. But I never saw him in Pershing Square. There are stories that something had happened between him and Sergeant Morgan— stories that after an incident of which there are different versions, Sergeant Morgan ran him out. Skipper merely said: "That park's for chippies, man!—hell, they go for pennies there!" . . . One night, high, he had talked everyone into driving to Hollywood, and then, moodily, had put it down: "Hollywood's nowhere." . . . Off and on he stayed at Trudi's near Silverlake—a neat, feminine unit in a flowery court, paid for by Trudi's "daddy." And in that world youll hear that Trudi's daddy really wants Skipper but wont admit he (the daddy) is a fruit, and so he makes it with Trudi, forgetting, maybe—which is easy—that Trudi, too, is, technically, a man. Once I had gone to score marijuana at Trudi's house —she always had some—and Skipper was there, sitting at the table eating, while Trudi lovingly served him like a young infatuated wife. . . . When Skipper was gone for longer than a few days—and he would disappear periodically—Trudi would come into the bars, hardly madeup, looking like a mournful little girl, asking if anyone had seen him. When theyd tell her no, she'd shake her head: "Those goddam beads," she'd mumble. Other times, at the 1-2-3, she would come in Grandly, completely madeup, to meet Skipper.

There is a consuming franticness about Skipper which seizes you the moment he begins to talk—the words coming often in gasps—his eyes burning—at times as if about to explode with intensity, at times on the brink of closing, giving up. Constantly, he flexes his body, looking down at it, studying it, as if to make sure it is still intact. . . .He hangs around in one place only a few minutes; if he doesnt score immediately, he'll leave, go to another bar; come back—and when he is sitting down, he constantly drums his fingers to the frenzied music— and even when the music is slow, the frantic drumming persists, as though the sounds he hears are coming from within; veiling his eyes—lowered lids—or looking down at the bar— as if he doesn't want to see too Clearly; creating circles on the surface of the bar with the water from the glass, then erasing them abruptly with his hand. . . . By midnight, he is usually drunk.

After being around him a few times, I began to avoid him; stifled by the knowledge of the sad, sad loss of Youth, of the terrible hints that life, perversely,. may make one a caricature of oneself, a wandering persistent ghost of the youngman that was, once—the attitudes of youth lingering after the youth itself was gone, played out. With Skipper, this loss was concentrated, emphasized because life had given him nothing but physical beauty, an ephemeral beauty relying on Youth. . . . That sense of loss had seized me acutely one day when, sitting with him and two scores, I watched him remove from his wallet a set of photographs, about six of them, all of him in different poses, showing him—almost nude, much younger— a glowing youngman of about 20. "Thats me!" he had said, almost challengingly, as he passed the photographs to the two scores. And he carried, too, mysteriously, some frayed clippings, in an envelope, an envelope which, once, I saw him replace with a newer one, with great tenderness: the frayed clippings becoming older and older—the envelope, new.

There were hints, in his conversations, of closed doors behind him, doors which had opened temptingly and *Slammed!* with great finality; hints of painful resignation. Behind the sullen look with which he nailed the people who bought him was the unmistakable awareness that he was on the brink of facing his doom: of facing Death. . . . And Death for Skipper was the loss of Youth. . . . The years that would follow the knowledge of his premature death would be played out by him like a ghost. . . . Watching him rush out of a bar once, Chuck had said: "Man, that stud walks more miles in a day than I do all mammy-screwin week long!" And Darling Dolly Dane had added, sighing deeply: "Yeah, baby, but he always ends up where he started from. . . ." Perhaps realizing this, Skipper constantly veiled his eyes.

I watch the skinny man now talking to Skipper. And I see the damning smile on the fatman's face as he motions them over. As Skipper walks toward us with the skinny man, I notice immediately that Skipper is already drunk; he stumbles, curses. His eyes are smoldering with the hinted awareness of tonight. . . .

"Hi, jack," he says to me. "Hi cholly," he says to the fatman. This is Skipper's way of putting a score down. The world is divided into "jacks"—of which he is one—and "chollys." A "cholly" is the necessary enemy in the life of a "jack." . . .

"Hey, don I know you from somewhere?" he says to the fat-man.

"Ive seen you—around," the fatman says. He stares at Skipper—and the smile on the fatman's face contemptuously belies the piercing hatred in his eyes—hammering their gaze at Skipper.

The fatman put a fresh cigar in his mouth, snapping his cigarette lighter on, clicking it loudly as if he were cocking a gun aimed at Skipper. In the flickering light of the flame, which the fatman held before Skipper's face, you can see the beginning tracings of lines around Skipper's eyes.

Sensing this and the unyielding stare of the fatman, Skipper moves slightly back, into the orangy twilight that floats in smoky pools about the bar.

2

On the table, in the booth where weve been sitting since Skipper came over—myself and the fatman on one side, Skipper and the skinny man on the other—there are the empty bottles of beer, empty glasses; the ashtray is crammed with smoked cigarettes like dead bugs. The mixture of beer and hard liquor Ive been drinking has worked its peculiar magic on me: I feel alertly high: The world now seems compressed into this immediate spot, as if in a giant painting everything but one tiny area has been blocked out—and the unblocked area is now in sharp focus, locked for minute observation. And as usual in that state, I feel tied in fascination to the scene. . . . The dim smoky figures beyond this booth have re-treated farther and farther into the amber darkness of the bar.

"And then what happened?" The fatman has been ques-tioning Skipper with the tone of voice one would use to goad a child to relate a fantastic story for the amusement of adults listening with mock interest—the child, unaware of being used, becoming more and more responsive to the attention.

I know that, sober, Skipper would have left long ago—as I would have left—but in the willing surrender to drunkenness, he is answering the fatman's questions as if testifying in his own defense. Sitting next to Skipper, the skinny man has com-pletely abandoned his previous role of novice. He has given in, under the impact of the liquor and the fatman's brutal attack, to the life the fatman has badgered him into. Watching him—his skinny form propped there resignedly against the brownish leather of the booth—I feel even more sorry for him now—

now that the pose which up to tonight had made his existence
more easily possible has collapsed under the ramming words
of the fatman. The fatman, aware of his triumph there, has
pushed the skinny man into the background. Now he is questioning Skipper with the certainty of a prosecutor interrogat-
ing a witness who has already confessed.

"So then what happened?" the fatman repeats: He sits
there, a giant caricature of Buddha. He has been sipping one
drink since we sat here; and he holds that drink cupped in his
fat-hand as if it were his sobriety, which for the purposes of
tonight he was guarding.

Skipper mutters: "Yeah, well, see—it was just after I got
outta the marines—and I met this guy in L.A. And I—"

"Louder," the fatman says. "I cant hear you."

Skipper raised his voice. Hes creating the familiar circles on
the table with the watery glass. "I knew this guy in L.A.—see
—that I stayed with. . . . See, when I got outta the service, I
made this Main Street scene. I met—lots of guys—you know
—go with them—hang around here—Main Street—all the
time. . . . Thats when I met this guy—right here, too, right
here at Harry's was where I met him."

"Oh?" the fatman says. He never removes the cigar from
his mouth, except when it becomes a stub, and then he seems
for a moment to be deliberating whether to swallow it—his
lips tossing it about his mouth uncertainly—and then he spits
it out, replaces it. Occasionally he winks at me: For his immediate purposes—tonight—he is trying to separate me from
the questions hes hurling at Skipper. But I know his contempt
could easily—would easily—turn on me. . . . "And so this
man—you stayed with him?" the fatman says.

"Yeah," Skipper said, downing the drink in his glass.
"Wannanother," he says. "Nother drink."

The fatman hands money to the skinny man. "Get some
more drinks, Mary," he says, and the skinny man—obediently
now, unprotestingly—goes automatically to the bar, returns
shakily balancing the drinks. The fatman slides his own drink
toward Skipper. "Heres two," he said. "Mustnt run out."

"Mustnt run out," Skipper echoed, shaking his head, whether
for some kind of clarity or whether because, for him, the
words have a more immediate meaning. "Mustnt—run—out."

"And then?" the fatman persists impatiently. He seems to
be delving into Skipper's life for some mysterious vindication
of his own.

"Well—see—like I say—I was just outta the marines.

Busted. I kept going awol. Christ, man—I was restless to start living. You know—really Living. . . ."

"We all want to live," said the fatman sneeringly. "Thats not strange."

"Yeah," says Skipper. "Sure—but see—when I got outta the service—busted—I was just making it. No gig. . . . So I made this Main Street scene. Then I met this guy—this guy I told you about—right here I met him—see—I just got busted out of—out of the marines—I—"

"You told us that," said the fatman.

"I would have liked to be in the marines." the skinny man said wistfully. "But—"

"We know, we know," the fatman dismisses him, "they put you in the wacs instead." He turned to Skipper. "You were out of the marines, and you met lots of people—who 'helped' you—"

"Well—this guy," Skipper said, "there was this one guy—he— . . . Man, he used to call me an 'angel'—dig—and he says he wants a picture of me—for this—for this crazy album he had—of guys— . . ."

And suddenly, in double, near-drunk pity, I want to laugh. . . .

And Skipper is saying: "So this guy takes me to this photographer, who takes these body pictures—you know—hardly any clothes—and he—this photographer—he asked me to come back—gonna take more pictures. . . ."

"I wouldnt have minded being in the navy," the skinny man muttered. His cigarette holder has lost its magic. It rests before him, discarded, dead, along with the previous pose.

"So this guy—he was Okay, this photographer—he wants to help me—he tells me someone called him—wants to meet me —this big Director out in Hollywood—and I go out there. . . . Got this real mean pad—I mean, swimming pool—the size—the size—" He looks into the bar. "Bigger than this bar," he finishes. "And this Director, he calls this photographer—wants to meet me. See, those photographs—they were in one of those body magazines—"

"What was this director's name?"

Skipper answers.

(I had heard the director's name—everyone in that world has. He is one of its kings. Later, in the Hollywood bars, when I would make that scene, I would hear the giddy fairies excitedly—enviously—narrate who the director's newest "discovery" was. Still later, with an old auntie—a prissy old man

—I went to the director's home, his mansion. That day, another youngman was there—the director's current "discovery" —living with him. And later, when I think of Skipper, I'll remember that other youngman. Life reveals itself, if at all, slowly—and often through patterns discovered in retrospect. . . .)

Closing his eyes completely now as if for him the memory of the past is too special to allow it in this bar, Skipper says: "It was a Beautiful home. . . ."

(The director's house reigns over the enchanted hills. You park by a thick stone wall, shutting in the famous-director's world: Within that wall, he reigns Supreme as a monarch. You lift a telephone in a niche, announcing yourself. A maid opens the door if youre expected. And you walk into a garden— sprawling beyond the door in three levels, outlining the house. About the garden are statues, nakedly white in the green of the trees, the grass—the lush flowers. A swimming pool dominates one level of the garden, bordered by marble benches. In a cave of shrubs, a long bar displays bottles like gaudy jewelry. They stand at attention as if awaiting the presence of the director. From the pool and the bar a gradually ascending flight of stairs swirls into an alcove, short white pillars creating a ceilingless rotunda. Beyond that, the trees spill deceptively into green-shrugging hills. . . .)

Skipper faced the wall momentarily, turning from the shrill sounds at Harry's bar. A piece of plaster has begun to crumble from the wall. He places his hand over it, covering it impulsively. "Man," he says, "I was nervous that first day—I went alone. See, the photographer—he couldnt go—this Director wants to talk to me—alone. The maid let me in. I just —stood there—it was like—a palace— . . ."

(And then, that afternoon, the director makes his entrance, emerging out of the white walls of the house in slacks and sport shirt: a tiny, skinny, wiry old man with alert, determined eyes. He looks at Skipper appraisingly. "Youre much better-looking than your photographs, youngman," he says, "and I might add you look good in clothes.")

"I knew it was the Bigtime," Skipper sighed.

"The Bigtime," the fatman repeats—as if in his role of prosecutor, of Avenger, this phrase gave him a clue.

"Yeah, sure," said Skipper. "Everyone's hearda this Director—"

"Even in New York," said the skinny one, "everyone knows

about him. I heard hes got this great pool—boys there all the time. I heard—"

(Later, when I went to the director's house with the auntie—several weeks later—the director would be redecorating his house. "Ive grown fond of it," he'll explain to us, "but it needs much work on it, so Im redecorating it—all." The auntie will say: "You know exactly how to live." "I do, I do," the director will reply.)

"Did this director put you in the movies?"

Skipper sighed almost inaudibly: "Yes."

(It's a summer day, the warmth hugs the director's house, this garden, loving the luxury, too: a Special warmth. And Skipper looks about him hungrily. The director senses the Craving in Skipper's eyes—which he knew would be there even from the photographs—as he has sensed it many times before in others; and he looks around at his house, his garden, his pool, owning every inch of it, possessing it. Now he looks at Skipper in the same way. "Would you like to take a swim?" he asks Skipper. And Skipper, in his early 20s then, goes swimming in the director's pool, and the water embraces him as if he, too, were meant for all this luxury. When he comes out of the water, laughing—the director places his hand on Skipper's shoulder and says: "I have a feeling youre my new Discovery.")

"He asked me to move in with him," Skipper was saying now, spewing out for the fatman with the cigar the steps by which his life had led him to squint his eyes now at Harry's bar.

"How long?" the fatman shoots at him.

"I moved in the next day," Skipper said evasively. "He said I'd be real big in the flix—I heard him—he told everyone I was his Biggest Discovery."

("Youre a Very Beautiful Boy," the director tells Skipper. "And in this town thats All that matters.")

"He took me around—showed me off," Skipper said. He smiles, the phantom smile of the youngman who believes hes seeing materialize fully the world hes been searching. "Man —I was really Someone!"

(Skipper learns how to make drinks—like the youngman who would be there when I would meet the director later. He learns, at dinner, to cue the director's best stories: "Remember when you were filming Angels in Paradise?" he may say, and the director: "Oh, yes—it was very amusing. The star was— . . .")

"And what did you have to do in return?" the fatman said. "Or did you just live there?" he asked derisively.

Skipper's eyes rise slowly from the surface of the table—he erases the circles of water in one sweeping move of his palm—and focuses his eyes evenly on the fatman. "I—" he started, and then instinctively he wiped his lips as if in physical disgust at the remembered contact. "Nothing!" he almost shouted.

(Skipper learns, for the first time, to reciprocate in bed—to close his eyes in order to stem the revulsion—to concentrate on the doors swinging open before him, leading to that glittering world. . . . Those first weeks he and the director will be alone. The groups of other youngmen are no longer invited. And in the afternoons, when hes not at the studio, Skipper will dive into the water of the pool, which, warming him, will reassure him. . . .)

"How long did you stay there?" the fatman persisted.

"A month—more—maybe two—" Skipper says at last.

"Why didnt you stay longer?"

Again Skipper dodges the question. "Well—see—this director—says I got the looks—the personality—but Ive got to study—lots—to get ahead in the flix—and—see—well—I was in one of his movies—"

(The director says to Skipper: "Youve got what really matters—Looks. But youll need training. Talent is important, too—there are many very beautiful boys in this town. . . . I know a man, a wonderful drama coach—I'll take you to him." And Skipper will have publicity photographs made, and the coach will tell him, "Youre a very beautiful boy—and thats Important." And the director tells Skipper theres a part for him in his new picture: "Not a big part—but the next one, when youve learned more—" He smiles reassuringly. "Theyll get to see you, at least, and thats important. In my next film therell be a bigger part, youll get to speak—theyll hear you this time." And Skipper tells himself he is certainly meant for this life.)

"What movie was that?" the fatman says.

Skipper looked into his empty glass. He turns to the bartender. "Hey! More drinks!"

The bartender calls back: "Come get em yourself, honey; I ain no waitress!"

The fatman extends money again to the skinny man. "More drinks," he orders.

The skinny man rose—the cigarette holder rolls and drops on the floor, and he almost stumbles on it.

"What was the name of the movie you were in?—I might have seen it." The fatman again shoves his own drink at Skipper as the skinny man sits down, sinks into the booth resignedly.

"It was called—" said Skipper, "—it was called *That's Life*." He laughed mirthlessly.

"I dont remember you in it—of course, it was such a long time ago," the fatman said inevitably. "What role did you play?"

"I didnt have a name," Skipper said.

"Why, I was sure you were going to tell us you got an award for it!"

"Shit, man!" Skipper blurts drunkenly, "you couldnt—couldnt even see my face!"

"And afterwards?" the fatman's implacable questioning continued.

(One evening, a cool breeze invading the garden from the hills—one evening, Skipper will refer to "his" room, like the youngman I would see there later—and the director will frown, look at Skipper: "You mean the east bedroom," he'll correct him ominously. . . . Soon Skipper detects the impatience in the director's eyes, he sees the new group of youngmen from the studio that come again to swim in the pool—and one especially—and he hears the director announce to that new youngman, emerging out of the pool while Skipper sits on the marble bench: "I believe youll be a sensation in the movies." And he turns to Skipper and says, "Go tell Mattie we'll have a guest for dinner.")

"Well," said Skipper, "see—after that—he tells me I need more lessons—I gotta—gotta learn more about acting."

("He hasnt got the Magic," the director will say to his friends later about Skipper. "But there is this young boy at the studio, I just talked to him today about his Possibilities—and: he is A Very Beautiful Boy.")

"You must have been a very beautiful boy," the skinny man muttered.

Skipper winced. He looked at the skinny man, startled. He looks in bewilderment about him—as if the echo of the words he had heard through those precious years of his life had momentarily transferred him somewhere else: the director's mansion, the homes he had been in, progressively less and less extravagant. In his look now I see, blurred, the slow surrender.

"What happened then?" the fatman said. Exhaling two fat

cylinders of smoke through his nostrils, he resembled a charging bull.

"Oh—I—well—later—I moved out. But I kept going to this acting teacher—and, well, see—I moved in with him—and then—see—I had met lots of other people—when I was living with this Director—and then through this teacher—and—I—well—they liked me. . . . Shit, man," he said suddenly, "I lived with them all, one right after the mother-fucking other."

"And after them?"

"Others," Skipper said dully.

"And then?" the fatman persists.

"Then—then I got fed up, see? Put it all down—I split. Then—when I came back—hell—I didnt even wanna—didnt even wanna see those people. And some of them—" he adds bitterly, "—they didnt wanna see me. Theyd call someone else—put me up for a while—with a friend of theirs. . . . Then I hung around Schwartz's, that movie drugstore—Hollywood Boulevard—the beaches: the whole scene. . . . So I came back—to Main Street—I didnt even wanna see Hollywood anymore—not even think about it. . . . Then—Christ!—I even got inna mess in fuckin Pershing Square. . . . Pershing Square!" he says contemptuously.

"Hows that?"

"This cop—this Sergeant Morgan. Man—he rousts me once, takes me downstairs—where they interrogate you. We're alone—tries to put the make on me—I slug him. Man! A cop! But, hell—dig: hes scared shitless—scared Im gonna tell on him. He lets me go—tells me if I ever show, he'll bust me— . . ." He holds his glass in both hands, squeezing it tightly. "Mother-fuckers," he says, shaking his head, as if he were passing judgment on all the people crammed into his life.

The fatman eyed him stonily. Then he yawns, looks at his watch. "It's past one," he says. . . . About us the desperation to find a partner has begun: Make it! During the past hour many couples have left, for the hotels along the block, for apartments, homes—parties that will last into the next day. But the bar is still jammed. The music seems louder, the laughter is more piercingly shrill, more forced. A sustained roar of words crowds you almost physically. The poses have become more effeminate on one side, more masculine on the other.

Like a bull ready to charge, the fatman lowers his head, places his hands on the table. "I'll tell you," he says to Skipper, and in acute awareness of what will happen, I want suddenly to stop his words. I start to get up, but the fatman is already saying to Skipper: "My friend here," indicating the skinny man, "would like you to go home with him. He hasnt got the guts to ask you, and so I offered to buy you for him—no big deal like youre used to: just for tonight."

The skinny man, even drunk, blinked incredulously.

Skipper passes his hand dazedly over his face, as if trying to place the scene in his mind. "Yeah?" he mutters. "Yeah?"

Again I want to leave quickly. This blacked-in scene, in focus, has become excruciatingly real. But helplessly aware that the bull is already charging—the beer and hard liquor churning vilely inside me—I hear the fatman's words go on ineluctably: "Will you go with him?" he has asked Skipper.

The skinny man, grasping all at once for the vestiges of sobriety, said, almost in tears: "Leave me alone, will you? Will —you—please—leave—me—alone—please!"

"Well?" the fatman asks Skipper.

"I'll go with him—" Skipper muttered.

"Good," said the fatman. But he seems disappointed; as if somehow he has expected another climax.

"—for thirty bucks," Skipper finishes.

And by the way the fatman blows out the smoke in relief, I know this is what hes been waiting for. "Thirty dollars!" he roars. "One for every year, huh?—and a few years thrown into the bargain? Is that how you figure it?"

"Thirty bills," Skipper repeated. His head almost touched the table.

"I can get several for that price," the fatman boasts. "Any of them! Take my pick of em!"

"Leave me alone," the skinny man is muttering.

"Twenty-five bucks," Skipper said, clenching his fists.

"Too much," the fatman says laughing.

Painfully, I see the bewilderment on Skipper's face as he looks up now from the table in amazed stupor—to face the fatman, the score—the Enemy. . . . As Skipper reaches into his pocket, removing the group of pictures from an envelope, I hear something inside of me shout to him: *Dont!* . . , realizing that Skipper is about to barter for his Youth. But already there are two frayed clippings in Skipper's hand. "Look," he says triumphantly to the fatman. "I was in the columns."

The fatman reaches for the clippings. He looked at them carefully. "Oh," he said dully, "you escorted a young actress to a nightclub." He reads the other. "This one doesnt have a name. All it says is that she was escorted by a young actor."

"Yeah," says Skipper, "but it was Me. . . ."

The fatman returns the clippings to him.

Now Skipper shoves the pictures at him, they scatter on the table, among the bottles and the glasses and the smoked cigarette butts. "Thats Me!" he says. The figure of a youngman —Skipper—lies among the debris on the table: the almost-naked body caught gleamingly young by the camera.

The fatman stares at the pictures indifferently. "You werent wearing much, were you?"

"They were in the body magazines," Skipper said. "I even made a movie for them—and there was more pictures—you could order enlargements, even—pay for them—and—"

The skinny man drunkenly reaches for the pictures. He studies them carefully. "Why—this looks like—isnt this the same—?" he started.

And the fatman interrupts him abruptly: "Give him back his pictures!" he shouted angrily.

"Yes—it looks like—just like the picture youve got framed in your room—the big one!" the skinny man said to the fatman. "It is—it's the same pic—"

"Give him back his pictures!" the fatman commands, snatching them from the skinny man. . . .

And now, his motives discovered, the fatman turns with undisguised ferocity on Skipper. "You were much younger then," he said.

"I was! . . . I had just got outta the marines—I told you—I —when—see—"

"Thats a hell of a long time ago!" the fatman shouts.

I see Skipper's face turned down again toward the table in crushed defeat—and I hear the fatman say to him: "I'll give you ten bucks—and I dont want you myself—I'll buy you for that one—" He points at the skinny man, who recoils from the fatman's finger extended pitilessly toward him. . . . "Ten bucks—for you— . . . and the pictures. . . ." the fatman says pitilessly, trying now, by degrading even the memory of Skipper's youth, recorded in the photographs, to erase his own years-long desire.

"Not the pictures," Skipper muttered.

"No deal then," the fatman announces victoriously. He still holds the photographs in his hand.

Suddenly Skipper lunges across the table, snatches the photographs from him. "Take your filthy hands off them!" he shouts. The pictures scatter on the floor.

The fatman looks with undisguised cold hatred at Skipper.

He organizes his spilling flesh, to rise—ripping his gaze away from Skipper.

Skipper gets up unsteadily now. In one swift unexpected motion, he shoves the fatman into the booth, the leather creating a sucking protesting sound as the fatman's form sinks into it.

Skippers shouts: "Sit down—*fatso!*"

In an instant the demonic composure of the fatman shatters like a wall crumbling under the impact of a wrecker.

"You son of a bitch!—dont call me that!" he whines.

The people in the bar, sensing excitement, crowd about the booth.

Skipper stands menacingly over the fatman. "You even *smell* fat!" he says.

They stare at each other like two soldiers in opposing armies who realize that neither will be the victor—that each has been mortally wounded.

Skipper repeats: "You even smell fat!"

The fatman—the bull rallying once more after having been stabbed—yells at me: "Well—you comin with us or not?"

"Fuck yourself," I said.

He roars over to the skinny man, lifts him from the booth, dangling him like a puppet. The skinny man, lashing out with his nails, burying them into the fatman as if to puncture the inflated body, wrests himself free of the bear clutch.

"You do!" the skinny man shouted—and he is crying now. "You really do! You really smell fat!" He begins to laugh, repeating over and over: "Fat, fat, fat, fat, fat, fat . . . FAT! . . ." until the word was drowned in the hysterical laughter, as the fatman—dodging Skipper's drunkenly aimed fist—thrusts his arms almost pitifully into the encircling crowd and rams his way into the escape of the sheltering night.

As he stormed out, I heard a familiar voice saying, "Let me through, let me through," and in the fatman's wake—pushing her way insistently toward the booth and Skipper—Trudi emerged out of the curious crowd. Small, frail, completely made up—understanding instinctively what had gone on—she gathered the spilled photographs from the floor—neatly—with the clippings, and she put them carefully into the envelope. Her head barely reached Skipper's shoulders, and she looked at him with the compassion that only one outcast can feel for another. Now she put her arms about his waist, whispering softly to him: "Cummon, baby—screw the beads —lets go home." She leads him through the crowd, unsteadily but firmly—Skipper willingly surrendering now completely to the drunkenness.

Outside, the air is cool. Night embraces Main Street blackly. . . . I stand watching the people as they leave the bar in pairs or in desperate aloneness. A few feet away, I see Skipper bent over the curb, vomiting.

Now a queen passes by, stands staring at Skipper. . . . And I hear Trudi—holding Skipper lovingly as he vomits rackingly into the street—challenge the queen's suddenly bewildered stare:

"Whats the matter, queenie? . . . Aint you never seen a *man* puke?"

CITY OF NIGHT

AFTER ALL, THERES THIS TO CONSIDER: *The world's no fucking good. "Youve got to pretend you dont give a damn and swing along with those that really dont—or you go under."*

I needed hungrily to feel wanted—but when someone tried to get too close—someone met in that daily excursion through moviehouse balconies, bars, the park—I immediately moved away from him. I seldom saw the same person more than a few times during those months.

Recurrently, around the others hustling those places, I felt a peculiar overpowering guilt because I was convinced I was not trapped by that world, as I was certain they were. Yet there were those other times when I felt even more hopelessly a part of it for having searched it out. It was a quandary so strangely disturbing—so difficult to understand—that I tried to force myself not to think about it—perhaps because I sensed even then that the answer to the riddle would entail something much too harsh to face.

Increasingly now there were moments of craving for a form of revenge on life—to get even with it. And for what reason specifically? I didnt really know. More and more, revenge became a conscious craving.

There is a bar in Los Angeles a block from Pershing Square, on Sixth Street. It's called the Hodge Podge. At that time it wasnt exclusively a hustling bar—many went there to make out mutually with each other. But often you can score much better in such a bar.

From the street, you descend into it, as if into a cellar. It is dark and like a cave: partitions separating it into small ghettos, where groups huddle in the semidarkness. As you walk in, a youngman who looks like a hood may check your I.D. Because he hadnt seen me there before, he asked me for mine. Before I could pull it out of my wallet, a Negro queen I had

169

seen briefly, at the most twice at the 1-2-3—Miss Billie—comes rushing over to me and the youngman checking I.D. "Oh, baby," she says to him indignantly, "hes All Right—why, Ive known him *for years!* You just go ahead and let him in like your sister says, hear?" She turned to me: "Im working here now, baby—to attract a new crowd—and you just rely on Miss Billie whenever you need help to get in this bar." Someone called to her for drinks. "I'll talk to you later, sweetheart," she said, moving away.

Before you can make out the faces here, your eyes have to wait a few moments to adjust to the light. As my eyes focused, there was one person I saw immediately, and he was looking at me: a well-dressed man, not yet middle-aged, sitting alone at a table. . . . Immediately I realized I knew him—from somewhere, sometime. It could even have been New York. Perhaps I had merely talked to him somewhere—Main Street, the park. But I knew it wasnt just "somewhere, sometime." I knew him from a time somehow important. . . .

"*Baby!*" I saw Pauline coming toward me with two drinks, one of which she handed to me. She is fiercely madeup around the eyes tonight—still trying to look like Sophia Loren, her lips round and pouting. I wonder what shes doing away from the 1-2-3 and Ji-Ji's—the two places preferred by queens because they could get away with higher drag. "I *knew* I should come here more *often.* Ive *heard* it's *really* getting to be a *kicky bar.*" She comes on like this with everyone—soon she'll be promising me all kinds of things. She'll be talking about her beauty shop—still Soon To Open. And she'll be telling me, as she tells everyone else, how Im the *only* person she has *ever* loved.

"I *just* moved into this *grand* apartment, out in *Hollywood,* baby," she gushed, "and you *must* come out and *live* with me. And we'll live in *grand* style. . . . You know, my Beauty Shop is *about* to open—and my customers are the *wealthiest* women in Beverly Hills, and I *just*— . . ." She goes on familiarly.

The man at the table is still staring at me. I wonder if he too is trying to remember from where he knows me. As much as I tried to avoid looking at him, I kept turning to face him. In that bar—among all the giggles and the loud laughter, amid the jukebox rocking—he appears strangely to me now as if sitting in some kind of judgment. On me? But I still cant remember.

"Ive got to split," I told Pauline abruptly.

"But you *just* got here, baby!" She poses at being offended.

"Are you being *unfaithful?*—to the person who loves you the *most* in this wide, wide world? Now, *confess*—are you being *unfaithful* to me? . . . Youre *bugged* by this place, arent you? I can *tell.* . . . I'll tell you *what!* I am *loaded* tonight, sweetheart. Lets go out to this *real wild* place I know of, where we can pick up some *really fine* maryjane. Then we'll go to my *pad* and get *high.* . . . Of course, I *wish* I could take you out to my *new* apartment—in *Hollywood* (though *actually* it's closer to *Beverly Hills*)—but as a matter of *fact,* I havent *really* occupied it, *yet.* You see, theyre *remodeling* it and the interior decorators want it to be *just so*—you know how those girls are—and *so,* in the *meantime,* Im still living on *Spring Street.* . . ."

We walked out together, Pauline shrieking to attract attention as she makes her exit. At the landing leading up the steps to the street, I glanced back at the man. He was still looking at me.

This time, for once, it turned out Pauline is telling the truth. She was indeed loaded. We took a cab to a place on upper Broadway.

The bar turns out to be mostly a spadebar.

On the dance floor, spade chicks with classic butts squeezed into gold and orange and red hugging dresses dance with gleamingfaced Negro men. This is not a queer bar—it is an outcast bar—Negroes and vagrant whites, heads and hypes, dikes and queens. On the dancefloor, too, lesbians—the masculine ones, the bull-dikes—dance with hugely effeminate queens, the roles of course reversed but technically legal—broadshouldered women and waspwaist-squeezed youngmen. The dikes are leading the queens.

"Isnt this *positively* mad, honey?" says Pauline, playing for tonight—or until her money lasts—the wealthy woman out on the town with her "escort." "I have a *fine* connection here, baby, and we'll get *tanked* on *bees* and *pod* and *then* I'll *really* show you a *sex-scene.* Ive been *waiting* since the *first* time I *saw* you. . . . Huccome youve never made it with me, baby? —youre the *only* one Ive *ever* loved! . . . My *God!* Those *queens* dancing with *lesbians*—ugh! They must be *perverts!*"

I went to the head, and there, sweat-bright spade and fay faces focus intensely on dice, cramped bodies in the tiny room exploding with the odor of maryjane smoke. A droopy-eyed Negro hands me a tiny joint, offers what is hardly a roach now: "Turn on?"

"You took so *long,*" said Pauline when I returned to the

table where we were now sitting. "I hope nobody was being *naughty* with you. I'll scratch their *eyes* out!" She goes on like this—but I wasnt really listening. I was still thinking about that man at the Hodge Podge. Somehow, whatever had happened with him, whenever and wherever it had happened, or not happened, was important. I knew that much with certainty.

"Why are you so *nervous*, baby?" Pauline asks me.

And then I remembered, suddenly and distinctly. Abruptly, I got up from the table.

"Where are you *going?*" Pauline asked.

"I just remembered," I told her, "I have to see someone downtown. Ive got to split, Pauline. I'll see you some other time—at your Hollywood pad, okay?"

"Why, *baby!*" she exclaimed. "You havent even *finished* the drink I *got* you!"

I drank it in a gulp.

"Something is *wrong*," she said. "Or dont you *love* me anymore?"

"Ive just got to go back," I said. "I just remembered someone I have to see, thats all."

And now she became mad. "Go to hell, for all I care—youre not so dam tough anyway," she growled in a man's voice.

"Sorry, Pauline—Ive got to go."

At the door I looked back, and she was storming across the dancefloor; stood staring back at me for a moment, to see if I would follow her. Realizing that I wasnt going to, she rushed into the ladies' room, dabbing at nonexistent tears. The scene, for her, although not what she had intended, was nevertheless complete. She was now the hurt, wronged woman. . . .

Shortly after, I was back at the Hodge Podge. As I walked in, looking through the dark clouds of smoke, I thought for a moment that the man had left, and my heart sank. But then I saw him. He had merely moved farther into the dark. And now that he was high—as he had been the first time I had seen him—I was certain who he was. I had the sudden feeling that he too was waiting for me. I stood near him.

"Drink?" he said. I sat down. He called Miss Billie. "Hi, hon," she said to me. "Why'd you leave so quick justa while ago? . . . And come to think of it, why aint I seen you in such a long time?—but then of course I've been in the hospital myself for about a week. I had this operation—and when I—"

"An abortion?" an eavesdropping white queen asks.

"Shut your nelly mouth, Mary," said the Negro queen—
"or I'll have you eight-sixed out of this bar so fast you wont
even be able to hold on to your makeup!"

"Honey," said the other queen. "I wasn't trying to dish you,
sweetheart. . . . Why, dearest, *I'd* like to get pregnant myself!"
They all tittered now, including Miss Billie: suddenly all sisters
again.

The man Im sitting with doesnt speak for a long while. He
doesnt even look at me. He stared down at the table, playing
with his drink. . . . But Im almost certain that he remembers
me too—that hes been waiting for me to fulfill something
vastly, if perversely, important.

"Will you come with me?" he asks me.

Without answering, I stood up. We walked out.

We went to a hotel nearby, much better than the ones on
Main Street. Coldly, we went up the elevator, into his room
. . . Outside, he hadnt appeared as drunk as he seems now,
and I wonder if somehow it's necessary that he be drunk—
and if not really that drunk, that he pretend to be.

He removes only his coat, places it carefully inside-out on
a chair, his wallet showing half-out from the pocket.

In bed, when he touched me, it was all quick, frantic. . . .
Then he lay back as if in drunken sleep.

Instantly—doing what I had come up to do—I reached for
his wallet. I removed all the money. I left the wallet, open,
on the chair.

And I walked out feeling strangely triumphant for having
just clipped the man with whom, that first afternoon in Los
Angeles, I had failed the world I had searched.

Part Three

"He's got the wind and the rain
        in His hands,
He's got both you and me
        in His hands,
He's got the whole world in His hands."

—*He's Got the Whole World in His Hands*

CITY OF NIGHT

HOLLYWOOD BOULEVARD IS THE HEART OF the heartless Hollywood legend. Like special moths attracted to the special glitter of the nihilistic movie capital, the untalented or undiscovered are spewed into the streets by the make-it legend.

You came here to find the wish fulfilled in 3-D among the flowers; the evasive childworld projected insistently into adulthood (some figurative something, that is, to hold hands with like you used to with Mommie until you discovered Masturbation); the makebelieve among the awesome palmtrees that the invitation of technicolored gold-laced Movies (along with Sodafountains and Stardom and the thousand realized miracles which that alone implies), of perpetual sun (seldom the lonesomeness of gray . . . lost . . . winter, say, or of the shrieking wind), and the invitation of The Last Frontier of Glorious Liberty (go barefoot and shirtless along the streets) have promised us longdistance for oh so long.

The invitation to rot obliviously, to die without feeling it, to grow old looking young, is everywhere in this glorious, sunny, many-colored city. And you sense this even before you enter the technical boundaries of the world called Hollywood: The sign on Crenshaw, surrounded by giant roses, said: WE TREAT THE SOLES OF YOUR FEET FOR INNER PEACE—and on Melrose you see a happy-faced Christ before a church: His splendid robes uncommonly festive.

And what you came hoping to be cured with (which is, importantly, what someone else came to be cured of—your sickness being someone else's cure) is certainly here (although you may not find it): all here, among the flowers and the grass, the palmtrees.

The blessed evenings. . . .

Hollywood—the fringe world beyond the movie lots.

Hollywood: Sex and religion and cops and nymphos and cults and sex and religion and junk . . . and sex and sects and flowers and junk and religion . . . fairies and nymphos and sick, sick cops . . . and sex.

Hollywood Boulevard is the imitation of a Dream.

Immediately, youre disappointed—expecting to see The Stars (in hope-materialized limousines), but the only ones you see are the bronze stars set into the sidewalks, exhibiting the names of the Memorable—but sometimes not so Memorable—Hollywood Personalities. You see, too, the long sequin-lighted rows, on either side, of stores and counter-restaurants, B-girled bars, Red Devil hotdog stands, moviehouses. . . . But you wont be disappointed for long if youve come to burrow beneath the tourist-neon surface of these streets.

Off Las Palmas, along—but on the opposite side of—the outdoor newsstand—where professional existentialists with or without sandals leaf through a paperback book and the fairies cruise each other by the physique books, while the lady from, say, Iowa (who will sigh Ahhhhhh as the Premiere searchlights screw the sky), here to attend a PTA convention at the Biltmore, buys a moviebook—off Las Palmas, on Saturday nights especially, the oldman graduate of Pershing Square writes Bible inscriptions on the street: in chalk; neat, incredibly beautiful letters. The young highschool delinquents with flattops proclaiming their Youth heckle him cruelly in merciless teenage fashion while he dashes out his prophecies of not-unlikely Doom: the booming words like the musicless theme of this street. . . . The fairies, half-listening momentarily to his shouting threats of imminent Judgment (while surveying the crowd for someone Cute), cross the street on their way, perhaps to the Green bar (where Miss Ana Mae—in Congenial Surroundings—will drown those echoing Threats as she plays her organ coyly), and they may say bitchily about the judging prophet: "My dear! Isnt she Too Much?—she should get a Man and settle down"—and swish on giggling—hoping for a Man to settle down with—wondering nervously does tonight's sexnervousness show beneath the giggles (and this can easily ruin a birl), and will they make it tonight and if so will it be someone Nice and early please God so they wont have to add to the shadows on Selma.

And Selma Street is a dark purgatory to which those who havent made it in the bars or on the lighted Boulevard sentence themselves in the desperate hours after midnight.

Along a distance of about four blocks on that street,

throughout the late night and into the first morning hours, male ghostforms haunt Selma along the apartment houses and the outlined trees (all appropriately flimsy in the night like movieprops); stand waiting for a car to stop, for someone to ask them what theyre looking for: If what you want is what hes willing to give, you go; if not, you wait for someone else to emerge out of the shadows. . . . Faces stare out of dark parked cars you think at first are empty, until a match, lighted suddenly, erupts, revealing a pair of staring eyes in the matchshadowed face. . . .

But Coolly: The plainclothes detectives also cruise this street. . . .

Toward the end of the stretch of more-or-less activity, back now on the Boulevard, before it sprints a short distance farther, diminishing in fluorescent splendor and turning into softlawned apartment units with pastel lights (where starlets live lonesomely wondering will they make it, finding no substitute for stardom in the carefully rationed joints of maryjane for manufactured dreams)—there (before the softlawned swimming-pooled apartment houses) is a coffeehouse primarily for teenage queers and those who want them: Inside (stained-glass windows like in a church), a dike (a squareshouldered butch lesbian, stocked up on bees—with poised pencil and pad) writes lovepoems to the femmetype teenage fairies. . . . After two in the morning, they wait in line to come in.

On the side streets off the Boulevard, that world's bars make turn-down business on weekends—even when their patrons keep moving from bar to bar, making it sometimes in one hectic night through more than a dozen of those bars—some catering to the hustlers (and one, near the U.S.O., to the hustling servicemen), some to mixed groups, others to the more effeminate or "arty" chorus-boy fairies; some to those with pretensions of Elegance, others to the goodlooking, masculine movie "actors"—whether ever in a movie or not. . . . A private "club" in the hills up a twisting dirt road, where men dance with men, women with women. . . . And there are, too, the "leather bars": black-jacketed mesh inside, moving pictures of youngmen wrestling realistically, murals of motorcyclists at a race, their faces sexually aroused; motorcycles parked in menacing rows outside. . . . After the first inadvertent times, I avoided those last bars.

And when the bars close, the crowds invade the Boulevard; those still without a partner stand as if looking into the gaudy-shirted shopwindows—or idle in the outside lobby of

Vic Tanny's gym—or outside the sandwich stand toward High-
land, which attracts, mainly, young hustlers and the scores
hunting them. . . . Or go to one of the all-night coffeehouses:
especially, then to Coffee Andy's, which throughout the day is
more or less a straight restaurant, but, after 2:00, becomes a
meeting and exhibition place for the nightworld.

Or, in the late weekend evenings, a portion of this world
will move to one of many parties, usually planned in an instant
in a bar or at Coffee Andy's, and usually lasting until Monday, when the previous-day's faces will have changed, possibly
completely replaced: in which some chosen house will turn
into a closed-in world: servicemen picked off the streets or as
they wait for the bus outside the U.S.O., masculine fairies,
queens, scores, dikes, straight but often frigid girls, straight
but curious men, malehustlers, nymphos. . . . Bedrooms suddenly locked, opening to expel one person, quickly replaced
by another—or sometimes by two, three. . . . Lights suddenly
turned out, bodies anonymously sprawled on the carpeted
floors.

Lulled into an emotional trance by the liberating victory of
having at last stolen, I felt myself in a constant state of highness—and I no longer sought either the joints of maryjane
or the pills: senses on pinpoint as if I were drunk without
liquor.

And what I was high on was the furious unsurfeited search.
Now the subterfuge that I did it only for money—even though,
as early as New York (especially when the act was executed
in public places), I had not strictly adhered to it—began to
disappear. It was now a matter of numbers.

Often—satisfied merely to know that I could have scored,
and turning down the person who asked me—I returned alone
to, now, another rented room on Hope Street, in another hotel
this time; and in that room, I lie in bed aware of myself . . .
sexually aware.

Often, too, the longing to return to El Paso would grasp me
without warning. I would imagine my Mother standing before
the glasscase in the living-room. Longingly, I remember the
mountain I had climbed as a boy: the statue of Christ under
that most beautiful sky in the world. . . . The memory of my
father. . . . I would touch the ring he had given me.

And then I would see El Paso racked by the savage wind.

In a dark moviehouse in Hollywood, a thin youngman picks

*me up, asks me to wait in the lobby for a few moments, returns
shortly with another youngman, and takes us both to his place
in the hills, where he comes on with both of us—and later, with
someone met while Im hitchhiking (as cars like glowing-eyed
bugs curve along Sunset Boulevard as if in general alarm), I
go to his house, where—he being hung up on pictures—I
merely stand while he peers behind the clicking camera, and
I wonder, Is this all?—and it is, because now Im in Echo
Park, where a queen, camping by the head, calls out, "Hi
babe—welcome to Jenny's tearoom—and, you understand, Im
Jenny, and this is my tearoom"—indicating the head (across
the street from Aimee Semple McPherson's Temple of appropriately Brotherly Love); going on: "I come here, oh, every
day," brazenly, "And I run away all those other hungry nelly
queens first so I can have my pick of the cute tricks—and so,
sweetie-love, if youve got A Mind To, would you join me in
my tearoom for a few happy Wholesome moments?"—and
soon after (mornings afternoons, nights fusing into a boundaryless existence) Im sitting in the balcony of a moviehouse in
Hollywood—waiting purposely for someone to come on, turning him off to replace him with someone else—needfully adding numbers; and I leave the theater—alone—going back
to that rented room in fulfilled—but only momentarily fulfilled—Awareness; and I meet a youngman, high on grass, and
we drive to the hills, where the houses being built are mere
skeleton frames against the grayish ghost-moon, where we
turn on, smoking under the oppressive sky, and he comes on
right there while I smoke looking at the stars, so few that I
begin to count them—no longer looking at those stars now at
a party that lasts two smoky nights, where I get so drunk I
forget who I came here with, where I wake in a rumpled
room, with people sleeping on chairs—and a pale wide-eyed,
opportunistic, up-two-nights-in-a-row queen is saying to me
almost worriedly: "You feel better now, honey?"—and I
wonder what Ive said or done—but I no longer wonder when,
only minutes later (or so it seemed—but it could have been
hours), Im on Mulholland Drive in the parked car of a man
just met: cramped in the car by the edge of a cliff overlooking
the city—and another scene follows that rapidly, this time at
Westlake, where two anxious fairies cruise me—one coming
up saying hurriedly, "Right here—behind those trees—my
'sister' will watch out for us"—and the sexnoises are stifled
by the sounds of the ducks nearby shivering out of the lake-
water, sounds of cars rushing along Wilshire—the park so*

dark, so dark, so dark, under now a starless night—that star-
less heaven soon replaced by the smoke-hugging ceiling in the
bar where Im with a man Ive just scored from, where another
score, with a youngman, talks to the man Im with about ex-
changing partners, and we all four go—and now coming out
of a theater (the dungeon sex-head where they exchange
partners, too), Im stopped by a man whos followed me and
offers me "ten bills for just a few minutes—just a short time"
—and I feel depressed, and I put him down, regretting it lone-
somely as I go home and try to sleep and feel the Terror like
a heavy blanket smothering me; but soon—and it's an after-
noon—Im hitchhiking again on Sunset (not going anywhere
—or, rather, going anywhere!), picked up this time by a very
young fairy, with whom—because, he explains, he has A
Jealous Lover—I go, instead, to the house of a friend of his—
who surprisingly turns out to be a dark girl with gobbling
eyes: the three of us making it, the nympho coming on like
a starved fairy but not wanting to be screwed: and Im wonder-
ing why as I ride in a car with three men who will soon now
come on, and I will feel hugely excited and momentarily sur-
feited, to be, oneway, the object of their desire—but surfeited,
again, only for those few moments; and out on the streets
to add more numbers, I get stopped, instead, by two cops
—one frisking me Intimately against the car with the red
light like an angry science-fiction eye; frisking me, his hands
sliding between my legs, and I say, high on Sex: "Are
you getting your kicks?"—which ges me aken to the station
—not booked but fingerprinted illegally—and the cop, search-
ing records to find a suspect who fits my description, says I
gave him a fuck-you finger as he passed in His Car (which
is not true), causing the detective there (more cool than most
and not too fond of the paranoic cop anyway . . . perhaps)
to break up derisively in laughter, and he lets me go—the cops
driving me back to where they picked me up—and where, soon
after I have stepped out of the copcar, I meet someone else
with whom I'll soon make it. . . .

All this happened within perhaps a week. And more. More
—forgotten . . . incidents stretching into a crowded but somehow vastly empty plain.

Within that period there appeared a face which at the time
had little significance but which I would remember later.
Outside of Coffee Andy's—a good pickup place if you can

avoid the periodically rousting cops—a very young boy whom
I recognize as a hustler asks me for a match.

"Howre you making it?" he asked me.

"Okay." I distrusted him.

"Made it today?"

I hesitate.

He said impatiently: "Oh, man, dig: You dont have to play
square with me. Save it for the hicks. Im cool—Im making
the same scene you are."

He was at the most 18. He looked like hundreds of other
youngmen in Hollywood, not tall, almost thin—slouched; his
pants, beltless, loose below the waist: a street-hood type with
brown hair—not really handsome but of a type that scores
find attractive. He has a look that may be meanness or a premature bitterness at the discovery of what life is really like.

"Man," hes saying, his eyes shifting scanning the street for
a prospect, "you know what Im gonna do tonight? Im gonna
find me a rich queer and clip him for every coin—I mean, Im
gonna leave him pantless! . . . But, see, I aint been here too
long—and I dont know the scene too good yet. So, see, what
I'd dig: I'd dig finding some swinging cat wholl help me clip
the queer—you know—take him to a dark street—or some
cool pad youre Sure of. . . ."

I know what hes leading to, even before he says:

"You wanna help me? . . . See, one of us picks him up. Both
of us jump him—split the bread. You make it much better
that way." Typically, hes talking tough—impressing himself
—but he needs someone to give him courage: another's rashness spurring him on to the action. . . . I havent answered him.
For some reason, I dislike him.

"My name is Dean," he was going on now, extending his
hand, trying to be friends. "I just got into town a few days
ago, like I say. I hitchhiked—that cocksucker that gave me a
ride, he laid some bread on me," he boasts, "and he told me all
about this scene." Despite the masculine street-hood exterior,
the tough jive-sounds, there is something vaguely, subtly soft
emerging about him. "But, shit, man," he says, "you know
what Im gonna do, man, when I really get to pinning this
scene, man? Im gonna find me a real rich queer so I wont
have to hassle it, man. Hell, man, I been sleeping sometimes
in the flix, until they kick me out—and, man, I dont dig that
scene. It's hoomilating! . . . And, see, if that queer aint rich
enough, man, I'll meet another one through him. . . ." He

goes on Bigly like that. Then: "Whattayasay, man? You wanna help me tumble a fruit?"

For a terrible moment, I felt a soul-corroding temptation, but quickly stifling that disturbing flash of excitement at the prospect of violence, I said no to this boy next to me.

He shrugged, moved away. I saw him talking to another youngman hustling the street. That other youngman looks interested. Together, they walk along the Boulevard, turn toward Selma.

I wonder what will happen tonight on that street.

And that season, which—lulling me with the false Highness —I had thought would be largely a period of drifting and blotting from my mind all thoughts beyond Today, became, instead, a time that would lead me through a series of self-discoveries, culminating in violence outside of San Francisco.

LANCE: The Ghost of
Esmeralda Drake III

IN THAT SHADOWED WORLD OF DIM bars characterized by nervous gestures, furtive looks, masked Loneliness—the World of the Gay Bars—over which the image of an intensely adoring Mother hovers nebulously like a figure created by the clouds of smoke—in that world, Lance O'Hara had sparkled in its cloudy heaven: A Legend. True—although he had been a part of the world of glittering moviedreams—Lance had never Made It Big, and you will not remember his name among the enchanted moviecredits.

He had been a chorus boy at first, later a dancing partner for the Goddesses of the Screen. Nevertheless, in his world— That World—Lance had been a Star: "the greatest beauty in Hollywood," the most Desired and sought after. . . . From the beginning, Lance O'Hara (secure in his own desirability, which was recognized and whispered about, longed for enviously or wantingly even among The Stars) had valiantly dropped the mask: He desired young males like himself, and he admitted it openly.

About him, in the fringes of that world which Lance had ruled unquestionably—and sometimes mercilessly with the disdain of those who know that beauty rules anarchy—the "extras" had existed to carry his legend into the bars—because that world of bars, extending like an underground from New York to Hollywood with fugitive stops in other cities, is a world of whisperers deliciously recording each conquest, each new skirmish of its stars—but, also . . . a chorus waiting eagerly in the wings to enter and announce a new Downfall.

And it waits to be alerted of an imminent Fall.

Off Hollywood Boulevard—in a pseudo-New-Orleans decor of grillwork and French posters, draped scarlet velvet, dusty winebottles—the gay world of Hollywood finds its head-

185

quarters at the Splendide bar: In the subdued amber and pink lights, friendly to its overwhelming, if imposed, guilt, it finds its haven; in its members, it finds its fleeting nightlong meaning (*the unsatisfied hunger, the hurried goodbyes after sexual intimacy . . .*). Among its patrons are the Young, the good-looking, the masculine—the sought-after—and, too, the effeminate flutterers posing like languid young ladies, usually imitating the current flatchested heroines of the Screen but not resorting to the hints of drag employed by the much more courageous downtown Los Angeles queens.

It was at the Splendide that I first heard of Lance O'Hara.

Next to me at the bar sits a blondhaired effeminate fairy talking to a thin dark youngman.

"Guess *who* is back in town?" asked the blond one, answering himself: "Lance!"

"Lance O'Hara?" said the dark one, pretending nonchalance. "I didnt even know he was *gone!*" He sipped his drink studiedly.

"Well," said the blond one, propping an elbow on the bar, hand dangling loosely from the wrist like a tulip, "he *did* go to New York. He was going to do a Show—but—" He shrugged his skinny shoulders, glancing nervously around. It's almost the desperate hour and he hasnt made a conquest for Tonight. "Well, you know about Lance's 'shows'—they never seem to get Produced any more. . . . I heard hes working again at one of the studios—but *not* as an actor."

"How does he look?" asks the other, his head like a swivel, his eyes searching the bar. (When two homosexuals who have no Sexual interest in each other talk in a bar, they seldom look at each other—their eyes scan the bar for a new, Available anyone.) "I havent seen him in years! I thought he'd—Retired!"

"Youre exaggerating. We went to his house last summer—remember?—when he acted like he didnt want to see anyone. Anyway, he looks Awful!" he said gleefully. "Youd never believe he'd been the Raving Beauty. Hes simply oh-ful!"

"Really?" said the dark-haired fairy, intensely interested now. He touched his face as if to feel if the skin is still smooth. In this world, more than in any other, Youth is a badge; Beauty a treasure.

"He might be coming in tonight—and then you can see for yourself."

"I heard he doesnt go to the bars any more."

"Well, he *does!* . . . Oh, look, theres Teddy. (I think hes very cute, dont you?) Teddy! Teddy! (But too femme for me, I like them butch.) Teddy!"

"You take what you can get, honey."

"Dont be bitchy. I dont notice anyone cruising you—" and then in a lisping whisper, "—and look at that number near me, hes been staring a hole through me."

"How interesting: a new hole."

And the blond one squeezed like a snake through the thick crowd, to a tight little group, where Teddy obviously was; and hisses: "How *are you?* . . . Guess whos back in Hollywood? *Lance!*"

"Lance O'Hara?"

"Hes back from New York?"

"That bastard!"

"How does he look?"

"Hes a *Mess!*"

"Well, it's about time!"

And so the chorus, alerted now, prepares At Last to announce the Fall of Lance O'Hara—"prepares," because Lance, in the waiting eyes of the whisperers, had not yet become Ridiculous.

And for the chorus to claim its victory, the God must admit his fall. . . .

It was through the vindictive whispering chorus that I heard, soon after, of Esmeralda Drake III.

"I saw Lance the other night, and it's True: He looks Awful," a fairy I was with said at the Ivy bar. A small group huddles by the unlit fireplace. "And you know what I heard?"

A long, long pause. "That Esmeralda Drake is dead!

"Esmeralda Drake the Third!" someone corrected.

"Yes—I forgot: The Third!"

"Well, it's no wonder: She was at least 100 years old!"

"Older!"

"Dont exaggerate."

"Figure it out: She admitted to being over 60. . . ."

Then the group disbanded like birds fleeing a nest, and the invoked shadow of Lance blends into the other shadows.

"Theres Lance!"

He stood at the draped door of the Splendide as if undecided whether to come in. He was an imposing figure: tall, slender, broad-shouldered. But I couldnt see his face from where I sat.

"It *is* Lance!" another fairy at the bar said.

"How does he look?"

Impatiently: "I cant tell any more than you can till he comes in!"

"Lets go talk to him And See."

They hurried toward the shadow entering the bar. I can see him better now. From the distance—despite the damning whispers I had heard—he was an extraordinarily handsome youngman: black wavy hair, thick arched eyebrows, features perfectly molded. . . . He acknowledged only cursorily the two fairies who had rushed-gushed toward him—leaving them indignantly widemouthed as he passed through the crowd, briefly greeting the constantly turned curious faces of the many there who knew or recognized him. He made his way to the far end of the bar at the back of the room, and sat there alone.

Despite his handsomeness, he looked somehow like a ghost —or, rather (and it could have been the mellow light which bathed him), like someone who is haunted.

2

At the Splendide again.

This time I was with Chick and Jamey, whom I had met just a few minutes earlier on the Boulevard. They had come on with that bulldozer approach of the type who believes firmly that everyone—almost anyone—can be made. And they asked me to have dinner with them. By then I had already been in Hollywood long enough to be pegged as one of the many Hollywood drifters who fall into this world out of at least announced convenience, not strictly "belonging" to it—yet. . . . I say "announced convenience" and "yet" only to be fair to that world, because in it most active members are convinced that eventually those unreciprocating vagrants and wanderers into their world will cross the sexual boundary that separates them now—and they wait almost vengefully for the crossing of that line—to the Other Side—*their* side. . . . So Chick and Jamey asked me to have dinner with them, and I told them I didnt have any money, which was untrue, and they sighed, and Chick said: "We know, we know—weve all read the script many times." . . .

Chick is possibly in his middle 30s—would be almost-fat but squeezes his waist mercilessly so that he is like a caricature

of Mae West. Jamey is younger. Tonight he is wearing a cowboy hat and boots, and because hes quite effeminate, despite
the costume and the pose, at best he looks like a slightly
masculine cowgirl.

"I heard something really delicious about Lance," Jamey
said. "I heard that Lance—the beautiful Lance who wouldnt
dream of falling in love—remember, Chick?—well, hes
Flipped! Hes in love with this young kid. . . . Can you
imagine, Chick? Lance—in *love?"*

"Frankly, no—I dont believe it. I think it's just gossip,"
said Chick, "though I will say—as much as Ive always adored
Lance and still do and everyone knows it—I will say it might
be the best thing that ever happened to him."

I remember the poised man I had seen that previous night—
who had sat alone and walked out by himself a few minutes
later—and even without knowing him, I couldnt imagine
his being in love.

"And have you heard about Esmeralda Drake the Third?"
Jamey said.

"Well, what about her?"

Jamey said: "I heard shes dead."

"Why, I just saw her the other day," Chick said. "She was
hobbling along the street with her cane. If shes dead, she got
run over, I bet. . . . Which reminds me: I went to this queen's
funeral once, and they had dressed her in drag!"

"Youre too much!" protested Jamey.

"It's the truth. That was how she wanted to go: dress, high
heels, gloves. It was in her will." Then: "This kid you say
Lance flipped over—do you know him?"

"Oh, yes!" squealed Jamey. "And everybody's had him. Hes
one of the Hollywood Boulevard tramps— . . . Oh!" He
covered his mouth naughtily, the cowboy hat almost falling
off. "Excuse me, baby," he said, patting my arm, "I forgot
we just—uh—met *you* on the Boulevard," and he grinned
treacherously. "Anyway, the kid is a tramp! . . . Why, Chick,
didnt you and I try to pick him up one night—at Coffee
Andy's? . . . Or was it you with me? We bought him a ham-
burger, then he left. Why, his name is Dean—Dean something.
. . . No, you werent with me. I was with Rick that night, I
remember. Rick liked him, I didnt. . . . Anyway," he repeated,
"this Dean is a tramp."

Dean? Dean. . . . I remember that name.

"I dont believe it about Lance," says Chick, with touching

loyalty. "Youre just being bitchy, Jamey. Lance may not be as Young as he was, but hes still too special."

"All I can say," said Jamey, "is that he certainly had his day."

"Babe," Chick said to me now, "Lance was the handsomest boy in Hollywood."

"*I* never thought he was *that* good," said Jamey.

"He was," says Chick staunchly, explaining to me: "He had them all scratching at his door. He was in the movies—we all were, then—he wasnt a Star, but everyone knew him. Why, he had an affair with Pierce Flint—the big moviestar. And Pierce loved Lance so much that when Lance left him, Pierce got married—*to a woman!* . . . Thats when Lance met Esmeralda Drake the Third."

Jamey interrupted Chick: "Were you on the set the day Esmeralda first saw Lance?"

"You know damn well I was, bitch, you tried to push me out of the camera each time you came on—like every other nelly upstart chorus boy. It was that Betty Grable musical we did—"

"Rita Hayworth," says Jamey.

"Well, one of those, who cares? It couldve been Shirley Temple!"

Jamey began to hum a tune from a musical, to sway his body to the rhythm. "I was just a Kid, then, but I remember it like it was this morning."

"You werent *that* Young," Chick said; then to me: "Lance was doing this number with Betty Grable—or Rita Hayworth —one of those—that was right after he broke up with Pierce. Well, babe, I mean to tell you, dont let anyone tell you a moviestar isnt Powerful in this damn town. Why, when Lance left Pierce, Pierce fixed it so Lance couldnt get any work, hardly. Lance might have been a Big Star today if it hadnt been for that. Anyway, they had to finish this movie—and Lance knew he had to do Something, but quick—Lance always looks out for himself—"

"Except maybe that time in Laguna," Jamey said.

"Well, you dont know what really happened, and dont pretend you do. You want to believe the worst about Lance. . . . Youre just: Jealous!"

"Me? Jealous? Ha!"

"Anyhow," Chick continued, "Lance is doing this dance with Betty—or Rita—when Esmeralda Drake walks in—"

"Esmeralda Drake the Third," corrected Jamey.

"Actually," says Chick, "her real name was Gregory—Gregory Drake—and she came from A Fabulously Rich Family—the Drakes—and she was The Third—"

"And the last—"

"Yes, it's sad. She was the only man left in the family—and, honey, she was queerer than I am," said Chick.

"Impossible!" said Jamey, throwing up his hands, this time completely knocking the cowboy hat off. "My *chapeau!*" he squealed; goes on: "No one—not even the dead queen who got buried in drag—is *that* queer!"

"Shut your hole, Mae; youre swishing so much youre going to make a hurricane—not that a breeze wouldnt be welcome in this place." Chick begins to fan himself with Jamey's retrieved hat. "Anyway," he continues, addressing me, "Lance nicknamed Gregory Drake the Third, Esmeralda Drake the Third—she was that nelly. Oh, babe, she was such a faggot! Awful. When Lance met her, Esmeralda was a very old man—"

"Tell him what Esmeralda looked like," Jamey said delightedly, and goes on to tell me: "She was a skinny, bony, old old man, with cheeks that looked like caves—"

"And can you imagine?—that lecherous old man fell in love with Lance. The moment she saw him on the set, she Flipped—and let me tell you, Lance looked Magnificent!"

"Tell him what Lance did to Esmeralda."

"Im coming to it, if you let me. . . . Nothing like a nervous queen on Saturday night when she thinks shes not going to Make Out and have to go home and jerk off," Chick chastises Jamey. "You *are* going with me, arent you, baby?" he asked me. . . . "So Esmeralda Drake—Lance gave her that name right after he met her (he called her that to her face; we all did)—well, Esmeralda Drake flips over Lance—and I mean, babe, she *fullipped!* And Lance couldn't get a job, because he'd tossed Pierce over. So he decides to play the old daddy for everything shes worth. Lance let her take him out to dinner, every day. . . . But this is the twist: He wouldn't let her put a finger on him."

"Thats what Lance claimed, anyway!"

"It's True. Everyone knows that: Youre just being bitchy. Everyone knows Esmeralda never so much as touched Lance!"

"I think you were in love with Lance, if you ask me," said Jamey. He shrieked in pretended annoyance when someone passing by said to him: "Honey, I didnt recognize you in that cowgirl drag!"

"Who wasnt in love with Lance?" Chick said. "And who was it that followed him into the dressing room that time and locked the door and—"

"Vile gossip!"

"We all saw you, and Lance pushed you away so hard you fell and threatened to sue the studio and they promised to put you at the front of the chorus line."

"Thats not true. I could have had Lance just like that—" Jamey snapped his fingers.

"Dont listen to her, babe," says Chick. "Shes just Nervous cause she'll have to go home alone," He turns now to Jamey: "That cowboy drag youre in was a definite mistake, honey— you look like an extra on the wrong set. . . . Anyway, let me continue—if this giddy bitch lets me—Lance was getting money from the old auntie, but Lance is Smart. He got the old man so fuckin hot after him that the old man was going out of her head. She bought Lance a car, everything he wanted, and, babe, this isnt gossip. It's The Truth. Still, Lance wouldnt let her touch him. Then Lance made this deal: He'd move in with Esmeralda Drake—"

"—the Third."

"—the Third. He'd move in with Esmeralda if Esmeralda would have the papers on the house made out in both Lance's and Esmeralda's names. The next day, Esmeralda was with her attorneys, and Lance moved in. Then Esmeralda tries to make out—and Lance says nothing doing, He promised to move in, and he did. But Touch him, no. . . . The old man was a case, I mean Ive never seen anyone so nervous. And she says to Lance he can have Anything. All right, says Lance, he wants the house in his name only. It was a magnificent house, babe: Lance still has it: all gorgeous modern furniture, original paintings (all the way from New York)—drapes like in the Movies—everything! . . . So the old man calls her attorneys again, she has the house put in Lance's name—And Then Guess What?"

Jamey gulps his drink in anticipation. "Youll never believe it!"

"We were all there—Jamey was there—all the kids from the set. Lance gave this party, to celebrate his new house, and Esmeralda is there hobbling around on her cane, following Lance, smiling, nodding—thinking at last shes made it. Well! It was real late, and Lance goes to Esmeralda Drake the Third, and says to her—"

"He really said this, we all heard it."

"—and says to her: 'Get out of my house, I dont want to see you here again!'"

"And the old man looked like a ghost—"

"Yes, like he was going to die right there, and Lance saying: 'I mean it, I mean it, get the hell out, youve bugged me long enough, get out.' And he shoves Esmeralda Drake through the door right in front of our startled eyes. . . . Well, you know, Lance is a big fellow. And he had no trouble. The old man almost stumbled on her cane. Well, it was about four oclock in the morning—"

"It was later—dont you remember someone had just said lets watch the dawn?"

"Yes, youre right. We were so tanked, remember?"

"Yes, and remember how Ronnie slapped you when you tried to make his boyfriend?"

"*Ronnie* slapped *me? I* slapped *Ronnie!*"

"Thats not what I saw," sang Jamey.

"How would you know, Miss Mess? You were trying to make everyone; they couldnt drag you out of the toilet. . . . Now shut your hole and let me go on. . . . So, babe," Chick says, turning his back on Jamey, "Lance shoves the old man out, and about seven oclock the poor old bastard (well, yes, I couldn't help feeling sorry for him)—the poor old bastard comes beating on the door with her cane—Lance had locked the door, and Lance yells at her, 'Get away from me, you lecherous old man!' "

"No. He called her a dirty old man."

"All right, all right—it's just a polite way of saying the same thing. And dont talk so damn loud, everyone's looking."

"And whats wrong with That?" says Jamey, striking a pose.

Chick went on: "And the old man is beating on the door. Then Lance went to the telephone and calls the police and says, 'Theres a man trying to break into my house, I want him arrested!' And the old man keeps beating on the door with her cane and shouting, 'Let me in, let me in!' "

3

The legend of Lance O'Hara was running through the bars —rather, the echoes of the legend. Incidents are being remembered, motivations supplied; and some, who had envied and Desired, now are obviously pleased: Who cared, for Now, if each new day another "great beauty" stormed their world? What mattered to them, for their momentary justification was that the "beauty" of *their* time, the one who had relegated them brutally to the background (and who, importantly, from the very beginning, had announced himself as one of them), must soon relinquish his throne. . . .

In Lance's life—as I was to hear it from the whisperers— in Lance's life (which, measured by the conquests that equal Success in that world, had been a meteoric, blazing ascent), there had been one very significant incident which in that tight-knit world was now being recalled with vindictive delight. The trap was being set, and this incident was chosen to mark the beginning of the downfall. Although it had happened many years before, during the time of Lance's unquestioned reign, it was the point which the whisperers chose to focus on.

In Hollywood, Randy is a well-known figure—a still-good-looking, masculine homosexual who, the whisperers have it, pushes narcotics. His thicklashed lids are always about to close, when he reveals his eyes from behind the familiar dark glasses. Once, he had played the drifting scene—the wanderer into the world of the active homosexual, all the more desired because he did not yet belong to that world—then. Because that was Yesterday. Now, in his 30s, he had crossed the line. And Randy, in the expression of the whisperers, Had Been Had. He had shifted roles. He was now a hungry searcher. Nightly youll find him, high or almost high, in one of the queer bars. Whereas once he had drifted into the lives—and masturbatory dreams—of others, now others drift in and out of his life. Randy had long acknowledged the hunger: His life was the cramming of night experiences. In recognizing this, Randy had acknowledged his fate and now hurled himself willingly into it.

I was walking into the Pirate's Den one night with Randy when a lisper gushes: "Randy-dear! You just missed Lance." Randy didn't answer. He moved hurriedly to the back of the bar. "Still not talking to him?" the lisper called after him. "Well, youre too much. Cant forget Laguna Beach, can you, sweetheart?"

Randy and I sat at a table, near the jukebox—its bright colors splashing courageously into the dark bar. Suddenly Randy said bitterly: "That fuckin Lance! Why doesnt he go away and stay away, or die—anything; just so I wont hear about him any more, wont know hes even around." He removes the sunglasses, squints at the people at the bar, puts the glasses on disgustedly. "Same fuckin faces, night after night. Man, if I pin the scene with you, you can still get out before it's too late. And I dont give a damn how cool you think you are, youll get Caught and get Caught royal. Shit, man, I wasnt queer when I came on this scene. Sure, I'd make it with the fruits, take whatever I could from them—but I wouldnt put out. . . . Then I met that fucker Lance. . . . But I got one big satisfaction: If that son of a bitch had stuck with me at Laguna, he wouldntve got into that mess. Thats what that silly nellyass queen was coming on about when we came in."

In a world as ingrown as that of the bars, it is not rare for two people who have just met to pour out the intimate details of their lives; and Randy says: "See, man, I was going with Lance—more or less going with him, thats about the only way you can describe it with Lance. And we used to go out to Laguna Beach that summer. Well, man, someone told him something about this Esmeralda Drake—this old auntie whod kept him. Someone told him Esmeralda Drake had just had a heart attack or some other fuckin thing; got taken to the hospital. Well, hell, Lance never gave a damn about that poor old bastard—he took that auntie for every cent, then he threw him out of the house he'd given him. Well, we were on the beach with Chick and them, and Lance had a great tan—always in the sun—but when he hears about how Esmeralda Drake just had a stroke, he turned yellow, like he was painted or something, and he says, 'Ive got to go to him right away.' I said what the fuck's the matter with you? that poor old sonofabitch doesnt want to see you, after what you did to him. Man, Lance locked that bastard out, called the cops that he was breaking in. Anyway, Lance says: 'Youre right, he wouldnt want to see me.' And thats when it started—like suddenly it wasnt Lance any more. He began cruising up and down the beach like some hung-up fairy that hasnt had any dick in months. He went in swimming, splashing around, showing off. He'd never done that—he didnt have to show off. He was so greatlooking, man, everyone came to him; he didnt have to say a word. He could be in a bar, alone—not talk to anyone, just glance at who he wanted and sit there and wait, and you couldnt take a bet in that bar that in five minutes he wouldnt have the cat he was after. But, Christ, that day, at Laguna, hes talking to everyone, rushing into the bar by the beach, drinking. And Lance didnt drink, man—thats the truth. I said, 'What the hell's wrong, you wanna get drunk?' He says, 'Yes, I wanna get drunk.' I said, 'Why?' 'To celebrate,' he says—he actually said that: To celebrate! And, man, all this cruising is bugging me. Like I say, I hadnt been strictly gay then, but Lance is a charmer—he was bringing me out fast —wowee! . . . Now there I was with him, and that mother-fucker is cruising up a steaming storm. Well, it got real late, the sun was going down, and it got cold, and we went into the bar—that queer bar on the beach. And Lance is still drinking. I tried to get him to come back to the hotel. But he wouldnt, he kept saying, 'The celebration isn't over!'—and, yeah, he keeps saying something about his new life is starting. . . . Then these two wise-ass marines walk into the bar—they werent queer, they were straight; just pinning the queer scene for kicks. And Lance says, 'I want those two.' Well, hell, I told him get the fuck away from me. And Im watching him coming on with those two wise-asses. Finally I split, didnt even go back to the hotel. I went back to Hollywood. And the next day I read how this actor (you know how the L.A. papers play things up: if a guy's in the movies, they call him a moviestar —well, Lance never was that tough in the flix, but the papers played it up like he was—and it must have been some bitch-ing gay editor anyway)—so the papers say how this movie-star nearly got killed out in Laguna, how he jumped off a cliff, broke both his arms. It didnt give the details, but it was clear what happened, man. You didnt have to be there to know. Lance is coming on with those two, and those two straight studs like: ugh-uh, no-sir, much-later, not-having-any. And this is putting Lance on—hes got this high opinion of him-self—and he says he'll drive them to the base, starts to put the make on them—in the car (which wasnt like him, then—I have to say)—and they still: not-having-any. So Lance says get the hell out of the car. And they come on mean with him —like clip the fuckin fairy. And Lance gets out of the car— he was drunk, anyway—and those two try to roll him. But he was broke—I know because I'd been with him—and they throw him over the cliff—like some common, helpless queer getting rolled. . . . Well, shit, I know you hear other stories— how *they* tried to make him, and he fell over by accident. Bull-shit! What I told you is The Truth. And I know it, because I know that sonofabitch. . . . Anyway, I havent said a fuckin word to Lance since that night, and thats been years, and I dont even wanna see the bastard. . . . And, man, like I say, I still havent pinned what the scene is strictly with you—but I wanna warn you: Thats one cat to keep away from—that fuckin Lance O'Hara. . . ."

"I saw you talking to Randy the other night at the Pirate's

Den," says Chick to me. I ran into him at the Green bar. "Babe,
let me warn you about Randy, hes one of the most dangerous
people to know in Hollywood. The cops watch him all the
time. Everyone knows he pushes—and takes the stuff himself.
Hes always high—and he was probably trying to get you to
push with him. Well! Hes trash! He uses marijuana—and
worse!—to make his tricks—hes that low—at least I buy them
Food. . . . And by the way, have you eaten yet? . . ." He was
maneuvering me toward the corner. On our way there, he
catches sight of Jamey standing by the bar. This time Jamey is
dressed like a motorcyclist, and this time he looks like a slightly masculine female motorcyclist, but not as rough. "Oh, my
God!" says Chick, covering his face in pretended horror. "Isnt
she a sick girl?—the bitch. I dont even talk to her any more.
Shes evil. . . . Anyway, I was telling you to keep away from
that Randy—For Your Own Good—no matter what he promises you; hes a liar. I know this cute kid he told he was going
to take to Las Vegas and spend all kinds of fabulous sums on
him (which he hasnt got)—and thats how he made the kid—
and then he gives him a phony phone number, after he'd already made him. . . . Do you have my phone number babe? . . .
Now listen to me, baby; listen to your mother—shes older and
wiser, shes been around much longer than you have, and she
knows what shes saying: That Randy'll get you to push for
him; hes ruined more fine trade that way, and then all theyre
interested in is that dirty marijuana and everything, which
makes it very difficult on we girls who havent got any—I mean,
not that I'd ever resort to such vulgar tricks—because, like
I always say, whatever I do in Bed doesnt harm anyone, but
those narcotics—well! . . . Besides, hes been spreading all kinds
of stories about Lance, since that time at Laguna Beach, and
you know, whatever they say about Lance, I love the guy—
always have, always will. Hes done some pretty horrible things
in his life, Im the first to admit that. Still, theres something
about Lance that makes him Special. . . . Anyhow, it was
Randy who started that story about how these marines tried
to roll Lance at Laguna Beach (actually, when it happened,
they were out toward Malibu)—and how they threw him over
the cliff, and lemme tell you thats a beachy—I mean, bitchy
—lie. No one ever even *tried* to roll Lance—no one could
even *think* of it! He had too much Dignity, baby—he was like
a King, and you knew it. But Randy goes around talking all
kinds of dirt—like that those marines were straight. Babe, let
your mother tell you: They were as queer as I am. And *they*

put the make on Lance—whod been drinking anyway, and
Lance hardly ever drinks. Well, something happened on the
beach that day, someone whod just come in from Hollywood
told Lance how Esmeralda Drake the Third was dying or
something, and Lance started drinking. It surprised everyone
—Lance never gave a damn, and like I say he never drinks—
but maybe he was just expecting he could get more money
from the poor old bastard before she'd die—or maybe it was
something else—who knows?—and Esmeralda didnt die, then
—though someone told me the other day she got run over by
this car crossing Hollywood Boulevard, and all I can say is:
If shes still cruising the Boulevard, at her age, well, baby, she
couldnt expect otherwise. . . . Well, when Lance heard about
Esmeralda in the hospital, he tries to leave—and all we kids
talked him out of it. Lance was great fun to be with, he would
make a party. So Lance stays, but hes getting drunk. And
these two marines at the bar start insisting they want to make
it with him. Well, babe, I dont blame them: Lance was Famous
from here to New York!—he'd been Pierce Flint's lover, and
he had affairs with Bruce Storm and Kipp Rugged—all those
big Movie Stars. So, anyway, Lance keeps saying no to those
two marines, he wouldn't stoop *that* low—and they were common. But, remember, he was drunk—high! high! High! . . .
Hi, Teddy! (Isnt that funny?—Teddy thought I was saying
'Hi' to him.) . . . Anyhow, I kept saying, 'Dont go, Lance,
youve been drinking.' But he wouldnt listen to me. So they
went off together, all three—and Lance was just trying to get
rid of them without a public scene, I can tell you—because
Lance never showed any Interest in them, he never showed
any Interest in anyone, really—or he never used to," he adds
wistfully, then quickly: "Not that I believe all those rumors
about him. Of course, Randy got real bitchy about that, and
he started spreading stories like how he was straight until
Lance brought him out—and, babe, that Randy was born sitting in the mensroom with the door open, thats how straight
he ever was! . . . Not that I blame him being annoyed at Lance;
he was with him at Laguna—*after all!* . . . Anyway, from
what I know—and I know it like it happened to me—those
marines start putting the make on Lance—*in the car!!*—and,
babe, drunk or sober, Lance doesnt go for that common stuff,
he puts them off. They tried to force him to stay—and thats
when Lance jumped out of the car, and they chased him—
drunk themselves and hot after him and I dont blame them
—and Lance didn't know he was on a cliff, and he jumped.

An accident. Thats all it was. He broke his arm. And, babe, those evil jealous faggots went wild spreading stories. But everyone knew they werent true. Lance propositioning anyone! Thats Ridiculous! Ive known him for years—better than anyone else—and Lance just doesnt proposition anyone. Well, anyway," he sighed sadly, "he didnt then—but I wouldnt know Now. Everyone changes so. . . . Look at me." (Sigh. . . .) "You want? to go? to eat, babe? . . ."

4

The Chorus chooses sides, the Fates prepare to cast their lots: And when It happens—if It happens—will they allow Lance a graceful fall? Or will he topple from the heights on the debris of crushed egos? . . .
The Chorus waits for news from The Cliff.

Jamey was bursting with excitement at the Leopard bar. "I just saw Lance!" he announced to a large group. Tonight he is wearing beachcomber clothes. "And let me tell you!—hes stinking drunk!"

"Not Lance," someone protests.

"Lance O'Hara—I just saw him. He looks like hes been drinking all day. Hes a mess!"

"Ive never seen Lance drunk," said another.

"Except that time at Laguna Beach," someone remembers.

"Hes been drunk all his life—with himself."

"Well!" said Jamey, "Hes worse than all that. He almost collapsed at the Pirate's Den, and they wouldnt even serve him a drink. They had to bounce him out! But thats not the best: He started fighting with Eddy—that cute bartender—and you know Eddy's not too big and Lance is, and finally the three bartenders had to push him out, and Lance yelling—guess what he was yelling? Well! He says hes looking for someone! Isnt that: Too Delicious?"

"Did he say who he was looking for?" someone asked eagerly.

"Yessssss. . . ."

"Who?"

"Who?"

"Who!"

Jamey looked smug for a silent moment, like a messenger bringing the news of a battle won. As if spitting out poison, he blurts: "Dean!"

"*Dean!*"

"That little tramp?"
"Everyone's had him."

"He's a thief."
"Is that the guy that clipped Eddy?"

"Hes just a kid—"
"Honey, hes a Mess."
"I'd be ashamed to be seen *talking* to him!"

"And Lance
O'Hara was looking for *him?*"

"Thats what I told you, isnt it?" snapped Jamey, and the buzzing continued. Delectably aware of the excitement he'd created, Jamey slithers away, pretends surprise at seeing me nearby, and confides to me: "Ive got to talk to you, babe. I saw you the other night with Chick, and Ive got to warn you about that mad fruit—For Your Own Good. Shes vicious. Let me tell you what she did to this cute kid I know. She promised to take him to Las Vegas, spend all kinds of money on him if he'd let her make him—and then she gives the kid a phony phone number— . . ."

I left the bar—later—with Jamey and someone named Tim whom Jamey had just picked up. Alternately coming on with him, then with me—about how much Influence he still had at The Studios, Jamey, I figured, was taking no chance tonight: He would make it with the more readily available. As it turned out, though, Tim and I ended up together at another party—much later: toward early morning—in a house somehow like Death—or like that house in the Gloria Swanson movie where she went Mad: the death-house has bear rugs and crossed swords, a leashed monkey jumping on the stuffed velvet chairs. From somewhere, weird organ music is being played. On the floor, male couples danced holding tight to each other. I was getting high, and the figures on the dancefloor, hardly moving, gliding over the waxgleaming floor, were like shadowy sailboats on a frozen black lake. Beyond the tall wide windows, a garden slides into the side of a hill; and figures that I took at first to be statues would move occasionally, come together, separate like dark clouds. A youngman stormed in from the garden, tears streaking his face, yelling hysterically. "Im through with him, hes out there with Rick— I Am Through With Him—This Time For Sure!"

"Isnt it a drag?" I heard Tim say drunkenly—although obviously new to all this, he stares around him in fascination.

The host came to us. Appropriately, he looked like Dracula,

with piercing unclothing eyes and red red lips. "You two dont
seem to be enjoying yourselves. Come on, boys. . . . Still new
at this? Well, I *adore* you for it!"—tapping us understandingly
on the back. "Would you two like another drink?" He faded
away, returned with two small cups topped with whipped
cream. "This will make you Happy," he said. His eyes are like
darts aimed between our legs. "Come on, lets get drunk! . . .
Or would you rather take a rest, maybe? No one is using my
Bedroom, Ive locked it up For Just Something Like This
(arent I naughty?)—and we three could— . . ." But he was
getting nowhere. With a sigh Dracula moved away, melting,
disappeared into the garden. . . .

Suddenly I was on Hollywood Boulevard. The bright early
sun crashes on me, colors burst like tiny rockets. It was Saturday. Vaguely I remember Jamey telling me last night that he
would be at the Rendezvous Room this morning. I walked
down the Boulevard, turned on Cahuenga.

And behind me I hear the screeeeeeeeching of a car out of
control: Brakes jam!—the car swerves jerkily into the opposite
lane. The motor: Stops! I saw the driver's head sway toward
the steering wheel; he seemed to pass out momentarily, re-
covers. I recognized Lance O'Hara.

Then the motor started uncertainly, the car sped away,
around the corner, into Sunset Boulevard, as I entered the
Rendezvous Room.

On weekends the Rendezvous Room begins to fill early:
Those who hadnt found someone last night are still trying—
their faces drained of all color from the night-long hunting.
Others, still unsatisfied, still sexhungry, are beginning the endless pursuit early. Most have come from parties lasting into
the morning, parties often still going on; and they comb the
bars for new, possibly fresh recruits.

The parting of the drapes at the door, announcing the entrance of someone possibly interesting, acts like a kind of
electronic device pulling all alerted units in its direction. The
heads swivel as the light darts frightened into the dark bar,
scurries, rushes out again. . . .

Inside, there are certain familiar faces. Jamey, Randy, and
Chick are sitting together. I sit at the bar with them. The jukebox is playing: "Children, go where I send you—how shall I
send you? Im gonna send you one by one— . . ." Then the
curtains parted, and the lightning streak of the sun flashed into
the bar.

"It's Lance!"

　　　　　　　　　　　"Whats the matter with him?"
　　　　　　　　"Is he sick?"
"Lance, baby!"
　　　　　　"Come on over here, Lance. . . ."
　　　　　　　　　　　　　　"He looks Terrible!"
　　　　　"Hes drunk!"

Voices fluttering through the smoky bar like lost birds.

Randy, who had been tapping his fingers to the rhythm of the jukemusic, flattened his hand on the bar with an angry: *bang!!*—the fingers suddenly tense, motionless.

Jamey slid off the stool quickly, walked to the tall slender figure now inside the bar and said: "Why, Lance-baby, I thought you were in New York—what happened to your show? I thought—"

The slender figure moved past him, staring anxiously around the bar.

"Whats the matter, Lance?" Chick whispers, following him as if to shelter him; aware of the chorus waiting.

Lance O'Hara squints dazedly, reels toward Chick: "Chick —I—" And then. "Have you seen . . . Dean?"

Voices, the music—the deafening sounds. Smoke like a gray shroud. . . . I walked out quickly.

Across the street, the cops were frisking three youngmen. I started to walk back toward the Boulevard, and then I was aware of someone close behind me. I waited. I felt someone's hand on my shoulder, and I turned to face Lance O'Hara.

"Youre not: him," he sighed.

The cops were looking in our direction now. Lance was leaning heavily on me, about to pass out. "Come on," I said, leading him away.

"No—wait. Will—you—drive?" he mumbled. "Please— come with me. Im parked—parked—somewhere!" He began to laugh at not being able to remember where his car was.

I had seen him turn on Sunset earlier, and I led him around the corner.

"There—" he said. "Thats my car." He handed me the keys, got in stumbling; leaned back, covering his face: "Whew! I cant—cant—drink. . . . Lets go— . . . *anywhere!*"

I looked at Lance O'Hara now.

When I had first seen him at the Splendide, the subdued light had chosen mercifully to bless him—and I had seen the youngman who had reigned securely. Now, in the glare of the summer sun, there was little mercy. I see the crushed Lance

O'Hara of the now-fading legend: tall, yes—slender; but his face, bloated from drinking and sleepless nights, had the look of alarm which only the faces of the once very beautiful and anarchically disdainful, on the brink of relinquishing their claim to that anarchy, can have: The skin was yellowish in the bright light, lines converged under the eyes forming small sagging sacks; his dark hair was matted at the forehead with perspiration. But the haunted eyes looking at me, a clear blue that melted almost indistinguishably into the white, are what I notice most: They are the astonished eyes of someone who after years of wearing sunglasses is forced suddenly to remove them in the savage stare of the sun. . . .

"Lets—drive—somewhere," he said. "Anywhere—nowhere —sooooooooommmmmmmmmmmewhere—over the rainbow!" Laughing chokingly, he swerves sideways on the seat— "Ooops!"—retrieves a bottle of whiskey which had rolled under the seat and drank thirstily from it. I started the car, moving toward the Strip on Sunset. As if on its own, the car speeds past the California palmtrees, silent witnesses to speeding life, fleeting Youth. Lance opens his eyes suddenly wide, seeing me, I thought, really for the first time. "You dont even look like him," he said. "Not at all, really. I followed you out. When I saw you leave—leave the bar, I thought—I thought you were—Dean. . . . Hey! Lets make it: A Party—havent had—party in—oh, long, long— . . . I wanna get realleeee drunk!" He held the bottle to me and I drank from it. His panic was infectious. Im aware of Flight now, acutely—of Lance's, mine. "Wowee," he said, "youre drunk too—thats it —wowee!"

We were on the Freeway now, cars racing before us, toward us, next to us. The world, everyone on the Freeway, is spinning in wide swirls . . . Away! . . .

"Bumpity-bump," said Lance, drinking again from the bottle, handing it to me. "More I drink, more you look like him. Dont care who you are—so—long—as—you—driiiive. Oops! Liquor hit—my head! Bumpity-bump. Hey! Lets ball! . . ." Then he was silent, eyes closed. "You dont know—Dean —do you?" he asked me abruptly. "Havent seen him—since —whee— . . ." holding the bottle for me again. "Dean," he said furrily, and again he seemed to pass out.

Now my vision became fantastically clear—which is that stage preparatory to my becoming drunk, when each object becomes sharply real. The traffic had thinned, and we were

moving past many-colored fruitstands strung along the highway like a gypsy caravan.

Now we're in the mountains, here lushly green, there brown-
patched, leprous—past, occasionally, areas of burned-down
trees: Dead. The road winds treacherously in a series of tight
S's—the sky is blue and clear: a cool inverted inaccessible lake.

At a turn in the road, the car almost swerved into the trees.
Lance sat up: "Have—a—baaall!" he laughed. "Crash the
fuckin car!—lets go up in flames!—aim for Heaven!—get
there with a Wham!"

Green scenery rushing toward us, retreating. Vast blue of
the sky like shifting panels. . . .

"Im drunk," Lance said. "You too? . . . Here—if we drink
more, we'll be on the way back—cold sober again. . . .
There. . . ."

Crack of wood!

Green shrubbery trembles. The car has stopped. I leaned on
the wheel, surrendering to the dizzy carousel of green. Dots of
sun needled my eyes as the leaves shifted dazedly about us.
Lance staggered out.

"Great to be Drunk!" he says, making his way down the hill.
"Great, great! Everyone should be drunk—all the time—
right? . . . Whole fuckin world on one great big endless: Dur-
rrunk!"

I pushed against the door, against the bushes. Tall trees
sheltered us from the sun. At the foot of the hill, some water,
very blue and clear like the sky, winds serenely along the
trees. I knelt, throwing water on my face, trying to stop the
green merry-go-round whirling about me.

And in one wild instant Lance was hugging me to him, sobbing urgently. "Dean—dont—go—away—"

"Im not Dean," I kept repeating.

But he didnt hear me. "Dean—" he was sobbing, holding
me tightly. The scenery stopped spinning now and collapsed,
came crashing over us—the trees burst, shattered. Again,
once, the sun pierced the leaves in a myriad of light—pinpoints bursting in the water shimmering. And Lance's arms
squeezed me tightly—and he whispered over and over:
"Dean . . ."

I felt my hand in the water, my one contact with reality. I
let my fingers dangle in the spring. . . . And the scenery which
had closed in on us green, blackened, and . . . the . . . pinpoints . . . of . . . the . . . shattered . . . sun . . . are . . .
closing.

I awoke and the sun slashed through the trees blindingly at my eyes. Beside me, Lance's head almost touched the spring. I pulled him away, threw water on his face, and he opened his eyes abruptly, stared at me, surprised, trying to remember. And then he turned from me and began to sob.

I walked back to the car and waited, and finally Lance returned. "Who are you?" he asks me.

"I just met you—early this morning."

He was silent.

"You asked me to take your car."

"I remember—something like that." His eyes stared ahead in the dreadful limbo of after-drunkenness and near-hangover. "Where are we?" he asked.

"Near Arrowhead—I think."

He still avoided looking at me. "I remember now—I saw you in some bar. I mistook you for Dean. I dont know what I was doing looking for him in the bars—hes not even old enough to get in."

"I was drunk too," I said, to ease his obvious embarrassment.

As I drove his car down the mountain, he became friendlier, his embarrassment relaxing. "I dont remember everything," he said, "but whatever happened—if something was wrong —Im sorry. I cant drink," he explained.

We stopped at one of the water faucets along the road and got out. The world shrugged beneath us: expansive and unconcerned.

"I—fell off a cliff—once," Lance said dully, staring down. He laughs bitterly. "If youve been around the bars in Hollywood at all, youve probably heard about it."

I was silent.

"No comment? That means youve heard. Hell, I dont care. If I only knew what really happened. I was drunk that night too. Some marines—I was with them—I dont even know how —I was frantic; drunk. Someone had just told me that—. . ." He stopped for a long while. "I remember shouting something to the marines; I remember—. . . The car stopped. There was a cliff. . . ." He stood staring down at the impassive world. "Sometimes—sometimes I think—I think I knew that cliff was there when I jumped. . . ." He was silent again. "When you look down like this," he said, "it's almost as if the world is waiting for you to jump, and the only thing you can do is turn back and postpone it—for a while—or throw yourself on it and get it over with. . . ."

He turned and smiled at me—the enchanted smile of the legendary Lance O'Hara—and he put out his hand to me in a gesture of friendship. "Thanks for coming out here with me."

In the car, he said abruptly. "I know! Lets go there now—to Laguna Beach! I havent been there since that day. Weve still got time! I'd like to see it again."

When we reached Laguna—that city like a slick patchwork quilt—the beach was deserted and cold.

We walked on the darkening beach. Lance stared ahead at the ocean. We lay on the sand silently. Then Lance got up, moved to the very edge of the water, which advances murmuring toward him, retreating, advancing closer now more violently. He stood against the sky, a shadow, the water lapping at his feet. . . .

As we drove back, Lance seemed happy. "I want you to stay with me tonight—will you?—and tomorrow Im going to give a party. I want to very much suddenly. I want to invite them all—and theyll all come, if only out of curiosity. But they wont see what they want to see. . . . Will you stay with me tonight?"

5

This is the house of Lance O'Hara—the house of Esmeralda Drake the Third. . . .

In the hills, serene.

The smile on Lance's face seems serene too: belying the existence of a ghost, tapping along the house with a cane. . . .

Most of the morning, Lance was on the telephone. "Yes, it's me—Lance! Im having a party. . . . As early as you like. . . . Here, in my house—you know where I live. . . ." And most of the morning, and into the afternoon, the telephone rang as if itself aware of the party.

Since yesterday at Arrowhead, Lance had not mentioned Dean—except once, last night, when, in bed with me (as he tried, I knew, to stifle with sex the screaming memories), he had called me by his name. But each time he answers the telephone today, the smile freezes, he closes his eyes, breathes deeply to contain the welling panic. He stands moments over the telephone, his hand uncertainly over the receiver. The "Hello," coming finally, becomes a wrongly answered question. . . .

Chick, naturally, was the first to come.

"Baby, I didnt know you even *knew* Lance!" he said, winking at me knowingly—and then he swept toward Lance, embracing him with genuine affection. "Lance, baby, oh! I could cry to see you looking so Great. What a grand idea to have a party! Remember the Old Times? Remember when we were dancing in the Movies together? . . . Party every night. Never went to bed except to party some more. . . ."

And now, it seems, they are all here: the handsome masculine ones desired alike by men and women; the gushing swishes, hands aflutter like wings; the few stray women secure among the men who will idolize them but not love them; and as in any group of homosexuals and those lured for whatever reason to them, there is here a mood of superficial good humor, of euphoria bordering on hysteria.

So the motley chorus has invaded the stage.

But looking at Lance, strangely sparkling now, the Furies are forced to abandon their dour prophecies. Only momentarily. They wait, They know. They have been alerted by life itself. Like criminals returning to the scene of the crime, the whisperers know they have returned to the scene of the beginning of the fall.

Jamey burst in, in a very brief striped bikini. "I went to the beach," he explained breathlessly. "I just heard about the party, and I was told it was going to be *very* informal—so *voilà!*"—striking a bathingbeauty pose. He catches sight of Lance and rushes toward him. "Well, Lance, welcome back— it hasnt been the same without you. And the other day, when I saw you—you know, at the Rendezvous Room (though I hardly expect you remember), I said, My God, whats happened to Lance!—he looks terrible," He stares calculatingly at Lance, and what he sees displeases him: It is again the Lance of the legend which Jamey must see destroyed. "And by the way, Lance-sweetheart, did you find him? . . . Oh, you know, whoever you were . . . looking . . . for . . . remember? —oh, look, theres Chick!" rushing away from Lance, leaving the words suspended behind him like a curse. "Chick, honey!" Jamey gushes. "I didnt expect to see you here—after that awful scene you had last night. I heard all about it! Did that tramp *really* rob you? Youve got to be more careful about picking anybody up on the Boulevard these days," he says loudly, aiming at anyone here who might have been picked up on the Boulevard. Later I hear him say to someone else: "I think Lance is trying to fool us—hes not as happy as hes pretending. And what the hell's happened to that little tramp Dean?"

"I dont know," the other answers. "I thought maybe he'd be here. . . . Youve go to admit," he said, "Lance looks good."

"Dont let him fool you, honey, hes just *pretending* to look good. Dont you notice how there isnt too much light in here?"

"Thank heaven for that, sweetie—you dont suffer from the dark yourself."

The stage is set. Lance O'Hara is surrounded by the waiting chorus. . . . But so far, Lance was perfect—laughing, moving from group to group, recalling incidents, love affairs, shamelessly flattering the extravagantly gushing women. "Didnt I tell you theyd all come?" he whispered to me. "The vicious fairies. And theyre disappointed it's not a wake yet."

Like a summer storm in those areas where in one instant it changes from bright to thundering dark, it happened.

Dean stood at the door—the same youngman who had talked to me that night on the Boulevard.

Lance had been talking to someone. The sudden silence descending over the room like a blackwinged bird made him stop instinctively. All eyes alternated between the youngman at the door and Lance. Lance was suddenly livid, the circles around his eyes deepened. He whirled about, smiling—moving toward the youngman. "Dean! Youre just in time for the party!" His voice shook. The breathless chorus rehearses its lines. "Where have you been?" he asked casually, placing his hand falsely steadily on the boy's shoulder.

"Away," Dean said curtly, and that word, thrust at Lance like a stone, makes the whisperers realize they have not turned up in vain. Lance dodges the stone, clings to the façade of composure. The conversations of those who understand— and soon, aware, of those who dont—stop abruptly as if the needle had been removed from a record. The whispers, ready to be released at any moment, are balanced like a great rock on a cliff, ready to tumble disastrously. Jamey, who had left the room before Dean came in, walked in at the wrong time: "My God," he says, "I was almost Raped in the powderroom." But no one laughed. It was as if someone had coughed during the crucial moment of a drama. "Whats happened?" he said, and then he saw Dean and Lance staring tensely at each other. And Jamey squints his eyes victoriously.

Dean marched past Lance, past the staring eyes—into the bedroom. Lance is behind him, gliding past the stares knifing him brutally, ready to repay him now for his beauty, for the anarchy of that beauty. Chick steps quickly before Lance, whispers frantically: "Lance!—dont go after him!—*theyre watching you!*" But Lance brushes him aside and follows Dean into the bedroom.

The door closes.

From behind that closed door come voices, alternately raised, lowered. Now the door of the bedroom swings open, and Dean walks out, his clothes thrown carelessly over his arm. Lance stands momentarily at the door.

And now he will do what will delight all of you who have hated him for his unquestioned reign: Lance will follow Dean. . . .

He catches up with him, pulls on the clothes draped over the youngman's arms. The clothes spill on the floor: Lance's façade crumbles before us. "Dean—dont—go—" he pleads. (And is he pleading as much for his life as for Dean? I wonder.) "I have to talk to you—come back into the bedroom—I —" The pressure of Lance's hand noticeably becomes heavier on Dean's shoulder. Dean jerks viciously away from him. And he lashes:

"Dont touch me, you fuckin faggot!"

And the door, slammed by Dean, refuses stubbornly to close—swings open, wide open, admitting the coming night.

The whispering has not yet been unleashed. Lance must admit his fall—with a look, a word.

He stands before the door, his back toward us, facing the night. . . .

And what is he staring at beyond the door? Is he looking at the disappearing figure of Dean? Or is he staring past the youngman? Does the same ghost that had hovered that afternoon on the beach, that night on the cliff, loom now at that door? . . . Lance doesnt move. Perhaps he cant face the buzzing bees behind him yet. Or is he acknowledging at last the old, old man who has waited patiently for his revenge? . . .

And in anticipation of the crushed look which will bring down the curtain on the reign of Lance O'Hara, Chick rushes crying into the next room; and Jamey sighs: "Well!' and that sighed word really means: "At last!"

Now Lance will turn to face you, and the look of defeat will confirm the news that the reign of Lance O'Hara is over— that the charmed life has ended. Tomorrow, in the bars, you will write the epitaph.

Lance closes the door with the intended *slam!* of Dean— perhaps with that gesture trying to push the ghost away: *Not yet!* . . . And with the false courage of someone who has just dodged one bullet in a rain of bullets, he stares now challengingly at the chorus in a desperate effort to squelch their triumph—and in this crucial moment: mercifully, mysteriously, Lance looks Radiant—as if he, who has always relied on miracles, still expects some miraculous salvation.

And it comes.

Before the whispers of false sympathy can conclude his reign, the door opens behind Lance, and a meek Dean appears, the few clothes dangling pitifully from his arms. He walks slowly to Lance—waits—whispers (but we can all hear him in that dreadfully quiet house):

"Lance—Im—sorry. . . . Lance? . . . I dont really want to go. . . . I—I just get kind of afraid sometimes. . . . I thought youd kick me out first. . . . Lance? Can I come back?"

Lance faces Dean—gratefully and with a look that could be only compassion, flickering, but unmistakably there.

"Tonight," Lance said, "you can stay tonight—if you havent got a place—but—for your sake—itll be better—tomorrow—if you do leave."

Now Lance turns to the startled faces before him, as Dean disappears into the bedroom.

"Whats the matter?" Lance said smiling—disappointing—oh, deeply, deeply—the waiting chorus, forced to retreat. "Whats everyone so somber about?" He leaned against the fireplace, like an actor aware of his enthralled audience.

"Our life," he sighed, "is meant to be a series of love affairs —nothing more. And you all know that. And who knows whos just around the corner? . . . Come on," he said, passing gracefully from one awed person to another, "drink up!"

And the buzzing has not come, the chorus is bewildered— as Lance O'Hara says, his back solidly to the Ghost tapping at the door to be let in (or—is it possible?—will it retreat now in peace? . . .):

"Lets have a gay time!"

CITY OF NIGHT

IT WAS SUMMER NOW.

Summer, which in Southern California does not come Magically as it does in the East. Warm days merely fuse with warmer days—and your resistance to life dulls. And like mangoes rotting imperceptibly in the white sun, bodies turn brown along the wide-stretching California beaches. To La Jolla, to Malibu, to Long Beach, to Venice West, Laguna—from the canyon beyond Malibu as the morning fog is swept away into the ocean; from the hot Los Angeles streets where the heat gathers in steaming pools; from across now-vacationing America, they come.

The Southern California beaches are a way of life.

Strips of sand fleeing from the mainland are cuddled by the distant outlining palmtrees. Like a restless, futile enemy of this sunny stagnation, the ocean invades the passive sand. As it grows late in the day and the bodies cluster away from the water lapping slowly inland, night comes like a blackout. The water, dark, capped by creamy froths, will lash turbulently at the beach, and youll hear that mysterious, disturbing murmuring of the wind and the water like a personal judgment.

Those summer afternoons on the beaches, time drifts unreally. Days are measured by the deepening color of your skin.

La Jolla. . . . Semicircling the water, cupped in a handful of sun. And only a short distance beyond it and the navy base: San Diego, a familiar row of tattoo parlors, loan shops, stores —typical of all the lonely servicemen towns in America: sailors roaming the nightstreets—whiteclouds of drifting uniforms.

Long Beach. . . . The amusement park near the beach, the hectic-whirling scene—the rollercoaster plunging ineluctably like a bullet along the murderous rails. The park . . . the hot public heads . . . a bar where on Sunday afternoons a mad queen did a dragshow with balloons and feathers.

Laguna Beach. . . . Bordered by squat jagged cliffs. . . .

211

Homosexuals ritualistically Protectively assembled in one close area—like flotsam on the beach—as if symbolically defying the world that shut them out—a world with so little compassion.

And Santa Monica.

From a slim green flowered park (a statue of Saint Monica serenely eyeing the long lines of cars turning from Wilshire Boulevard toward the beaches), the sand gleams expansively white—and Pacific Ocean Park gathers itself like a small facsimile pleasure-island: rides, a simulated sea, Neptune holding court over rainbowed fish, make-believe jungles. Between it and the row of fresh-fish restaurants—beyond muscle beach, where the men with balloons for muscles posed for each other with set faces—is "Crystal Beach."

Along an area of perhaps two blocks, one block of sand wide from the parking lot to the ocean, the initiates of the world I lived in gathered from the early morning (a face sometimes emerging eerily out of the fog in the first sudden blaze of oceansun) into the late sun-clinging afternoon. All the representatives of that world are here: the queens in extravagant bathing suits, often candy-striped, molded to the thin bodies—tongued sandals somehow worn like slippers; the masculine-acting, -looking homosexuals with tapered bodies and brown skins exhibiting themselves lying on the sand, trunks rolled down as far as possible—or going near the ocean as if undecided whether to dive in, posing there bikini-ed, flexing their bodies, walking the long stretch of beach, aware of the eyes which may be focused on them; the older men who sit usually self-consciously covered as much as the beach-weather allows, hoping perhaps for that evasive union, more difficult to find now—ironically now, when the hunger is more powerful, the shrieking loneliness more demanding; the male-hustlers, usually not in trunks, usually shirtless, barefooted, levis-ed, the rest of their clothes wrapped beside them, awaiting whatever Opportunity may come at any moment, clothes, therefore easily accessible for moving quickly for whatever reason.

Periodically, throughout the day, the representatives of that world, now centered on the beaches, will move to the small sandwich shop across the parking lot, looking back to see if anyone has followed them there. But, mostly, they will move into the bar a block away: and this is Sally's bar.

As the magic-tanning sun diminishes, Sally's bar on weekends is crammed with oiled malebodies rubbing sensually against each other, hands openly exploring.

Forced laughter drowns the vomiting of the jukebox.

I had seen in Lance's look—in that look as, perhaps, he tried to expiate his guilt and calm the haunting vengeance of a sad old man—I had seen that faint glimmer of compassion, for Dean—and therefore, now, the barest hint of a capacity to attempt to love—someone! . . . That look had frightened me. And I fled from it.

And during those summer-beach days, I drove myself furiously: sometimes making it and quickly returning to the beach, leaving again with someone else: faces confused with others, the hurried intimacy remembered perhaps days or weeks later.

Those summerdays spent mostly in Santa Monica, I would hear often of a youngman named Glen—a smallish blond youngman I would see every day on the beach. A few summers ago, he had been one of the most desirable hustlers on the beach: "Simply everyone," a score told me, "wanted Glen—then—but, now—well, everyone's used to him: There are so many new faces each summer. If Glen were smart, he'd move somewhere else, where they dont know how old he is. At first, Glen was strictly trade. Now—well— . . . He'll do everything!"

"After a while," another man told me, "Glen will be out of the hustling ranks. He'll quit going around with the teenage girls he still tries to impress us with—and he'll have a steady young boyfriend. Watch and see."

"After all," another man added, "*pretending* that you never, never, never do this or that is fine—or if you dont now, that you never will. But *really* never, never, never doing this or that—well, it's slightly insane. It's a perversion in itself."

And so, that summer, it was an insistent refrain: the premium on Youth. Often, it was brought up bitchily by scores after the sexscene—but other times it was said from an acute awareness of the life they—we!—lived. . . . Mr. King had brought it up, but that had been at the beginning of the journey, and its meaning had been remote then. It wasnt *how* I would live that terrified me. It was, instead, the horror that the youthful cravings would extend into a time when what made them possible of gratification might no longer be.

And one of that summer-wave of people who would emphasize that refrain was an evil old auntie—whom I will remember as an impeccably clean dirty old man—whose name is Hubert, but who says self-affectionately: "Call me Hughie, dear—everyone does"—a rabbity-looking, mincing, effeminate, beady-eyed little old man of about 60.

As he tried to flash brilliantly before me, confusing T. E. with D. H. Lawrence, I couldnt help—and what the hell?—coming on intellectually, and I corrected him. "Oh, dear me," he said, "how frightful—an Intellectual! You should have kept your mouth closed, youngman. My oh my—oh!—the mind of an old man and the body of a young boy. Dear, dear me!" And I struck back at him: "Better than the mind of a young boy and the body of an old man!" "Ouch!" he winced, "dear me, dear dear me," as with rabbity gestures, he cuddled himself on a chair. . . .

Although I had dinner with him several times after that, he indicated no sexual interest in me then.

And it was with him, soon after, that I went to the mansion of that famous director whom Skipper had known. Derisively, the old auntie announced to the director: "This youngman is an Intellectual—watch out," and the director had immediately sneered: "The last time I even *talked* to one—a writer," he said, "I ended up in *Confidential* magazine." "Oh, dear, oh, my —listen to *that,* will you?" the little auntie fluttered: "Oh, the wages of Fame—tsk-tsk!" The director commanded the youngman living with him at that time: "Go tell Mattie we'll have lunch outside"—with a coldness and an undisguised contempt —a paid owningness—that made me cringe. The youngman moved away obediently—after having fixed our drinks.

That whole evening turned into progressively less veiled hostility between myself and the director, as—throughout his brutal imitation of a star then involved in a frontpage sex scandal—the face of Skipper—somewhere drunk in downtown Los Angeles—scorched my thoughts.

Later, in his own house, when Hughie tried to come on with me for the first time—nibbling, appropriately rabbit-like, at my chest—I pushed him away, despising him strangely.

"Youre too old for me anyway," he said. "I prefer them *very* young and very, *very* dumb, dear," he went on cuttingly. "In their 20s, theyve already been had too often—and in too many ways. I like the little boys who can still get aroused by dirty pictures. I like to watch the naughtiness awaken. . . . Theres a family near me—three boys, the oldest seventeen, the youngest twelve," he bragged, "and Ive had the first two, now Im working on The Young One. *They* read comicbooks—not

D. H. Lawrence!" He smacked his lips lecherously; and noticing my reaction of disgust, he said laughingly but still seriously: "Blame the aunts, dear."

"The aunts?"

"Yes—I was raised by two maiden aunts—they taught me to play with paperdolls. Each time I seduce a very young boy (oh, anywhere around fifteen years—anyone over that is, well, just extra)," he aimed at me, "each time, you know, well, I Offer him Up to The Aunts!" . . .

And so all those reminders of the premium placed on Youth mesmerized me, made me focus on that particular summer, as, later, I would try to focus on whatever particular season it was. I canceled out the future—or tried to—as if only the Present existed and would go on forever. I was crazily convinced that somehow if I concentrated only on Today, the specter of that shattering tomorrow would disappear. . . . But in a life that can date you when you begin to look over 25, I felt myself clawing to hold on to the present. . . .

At the Ranch Market on Vine Street, a cockeyed clock winds its hands swiftly backwards. Longingly I stand before it.

It was that summer that I met Dave.

On the beach one morning I had met a malenurse who was going on a splurging scene with several credit cards (which may or may not have been stolen), and I got in on it: Wellington boots, khaki levis, shirts. Because he was staying at the home of the man he was nursing, we went that night to the apartment of a friend of his—a giddy short Italian.

Lying on a couch was a darkly handsome, masculine youngman who looked immediately to me like a hustler. We acknowledged each other with a nod. When I came out of the room with the malenurse and the giddy Italian, the dark youngman I had seen on the couch was gone.

A few days later, in an all-night coffeehouse on Sunset, he sat next to me.

His name was Dave, and I had been wrong about his scene: He was not a hustler. He worked in an airplane factory, he told me, and he went to school at night. He quickly explained that he merely shared that apartment with the giddy Italian; that there was nothing between them.

For a long while we spoke about many things—but not about the homosexual scene. I was beginning to think he was straight, despite his roommate. Then he said: "That malenurse you were with that night, he just likes hustlers." He wa. obviously trying to find out about me. I said nothing. "I cant see just going to bed with a lot of people—different ones every night," he said. "I mean, a person, whether hes queer or not, hes got to find someone. . . . Nothing like a lonely fairy," he said smiling. I liked him right away.

And for that reason—resisting the temptation to say no (I had known immediately that he was not a score—and I sensed, although I dismissed it, that sexually he would be attracted only to someone who would be equally attracted to him, and I sensed, too, that he would look in that person for more than a night-long partner)—I went to his apartment with him when he asked me if I felt like talking some more.

In the apartment, when he touched me, I told him quickly I had to leave.

He looked at me steadily. Then he smiled. "Sure," he said. "Maybe youll want to go to Arrowhead with me tomorrow." Surprisingly, he was not annoyed that I had put him off. "It's Sunday. I'll pick you up if you want to."

I said yes, suddenly anxious to leave. As he drove me to the hotel on Hope Street, I felt certain I wouldnt be there when he came by.

But I was.

And after that, I saw him more and more often. When he wasnt working or going to school, we would drive out of the city. . . . And I began to discover in him an honesty that constantly amazed me, an integrity and decency rare in the world of the bars and streets: It pleased me strangely that soon after I met him, he moved into another apartment, this time alone. Although he openly acknowledged his interest in other youngmen, when it was a mutual interest—and he was a very desirable member of that group—I could tell that his was not the furious hunger that it very often is with others. Since that first night, he hadnt attempted to come on with me, and we rarely ever spoke about that scene.

He told me about himself: about the stone-cold woman who was his mother; the ranting father, consumed in flames one nightmare night: a cigarette dropped drunkenly on the bed. He told me this without selfpity, merely as the recitation of his life.

And I found that I was revealing myself to him, letting slide off more than ever before the mask I had protectively cultivated for the streets and bars. At times, I felt he knew even more about me than I told him, which alternately pleased and disturbed me.

"Why do you hustle?" he asked me once. It was the first overt reference he had made to that, and it was the kind of statement that, from almost anyone else, I would quickly have put down.

I was tempted to point out that I hadnt asked him for anything. Instead, I merely said. "I have to."

"Thats not true," he challenged. "Youve told me youve worked."

Annoyed far beyond his question, I said: "Okay, then, I prefer to."

More and more, I was now in the bars or on the hustling streets only when I had to score. I avoided Main Street altogether. The craving for the sexual anarchy began to diminish for the first time since I had begun that journey through nightlives. I felt a great friendship for Dave (and an amount of pity for the paradoxical fact of him in a world of furtive contacts; he should be married, the father of adored children). . . . But all this, I told myself, was merely a welcome friendship in a period of ennui with the turbulence of the chosen world.

Still, there were those times when a different kind of fear began to seize me.

Im sitting with Dave in the outside arena of Pacific Ocean Park in Santa Monica, watching the animal circus. It's a bright breezeless afternoon, when, miraculously, the usually hazy Los Angeles sky is purely clear, like a childhood-remembered Texas sky.

"Miss Pinky! The Graceful Elephant!"

The announcer, who has just introduced the next animal performer—"Miss Pinky"—leads a small elephant into the arena. Painted a garish purplish pink, the elephant wears a small, multicolored, flowered hat perched absurdly on the giant head, slightly bowed as if in shame. The liveried trainer puts the pink elephant through a series of dance routines, accompanied by music. The elephant with the ridiculously flowered hat goes doggedly through the motions of a hula, a mambo, a waltz. The trunk sways clumsily, enormous legs execute the steps ponderously. The flowered hat fell over one eye, and the trainer coaxed the elephant to push the hat back on with its trunk.

The audience rocked with laughter.

As the elephant lurched from side to side, the great ears as if rejecting the hat, the announcer says: "Miss Pinky isnt really a dainty young girl, Folks! She is really a boy-elephant. But he has such A Special Appeal—such Graceful Talents— as Im sure youll agree—" (Applause!—and the elephant is persuaded by the trainer to bow his great head in thanks.) "—that we think it would be a shame to waste them. And so, Folks, a Great Big Hand for Miss Pinky—the graceful boy-elephant!" . . .

I see Dave stare solemnly at the elephant being led off the small arena, the flowered hat perched crookedly over one ear. . . .

"It's sad—that great big male elephant painted pink—and that hat on his head," Dave said.

Suddenly Im frighteningly moved by this youngman beside me. I feel that impotent helplessness that comes when, through some perhaps casual remark, I see a person nakedly, sadly, pitifully revealed—as I see Dave now.

We were both silent as we drove to his apartment.

Along the hall of that building, a door is open. Two young-men had moved in—and the mother of one, Dave had told me earlier, had come to visit them, staying there with them, aware that her son and the other youngman were lovers. Through the open door as we passed it, I heard the voice of one, whining peevishly: "Mommee! listen to what Duane is saying to me!" . . . I cringed visibly. Dave noticed this. "They fight all the time," he told me. "Duane thinks Rick is making it with other guys—and Rick's mother always takes Rick's side."

Inside the apartment, Dave said unexpectedly:

"It sure is great to be with you!" He put his hand fondly on my shoulder, letting it rest there—the first time he had touched me even this intimately since that first night.

For a long moment, I didnt move, feeling his hand increasingly heavier. . . . I jerked away from him.

The words erupted out of me: "Maybe so—but it's all stopping!"

Even when I saw the look of amazement on his face, even when I wanted to stop, even when I felt that compassion, tenderness, closeness to this youngman—even then, I knew, as much for me as for him, that I had to go on; that although, inside, I was cringing at my own words, in hammerblows I have to destroy this friendship. "I mean—well—Ive spent too much time with you—thats all."

And crazily through it all, I keep thinking about the pink elephant at the park—the ridiculous flowered hat!—the sad eyes! . . . And the echoing, petulant, girlish "Mommee!" that had emerged from the half-open door along the hallway. . . .

"Im sorry, Dave," I said at the door, which I was opening now, to clinch the Escape, to get *myself* away from *him.* "Im sorry," I repeated, "but this scene is nowhere!"

Outside in the hall, I close the door behind me. I pause for a moment, not knowing why. Then I walked out of the building quickly.

Im back in Santa Monica, alone, facing the wind-tossed ocean.

SOMEONE: People Dont
Have Wings

I HAD SEEN HIM ON THE BEACH several times before.

He never wore trunks. He was always dressed neatly in summer sportclothes. After I began to notice him—and even on the crowded beach he stood out—I realized that during the last week he had been here daily.

He would stand on the sidewalk before the beach, looking, it seemed to me, not at anyone in particular but at the whole beach and everyone on it. After a few minutes, he would drive away—alone, without having spoken to anyone. Occasionally, that same afternoon, he would return. Soon, I began to watch for him to appear.

Once, going to Sally's bar, I saw him closely. He looked at me; and realizing I had noticed, he quickly turned away. He resembled a highschool coach: neatly cropped hair, ruddy face, trim build. He was possibly in his late 30s. He didnt look like a score; he didnt look like a masculine homosexual (that is, his masculinity did not seem posed); he looked completely incongruous—and I suppose this is why I had first noticed him. After seeing him so often, standing in almost the same spot those afternoons—I began to be strongly intrigued by him.

That afternoon, when I saw him again, I was lying on the beach with two fairies who had spotted me for a teahead and were trying to get me to go with them by telling me they had some marijuana at home—changing the subject when I kept referring to being "broke": the standard hint when youre not entirely sure someone will pay you for making it. . . . Both of them were youngish and slender; they looked masculine, but their coy gestures, their rolling eyes, their suggestive, high-pitched comments canceled out their initial physical appearance.

"Well, hon," said one, "if you dig—uh—pod, we will—uh

—turn you on—and have a—real smash—I mean blast—at our—uh—pad." He spoke the jivewords as if he had memorized them.

Im still looking at the man standing before the concrete ledge separating the beach from the sidewalk. . . . I said to the gushing fairy lying beside me on the sand: "Well, see, I *would* dig making it to your pad—but I dont know how far out you live, and I dont even have enough bread to make it back downtown."

"Well," said the other one, "no problem there, honey—well be glad to give you a lift back!" They were either very dense or determinedly avoiding the hint—and I leaned heavily toward the latter theory. In a few minutes I would leave. I had stayed this long largely because the sun kept me glued to the beach—that lazy, pleasurable, sensual feeling hugging me as I felt my skin turn browner.

"Who are you looking at?" the first fairy asked me.

Startled to find that I had been so obviously staring at the man on the sidewalk, I turned quickly sideways—but following my gaze, the fairy had already discovered where I had been looking.

"Look," he said to the other one, "theres that strange man again. Hes here every weekend—just stands there. Ive never seen him go with anyone. He just stands there."

"I wouldnt be too Interested in him, hon," the other one warned me. "He may be welldressed—but he doesnt look like a score." And now I knew they had been hip to my scene all along, trying to con me with the weed. "Hes kinda cute, too—but not Young enough," he added.

"He looks like a plainclothes dick to me," said the first one —then turning to me: "Is 'dick' the right word, hon?—it sounds so strangely dated or something. Or would a plainclothesman also be referred to as 'fuzz'?"

" 'Dick'—like Dick Tracy," I said with a straight face.

He was right: The man did look like a plainclothes detective. Obviously, others had noticed him. The fairy next to me is saying: "Thats all he could be—a plainclothes dick!"

But the other one was already dismissing him: "Why dont you take your pants off, hon," hes saying to me, "so we can see what you look like all over—before buying?" And so hes decided this is the only way.

"Im not wearing trunks," I said.

"Thats exactly what I mean," he said, throwing up his hands in glee. "Lets see what you *really* look like!"

That did it. I mumbled something about having to leave, and I walked away. They said something, but I didnt hear what it was—undoubtedly something Bitchy.

But had I left really because I was annoyed at what he had said?—or was it that I had wanted all along to do what I was now doing? . . . I sat on the concrete ledge—near the man in sportclothes. Glancing up purposely suddenly, I see him looking at me. I wiped the sand off my pants, I light a cigarette —stretching the time that I could stay there without being obvious. This time I look at him directly for a response. He smiles at me.

For no apparent reason suspecting strongly that the fairy just now had been right—that this man was indeed a detective —I put my shirt on, got up, started to move away without looking back. But soon Im aware that hes taken a few steps toward me. I faced him. He opened his mouth to say something, and then, in real or pretended embarrassment, he merely smiled again. Reacting to him as if he is a cop, I look at him coolly.

"Im leaving the beach," he blurted. "Can I give you a ride somewhere?"

Now, Im not at all sure hes a cop—not because of what he said (Southern California is notorious for entrapment—theyll even offer you money and bust you later)—but because of the diffident tone of his voice; he appeared embarrassed the moment he had spoken. It is usually relatively easy, once youve made the scene in the bars and the beaches, to peg someone quickly at those places. But not this man. I keep shifting my suspicions.

"Which way are you going?" I asked him.

He shrugged. "Oh, anywhere. I havent got anything to do. I'll drive you wherever youre going."

I want very much—because of a strong curiosity—to find out about this man. On the other hand, if I leave the beach now—and he merely drives me back downtown—I will have left for nothing, and it's still early: the golden-tanning sun still holds the sky.

He sees me hesitating—saw me looking at him trying to pin him—and he said completely unexpectedly: "Dont worry, Im not on the vice squad."

"What makes you think I'd care?" I said, annoyed.

"Honestly," he said. "Look." He drew open his coat, so I could see there is no badge—although of course it proved nothing. It only irritated me further.

"What makes you think I'd care if you are?" I challenged him again. The implication that he *knows* I have something to fear in that direction bothers me. It indicates, too, that, whatever he is, hes familiar with that world. But then, merely his repeated presence on this beach revealed that.

"Oh," he said uncomfortably, "well, I mean, it has nothing to do with you, really. I mean—well—this beach—and I *have* seen you several times—you leave with different people—and they—well— . . . ." He went on apologetically, making it worse. "Lets go get some coffee somewhere," he said hurriedly.

We got into his car, a new stationwagon. There is a suitcase on one seat.

"Im on vacation," he explained. "I dont live here. Usually I come down on weekends. I didnt have any plans for my vacation—so I thought I'd just drive around. Ive only got four more days left."

At the restaurant on Wilshire—as we stood waiting to be served (surrounded by tanned faces rejuvenated by the Sun), he doesnt look at me like the other people who would usually pick you up, doesnt talk like them. . . . Of course, there are many men in that world who, outside of pickup places, wear a mask convincingly, but in the atmosphere of the beaches, the bars—or when theyve made a contact—the mask usually slides off—if only slightly: They remain masculine, yes, but there is usually at least the subtlest hint of the façaded sexhunger. About the man Im with there hasnt been that slightest hint.

"Have you eaten yet?" he asked me.

"No."

"Why dont you then?" Even this is said merely graciously, not buyingly.

Too, there is always the threat of meeting someone who looks perfectly "normal" and who turns out to be psycho— like the man in the raincoat in New York who had pulled a knife on me. In a life that thrives on the arbitrary stamp of "differentness" imposed on it by the world that creates it and then rejects it, the more "regular" the person (the more he defies the usually easy classification of masculine homosexual, queen, score, hustler, fairy), the more suspect he becomes.

He talked very little while we ate; and because of my complete inability to make him out, I had eased the hustling stance. That pose can blot out all but sexual communication. Yet, those usual times, you know—youve learned!—that it's necessary. . . . This man, though, is different.

Outside again, we stood on the sidewalk. The sun is fading behind the strip of park, beyond the sand, into the ocean. Toward the horizon, the fog lifts itself gracefully like a veil welcoming the night.

"You want to stay with me for a while?" I heard him ask me. His look, unshifting on me for moments—asking—softens into one of the familiar expressions. It reveals him at last.

"Sure," I said.

We walked across the street, along that green park—the flowers bright and alive—past the many afternoon people sitting on benches. We stand looking out toward the beach. The crowds on the sand are thinning. Across the bridge from the beach to the streets, they come with their towels bundled, fleeing from the lifting nightfog. They seem to gather on the beach for some kind of huddled protection, and when groups begin to leave, when that sense of mutual protection begins to diminish—as if this were a summons, the others leave too. A few will linger on, as the breeze from the ocean rises. The sun is frozen-white, spreading its light desperately before expiring into the ocean. Now the roaring waves will try to claim the sand throughout the night. . . .

"Why did you begin to walk away from me on the beach?" he asked me.

I was about to say: "You didnt look like a score." . . . Instead, I said: "You dont look like you belong on that beach."

He was silent, looking into his hands, studying them. "Let me explain something," he says. "I guess—" he went on uneasily "—I guess maybe youve noticed me on the beach. I mean, I must stand out because I come there so often—and leave, come back. It's just that— Well, in a way, it's all—it's all new to me." Still studying his hands, he said quickly: "Im married, I have a kid—a little boy."

This is a familiar story. Many tell you this for whatever purpose. Hustling, it emphasizes your masculinity for a score. For the others—even, sometimes, the very effeminate—this may be a symbolic subterfuge to emphasize the quandary of being in that world. . . . With this man, though, Im convinced beyond any doubt that what hes just told me is true. . . . I notice an untanned circle about his finger from which he has probably just removed a ring.

"Ive only been with two men in my life—that way—" he went on slowly. "And those two times, nothing really happened. I just— . . . And, once— . . ." He broke off abruptly. "What I mean is that Ive never really *done* anything," he said. "Oh, sure, Ive *known* for a long time. I guess—I guess thats largely the reason I got married, but I didnt *really* know, then. . . . Now Ive got a kid nine years old. . . . But things—from the beginning—they didnt go right. Thats mainly why she wanted a kid. . . . And then I started driving to the beaches, I guess to make sure there was a whole world ready to welcome me when I finally decided to join it—if I ever decided to. I always came there with the intention of meeting someone. But then I would see a screaming fairy—and suddenly I'd be ashamed. It's very strange—but I couldnt bear to look into his eyes, afraid, I guess, that he'd look back at me with recognition. And I didnt want a fairy, I knew that. I didnt even want them to look at me in that strange, piercing way. So I would drive away—but then I'd come back. . . . I'd seen you before. One time I almost talked to you. You see, I'd see you there alone— then youd go off with someone youd just met. So—well—I knew—well, that if I talked to you, youd at least talk back to me. I mean—those people I'd see you with, many of them were—well—obvious, and so—"

Turning to look at him—a man still not middle-aged, with still the hint of the attractive youngman he had been—I understood something of his struggle. That thought disturbs me, and I say quickly: "It's getting cool, isnt it?"

"Very cool," he said.

A long silence.

"Will you stay with me tonight?" he asked me.

The breeze is rising rapidly. The sun is now a blaze of white fusing with the glaring ocean.

I cant help asking: "Are you sure you want me to?"

"Yes," he said—but uncertainly. "I think Im sure. Yes, Im sure." Quickly, as if once having said that, he was resisting the instant compulsion to reverse himself, he said: "Im on vacation—I told you that already, didnt I? My wife—she— . . . Ive begun to wonder if theres any use even staying with her," he said.

"Does she know?" It was a square question—the kind of question I would not ordinarily have asked; but, having eased the street pose, Im reacting completely differently to him, responding to that evident struggle within him—the eminent Aloneness. . . .

"Theres nothing to know," he said almost sharply resentfully. He sighed, relenting. "Well. I guess I dont really know myself if she knows or not. She knows something is wrong. She couldnt help knowing that. The kid—hes the one that worries me. I mean—he—well, what would it feel like to find out your father is a— . . ."

"Lets get off the street," I said, stopping him.

"Ive still got to rent a place to stay tonight," he said. "Ive been staying at different motels. It's been about a week since I left—home—and, until today, I havent spoken to anyone. . . . But, God! how Ive wanted to. . . . I guess—" he smiled. "—I guess I look too suspicious for anyone to speak to me. I heard someone on the beach say I looked like a plainclothesman."

I wonder why I will stay with him—and I knew I would. At the same time that I feel he needs me—someone—that he is desperately alone—something else in me insists that I leave.

"We'll get a motel here, all right?" he asked.

"Sure," I said.

"And we can go to the beach tomorrow. . . . Will you stay with me the rest of my vacation?" he asked hurriedly. And as if understanding something, as if defensively beating me to it, canceling out the possibility that I would bring it up— which I would not have—he said: "Ive got enough money for both of us. I mean, after all—friends should— . . ."

Friends! I had just met him, such a short time earlier. I wanted to say something that would be very right—to do something: even, I thought cornily, to shake hands with him. But I could find nothing to say, nothing to do.

At a motel across from the beach, the man at the desk asked: "Two beds?"

"Yes," the man Im with answers embarrassed.

Through the wide window inside the room, I can see the ocean extending to the end of the sky.

The man turns the television on. For minutes we remain wordless. Several times I still want to leave.

He said as if reading my mind: "Do *you* want to stay with me?"

At any other time I might have interpreted this as a kind of rejection, implied. With him, I was convinced he wants me to stay.

"Yes," I answered.

I sat back on one bed, he sat back on the other. For several hours, making occasional forced comments about the programs, we watched television.

Outside, the night has shrouded the sky. I can hear the rumble of the ocean—the sound of the wind . . . speaking its personal language to each person who listens. . . . The insistent sound . . . that wind carrying us along. . . .

"This must be very boring for you," he said.

"It's fine," I told him.

"Are you tired yet?" he asked.

"Yes. I like to sleep listening to the ocean."

"I know what you mean," he said, pulling the blinds, shutting out the night. "It's the same with the wind, isnt it? —when youre inside and just listening to it. . . . It used to scare me when I was a kid. You cant stop it."

"It scared me too," I told him. "I even—crazy—used to wish there was something you could draw across the sky to block it."

He laughed. "Nothing can stop it, though," he said.

I took my clothes off, not facing him, facing away. Quickly I got under the covers. He went into the bathroom, he came out wearing pajamas.

He turned the light out.

I close my eyes. . . . I felt him sit on my bed. Somewhere beyond the window, someone was laughing. . . . A car honked. . . . Over it all I can hear the private murmuring of the ocean . . . the lowpitched whistling of the wind.

I feel his hand on my leg over the cover. Suddenly I wish I hadnt come here. . . . And yet will there always be the perversity?—because I keep thinking with crazy excitement: *This is the first time hes done this!*

Hurriedly, he draws the cover from my body, bends over me—*as if driving himself!* I think—and the thought blots all the perverse excitement of his newness.

"Dont you want me to?" he asks me.

"Do you want to?" I asked him.

"Yes," he said.

2

It was Sunday.

I woke up, and the glare of the sun on the ocean was flooding the room through the slanted blinds. The man was sitting propped on one elbow on his bed looking at me.

Several times during the night I had wakened, wondering apprehensively what his reaction would be in the morning. Immediately after—last night—he had sat smoking in the dark, and I had pretended to fall asleep. Throughout the night, he would sit up, light a cigarette. . . . Now I see him smiling at me. "You want to sleep some more?—it's still very early," he said. "Or you want to drive somewhere and have breakfast? . . . How about Arrowhead?"

I had been there not too long ago with Dave—whom I pushed more and more from the immediate presence of my mind, but, even now, when I saw someone who might be him, I would panic. But it was never him. He seemed to avoid the places where we had gone.

We drove to Arrowhead, early that morning—to the lake there and the beach, almost like a New England Village: imitation-cottage buildings, small logged shops. Today, there was no uncomfortable silence between us. My decision, from the beginning, to ease the usual street role had proved a right one. . . . There was an easy communication between us which the other scene would have strained. Usually, the appeal of the jivetalking street-hustler is stronger for the more jaded, in direct proportion, it seems, to the time they have actually been sexhunters. . . .

When he paid at the places we went to, this man did so without the flashy display of the score. It was not in payment for companionship that he did it—it was as if indeed I were his friend and he had money to share with me. Too, when he spoke about his job in advertising, there was not the usual note of many of the others I had known who pick you up and try to put you down by flaunting their real or imagined Position.

Eating breakfast as we sat by a window looking out at the clear greenness of the surrounding hills, he had brought up a subject which he had dropped yesterday afternoon: "Those two people I told you I'd almost been with before," he said, "when it came to actually going through with it, I couldnt— I walked out. I wanted to forget I had even—desired them. I wanted to take a shower right away, to get clean again— without having done anything. I'd return to my wife—but of course that didnt change anything—only for those few moments when I was so grateful for her. . . . Last night, after— well, after I came over to your bed—I wondered if it would be the same. And afterwards, yes, I felt guilty. . . . It was the first time—and it was all very strange—although, years ago, once, someone did that to me. . . . But I guess I always knew that I wanted to do it—that if I ever did go with another man, that would be the role I would play. Last night—after it happened—I sat there smoking after you feel asleep, and I thought, Well, Im not exactly young—and I suppose, as I sat there thinking—I suppose I told myself that it's wrong to fight yourself, when so much is fighting you already. . . . This morning, though, I feel great!"

When he got out his wallet to pay for breakfast, I saw the photograph of a young woman holding a child in her arms. . . . He closed the wallet quickly.

We returned to Santa Monica that afternoon.

Crossing the bridge leading to the amusement park, he said: "Im glad you decided to hang around with me. My vacation will be over soon—then I have to go back. I hate to think about it. . . . But if you want, I can see you on weekends, when I drive in. I'd like that—if you would."

Before I could answer—as we crossed the small bridge that spans the park into the beach—he said: "Lets not go to the queer part of the beach."

We sat close to the water where it rolled in fleecy waves toward the shore. Young girls were playing on the sand with their boyfriends. Couples sat with their families. . . .

Then we both saw it, almost at the same time looking up. Both stared into the sky, watching it.

A bird was swooping down from the blue, blue sky, swiftly as if determined to crash into the dark ocean. Within what looked like mere inches of the waiting water, it spread its wings gloriously and escaped into the blue of the welcoming sky.

The man said thoughtfully: "It's sad—isn't it?—that people dont have wings too."

A beachball rolled past us. A little boy, about seven, came chasing after it. The man grabbed the ball, threw it back playfully at him, stared after the kid rushing back to a man and a woman sitting watching the kid fondly.

"Lets leave," the man said.

We're now on the beach where I met him yesterday. In extravagant, colorful trunks, in brief bikinis, they lie on the sand, straining their necks to look at the new arrivals.

We lay there watching the parade. One fairy is wearing a suit in the style of the 20s, but made of a flesh-colored material which, when wet, was almost transparent. He would go into the water, just long enough to get the suit wet; then he would stand there at the edge of the beach, looking completely naked.

"Gay people—they—" the man started, interrupting himself: "I hate that word—'gay'—there should be another word: not 'homosexual'—that sounds too clinical—not 'queer', not 'fairy,' either— . . . Anyway, they seem to cancel out so much that could be. I mean: Ive seen some of them—not all of course, or even the majority—Ive seen them shrieking on the beach—neither men nor women. The effeminate ones—I told you this yesterday, I think—they frighten me. They seem sometimes to know so much. With a look, they can make you feel —so—well—so— . . . Like youre trapped," he finished.

I think of Miss Destiny—and I remember what Chuck had once said about queens—and I say now: "But you have to admire them for living the way they have to."

"Maybe so," he said. "But I dislike them. They make me feel as if I— . . ." But he stopped, noticeably uncomfortable. "Tonight I'll get the same room we had last night," he said, burying his hand under the sand and touching my arm, withdrawing his hand quickly in sudden embarrassment: The sun is too bright, too nakedly accusing.

As we walk toward Venice West, past the tourist "international" restaurants like a small hybrid town—beyond Pacific Ocean Park, past the beach stores and food counters, past the old retired people who sit on the benches dozing throughout the day, past bearded Bohemians playing bongoes softly, he asked me again if I would spend the rest of his vacation with him. I said yes.

"And weekends?" he asked.

I answer casually: "Oh, sure."

"Theres a bar around here," he said, "Ive seen it, but Ive never had the guts to go in. I think it's called the Merry-Go-Round."

"You mean the Carnival."

"Yes, thats it. Have you been there?"

"Yes."

"I'd like to see it," he said.

"Lets wait till later," I said. "The sun's still out—I want to get more sun." I tried to analyze a sudden ominous feeling at his mention of the Carnival bar.

3

The Carnival is one of many crackerbox buildings along a row of crumbling stores that make Venice West. Its windows are painted purple, green—black-smeared—so that you cant look inside. There is a forbidding wooden door. You push it open, and at the entrance is a huge bulldike like a truckdriver: a masculine lesbian with wide shoulders and hair cut in a man's ducktail. Shes wearing levis, a sweat-shirt, no makeup.

She may check your I.D.—and then in a gruff bulldog bark, allows you to pass:

And youre inside a bar with long splintery wooden tables, names carved on them; uncomfortable benches without backs —the actual bar, small, winding toward a side door leading to the head outside. The walls are colored dark purple. It's typically semidark; dimlights and thick clouds of smoke. From the ceiling hang three hideous monster faces and a facsimile of a giant snaring cobweb. Like an electric monster, a huge jukebox radiates fantastic colors.

Jammed into the benches are the malehustlers, usually shirtless, coming here directly from the beach; with them an occasional toughfaced young girl. Scores are here, too; and masculine homosexuals cruising each other; queens in semibeachdrag; lesbians—femme and bull types; even a few well-dressed women, slumming with their well-dressed husbands or escorts —but, usually, *knowingly* slumming. . . . Junk is pushed here —usually soft stuff: marijuana, pills—but you can also score for hard. Ratty pushers scrutinize the crowd for teaheads, hypes. . . . Some of the faces are like slightly mellower representations of the set monster-masks dangling from the ceiling.

In a small clearing surrounded by the tables and benches, a line of six young males danced the Madison: without touching —making it legal.

With the man, I stand purposely toward the back of the bar, expecting that he wont want to stay. But already hes suggested we sit and have a drink. The people on the bench move closer to each other to make room for us, welcomingly (their bodies can touch more intimately).

The Madison ends. The youngmen disperse into the bar. The jukebox is rocking, sounds monotonous but exciting: Africandrumming, jungle-moaning; the insistent beat-beat: sexually, primitively: the sound of this world, I think, not the moody sounds of jazz—but that monotonous pounding of cannibalistic music wearing at your senses. . . .

From somewhere, lured by the jungle sexsounds—a dark Latin queen rushed frenziedly onto the small clearing of the dancefloor: beach-hat with lurid dyed feathers, red-polkadotted loose-sleeved blouse tied at her stomach, white kneelength beachpants glowing purplish in the light, a gaudy gold butterfly pinned to her hip, several bracelets—beaded, multicolored, on her long brown arms. Dark body gleaming, thin and sinewy, she twists, grinds—lips parted, teeth gnashed. In convulsed, savagely rhythmic movements, accompanied by

guttural groans, she writhes the reptile body, contracts it suddenly—simulating a woman's orgasm. She crumbles near us
on the floor in a dark, sweating, panting, violently colored
heap. . . . More than a dance, it has been a demand for
Recognition of her mutilated sex.

I look at the man, and his eyes are staring down at the table.

Face shiny with perspiration, eyes almost demented: wide-
blackcentered—the queen removes her hat and passes it along
the crowd, collecting money—making comments as she moves
still writhing; dishing the women flagrantly, insulting the men
with them; calling the lesbians "mister," the fairies "miss";
camping openly with the masculine hustlers, withdrawing her
hat abruptly ("I'll take it out later in trade, honey")—subtly
choosing those from whom she will *demand* recognition—and
she is carrying it all off Triumphantly: her woman-act so
exaggerated, so distorted, so uncompromisingly brutal in its
implied judgment, that this crowd, hypnotized by her, momentarily sucked into her immediate world, responds mechan-
ically: As if buying away her scorching-eyed judgment of
them, they acknowledge her with the coin dropped into the
feathered hat.

She approaches us.

And she passes the hat before me—withdraws it quickly
with a wink and a kiss—and I breathe in relief at having expelled her implied judgment.

But she leans over the table, extending the hat toward the
man.

He doesnt move.

His eyes, rising slowly from the table where they had remained throughout the queen's dance, meet hers. Pale-gray,
they intercept the demanding look of the queen. With his look,
clearly, he refuses to acknowledge her with the coin dropped
symbolically into the hat, poised before him like a parody
sacrificial altar to what she represents. He is the only one
who will not acknowledge her on her own terms, the only
one who is refusing—with that look—to accept her judgment
and is therefore judging her. *Suddenly!* their eyes are tied to
each other, begin to grapple ferociously in mutual carnivorous
looks: deadlocked far beyond the immediate insistence of the
queen now, in view of the glaring, uncompromising, but un-
acknowledging look from the man, to get the token offering
from him. And the feared staring back by the queen is visibly
nailing the man in a strange way: more, I realized startlingly,
than the scene with me last night. The world he has joined

at last has stripped itself luridly Naked. The queen's look, the symbolic—now—seduction by the demanded acceptance of her, beyond the mere insistence of a dropped coin, emphasizes it savagely. Their eyes refuse to release each other. And now others on this bench are aware of that mysterious struggle between them. A vein on the man's neck begins to squirm like a tiny pinioned worm. The queen doesnt move, except for the heavy, now-racked breathing: Shes leaning— still leaning—across that table; and still both pairs of eyes are knotted frozen: the enormous burning dark eyes of the queen (and they are staring at the man with hatred, although her mouth is still spread in that wide-set forced smile); the pale eyes of the man icily refusing to acknowledge her, refusing to acknowledge that stripped, suddenly unmasked, rock-bottom revelation in that knowing, glazed look aimed so surely into him. I see the man trying to control his breathing. The squirming vein on his neck paused in its pulsing, as if the blood refuses to pound any longer. And even the frozen smile on the queen's face is threatening to disappear. The eyes—those eyes —those two pairs of eyes wrestling relentlessly for stakes which perhaps no one but them can really understand. Those eyes steady and fixed, almost unblinking, brimming with something too enormous to be contained much longer. Neither will break the deadlock. I imagine that a match ignited now will burst in a streak of cold white fire gluing their eyes to each other forever. The queen's tongue darts as she moistens her lips—darts hideously from the dark pit of her mouth like a lashing snake's. I see the man blink, his eyes moist with the intensity of the staring in this murky smoke-oppressed boxbar; and the queen's eyes open wider, slowly wider as if they will somehow be able to swallow the man: wider perhaps in order not to sever the emotional whirling currents forming an invisible vortex sucking the man further and further within himself. For moments that seems like hours, the staring continues—and even the people at the other tables are aware now; their eyes, too, focus on this scene. It cant last much longer, I keep thinking, searching for some way to stop it. But it goes on: that look like a doubly pointed knife on each side, stabbing each other mortally each moment it continues: the reflected pinpoints of each other's eyes magnified like searchlights into their very souls; the reflections boomeranging, finding new, undiscovered, secret areas—mirroring their mutually ripped lives. The perspiration is running down the queen's face in streams—the makeup melts from her painted eyelashes in waxlike smears: transforming her painted face now into a mask more terrifying than the ones that leer, eyeless, from the ceiling. And the man's face is now a bloodless, hollow, tanned shell. . . . *And his eyes!—the infinitely, infinitely, infinitely pale, unsurrendering eyes!*

Suddenly I brought out some change from my pocket, dropped it into the queen's hat.

And with an almost mortal groan, she rose from the table, her long legs thrust out into the clearing on the floor; and she swept the feathered hat in a loop. And with a peal of piercing laughter which seemed to emanate from the very depths of her slaughtered being, she placed the sacrificial hat on the floor.

And in an insane gesture—hissing demoniacally—she shook her beaded arms fatally before the man's face—and disappeared in a flash of tawdry colors beyond the door.

I surrender to the sounds about us, now released.

The man's hand holds the bottle of beer before him as if for some kind of futile, transferred protection. The vein on his neck has begun to pulsate again.

"Lets go," he said.

The sky is black.

We walked along the beach, wordlessly. An old bent man combs the sand for lost coins. The fog hangs gray and ragged over the ocean. . . . We walk through Pacific Ocean Park—the gay sounds of the many people still on that candy-colored strip only emphasizing the thundering silence between us. We're on Crystal Beach now. Inside Sally's bar, there are only about seven people. Two youngmen play the pinball machine, rainbow-shattered, tap-tapping the players' scores in colored numbers. The teeming screaming crowds have already left, but the beach seems somehow haunted, as if a part of their lives had been left buried in the sand, which will be carried into the ocean by the water and the wind which will rise.

The desolate beach was purplish before us. Where, earlier, the desperate people had strained to look at each other and the false laughter had risen into a crescendo that rivaled the beating of the ocean, now I see only one lone figure—a youngman in white shorts—walking the sandy lonesomeness. I sat with the man on the concrete ledge—where I had first talked to him, only yesterday: trapped almost physically now by the roaring sound of the waves against the sand and by the silence shouting between us.

Now there was another figure on the beach—a shadow obviously pursuing the youngman in the white. shorts. Soon, another lonesome figure appeared. The three formed a kind of strategic triangle on the sand—the focal point being the youngman in the white shorts. They disappeared toward the water. . . .

In the light along the bridge as we walk to the car, the man looks much older. The wrinkles on his face are sharply etched —or perhaps I notice them for the first time. Still wordlessly, we got into the car.

He drove a short distance, along the quiet park.

Then, brakes screeching, he stopped the car suddenly.

"Ive decided to go back tonight," he said. "Where shall I leave you?"

"I'll stay here," I said.

He was looking intently into his hands, as he had done— only yesterday—when he had told me about his son.

I opened the door, got out.

Without a word—and before I could say anything to him— he drove off.

But a distance of only a few feet away, he stopped the car sharply. And he waited there. . . . And with a knifing awareness I thought: *Just as I paused outside of Dave's door!*

Then the car, stopped only for those few decisive moments, roared away along the street.

CITY OF NIGHT

YEARS, YEARS, YEARS AGO, I HAD stared at my dead dog, buried under the littered ground of our barren backyard and dug out again, and I had seen in revulsion the decaying face. Now, as if I had dug beneath the surface of the world, I saw that world's face.

And it was just as hideous.

For many, San Francisco is an escape, in that coffin-shaped state, from the restless neon-forest of Los Angeles.

Its whitewashed, closely pressed houses cuddle each other as if from the chilly invigorating breeze that invades its streets every day around noon, washing them with rain-specked fog almost nightly. In the crystalline mornings, the sky blazes triumphantly clear. Whitewashed, rain-cleansed, breeze-swept, the city itself ascends vigorously in steep hills before diving toward the bay. All this gives San Francisco an aspect of purity—a magnificent impressionistic prettiness. Even its inevitably shabby streets—around Mission, say, or toward the Embarcadero, into Italiantown—exhale that fresh, fresh bay-air.

For me, San Francisco was the inevitable step in that journey toward the loss of innocence. Although I didnt realize it then (telling myself that I was coming here to separate myself —again!—from what had become a guilt-obsessed life; that there was a resurrective atmosphere in San Francisco which would make this possible), I understand now that I came here instead to initiate myself in a further rite which that world would only too willingly expose me to: hinted at subtly the previous time I had been here: when I had explored, but shortly, the netherworld of that city.

And I did get a job. Yet in fairness I must say that, even then, I knew that on the slightest pretext, if any—as before— I would quit.

Looking out the window where I worked on Market Street,

I saw an older man stop to talk to a boy who had been loitering at the corner obviously trying to score. Together, they moved away. Minutes later, I walked out on that job.

Away from those streets, I was wasting my Youth. The end of youth is a kind of death. You die slowly by the process of gnawing discovery. You die too in the gigantic awareness that the miraculous passport given to the young can be ripped away savagely by the enemy Time. . . . Youth is a struggle against—and, paradoxically, therefore a struggle *toward*—death: a suicide of the soul.

Like a repentant lover, I returned to that previous way of life. And so had I come, under the guise of separating myself from Los Angeles, to search, in this seasonless city, under that bright clear cold sky, not only the life I had left behind but a new aspect of it?

And the side of that world I will explore now in San Francisco is one that will scorch my consciousness.

There are, recurrently, things that you realize only in retrospect, things that could have been observed as signals at the time of their occurrence.

So it had been with several of the people I had been with, in New York and Los Angeles, but mostly in that previous time in San Francisco: the urgent whispered sexmutterings ("I am a— . . ." "Make me do— . . ." "Call me a— . . ."). There had been too, as clearly in retrospect, the insistence on pressure at certain moments, the hands reaching for you eagerly pleading for that pressure. . . . The motorcycled bars of Los Angeles. . . . Yet I had not really *wanted* to know.

Buzz is a youngish score in San Francisco, who generally made his pickups at the arcade on Market Street. He was obviously fond of his nickname, which, in its jivy sound, made him feel much closer to the youngmen he picked up than the ordinarily remote score. Among the hustlers, he was well liked. Whether or not Buzz still wanted you sexually after the first time (and he seemed to prefer many people rather than one), you could always count on him. On weekends he would be at the arcade playing the machines with the young vagrants. If someone was hungry and without money, he would give him enough to eat on, without demanding anything back. Unlike those other scores who, their desire satisfied, bitchily try to put you down for the very things that initially attracted them, Buzz was more like a friend.

I was with him two nights (going to the movies, eating with

him, driving around the city in his car) before he came on with me; but at the end of each of those previous nights, he had driven me to the Y on Turk Street, where I was staying, and he would give me money.

On the third night, at his apartment, we made it.

"Have you ever been busted?" he asked me in the morning.

It was a square question, especially since, last night, two youngmen from the arcade had come up to leave some mysteriously acquired things which Buzz had accepted unquestioningly.

"No," I answered.

"Im not coming on square," he said, as if reading my thoughts. "I dont give a damn, myself. The reason I asked is I want you to meet someone who can help you. See, San Francisco isnt like L.A. The street scene here can get pretty mean after a while. This guy I want you to meet—well, you cant have been busted."

The next day he took me to a Turkish bath, to meet the man he had mentioned.

The bath is in one of the seamier sections of the city— down a flight of gray stairs, leading to a small booth where customers pay to get in. I had walked through this area before —one of the hustling bars is nearby—but I had never realized there was such a place: It is almost hidden, gobbled by the other buildings on the street and then it sinks underground. To get to it, you have to know it's here.

Behind the registration booth, a short squat, muscular man of about 40 is working on a ledgerbook. Hes wearing a T-shirt. His arms are covered with a thick mat of black hair, and he looks like a wrestler.

"This is the kid I told you about," Buzz said to him.

"Wait for me in the lounge," the squat man said peremptorily. In the lounge were several couches—a coke machine in one corner, several doors leading to other sections: to a row of whitedoored cubicles, the steam room, the head, the showers. It was not a wellkept place, although it appeared superficially clean. Even the lights were grayish. It looked improvised, as if someone, deciding to open a bath, had merely adapted whatever was readily, cheaply, and most concealedly available.

As I sit there with Buzz, several men walk from one door into another, glancing at us: the customers—older men, starved-eyed youngmen—in towels, the attendants in sweatpants. I notice how different each of the attendants Ive seen

(and they all spoke familiarly to Buzz) is from the other—
markedly dissimilar as if carefully selected as to *type*.

Im struck by the atmosphere of overwhelming debauchery
here—beyond the feeling of the streets and the bars: a fantastic
apparent anonymity as the various attendants and clients move
about, somehow like shadows, lifeless manikin people. . . . It
was as if what revealed itself on the streets and some bars as
at least wild, alive determination had reduced itself here to its
rockbasis, a cold, unquestioned, unquestioning Availability.

The squat man appeared. "We can talk better back here,"
he said, leading us into a small room lined with shelves on
which are stacks of clean towels. "Im sorry I kept you waiting. One of my helpers—I told you—" he said to Buzz "—he
left abruptly—just didnt show up." His voice was incongruous
with the rest of him. He spoke clearly, precisely. He has put
on a pair of black-rimmed glasses and now resembles someone trying to look like an aloof businessman. He stares pen-
etratingly at me. Already I dislike him.

"Do you have a record—other than just being rousted?" he
asked me.

"Why?" I asked him.

"Because I cant hire anyone with a record," he said impatiently.

"Hire?" I asked.

The squat man turns to Buzz exasperatedly. "Didnt you
tell him?"

"Just that I wanted him to meet you," Buzz says.

"Ive got a vacancy here," the squat man goes on officially.
"That kid you sent me—the skinny one," he said to Buzz,
"hes the one that left."

Purposely Im looking blankly at him. He seems uneasy at
my attitude. Buzz notices it.

"Hes all right," he tells the squat man, "Ive known him a
long time." He puts his hand intimately on my shoulder to
emphasize it.

"Umm," the squat man said. "All youve got to do here," he
said to me, "is hand out towels to these guys—keep the place
clean. I dont pay you much. But I leave it up to you how much
you make—on tips."

Im still playing it square, not saying anything.

"You sure this is the guy you told me about on the telephone?" the squat man asked Buzz again impatiently. Buzz
nods. "Look, boy," the squat man says, "I'll tell you straight:
I need a small slender guy something like you—some of these

creeps prefer them; theyre pretty weird; you cant tell what they want. . . ." Hes trying to indicate that he himself is uninterested, disassociating himself from "these creeps"; indicating that hes outside of the scene; that this, to him, is a business. I wonder how Buzz can take it. . . . Several times the squat man twisted a wedding band on his finger, to bring attention to it.

As usual, I react negatively to being appraised that coldly, to being, if only by implication, talked about as if Im not around.

Suddenly, from somewhere beyond this room, theres a shout. The squat man disappeared. We followed him into the lounge. I heard excited voices coming from the cubicles—snatches of talk: "Ive warned you—not so loud!" the squat man is saying. A man emerged from one of the cubicles, going to the head. His nose is bleeding profusely. As he passes us, I see on his oddly smiling face—which he doesnt bother to cover with a hand or a towel—an unmistakable look of pained satisfaction. . . .

Back in the room with the toweled shelves, the squat man says to me: "Well?"

"Well what?" I glare at him, strangely filled with hatred for him.

"I believe youve got it all wrong," he says coldly. "I run a legitimate business. Sometimes things get out of hand. But the cops dont disturb me. It's just that these guys—" again contemptuously "—theyre 'strange'—and they like different types around them." Im still staring at him, enjoying seeing him put on this way. Then I walked toward the door, to leave. "You—" he started and broke off abruptly. "I dont think I'd hire you, you wouldnt do very well here," he said, opening the door—attempting to beat me to the gesture.

Feeling the perversity seething inside me, I shot back at him, aiming at what I knew would be his weakest spot: "Im not your type," I said, watching him blanch.

Outside, Buzz said: "Why did you play square? You wanted to bug him, didnt you?" It wasnt asked in annoyance—almost, instead, in amusement. "You knew the scene. You kept putting him on."

"I hope I didnt screw up anything for you."

"Hell, no. Wanna know something? I kind of dug seeing you put him down. Hell, most of the people hes got there—I got for him. When he needs someone, he calls me. He'd

called me that he needed someone—well—you know—your
type—to replace that kid that left."

"The skinny one," I laughed.

"Why did you play square?" he repeated.

In my mind I could still see clearly the delirious face of
that man with the bleeding nose.

"I don't know," I said.

Throughout the time I will be in San Francisco, I wont see
Buzz again. I'll hear a few days later that he was busted for
"harboring" two youngmen involved in a robbery. . . . People
just disappear, in one way or another. You seldom know what
really happened to anyone, except as your own life may have
touched theirs. . . .

And even then—

The fastidiously dressed man next to me at the Stirrup Club
on Turk Street has been wordlessly drawing on a piece of note-
book paper. Earlier today someone had mentioned this bar to
me, and I had come here for the first time tonight—knowing
what I would find. . . . Now the man slides the paper toward
me.

On it is the lightly outlined figure of a man wearing tall
boots, lovingly and in detail drawn so that they shine. The
figure also wears a wide garrison belt and an open jacket, both
as sharply and shiningly indicated as the boots.

About us in this malebar are a number of men—some
young, others not so young—dressed similarly: black shiny
jackets, boots. The goodlooking ones—and sometimes the not-
so-good-looking ones—pose imperiously for the others ogling
them. Just as the queens become a parody of femininity, many
in this leathered group are parodies of masculinity: posing
stiffly; mirror-practiced looks of disdain nevertheless soliciting
those they seek to attract.

I was ready to push the slip of paper back to the man beside
me, resenting it, when I heard him say: "Thats how you should
be dressed, youngman. Those Wellington boots youre wearing
arent nearly enough. Really, Im a good judge of character."

I faced him for the first time. In his late 30s, he looks like a
college professor. He is obviously trying to suggest elegance.

"I dont know what youre talking about," I said curtly.

"Dont you really?" he said delightedly. "How marvelous!"
He calls the bartender and orders two drinks. "Dont be annoyed," he said, pushing the drink toward me like the

momentary bribe it is. "I merely want to be friendly." He changes the conversation: "How long have you been in our fair San Francisco? . . . Are you working? . . . Where are you staying? . . ." He is trying to determine how aware I am of the scene and whether Im here to score. "You intrigue me," he said, his eyes flirtatious—and the more he speaks, the more effeminately coy he becomes. "Well, of course, a large part of it is that Ive not seen you before—and one grows oh so bored with the same tired nelly faces trying so hard—and so unsuccessfully—to look butch in leather. . . . But there is something else— . . . I wonder," he says cautiously, "if youd care to join me at my home for a drink. I have a bar there," he says to impress me. "We can talk—better—and I would like that." Seeing me hesitating, he says, waving his hand dismissing it impatiently, "Oh, dont worry. Ill make it worth your while."

We sit now on Russian Hill, in his apartment, which, like him, is impeccable. If I stand by the wide window, I can see the city, fog-covered tonight: tiny pinpoints of smothered lights trying to penetrate the mist.

Distrusting his Grand Show, I have asked for the money first —which he gives me unquestioningly.

"You really didnt know why I drew that sketch for you?" he asked me. "Or why I suggested thats what you should wear?"

"No," I said, but of course, vaguely, I did.

He went into another room. When he returned, hes holding a black jacket, high boots, black belt—the same items he had drawn so adoringly in the sketch. "Try them on," he said.

I remember the man on Times Square. But I know that this time I will not be expected to walk around the streets in this man's clothes.

"Please," he coaxed, extending the clothes toward me. A disturbing note—almost a whine—is creeping into his voice.

"I'd rather not," I said.

He shrugs. "Suit yourself. You will eventually. If not with me, with someone else. Remember that." And then burying his finger into the collar of his shirt to exhibit a tiny chain on which dangles an "M," he announced proudly: "Do you know what this means? It means Im a masochist. It means I adore pain." He spoke with alarming aloofness. "It excites me because I really do believe youre new to this—to this aspect of it," he adds. "And the best experiences Ive had are with such people."

In one fierce movement, he planted one of the heavy boots harshly on his crotch, grinding it in savagely. His previous look

—impeccable, composed—disappeared, became rapt. His face contorted ecstatically as he utters a pained *"Ugh!"* And he coaxes me: "Put them on please." His voice has become a complete whine. "Please—? Please command me to do whatever you want!"

I stare fascinated at him.

"Is that a glimmer of interest I detect in your eyes?" he asks me, laughing. The boot is still pinioned between his legs.

"You dont detect anything!' I said angrily.

"I feel cheated, then," he said. "Not because of the money—but because I somehow expected so much of you. . . . Wont you . . . let me . . . Idolize you?" he said slowly. "Won't you be brutal?"

I have always been repelled by pain, either inflicting or receiving it. Why then did I feel a dart of excitement at the man's words? To squelch that feeling, I walked out quickly.

There is a theater on Market Street that changes features daily: One of those enormous swallowing buildings with a dark, dark balcony. Its back rows fill quickly with men, and there is constant movement. The most intimate sexscenes are sometimes played out here, at times in groups gathered like dark vultures. . . .

As I sat down, halfway up the balcony, a man moved hurriedly from another aisle to sit directly beneath me, where my legs were propped on his seat almost straddling his shouders. In a quick movement, he turned his face sideways, brushing the Wellington boots with his tongue. When I didnt move, he got up, startlingly gasped at me:

"I like *mean* sex, I'll pay."

My stomach contracted violently. With excitement? With revulsion? . . . I didnt wait to find out.

Three people haunted me now much like that man whom I had first attempted ' steal from: the man with the bleeding nose, the man with the boot hammered into his crotch, and the man in the theater. . . . I told myself I had seen enough. I stayed away from the Stirrup Club.

In the afternoons, at the Y, I would go to the highest part of the sundeck where you could make it. Late at night, into the mornings, the showers ran unstopping. Eventually it became too hectic, and I moved out of the Y and into an apartment on Bush Street.

Now in the afternoons I would go to Aquatic Park: a short

beach curled along the bay, a section like a truncated stadium
—concrete stairs—where you sit and wait. . . . Other times I
would go to a cliff outside the city—where, walking along a
path that seems completely deserted, you suddenly may discover men intimately locked with each other.

With someone met in that journey through other lives, I
went to Carmel. To Monterey. . . . To Big Sur: craggy awesome cliffs outlined by twisted trees.

Back in San Francisco, to North Beach, usually to the
Raven bar—which, at that time, was the best scoring bar in
the city—especially on weekends, when a queen would go
through a parody of an opera, playing all the female parts.

Market Street by the magazine store, and you stand pretending youre watching the toylike trolley swinging around to
begin its weary ascent up Powell. . . .

Pickup places scattered from the Embarcadero to the fashionable sections of the city. . . .

Walking through North Beach one silver afternoon—a few
blocks beyond a flowered park where people on their lunch-
hours sit in the sun (and where another afternoon a sad drunk
woman, angered when I turned down her offer of a drink,
started yelling hysterically: "He tried to snatch my purse!
Catch him!"), I looked up at the huge statue of a monk before
a church.

And I went into that church.

There were only a few noon people inside. Automatically, I
knelt, crossed myself with the holy water: iron-binding echoes
of childhood you cant shed no matter how you try. Mechani-
cally I said some childhood prayers. It was serene and peaceful
here—yes—but it was also Empty, infinitely Empty. The
painted statues with blind eyes fixed into the air were remote
and distant, like that heaven which doesnt exist. Whatever was
to be found was not in here. It was in the World. . . . I made
the sign of the cross—again embarrassedly—and I walked out.

If I relented now in that journey through this submerged
world, whatever meaning I might have found would evade me
forever.

Now those three haunting faces which had invaded my life
were turning a searchlight into my soul. I had to follow that
penetrating glare no matter where it took me.

NEIL: Masquerade

1

"WILL YOU HAVE SOME TEA?"

The man who has just asked me that question is dressed like this:

In black mounting police pants which cling tightly below the hips revealing squat bowlegs; boots which gleam vitreously and rise at least a foot above his ankles—silver studs forming a triangular design on the tip of each boot, then swirling about the upper part like a wayward-leafed clover.

"One lump or two?"

The belt—futilely trying to squeeze his large stomach (squeezing it—although he was not otherwise excessively fat—to the point where even his breathing has to come in short, sharp gasps) but actually causing it to bulge out insistently over and under it in two sagging, lumpy old tires of flesh—is also black. Looping in waves like a wildly zigzagging snake, the ubiquitous studs (and each silver stud is haloed by tiny gleaming beads) join in front at an enormous buckle at least five inches wide on which is engraved a large malevolently beaked, bead-eyed, spread eagle.

"Do you take cream?"

Over a dark vinyl shirt, he wore a black leather vest, tied crisscross with a long leather strap from his chest to his stomach. On each lapel of the vest is reproduced the triangular clover-leafed pattern as on the boots (and each silver stud, again, is encircled by the beaded haloes). The vest, the shirt, the legs of the pants are so tightly molded on his stubby body that his movements are restricted. Cautiously, he reaches for the teapot, the sugar, cream—each gesture threatening to burst a seam somewhere.

"Perhaps you prefer lemon?"

He himself, when you can pull your gaze from the hypnoti-

245

zing costume in disbelief, is a florid rather short man, in his early 50s. Actually he looks much like what is depicted in American movies as the typical pre-war Bavarian who sits goodhumoredly drinking beer out of a giant stein, bellowing ebulliently in beered-up delight as a blonde-braided girl and a lederhosened man dance to the accompaniment of a merry accordion. . . . But dressed as he is, he resembles a somber, heavily silverlighted Christmas tree.

It is not Halloween.

It isnt even New Year's, and we're not even at a costume party.

No.

We're sitting, instead in the early afternoon, in the living-room of a neat house in a lushly treed area in Oakland, across the bay from San Francisco.

The room is decorated in "antique" style—but of what period, it is impossible to determine. Rather, it seems to have been decorated to suggest an indefinable time somewhere, nebulously, in The Past. Over a bursting metal sun pinned to the wall, are two crossed swords. A shield. A lance. The drapes are wine-purple velvet and droop to the floor in high-lighted folds. There is a small replica of a suit of armor by the brick fireplace. An oriental-looking statue of a monkey is poised as if to spring from a small, arch-legged desk. . . . The sun pours in through a windowed wall in a warm rush of light which accentuates the colors of the chairs, upholstered in striped gold and red, striped silver and blue. . . . It struck me that this room, which is all Ive seen so far of the house, is much like a conglomeration of movie furniture acquired from many period films.

(This is how I happen to be here now, drinking tea, self-consciously, with this man: Only a few nights earlier, at the Stirrup Club, I had noticed a man wearing knee-length boots, a dark leather jacket with a goldsewn insignia of a rapacious bird, a cap much like that of a policeman, and a silver chain around his left shoulder. I asked the person I was with who he was. "Neil," he answered, "the weirdest character in San Francisco. I'd keep away from him if I were you." . . . Later that night, Neil had come over—he knew the man I was with—and introduced himself. Brazenly, he asked me to have lunch with him the next day. Considering him the most ridiculous man I had ever seen—but still greatly intrigued—I said yes.)

"Shall I freshen up your tea?"

"No, thanks, Ive had enough."

"Tea is very invigorating in the afternoon, especially after a big lunch," he insisted curiouslv—and poured out another cup.

It seemed so ludicrous—this hybrid movie-set room (like a small-scale parody, at times, of a medieval chamber, with anachronistic touches of Contemporary California) and the man in the incredible costume—so ludicrously incongruous it all seemed, to sit sinning the carefully laid out tea (and cookies!) from the small lilac-decorated china cups.

Glancing over the teacup, into another room (to avoid looking directly at this man and thereby to thwart his excoriating gaze by not acknowledging it—and throughout lunch he had hardly spoken, concentrating merely on studying me), I catch sight of a foot—just the tip—jutting from behind the slightly open door.

I asked Neil: "Are you alone?"

"Oh, yes! Just you and me—and my cat," he answered, savoring the tea loudly as if to induce me to take mine.

I dismiss the foot, which hasnt moved. It is probably a shoe—or, more likely, a boot—tossed behind the door.

The telephone screams, and I almost drop the cup nervously. Excusing himself, Neil goes into the other room. He steps carefully over the jutting foot as he goes through the door. The door, slightly farther ajar now, reveals, still unmoving, what is definitely a boot.

"Hello?" he answers the telephone. A pause. "Hello?" again. Silence. I hear him hang the telephone up. There is a shuffling sound of moving in that next room. The boot disappears entirely.

"Ive been getting these Mysterious Calls," Neil explained, returning. "At least once a day—sometimes more often. Someone calls up, listens to my voice, doesnt say a word."

"Someone must be trying to bug you," I offered.

"Oh, no!" he exclaimed adamantly, obviating such a simple explanation. "Nothing like that! . . . Im convinced it's someone who just wants to know—*has* to Know!—that someone, somewhere—someone like Me—exists. Eventually," he predicted solemnly, "whoever it is will speak to me, and he'll ask me if he can come up. . . . Oh, you may not know it, but I am rather—well, I'll say it: Why not?" (Except that he said it like this: "Whu-I NOT-" and he shrugged his fleshy shoulders—or, rather, attempted to: The warning stretching sound of the shirt rejected the movement.) "I am rather Famous in California."

"Because of your costumes?"

" 'Dressing up,' " he corrected me coolly, "does not mean wearing *costumes!*" He finished his first cup of tea—offered me another cup, which I refused. "When I spoke to you the other night in the bar," he told me, "it was because I felt a certain propinquity—I mean," he added carefully, "a certain interest."

"You stood out—even in that bar," I said tactfully.

Again, it wasnt what he wanted to hear. "What I mean," he said testily, "is that I felt you were 'ready.' "

"Ready for what?"

He avoided the question mysteriously.

A furry amber cat curled like an ostrich plume about the man's boots, then jumped lithely on his lap. Neil began to stroke the cat absently. In the long silence that followed, I could hear the satisfied purring of the animal as it pressed itself against the leather costume. As if just realizing that he'd been stroking the cat, Neil pushed it away suddenly, thrusting it angrily to the floor. He almost lifted it away with the tip of his boot. "I hate him when he becomes snivelingly affectionate!" he said.

He rose precariously from the chair. The tight costume would not even allow him to walk easily. And when he opened a drawer in the antique desk, he crouched before it uncertainly, rigidly to keep his clothes intact. He brought out a box, removed a key from another smaller box, opened the first, and took out a stack of pictures which he brought over to show me.

I prepared myself. That world, being a world of fleeting contacts, has a great attachment to photographs, as if to lend some permanence to what is usually all too impermanent. But I know before Ive seen them that the ones Neil will show me will be far from ordinary—will, in fact, be a part of a game Im convinced hes playing with me.

Withholding the pictures dramatically, he said proudly.: "These are only some of my Converts. People just Radiate toward me. And I open the world theyve been hunting—hunting, mind you, without even knowing it sometimes. That way, I help them find Themselves." He spoke as if delivering a familiar speech. "You should see some of the ones that come to me—so timid: Just knowing someone like Me exists helps them. Even the first time, they walk out the door differently: Proud. Erect. Glad to be: Men! . . . I lead them carefully. I

open doors for them, slowly. . . . They call me up—I had a
call from a youngman in Seattle the other day. He'd heard
about me, through friends—and he wanted to come down
especially to see me. Why, I get calls all the time from Los
Angeles. . . . And, well, Whu-I NOT?" He attempted another
shrug, again frustrated. Dreamily: "I like to see youngmen
coming out—I like to see them—well, flower out— . . .
Rather," he corrected himself hastily, "I like to see them burst
out *Violently!* And I watch them move in the direction they
were meant to go. Theyre like Disciples, discovering The Way.
. . . Sometimes," he said wistfully, assuming a benign look as
he gathered his hands over the photographs on his lap,
"sometimes—I get the feeling that Im something of a— . . .
yes, something of a Saint."

I look at "The Saint" in the strange costume. His stare challenges mine. With a flourish, he spreads the photographs on a
table before me as proudly as a peacock spreads his tail.

There are youngmen dressed as military officers of long-ago
periods, cowboys, motorcyclists, policemen, pirates, gladiators.
. . . Single, they seem to have menaced the camera. In groups,
they depict scenes of violence. . . . I lay the pictures down
without looking at the rest.

"I took every one of them myself," he sighed.

The cat had returned surreptitiously, winding in and out of
Neil's legs. Again, he shoved it away with his boot, this time
much more violently. He watched as the cat moves away.

"*And now!*" Neil announced. "I'll show you My Real Collection!—the most complete in California—and (Whu-I NOT)
possibly in the United States!—though Ive heard theres a man
near Griffith Park in Los Angeles who has a pretty good collection," he condescended. "His name is— . . . Dan? Stan? Something like that. But Ive been told hes not at *all* like Me!"

He ushered me into the bedroom. When he pushed open the
door, past which I thought I had seen an unmoving foot
earlier, I start.

There are two men in the bedroom: a policeman wearing
sun-glasses and a motorcyclist, legs spread, hands planted on
hips, his head thrust forward as if ready to attack with gloved,
clenched fists.

Seeing me start, Neil laughs. "Theyre manikins!" he announced triumphantly at the deliberate deception. "They look
terribly real, dont they?" He went fondly to the dummy dressed
as a policeman, and he adjusted the cap, to one side; to the
motorcyclist now and changed his stance, lowering the head to

emphasize further the impending thrust. "I prefer this one."
He indicated the motorcyclist. "He looks more—oh, Rough!"

The room has about it a twilight darkness—the same indefinite antiqueness as the living-room. The bed is covered with
a shiny black-leather spread. Creating the illusion of a throne,
a high-backed carved chair faces a three-paneled full-length
mirror. Behind the chair, dark drapes brocaded along the
edges are held back majestically by a gold cord. The furniture
here belongs to that limbo-historical movie period. . . . The
manikins have been sedulously arranged so that their reflections, in the mellow light, are reproduced realistically from a
variety of angles in the mirrors.

"I had them made especially," Neil is explaining, eyeing the
dummies like an infatuated lover. "Theyre not always dressed
this way. I change their clothes to whatever suits my mood. . . .
Incidentally," he added proudly, "most of these clothes Ive
designed Myself (Im a very Talented freelance artist, you
know)—and then I have them custom-made."

Stirring himself out of his awe, he slid open a panel of
doors, displaying an incredible array of costumes—a mesh of
colors, of brocade, studs; jackets, pants, vests. He stands to
one side like a painter undraping his Masterpiece. "Dozens
and dozens and dozens," he points out, "all different sizes, all
different periods!" Beneath the costumes are about fifty pairs
of boots, all kinds, all colors.

From a shelf on top, Neil pulled a large brown leather box,
carefully pushing away stacks of hats (cowboy hats, military
and motorcycle caps; plumed helmets). Inside the box are
whips, leather gloves, handcuffs, straps. He exhibits these like
a woman showing her most precious jewelry—or her trousseau.
"All of this is insured," he explained. . . . He even had a
leather handkerchief.

He returned to the costumes, pulling out a jacket here, a
vest there, a pair of chaps, pants—holding them before me—
his expression rapt; his voice awed (the tone one would use
in a church); his movements ritualistically careful (as a bride
would touch her wedding gown). Throughout this display, he
studies me as he presents each item; awaiting any reaction he
can grasp, any clue as to my interest. I know instantly that I
would like to see myself in these costumes. And he knows it
too. He sighed contentedly.

"Would you like me to dress you up?" he asked me.

I feel suddenly apprehensive, but I dont answer.

"I'll use the very basic this first time, I'll go slowly, nothing too elaborate." He coaxes me like a doctor with a child. "Another time, when Ive studied you more, I'll really show you. This time I'll just open the door just—oh—about a fourth of the way."

He interprets my silence as acquiescence. With sureness, he removes clothes from the closet, becoming progressively more excited as he touches them adoringly, worshipingly, reverently. His trembling hands reject an elaborately studded jacket, which he held treasuringly for a long moment—choosing more "conventional" clothes; admonishing himself: "Not the first time, not the first time"—but vaunting each idolized piece of clothes he nevertheless rejects.

He has forgotten the restrained movements that the clothes hes wearing demand. His shirt is bulging out over his stomach. He has loosened the belt, the vest. Straps dangle. The shirt protrudes in a satanic tail behind him. Hes becoming sadly disheveled. The whole costume sags. Prespiration runs down his flushed face. Hes huffing.

Ritualistically, like a servant who adores his job, whose purpose in life is subservience, he begins to remove my clothes (not as another person might, for the sake of the nakedness emphasizing the sexuality of the act: no, not at all like that: with him, it seems to be the actual act of obeisance that is exciting him). He had led me carefully away from the mirrors. When Im stripped, he doesnt touch my body, hardly even glances at me.

First a pair of skintight black denim pants; a tapered shirt, russet-colored, which he leaves open halfway down my stomach. I wonder what this costume will ultimately be. It seems he is improvising for over-all effect: to create a fantasy which, like the furniture, will merely suggest something rather than be anything specific. . . . A pair of black boots which come to the knees; when he slips the boots onto my feet, his head bends brushing the slick leather with his cheek. . . . Black leather gloves. A hat which arches slightly on the sides. He added a thick large-buckled belt about my waist. Rushing to the leather box in the closet, he removed a long coiled whip, which he planted firmly in my hand. And he announced apocalyptically:

"A plantation overseer!"

Automatically I turn to face the panel of mirrors; but Neil blocks my view quickly. *"Not yet!"* After a few moments, he steps aside dramatically.

"I present you to you—to You as You have always wanted to be," he said solemnly.

Clearly, this is me as *he* wants to see me. But I feel excited by the reflection of myself. Possibly noticing this, Neil stands before me again, once more blacking my reflection, as though my own fascination threatens to shut him out of the fantasy.

"It's just a hint," he said in that awed tone. "Nothing extraordinary. Another time, I'll Really Show You!" I notice his voice is changing strangely. What is he trying to convey by those vaguely recognizable accents?

With a jolt of awareness which almost took my breath I realize that he is now speaking in the slightly slurred Southern sounds of a field hand! My first impulse was to laugh; my next, to remove the clothes and leave this fantastic man.

But Neil is already saying: "Now we're ready. Now we can really begin The Initiation." Like a well-trained acolyte, he bowed. His actions revolt and fascinate me. I am overwhelmed by the ritualistic attention, excited by the image of myself in the mirror. He knows it too. But I am sure hes misinterpreting that excitement, which is merely for *myself* in these clothes, narcissistically, not for what the clothes themselves must represent to him.

He approached me slowly. Fascinatedly, he moved around me, arranging the mirrors so that both of us can see the reflections from different angles; careful, always, to be in the framed image. He led me to the elaborately carved chair before the mirror.

He knelt.

Without warning, he flung himself stomach down on the floor, and now all his actions will become astonishingly feverish. His head burrowed between the boots; his tongue glides hungrily over the glossy surface; his hands caress the leather, reach now for the belt. He looped his fingers urgently behind it. Releasing the belt, his hands move treasuringly down the costume. His mouth gnaws into the opening at the top of one boot, then the other, his teeth cling to the straps inside. Frenziedly, he raised my foot with one hand, turned himself face up on the floor. And he held the boot poised over his face. From his throat emanate gasping groans; his eyes are deliriously wide, as if to magnify the scene beyond his ordinary vision. With one desperate hand, he pressed down on my leg from the knee, attempting to bring the boot against his craving mouth.

Swiftly—angered—I moved away from him—leaving him a shattered heap of studs and leather straps sprawled grotesquely on the floor.

"What's the matter?" he whispered almost inaudibly.

"Im not interested," I said harshly.

As I took off the clothes he had dressed me in, to leave, he eyed me curiously from where he still lay pitifully like a smashed doll on the floor.

2

But I came back.

He indicated not the slightest embarrassment over what had occurred the first time. In fact, he seemed to have been expecting me.

"Im glad you came over. I want to take some photographs of you," he said. Today hes dressed in a vaguely Western costume. "Oh, dont worry—I'll just dress you up for the pictures," he promised. "Nothing else." But he eyed me slyly.

He knows now that I am, at least, intrigued by his masquerade.

When he presents me to myself in the mirror (again: "You as you would like to be!"), Im an exaggerated cowboy, with spurs, chaps. Looking at myself, I feel slightly silly; but soon the seducing attention obliterates the feeling of absurdity: I feed hungrily on his glorified adulation, as Neil, speaking this time in a Western drawl, prepares to take the pictures.

We move into the other room.

The cowboy first. A Prussian officer. A pirate. He poses each scene at the point of arrested violence. A whip in my hand as if about to unfurl at him behind the camera. Boots always prominently displayed. Fists clenched. Body lunging. Now he brings in one of the manikins—heterogeneously "dressed up" —studs, straps, chains. . . . Neil executes—crouched, contorted, sweating—"to get the feel of it," he explained—the cringing positions that the dummy will ultimately assume, menaced, for the pictures. The camera keeps clicking as Neil vacillates from acolyte to High Priest.

"Now I'll improvise!" he exclaimed joyously.

When he was ready to take the picture, he announced triumphantly: "An Executioner!"

And Im standing before the camera in black tights, boots to the hips, a leather vest, a black braided whip in a swirl about the boots. Im surrounded by the shield, the lance, the metal sun, and a long medieval axe propped against the wall.

The shutter closes. . . .

Neil rushed toward me, his eyes begging, and in a terrifying, shaken voice he pleaded with me to execute with the whip the movement which the camera had just frozen.

But I didnt.

He was disappointed and nervous.

Sulkingly, he went about preparing lunch. Then something strange happened: As he stood over the stove, dressed as he was in the Western clothes—and an apron over all of that— he turned to me (dressed now in my own clothes—although he had insisted I leave the "Executioner's" costume on), and he asked me this:

"Tell me truthfully: Do you find me effeminate?"

I studied him as he stood by the stove. That apron over the costume— . . . He was holding the spoon limply in the air. Realizing that, he grasped it tightly. Seeing the look he was throwing at me, exhorting me to say what he wanted to hear, I said: "Of course not, Neil."

"Thank you very much," he said almost humbly.

Shrugging his shoulders, dipping vigorously into whatever he was cooking, he laughed goodhumoredly, looking very much like that ebullient, beer-drinking Bavarian. "One time," he said, "I was walking along Market Street—oh, I was really Dressed Up—a cowboy! And a carload of teenage boys drove by and shouted: 'Hi Tex!' "

I realized the telling of this story amounted to presenting his credentials for "realness." Yes, having seen him in the extreme clothes, I cant help thinking that what hes just presented as proof of his Realness had been, instead, more of a derisively hurled insult. . . . He was waiting for me to comment on the story. When I want, he said: "I *know* I look very Real"—but theres a questioning tone in his voice, as there had been, I remember, in Miss Destiny's when she too had proclaimed her "realness."

We were hardly through lunch when I heard the obstreperous roar of a motorcycle outside, then an insistent knock at the door.

"Damn it!" Neil said, looking out the window. "It's Carl! Whenever hes been drinking, he comes over!" Opening the door, he pretended surprise: "Carl!—how nice to see you!"

Carl, a large, masculine, somewhat goodlooking man in his 30s, strutted in arrogantly in motorcycle clothes. His breath reeked of liquor. "Just seeing how the leather half lives," he said, and sat down—unasked, and much to Neil's evident chagrin.

"Well, of course, Im always glad to see you, but we—" Neil began.

Carl interrupted: "Oh, just pretend Im not here."

"Difficult to do," Neil muttered. Then (and I can almost hear him thinking, "Well, Whu-I NOT?"): "Well. Carl, if you are going to stay—for a little while—you can take some pictures for us. That way I can be in them too."

"Sure . . . sweetie," Carl said. Neil stared warningly at him, evidently annoyed by the endearment.

Now both Neil and I are dressed in cop uniforms, and Neil is going down on me. Now we're cowboys, and hes on the floor begging (not) to be hurt. Now hes in a seventeenth-century costume, and Im a pirate threatening him. . . . He acted out each scene impassionately. . . .

Protesting again when I got into my own clothes, Neil is now dressed in a tight "improvised" costume—boots, belt, straps, glittering studs.

"Dont let him fool you," Neil said maliciously to me when the picturetaking was over and Carl had gone to the head. "Carl's not quite as butch as hes pretending to be. Hes really the end!—but even people like him serve a function. . . .I'll tell you something about him, before he gets back. Sometimes, when he plays the sadist (though hes more often the masochist now), he picks up the nelliest queens—the most effeminate types, types I wouldnt even *talk* to! Theres this one little queen —a chorus boy—who goes around telling about when he went home with Carl. Carl put on a uniform (he has an insignificant collection) and stood menacingly over the little queen and said: 'I am your fuehrer; you do everything I tell you. And the queen—ho-ho—you know what she said to him? She broke her wrist and lisped at Carl: 'Oh, Mary, youre too much!'—and she swished out. You can imagine how Carl avoids her like poison! . . . Youd never believe it, to look at him now, but when a friend first brought Carl over—oh, several years ago—you should have seen him: shy; he wouldnt do anything. But now! . . . Poor Carl—the things that happen to him. . . . I'll tell you something else—very funny—ho,ho! One time he stomped into a bar and slid on some spilled beer. (He drinks a lot now—and for some strange reason, as I say, he always comes here when hes drunk.) Anyway, he slid on the spilled beer and fell with legs up—and the queen was there and she shrieked: 'Highheels and all!' . . . Carl is the one who gave me that silly leather handkerchief. . . . And Carl, in the middle of summer— . . ."

Carl came back. Neil finished tactfully: "In the middle of summer I usually go to Los Angeles to see how things are going. Ive bought many fine items there." Now he turned to Carl, baiting him like this, perhaps to drive him away: "I heard something hilarious, Carl. You know what that little chorus-boy queen told me?—*you* know the one I mean."

Carl blanched.

Neil continued: "She told me that the height of sadism is the sadist who lets the masochist win! Ho, ho, ho!" He laughed raucously like a department store Santa Claus.

Carl, of course, wasnt amused. "Have you heard anything more about your stolen guns, Neil?" he asked. Neil winced. Carl apparently had aimed directly.

"No!" Neil said curtly.

Making himself at home—and smiling for having wounded Neil back in a way which I did not understand—Carl goes to a cabinet and brings out a decanter of wine, begins immediately to drink from it thirstily; and as he drinks, he becomes more pugnacious toward Neil—and his voice will become progressively more highpitched, his gestures airier—hinting, shockingly, because of his masculine appearance, at girlishness.

Turning toward me, Carl startled me by saying this: "You may have discovered this yourself (I dont know how long youve known Mr Neil), but hes insulated himself with his costumes, the way other old men insulate themselves with money—or dirty pictures." It is more than the previous embarrassing reference, by Neil, to the interlude between Carl and the chorus boy—more than the liquor—that is making Carl abandon so swiftly even the barest trace of civility between him and Neil, as though a years-long tacitly undeclared war had at last flared into open conflict. "Thats how youve prepared for your old age, isnt it, darling?" he asked Neil.

Sensing the direction of the conversation, Neil tried to remove the wine, but Carl reached for it quickly, poured out another glass. Resigned to the fact that Carl was staying, Neil said: "Lets take more pictures. I have a good idea for one! . . . And dont call me nelly affectionate names, Carl—Ive warned you before! And dont call them 'costumes'!"

Carl ignores him, goes on flaunting his deeply rooted anger. "Anyway," he says, "Neil lures people with his fantastic make-believe—and in a world— . . ."

Neil: "Why dont you tell us instead about *your* experiences —like with the chorus boy."

"—and in a world like ours that deals, from the beginning, largely in repressed sexdreams," Carl goes on, "Neil fills his sexual needs by attracting others with his— . . . Collection. Look at those boots—the belt— . . ." He shook his head, smiling wryly. "Has he shown you his collection in the basement?" he asks me.

"Carl, Im going to have to ask you to leave," Neil said angrily.

But Carl went on: "Do you know how he makes his contacts?—and, again, I dont know how he met you—" More wine. The masculinity has relaxed into a girlish wistfulness of the face, the body. "Well, sometimes, he advertises sales of leather goods, in the newspapers. Then he makes the people who turn up. Or he invites people over for . . . tea!" He chortles. "Neil is so buried in his fantasy that he cant acknowledge that several of these people come to him to get something else from him—at first: food or whatever—to stay if they dont have a place. . . . Why did you come?" he asked me.

"What youre saying isnt true," Neil said severely. "I get calls from Los Angeles—as far as Seattle—farther!—people wanting to meet me—just to talk to me, see my Collection!"

"Collect?" Carl asked.

Neil: "I said *Collection. My* Collection."

Carl: "I mean the calls from Seattle—are they collect?"

"Prepaid!" Neil said annoyedly. "Although," he added, making Carl smile, "if I help people out, what difference does that make? After all, a convert— . . ."

"Is a convert," Carl finished for him.

"Well, you dont have to talk as if *youre* not!"

Carl asked me: "Has he told you he considers himself a Saint?"

Neil: "I lead people in the direction they want to go. I fulfill— . . ."

Carl raised his glass in a toast. "To Saint Neil of the Leather Jacket!" He said to me: "I was brought over by a . . . 'friend,' and Neil—how do you put it so cleverly, dearheart?—oh, yes! He 'opened the door—a quarter of the way only'—the first time. And all that attention he heaps on you! Whew! And then —then he *pushed* the door open!" He made a harsh gesture of shoving an invisible door. He laughed, straightening up decorously on the chair, realizing he was getting high. "And it was quite a world, Saint Tex—oops!—I mean: Saint Neil of the—

of the— . . . What? Leather Jacket. Thats it: Saint Neil of the Leather Jacket!"

"You were *anxious* to come in, whether you knew it then or not," Neil hurled at him.

"Was I?" Carl said, passing his hand over his eyes for clarity. "It was such a long time ago. . . . Remember, Neil, when you advertised one of your phony sales—and the man called, and he came over with his mother and his wife? He'd probably been warned about you. Did you dress all three up?"

"You know I cant stand women," Neil said icily.

"Thats ruh-hight!" Carl turned to me: "Has Neil recited his poem—scuse me: I mean, speech—about the place of women in the world?"

"Nevermind," said Neil. "Youve been talking enough. Now *I'll* talk." He turned toward me, and I will be startled by the new tone of his voice, his look. He will no longer be the man who only minutes earlier in the pictures assumed the groveling positions. No. Watch him now as he becomes a politician expounding a noble movement; a general indoctrinating his troops.

Standing up—again reciting as if from memory, his voice welling with authority—Neil began: "Yes I do consider myself something of a Saint. The leader of a movement. Ive made Enormous strides here in Oakland and in San Francisco. Why, I practically organized the Stirrup Club—and that coffee shop nearby where all the cyclists go. And Im advancing rapidly in Los Angeles. Just look at all the leather bars there! . . . Yes, a magnificent movement! Previous such movements have failed. Mine wont—because I know The Secret. Youll watch this movement grow—the only truly militant current the world has ever known—and it will carry everything before it." He swept his hand across the air, frightening the cat who at that moment had been approaching him again. "Hitler failed," he said, pronouncing the inevitable name. Chin thrust forward, bowlegs spread, planted firmly like the hands on his flaring hips, he went on: "Yes, Hitler failed. But We will succeed. And women? Women will be out! They represent weakness!—but still they want to dominate their Masters— The Male!" He closes his eyes as if to contain the sudden hatred. "Women are vampires! Vicious, draining bloodsuckers!"

Carl shakes his head: "Listen . . . listen."

Neil: "Women will have but one purpose: to give birth to more of Us. That Is All! They say the great civilizations col-

lapsed when We threatened to take over. Theyve missed the
point. They collapsed because We didnt go to the inevitable
limit: which is complete— . . ."

Carl finishes for him again, as if hes heard it so often he
can tell it himself; he barks mockingly: "Complete acceptance
—right, honeypie? And not only acceptance!—but a rejection
of the other!"

"Exactly!" Neil boomed. "And Im not, of course, talking
about the ordinary world of simpering faggots and lisping
queens that exists now: Theyre weak! Sentimental! They disgust me! . . . Im talking about Power! . . . About a movement
that has had a glorious history. Why, the Marquis de Sade
(the Great! French! Nobleman!)—he and Dr Masoch used
to have some exquisite experiments with each other." His
eyes glimmer relishingly.

Carl comes in killingly: "Neil, Neil, Neil—youve been
wrong all these years: The Marquis de Sade and Masoch didnt
even live at the same time. Youve thrown history together for
your own purposes—something like the way youve done with
the furniture in this house! . . . Masoch wasnt even a masochist, sugarheart." He spills some wine on his chin, pushes it
with a finger into his mouth in a babyish gesture. He sucks
the finger loudly. "As a matter of fact, Saint Nick, they lived
in diff—diffrunt cunt—countries!"

Neil raised his eyebrows in gigantic indignation. His authori-
tative pronouncement is being torpedoed. Hes been talking
down to me, explaining things as if I were a potential convert
—"opening the door" for me. In my having gone as far as I
have into his world—by putting on his costumes and going
through the poses of violence—he thinks he senses, inchoate,
similar cravings in me. . . . But how, I keep wondering, does
he rationalize his talk of supremacy with his sexual subservience?

"At any rate," Neil tries to go on, "it will be the only movement toward the justification—"

"—of Mamma Nature," Carl says, like an impudent student.
He giggles sillily.

"Carl!" Neil says querulously, "dont interrupt me! Im talking *seriously!*" . . . In his imperial tone again: "There are the
weak and there are the strong. Pain is the natural inclination:
The inflicting of pain— . . ."

"And yet you play the masochist?" Carl asks the question
for me.

Visibly cringing, Neil blurts: "Ive explained that to you be-

fore! . . . Seduction! I have to show The Way of Strength—so
that The Movement will continue. Masochists—sadists—even
people like you, Carl!—theyll bring new converts to create
that Glorious Army, of which I—" (He expanded his chest,
the shirt protested, he exhaled.) "—of which *I* will be: The
Leader! Then—and only then—can I assume my Natural
Role!" He calmed down, mopping his perspiring brow with a
black handkerchief. "In my experiments—naturally—I have
to play many parts. I will not always be the—the—" he
blustered, and then he came out with the wrong word, which
he realized the moment he had uttered it: "—the low man,"
he finished. His look mellowed. "Will you have some wine?"
he asked me. "It's very good."

"No, thank you."

"Hummm. . . ." He became suddenly aware that his costume
had become quite hopelessly disarrayed. Urgently, he tried to
arrange it, tucking it here, smoothing it out there. One thing
would go in, another would pop out. He gave up with a loud
sigh of relief. "Still—" he struggled intrepidly once again to
come back philosophically, "youll have to admit, Carl, that
even the great writers—Dostoevsky, for instance—why, Dostoevsky even went so far as to condone murder—he— . . .
why, in— . . ."

"Re!-dem!-shun!" Carl shouted, still melodramatically mimicking Neil's previous tones. "In Dostoevsky, theres always
re-dem-shun at: The End!" He laughed uproariously.

"Well," said Neil, eyeing him meanly, "*you* may think so.
. . . And, well, I can see that theres no use trying to carry on
a Serious Discussion when youre drunk, Carl. And I dont
really see why every time youve been drinking, you come over
here. Everytime— . . ."

"You dont see why?" Carl asked.

"Well," Neil said, the authoritativeness vanishing as he
laughs very loud, shrugs his shoulders in a gesture that is now
becoming for me typical of him (as he always does, I notice,
when he feels trapped or ridiculous), "if you want to come
over when youre drunk, well, whu-I NOT?"

"But—" Carl came in obsessively "—this all started cause I
was going to tell you—way—away, way, way back there—
about Neil and what happened to his precious collection of
guns."

Neil: "Youve said enough, Carl. Ive asked you to leave;
and if you had any— . . ."

"I dont have 'any,'" Carl said. "And I wanna finish, Saint

Neil." He bows and spills the wine again. "Saint Neil of the
Leather Jacket sometimes makes his contacts at the famous
corner of Seventh and Market by the Greyhound bus station.
(Did he meet you there?)" he asked me; not waiting for an
answer, goes on: "And I guess—I guess the word has spread
—not *The* Word, Neil—just the plain old 'word'—has spread,
far and wide, and some youngman usually is there, waiting for
The Saint. There was this one kid recently. How old was he,
Neil? Eighteen? Nineteen? Anyway, Neil thinks hes made a
real conquest: A young kid he can really convert: from
scratch! . . . The kid let him dress him up, and Neil brags to
everyone hes got a Real Convert—the kid looks up to him,
respects him. So what happens? Oh, it's too much to tell!"

"Youre pitiful," sneered Neil.

"So are you, dear," said Carl. . . . "Anyway, Neil is going
through this wild scene; keeps yelling at the kid: 'Harder!
Harder!' (Is this how it happened, honeybunch—or am I con-
jecturing too much from the past?) Anyway, heres where I
come in—literally. I came over, the door is open (very unlike
Neil), and I find Neil on the floor—knocked out cold! The
kid was gone. So was Neil's car. And so—more importantly—
was his priceless collection of guns. . . . Youve started another collection, havent you, Mr Saint? . . . Well, they found
the car, abandoned—but not The Guns."

"That boy," said Neil indignantly, "did not just 'steal' the
guns. He *loved* them so much he *had* to take them."

"Did he also 'love' your cufflinks which he also helped himself to—and the car?" Carl laughed. "Would you believe it?"
he asked me. "Neil wouldnt even tell the cops about the stolen
guns—wouldnt even check the hockshops. He kept insisting
that his own love of costumes—and all the frills—was what
had made that kid steal the guns—that the kid wouldnt ever
sell them or hock them—never part with them, he loved
them so!"

"That dirty little bastard!" Neil blurted uncontrollably, sink-
ing into another of his contradictions at the memory of the
stolen guns. "I brought the little tramp home—hanging around
the Greyhound station—"

" 'Tramp'?—your 'convert'?—who respected you?" Carl
asks sarcastically. "I tell you, Neil, theyve heard about you."

Neil: "—and I brought him home for tea!"

"Tea!" Carl echoes, amused, reaching for the decanter. He
turned to me: "Have you found out why he tries to tank you
up on tea?"

"And *food!*" Neil interrupted. "And I let him stay here. Then he stole my guns. But it wasnt a common, ordinary, everyday robbery, as you seem to think, Carl: He *loved* those guns." The constant seesawing rationalization. . . .

"Everyone in the world has the same loves you have, huh, lovebushel?" Carl asked.

"Well, *you* do!—and Dont You Forget It!" Neil hurled at him.

Carl closed his eyes, sipped the wineglass empty, refilled it. "Their souls—our souls," he sighed.

Neil: "What are you babbling about?"

Carl giggled. "You. Im babbling about you. And Souls!"

"Besides," Neil said absently as if to himself, "he wasnt even any good. He just wanted to lay there—*naked!*"

"You told me he *loved* costumes," said Carl in mock surprise. "And your guns, remember?—he loved those too. You mean, Neil, he just knocked you out—just like that—you werent even going through one of your fantasies?"

"Naked!" said Neil contemptuously.

Carl: "Why do you hate the body so much, Neil?"

The phone rang.

"Hello?" Neil answered. . . . Nothing.

"Your new disciple?" Carl asked when Neil returned.

"One day he'll speak," said Neil pensively.

"Maybe theres lots and lots—and lots of em, Neil—all *women!*" He spat the last word at Neil. "Maybe theres a counter-conspiracy afoot! To drive you may-ad!"

"Shut up, Carl," Neil said.

"You really are a Saint," Carl said.

"You may say it sarcastically—youre so drunk you dont even know what youre saying. But I do bring people out."

"Hes really right about that," Carl says to me. "Have you taken him around yet?" he asks Neil. To me: "He will—if you stick around. (But dont, baby, dont!) He'll take you to the bars —he'll dress you up—he'll show you around. Hes already taken pictures of you! . . . And he'll introduce you to the motorcycle leather-crowd—show you their 'initiations.' The first time I went, they tied one guy up to a post, took turns— . . . The blood was coming, but he was screaming for more!" And still addressing me, he went on: "And then one day, Neil will show you his collection in his studio in the basement." He shuddered. "Did you know, Neil, that once, when I told you there was a guy who hung out in Union Square in leather and you went and sat there three straight nights in a row waiting for him—did you know that I made it up, hoping one of the park regulars would pick you up and really—and seriously—beat the hell out of you?" He says that in a jocular tone, but his eyes are fixed on Neil with unequivocal hatred. "And later," Carl sighs, "when *I* heard of someone new, *I* was waiting for him!"

Neil laughs—but nervously. He comes in illogically, whether to change the subject or whether still obsessed by the kid who had clipped his guns: "Sometimes, you know, sometimes I can still get aroused by the— . . . naked . . . body."

Carl's transformation has become complete: All the masculinity has been drained out of him as if by the liquor. His legs are curling one over the other. The once rigidly held shoulders have softened. The hand that had held the wineglass tightly, now balanced it delicately with two dainty fingers, the others sticking out gracefully curved. His look liddedly mellowed, and he began to thrust flirtatious glances in my direction. "Im Unhappy," he drooled in wine-tones.

"Strength!" Neil shouted, trying to square his shoulders. "Remember, Carl: Strength Is The Only Answer!"

"Strength?" Carl asked dazedly. "You know—know wotI-wan, Neil? Wanna know why Im Unhappy, baby?" he said to me. "Because Ive sunk too far into a world where sex aint even sex no more. . . . They talk about sex without love. What about sex *with* hatred? . . . Oh, it's perfackly—perfuckly—per-fect-ly All Right—per-fect-ly— . . . Start again: It's perfectly okay to be homosexual— . . . Oh, sure. But your world, Neil—your world! Whew!" He stopped; he stared very long at Neil. The drunk hatred melts into an abject smile. "Your world, Neil, where sex and love— . . . Well—love— . . . For-got what I was gonna say," he said. "Oh, yes—but you know why Im Unhappy?" he repeated. "Because—" he said, enunci-ating slowly, "because—I—wanna—wanna—lover. Yes! A Lover! And all this—this motorcycle drag—it doesnt mean shit to me. I'd wear a woman's silk nightie if it got me a Lover," he said.

Neil winced at the blasphemy, as if Carl's remarks had physically wounded him. "Be careful, Carl! Youre talking to *Me!*" he said.

"I know. The Saint." Carl went on: "Yes, I wanna Lover," he said, downing another glass of wine. "If he wants me to be a woman, I'll be the greatest lady since Du Barry. I'll be all things to One man! . . . I—am—lonely." He turned drooping eyes toward me and sighed lonesomely: "Will you join me in a toast?" He lifted the glass of wine; and holding it toward Neil, he said:

"To Saint Neil—from one of his—most—de—de— . . . Devoted— . . . Converts!"

The glass smashed on the floor.

He was still passed out on the couch when I left.

3

When the inevitable happened (which had lurked in my mind, and which at the same time—I am now sure, looking back on it—I had thought to thwart through that very contact with Neil: although I was becoming aware of perhaps the most elaborate of seductions—or, rather, I would become aware of it in retrospect: a seduction, through ego and vanity, of the very soul), when that inevitable happened, it happened swiftly like this:

I found Neil at home one late afternoon watching television: a western; the box set completely out of place in that bedroom suffused with the atmosphere of some dim past. I could tell that watching that program was such a ritual with him that I sat alone in the other room. Through the door, I could see him. He was dressed in full cowboy costume, replete with holster, gun. . . . As the sharp bang-bang! of the television villain's gun burst from the screen, Neil drew his own and made a motion of firing back.

When the program was over, we sat in the bedroom (he pushed the television set out of sight), drinking tea. . . . The manikins stared menacingly. Today, one was a military policeman; the other, whose costume I couldn't make out, was somberly dressed in black.

"We have a fine relationship, dont we?" Neil said.

The statement surprised me. The several times I had been with him since that afternoon with Carl—only briefly for lunch or dinner—I had felt an even greater tension and self-consciousness than before—especially since lately he had begun to talk to me in almost fatherly tones.

"Except," he went on, "that you hold back. Why? I *know* youre intrigued by Violence. I could sense your excitement when I presented you to the mirror. You saw yourself, Then, as you should be—as you would *like* to be!—as you *could* be! Out of my clothes, you know, youre very ordinary—like hundreds and hundreds of others. (Youre really not my cup of tea)," he added cuttingly. "But I can transform you—if you

Let Yourself Go!" he exhorted me forcefully. "Let me!—and I'll open the door—Wide!—for you. Youll exist in My Eyes! I'll be a mirror! . . . Why should we fight our natures, which are meant to be violent?" he went on in the strangely gentle tones. "The past—with its grandeur, its nobility—yes, its purifying Violence—that was the time! It wasnt the 'compassionate' hypocrisy of our feeble day!" he sneered. He rose to add a thicker belt to the dummy in black. (Almost every inch of the dummies is covered, except for the faces.)

He goes on, now speaking about the weak and the strong, how the former are to be used by the latter, extolling violence, drawing pictures of what his world would be like. "Power," he was saying. "Contempt!" he shouted. "Contempt for the weakness of compassion," he derides. . . .

Tense, cold in the warm afternoon, I found myself—although I didnt realize it until he said what he did next—automatically twisting the ring on my finger.

"Who gave you that ring?" he asked abruptly.

I hesitated to answer. Finally I said: "My father—a long time ago." Even to mention my father—to recall the memories of that ring—in the presence of this man suddenly seemed blasphemous.

Neil made a face of supreme disgust, and I felt anger mushrooming inside of me. "Things like that—which people cling to as memories," he said, "it's those things that keep men from realizing their True Nature. My movement will be an upheaval: Nothing is sacred, except Violence and Power. Sentimentality—false memories of tenderness— . . . Fathers, mothers!" he said contemptuously. "That ring you wear as a symbol of—whatever!" he spat.

My anger became hatred for him.

And did he sense this? And had he been counting on this? I didnt have time to consider that, because the scenes that follow will come suddenly like a movie in fast motion.

Suddenly Neil is crouching before me where I am sitting on the bed. He is sliding a pair of thick-soled, high-length studded boots onto my feet. I stare motionless at him as he winds a thick belt about my waist. (*I remember that other man in San Francisco: "You will eventually . . . if not with me, with some one else."*) This time, sensing my immediate mood—the mood he has cunningly put me into and will use—he will not even take the time to "dress me up" completely.

Swiftly he has flung himself on the floor, his head rubbing

over the surface of the boots—the tongue licking them. He rolls on his back. His face looks up pleadingly at me.

Automatically responding (the anger, the hatred like a live gnawing thing inside me)—feeling myself suddenly exploding with that all-enveloping hatred for him *(has he counted on this? does he always?)* and also for what I know I will do at last (senses magnetized on pinpoint), and, too, feeling a tidal-sweeping excitement at the reflections from the mirror which he has carefully moved before the bed so that it records from various angles the multiplied adoration of his face (an adoration augmented shrewdly by the remembered hint, the challenge, of its possible withdrawal: "Out of my costumes you're very ordinary . . .")—his eyes as if about to burst into flame, his tongue like an animal desperate to escape its bondage—I stand over him as he reaches up grasping, urgently opening the fly of my pants.

"Please— . . . On me— . . . Please do it!" he pleaded.

And as the meaning of the tea looms in my mind, I realize suddenly what he wants me to do. But I cant execute the humiliation he now craves. He rushed into the bathroom, turned the water faucets on fullblast. "Do it," he pleads. . . .

The sound of the water, splashing. . . .

The scene reels in all the incomprehensible, impossible images that follow.

A gurgling in his throat—and he rises on his knees, face pressed against the wide belt, which he unbuckled urgently with his teeth. Like a dog retrieving a stick and bringing it back to its master, with his teeth clutching the buckle, he slid the belt out of the pants straps—and he crouched on all fours brandishing the belt before me, dangling it from his mouth extended beggingly toward me. "Use it, use it!" he insisted.

Something inside me had been set aflame, a fire impossible to quench until it has consumed all that it can burn: something aflame with the anger he had counted on. I acted inevitably and as he had wanted all along: I pulled on the belt, which he clung to with his teeth, so that, released, it snapped in a lashing sound against his cheek, leaving its burning imprint. . . . He knelt there, eyes closed, expectantly. . . .

I dropped the belt, which fell coiled beside him, the gleaming studs like staring blind eyes on the floor. . . . He gnaws ravenously on the straps inside the tops of the boots, falls back in one swift movement lying again on the floor as he reaches for my legs with his hands, looping his fingers into the inside straps, bringing one studded boot pushed into his groin. He makes a sound of excruciating pain. Even then, his hands will not release my foot, crushing it into his groin with more pressure. "Harder!" he begs. "Please! *Do It Harder!!!*"

Rocked by currents inside me which sealed off this experience from anything that had ever happened previously to me—aware all the time that it was *I* who was being seduced by *him*—seduced into violence: that using the sensed narcissism in me—and purposely germinating that hatred toward him—he had played with all my hungry needs (magnified by the hint of the withdrawing of attention), had twisted them in order to use them for his purposes, by unfettering the submerged cravings, carried to that inevitable extreme—and disassociating myself from all feelings of pity and compassion, to which—despite the compulsive determination to stamp out all innocence within me and thereby to meet the world in its own savage terms; to leave behind that lulling, esoteric, life-shuttering childhood, that once-cherished place by the window —to which, despite all those things, I had, I know, still clung: to compassion, to pity—and knowing only that this was the moment when I could crush symbolically (as in a dream once in which I had stamped out all the hatred in the world) whatever of innocence still remained in me (crush that and something else—something else surely lurking—but what?—*what!!*) —that at this moment I could prove irrevocably to the hatefully initiating world that I could join its rot, its cruelty—I saw my foot rise over him, then grind violently down as if of its own kinetic volition into that now pleading, most vulnerable part of that man's body. . . .

He let out a howl.

A dreadful sound hurled inhumanly like a bolt out of his throat—a plunging bolt which buried itself instantly within my mind. His face turned to one side as if he would bite the floor in pain. Tears came from his eyes in a sudden deluge which joined the perspiration and turned his face into a gleaming mask of pain. And he sobbed:

"Why . . . hurt? . . . Why . . . do you . . .? I . . . did . . . for you— . . . did everything! . . . Wanted— . . . want— . . . Why? . . . hurt . . . why? . . . Wanted lo— . . ." Clenched teeth choked the word he had been about to utter.

The scene exploded in my mind. I was seized by the greatest revulsion of my whole life—a roiling, then a quick flooding invading my whole being like electricity; a maelstrom of revulsion—for myself, for him, loathing for him, for what he wanted done—loathing for what I was doing.

And hearing the racked baleful sobs which continue ("Why
. . . hurt? . . ." And again the unfinished word: "Wanted—
want lo— . . .")—seeing that writhing pitiful body, the boot
pinioning him to the floor (like a worm! like a helpless worm!
like a helpless worm tortured by children!)—seeing that face
gleaming with tears and sweat—and feeling, myself, as if the
world will now burst in a bright crashing light which will consume us both in judgment—I bent down over him, extending
my hand to him—my foot removed from his scorched groin:
extending my hand to him, to help him up—to help him!—
as if he were the whole howling painracked ugly crushed
mutilated, sad sad crying world, and I could now, at last, in
that moment, by merely extending my hand to him in pity,
help him—and It. Compassion flooded me as turbulently as,
only seconds before, the seducing savagery had rocked me to
my violated soul.

And as the man sobbing on the floor in the disheveled wet
costume saw my hand extended to him in pity, the howling
stopped instantly as if a switch had been turned off within
him, and his look changed to one of ferocious anger.

And he shouted fiercely:

"No, no! Youre not supposed to care!"

4

"I knew youd come back," he said victoriously.

I had walked out on him that day, and I had stayed away
for several days.

"I understand," he said. "In the first stages it can be difficult
—for some. And those are the ones that turn out to be the best.
This time you can use this whip." He brandished a coiled
leather snake. "And if youre ready, I'll show you my 'studio'
in the basement."

He had misunderstood my purpose in coming back—which
was to show him (and to show myself?) that he could never
seduce me in that way again. I knew it irrevocably when I
saw a black costume lying across the leather-spread bed. He
was bent over it folding it to replace it in the closet.

It was the costume, complete with swastika, of a storm
trooper.

"Were you wearing that?" I asked him.

"Yes," he answered proudly. "I wear it only on Special oc-
casions." But a note of nervousness entered his voice as he
said: "Today I went to an Execution."

I blinked incredulously.

"Yes," he repeated with bravado—but he appears even more nervous now. "You heard right: An Execution! If you had been here, you could have witnessed it. My cat—remember the furry one?—he was becoming too weak—constantly simpering, whining. I hate weakness. I despise it. I loathe it. . . . So I executed him."

"You put on that Nazi costume and you—?" I started.

"Yes! And I Exterminated him—as all weakness must be Exterminated! . . . I put that cat out of his absurd sniveling misery!" He went on deliberately: "I put him in a bag, I drowned him in the bathtub!" As soon as hes verbalized what hes done, he appears visibly shaken, as if an emotional rubber-band had been stretched to the point of snapping.

I felt violently sick. . . . The black uniform now being hung adoringly in the closet . . . the flushed face . . . the pitiful lumpy body covered with the absurd clothes . . . the terrifying words. . . . The dummies gazing blankly. . . .

Noticing that I was staring at him with undisguised contempt; surprised to see it so coldly aimed at him; realizing all at once that he had misinterpreted my returning here—and looking tense as if my look of disgust had thrown him unexpectedly off-balance—he blurted:

"There is no excuse for weakness! . . . Once you allow yourself to be touched by it, youre lost! . . . And you may think—like that insidious Carl!—that it's weakness to do—to do the things I do. But remember the importance of Seduction! The Leader of every cause has to set an example, whatever form that takes! He has to show The Way!"

I want to tell him what I see so clearly. I want to say: "Youve rationalized your masochism—masking your own very real weakness." But I merely stare at the posed obdurate face, chin thrust out like the caricature of a repugnant dictator —but a very uncertain dictator somehow.

"You killed that cat," I said finally—still not really believing it; rather, not wanting to.

He sighed wearily. The enormity of what hes done seems slowly to be dawning on him. But he fights back, shaking his head: "Once you let weakness touch you— . . ." he starts; and his whole body begins to tremble instantly, as if his jangled nerves were out of control, rebelling against him. He shook his head as if he were very, very, very tired.

And then he erupted:

"I'll give you an example of what weakness can do!" he

shouts as if to blot out his own guilty thoughts. *"The* Example! My own father! . . . He was weak! . . . But my— . . . mother!" He flung the word out with infinite revulsion. "—that—woman! —that loathsome despicable woman with her hatred of the body— . . . I couldnt go barefoot! I even had to take a bath in the dark! . . . That woman!—*she* knew. *She* was strong— and she used that strength, and she used my father's weak- ness—" He twisted his hands as if wringing out a piece of cloth. "—and she twisted and drained and twisted. And then he—my father—that weak man—would take it out on me— hit *me!"* He flayed himself with the thick belt he had removed from the dark pants. "But I showed him *I* was a Man! I wouldnt run away from him! . . . And he hit me and hit me and hit me with his belt—until I'd pass out." *Whack!*—again the belt against his thigh. He didn't flinch.

"And then I wouldnt even faint any more," he said. "I'd just— . . . let him. . . . And yet," he whispered as if in a trance, "and yet—do you know?—that weak, dreadful man— my father—he— . . . *He wore boots! Boots!*—a symbol of the strength he'd given away so easily, without a fight! *That piti- ful man—dominated by my mother—had the guts to wear Boots!* . . . And then I found the Answer—Strength! . . . And when I found that out, I— . . . You want to know what my first gesture of—of Freedom!—from him and that woman —was?" He threw back his head and roared with pained laughter. He continued as if hypnotized by the remembrance of that ugly past: "I had gone to the movies—secretly because I wasnt even allowed to do that! It was a period picture. . . . And the hero—a strong, handsome, masculine man (every- thing my father wasnt!)—he was wearing Boots too. But on him they were Right: No woman would have dominated *him!* . . . I sat through that movie several times especially for a scene in which that magnificent man was sitting in bed, putting on his Boots! He looped his fingers about the inside straps— and he slipped the boots on! I held my breath. . . . That night, when my father was asleep, I went into his bedroom. I stood looking at him: Even asleep he looked weak and dominated. . . . And staring at my— . . . father!—asleep—I hated him more than ever. I found his boots under the bed. I took them to my room. I got my mother's scissors. *And I snipped the straps off the insides of his boots!"*

He formed two fingers into a V and closed them with finality.

He looked worn out. The studded costume he wore seemed

like a ponderous burden on him. His face dropped toward his hands. Dispassionately, lifelessly, he echoed: "I snipped those straps from the insides of his boots. I cut them off, I stamped on them, I spit on them, I—I— . . ." And then he shouted:

"I pissed on them!"

His voice quavered, broke, halted. He turned his face away from me. His shoulders trembled as if in a sudden cold wind.

"So you see: power and strength—" he began weakly without finishing.

I sat next to him, where he had sunk onto the bed.

But is there anything you can say now to Neil?

It's too late. It's too late.

Through the open door of the bathroom I see a water-soaked bag on the floor.

CITY OF NIGHT

CHICAGO!
(San Francisco . . . the fog . . . the mourning wind . . . the
discovered violence, hatred. . . . I fled California. San
Francisco, which had lured me spuriously with its promise
of renewed life, had withdraw that promise.)

Now it will be Chicago—that savage city like a black fortress
erected against the blue of the sky, the blue of the lake.

And what have I come here to search for?

Something not yet clearly defined which has to do with the
antithesis of Neil's world.

And I'll search again through the labyrinthine world I had
found on Times Square, in downtown Los Angeles, Hollywood,
Market Street. . . .

I stayed in an apartment house on Dearborn next to the
YMCA. . . . And nearby was the beach. And nearby is the
hustling park.

On the beach (which is not so much a beach as a loop of
sanded concrete along the lake—to get to which you walk
through a subway tunnel—lights slanted on one side of the
wall flashing like interrogation lights in your eyes—and you
emerge, somehow guiltily, and see, through cracks in the
cement, weeds and patches of grass struggling to emerge for
one last breath of the expiring-summer air), I will meet a
series of new faces which will be added to the hundreds that
have already paraded through my life.

Near-autumn afternoons spent there waiting to be picked
up. (Behind me, the outline of the wealthy Gold Coast:
luxurious apartments glistening goldenly in the sun—resembl-
ing, for all their plush elegance, clean hospital wards: rows
of giant apartment buildings like monsters ready to march
snobbishly into the lake, their backs haughtily to the rest of
the city as they huddle—healthy and muscular but still somehow afraid—close to each other as if for protection.)

Sometimes, at night, I'll return there. Ghostly waves will seek out life, dashing against the shore (while teenagers swim bravely in the cold water, men fish, couples make love, tramps sleep along the expanse of cement ground). . . . And I wandered along the beach, idly, until someone spoke to me.

But, mostly—at night in that city—I will search the park between Dearborn and Clark: Chicago's Pershing Square, without the almost-healthy indolence of Los Angeles.

This park where in the afternoons the city's old and young vagrants serve their novitiate before the derelict jungles of the city. . . . They gather drearily here in bunches, frantic in the awareness that soon the weather will turn cold.

I watch and listen and join in.

A couple—"just in from L.A."—drink wine to celebrate "two years on the wagon." They offered me a drink from the bottle, and I celebrated with them. Behind us, a lame squirrel looked on quizzically, hobbled among the pigeons on the grass. A shabby, fat middle-aged woman said to her crony: "What good is A Beautiful Body?—it aint got me nothin," as she shifted the hills of her spent flesh. A tramp tells me: "You don gotta worry, boy—youre still Young, still got good hustlin in you—it's when you get my age— . . ." I stop listening, concentrate on a romance sprouting in tatters nearby. (An old man has called to an old woman: "Hey, hon, cummon over —I got somethin forya." She is sitting with him now, as he produces a bottle of cheap wine—and they invade Heaven together, momentarily before the harsh hangover. . . .) As I move away, one harpy in an overcoat grits her teeth and says to no one: "Moody woulda killed him if he'dda kep screwing with me—I mean to tell you, he woulduv." A youngman lies on a bench, asleep, the sun directly in his eyes.

Vagrants bunched like birds over a worm: young vagrants playing "rummy"—which means dice or poker. Their eyes trained to remain on the dice while still watching out for the cops. Trying to defeat Time. . . . As the dice tumble to the walk, a woman, huddled over in a wined-up terror, whines from the wasteland of her memories: "My daddee was— . . . My daddee was— . . ." Seeing me stare at her, she sighs: "You believe me, dont you?" I nod yes.

I begin to feel a hint of what, in expiation, I must find in this city.

Through the night-sheltered park (as, in the breezy night, shadows grapple with each other on the gray walks), a queen completely painted like a woman, wearing a woman's blouse and slacks, parades languidly but still unsurely—past the park-socialist shouting feverishly: "Jesus Christ—not Karl Marx—was the first socialist!"—and the tourist bus, full of middle-aged middle-classed ladies, roars away from the blasphemy as wellfed faces look back through the windows at the park in horrified Disbelief.

Hunting eyes outline the ledges of the park. Malehustlers assume that necessary tough veneer of hoods. After two in the morning, cars still go around the block to choose a paid partner from the stagline.

New in town (and in the waning summerdays, other faces have become familiar and stridently desperate), I splashed on the scene, going from morning to morning—in and out of the different cars that stopped after circling the block. . . . In and out of the different bars (Tommy's where the bartender will pimp for you after hes made it with you; The Cavern, into a pit of malebodies crushed dancing). . . . Back and forth on the streets (Dearborn, Rush)—back to the park, the beach. . . .

And these are some of the faces with which I'll try to blot out the guilt-ridden memory of Neil:

The pale face of a youngman who hands me a written note that says: "I'll pay you $10." I turn to answer him. He shakes his head, indicating hes a deafmute. . . . And about 20 minutes later Im back in the park again. . . . The bony face of the man driving a car around the block, stopping before me. Wordlessly I get in. Wordlessly we make it. . . . The face of the man who took me to his house in Evanston *(and it was here that I had stopped on my way to New York, here that I had felt the restless compulsive anarchy those afternoons walking by the lake with my friend, now gone)*, and afterwards I explored that lake by the University: The waves thrust themselves against the darkened beach. Pinpoints of cigarette lights reveal the standing forms. I make it there. . . . The face with swallowing eyes of the man who follows me out of the Cavern. "You dont have to do anything—just stand," he says. . . .

The faces of two youngmen I think at first are also hustling the park. One is a dancer. I score from both, separately, and the dancer gives me several telephone numbers. But I dont call them: The city—its streets, park, beach—invites me luringly. . . . The face of an oldish man in sandals—and he warns me against clipping him: "Thats *so* cheap!—so I must ask you: Please—dont—clip—me!". . .

The perspiring face of the man who takes me to an Italian

fair, where we're surrounded by dark faces. And he mops his brow and says: "Well, it's all right to *read* about teeming humanity—but to be *surrounded* by it!"—as he pushes his way anxiously out of the fair. . . .

The calculating face of the man I think I'll score from easily; who says: "Youre asking too much. I always smile at you guys, when youre new in town and it's still summer. I just wait for winter—then I can get anyone for hardly anything! . . ."

And the sad face of the score who thanks me afterwards and sighs: "I guess I'll never see you again. The nice ones just disappear—so quickly. It's the mean ones (oh. I get so mad!) that keep coming back like we owe them a living!"

The faces drinking beer at the place of a queen whos picked me up—faces there of three youngmen picked up by the queen's roommate. And released by the beer, the scene turns into a melée of bodies. . . .

And the others not now remembered.

And that search to find some immediate redemptive something to expunge what was discovered in San Francisco took me to the mangled sights of Chicago's hobo jungles.

Madison Street.

The enormous Kemper Insurance Building—a huge gray ugly building a block square along the river. Looming darkly. More than 40 stories high. A great bulwark, a fortress. A large square area windowless—Blind. Almost symbolically it turns its back arrogantly to the west side of Madison.

Cross the bridge.

And West Madison stretches in shabby tatters for blocks of leprous buildings. Networks of fire escapes cling to the crumbling walls like tenacious steel spiderwebs. Intertwined among the transient hotels and the harsh yellow-lighted bars are the missions. Each presents its scrubbed face to the stained desperate faces of the doomed tramps, waiting for the sermon and whatever else theyll get.

I pursued those streets as if hunting ghosts.

In one mission, a deacon-type athletic man, radiating health, shouts: "I got a friend in Jesus!"—while an old tramp, doubled over in a wrecked heap, experiences a religious (drunken-hungry) fit, howling: "Lord, Lord, Lord!"

Men outside pace the fetid street funereally, sleep under parked cars, trucks. I see a man roll onto the street, groaning, while the parade of wined-up zombies passes, ignoring him. Others stand like displaced sentinels; dismal mask-faces hanging lifeless outside of doorways.

Shadows huddle, drinking.

From the street, I looked up into the apartment buildings, into the naked windows of the tiny cubicle-rooms. More haggard faces peering blankly; skinny, maimed bodies of uncaring women in slips; men without shirts. All have the same look: the look of nolonger-questioning, resigned doom.

The world on its knees. . . .

A beat-up old man before me chases a wine bottle along its course into the gutter. He yells at it: "Go on, damya—into the gutter whereya belong. I aint gonna touchya no more."

Instantly, three men jump out of the shadows to retrieve the bottle. Discovering it empty, one smashes it on the filthy street.

I see the terrible cheated eyes.

Other ghosts to pursue through the bandaged jungles.

Beyond the tangle of the elevated, to State Street: carnival street: Tattoo joints; novelty shops (horror masks leering among rubber cobra snakes, masks less hideous than the human ones along the Madison doorways); arcades ("Parisian Movies," "Chauffeur Photos," "Art Films"). Tough girls shoot pool. Sailors stand on corners. Burlesque bars coax you with NO COVER NO MINIMUM. The Gayety Burlesque is featuring Teddy Bare and Borden's Ice Cream.

A tall gaunt man hands me a pamphlet. ARE YOU BORN AGAIN?

And I followed the ghosts into the burlesque theater.

Blondes! redheads! brunettes!—lips liver-colored in the changing light; shouting Ah-haaaaa like cowboys; hands edging toward the hypnotic spot between the legs, resting there caressingly; hips momentarily magnetized, suddenly released, swinging sex around; kneeling. . . . Fingers teasingly exploring the breasts, playfully pinching them, coyly affecting looks of mock pain. . . . G-strings like phosphorescent badges etched across the thighs; spread legs radiating their unfulfilled invitation; breasts like searchlights, completely uncovered; apocalyptically revealed pink-crowned nipples, presented cupped in white hands like an offering to the hungry audience; breasts bouncing playfully, jiggling temptingly like white-jelly. . . . *Night Train* from the jungle of exhibitionistic sex. . . . Hands at the back, naked breasts pointing Heavenward; tensed stomachs forming a tight "8"; legs arched open; fingers

sliding into G-strings; thighs thrust out groaningly simulating
orgasm.

Hungry unfulfilled eyes in the male audience, focused on
the promised but unattainable. . . .

Pursuing ghosts through Negro streets. . . .

Under the elevated at 63rd and Cottage Grove: nearby:
The Temple of Brotherly Love. A cross proclaims:
GOD'S CORNER.

And GOD'S CORNER is a tangled glob of steel tracks
thundering with the roar of trains. . . . I see only Negro faces
for blocks in that area. Jukeboxes shouting. . . . Vainly, the
afternoon sun tries to pierce the tracks into the street.

Wells.

Oak.

Franklin. Thirty-fifth.

Negro streets at night.

Past black faces staring through curtainless windows into
the dark streets . . . Negroes swallowed by the merciful dark.
Into the street—into torn porches—they escape out of tiny
cramped rooms, the dark stairways like mazetunnels through
the open doors. . . . A little Negro girl asks me derisively:
"Hey, mister, ain I seen you on TV?" In the hot nightair,
I feel the resentful stares. The silence explodes into laughter
coming from somewhere within the crushed darkness.

Pursuing ghosts on Clark Street. . . .

Panorama of ripped sights along the rows of ubiquitous loan
shops, poolrooms, "bargain" centers, billiard halls, cheap
moviehouses. Zombies in a ritualistic hungover imitation of
life. Men staring dumbly at nothing. A body lies unnoticed in
a heap by a doorway. An epileptic woman totters along the
block. . . . Staring startled eyes. Mutilated harpies wobble
along the street—past crippled bodies. A man beats a woman
ruthlessly as the man's two husky friends stand guard over
the scene.

NO DOGS OR OTHER ANIMALS—a sign warns outside
of a bar.

And I search through the ghosts at the Shamrock. . . . A
ripped bar with tables, tough outcast faces. One woman passes
out on the floor with a long, desperate sigh. A man slides a
glass of beer toward her. Instantly, she awakens—reaches for
the beer, guzzles it, passes out again.

Outside. . . .

Skeletons gaze through apartment windows down into the

street. *As if their gazes were somehow aimed directly at me in horrible judgment!*

Fun in Hell!

The Kings Palace on Clark Street. A skeleton awning (no canvas) and a drawing outside of what could be a mangled clown. . . . Inside, a huge dirty square hall with two oval bars —those harsh lights which only derelicts with nothing left to hide can stand for long. On the walls, faded paintings hinting of faraway Escape: sailboats, palmtrees, cactusplants, leis.

Hybrid of all the tarnished fugitives of America.

From a tiny improvised stage a mustached round man announces: "The Amateur Talent Show!" . . . First prize: Five Magic Dollars! It can buy much magic wine. . . .

A woman who looks like Mrs Haversham of *Great Expectations* sits woodenly like an elaborate stuffed bird with open eyes. On the stage a gravel-voiced man tries to sing: "Enjoy yourself, it's later than you think." A tramp nods, agreeing. A skinny old woman sits at the bar, sticking out her tongue at the world. A drunk man shoves a woman through a door with a sign that says PRIVATE KEEP OUT. She doesnt come out.

"Enjoy yourself—it's later than you think— . . ."

And while the man goes on trying to sing, a Negro fairy goes through the motions of a strip; and like an Indian doing a frantic war-dance, a harpy rocks and rolls about the neon-flashing jukebox—a badge across her desiccated breast proclaiming her name pitifully: "BEATRICE."

Mrs Haversham has rousted herself onto the stage to strum a guitar, producing an anarchy of sounds. A sadfaced man, surprisingly welldressed, guiltily buys drinks for all the derelicts around him, while a sullen old woman huddles against a cubicle, menacing with a fist anyone who approaches her.

"Beatrice," now on the stage, hopped like a puppet.

A fat old fairy stares longingly at the young drifters and bursts uncontrollably into tears, the sound of his crying drowned (his pain reduced to paroxysmal pantomime) by a brownfaced man who howls like an Indian as Beatrice hops loose-limbly on the stage. . . .

A mountainous woman calls out to a man across the bar: "Wottayalookinat?" "You, honey, I wanna kiss you." "Kiss-my ass!" she roars (and Beatrice, still on the stage, wiggles hers for emphasis). "Okay," the man says, getting up, "where?" The fat woman shakes her giant butt: "Cant miss it, baby," she says, "Im ALL ass." . . . Still hopping convulsively, Beatrice is ushered off the stage by the announcer.

A fastidious man, in elegant tatters, sends back his beer because the glass is dirty. The waiter stares incredulously at him.

Next on the stage are two skinny drunk men, leaning on each other singing plaintively: "Those far away places— . . ." Like a chipped record, repeating: "Far, far, farrrrr away places— . . . Far away— . . ." And cant go on.

A Negro woman, perched like a crow on a stool next to a tattooed sailor, feels suddenly beautiful at his attentions (she smiles, rolls her round eyes in pleasure) as he strokes her butt, which she squirms deliriously—but stops its movements abruptly at the thud of the two drunk men collapsing on the stage.

Against a wall a faded blonde woman—an exiled angel, the hints of beauty still lingering on her palewhite face—sits with blackoutlined eyes burning into the bar. A young tramp, drunk —the mark of premature doom stamped on his face which resembles James Dean's (1 have seen him before—hustling Main Street in Los Angeles—but he looked much younger then)—offers her a beer, paid for with a few coins I saw him clinch only moments earlier from the Negro fairy. The woman takes the beer wordlessly, her gaze piercingly buried beyond the bar.

Now on the stage a fleshy woman is trying to do a bellydance. Someone hooted: "TAKE HER OFF!" and misinterpreting the harsh command, she began to do a strip. . . .

The boy who looks like James Dean touches the faded blonde woman intimately between her thighs. She turns in demented raging fury, ready to slap him. He hurls the beer at her in a stream. "Dirty whoor," he yelled, "huccome you don wanna screw with me?" He slaps her. She smashes the beer bottle on the counter, threatens him with the sharp glassy teeth. He runs out. Someone calls: "Go join the army!"

Next in the competition on the stage is a giant of a man, introduced as "The Growling Bear." In a cracked, beerslurred voice, he begins to sing. Noticing the lack of response, in desperation (the five dollars! . . . the wine! . . .), he sprawls on all fours, pretends to be an animal, baving, while the master of ceremonies, trying to inject something of comedy into the tragic moment, hops on him.

Now the gigantic man groans like a dying animal.

I didnt wait to find out who had won The Prize.

Outside, I walked along the bleeding nightstreet, toward the park. . . . The faces of hustlers and scores . . . queens. Always waiting.

And I walked, that night, along the impassive nightlake—northward beyond the couples making love under the silhouetted trees. . . . Along the dark lake. . . . And I looked back toward the magnificent Chicago skyline: that magic cyclorama embracing the water. Even the buildings which earlier seemed like giants marching snobbishly into the lake, now softened, blended into a glittering network of lights, lighted checkerboard. . . . Black and mysterious, the water trembles toward the shore uncertainly. A distant light shatters the black water in a shimmering streak. . . . A man who has been following me propositions me. I say no. As he moves away, I stare beyond, along the drive, where cars move as if in slow motion along streetlights strung blue-white in a curve.

And I see:

Dominating the skyline, at the top of a tall building, a giant searchlight scanning the city.

It glides eerily, swirls over the black water. It floats, soars above the skyline, encircles the nightcity.

And crazily excited I wonder suddenly if that spotlight swirling nightly is not trying somehow to embrace it all—to embrace that fusion of savage contradictions within this legend called America.

And I know what it is I have searched beyond Neil's immediate world of sought pain—something momentarily lost—something found again in the park, the fugitive rooms, the derelict jungles: the world of uninvited, unasked-for pain . . . found now, liberatingly, even in the memory of Neil himself.

And I could think in that moment, for the first time really:

It's possible to hate the filthy world and still love it with an abstract pitying love.

Part Four

"In the land of dreamy scenes
There's a garden of Eden. . . ."

—*'Way Down Yonder in New Orleans*

CITY OF NIGHT

EACH YEAR, NEAR THE EARLY PART of January, a strange exodus prepares to depart from the Cities of Night. From East to West, a private call will murmur throughout the darkcities.

Along Times Square, in the midst of the dogged winter, when the wind lashes at the concrete City like an icy scythe, the tattered army of young vagrants will raise their collars shelteringly and receive the calling. . . . In the warm palm-treed Los Angeles nights, restlessly they will feel the secret excitement. In Harry's, Wally's. Along the Main-Street-blocks-long arcade. In Pershing Square. Along winking Hollywood Boulevard. At Hooper's in the stale greasy light. . . . On Market Street in dewy San Francisco, from Seventh Street to the magazine store at Powell, as they stand perhaps in the drizzle, fugitive spirits will respond to that now-faint message soon to become drummingly insistent. . . . In Chicago, along Clark Street. In the Square—as they huddle indolently in the frozen night for a car to stop and someone to ask if you want a Ride—that call will whisper to the outcasts like wind from the deserted concrete lake. Along Division Street. In the bars. . . . Sweeping through the other nightcities, the beckoning becomes louder.

And the summoning words are these:

Mardi Gras!

By early January, say (depending on when Lent will begin that year, and therefore Mardi Gras), lean young faces will dot the white-winter highways, fingers will point in the direction of Away, New Orleans. In the Greyhound buses headed South, youngmen with maybe guitars and patched bags if any will eye the young girls reading *True Confessions*. . . . Quilted jalopies will tackle the highways of many-masked America.

The exodus has begun.

Slightly later, the second wave of fugitives will have felt the stirring of this call to brief Freedom. New Orleans is now the Pied Piper playing a multikeyed tune to varikeyed ears. In those same darkcities equally restless queens, wringing from their exiled lives each drop of rebellion, will feel the strange excitement. ("My dear, the Most Fabulous Drags in the *world* go there," you will hear them say, "and the simply *butchest* numbers—and all kinds of rich daddies so tired of their frigid wives theyll pay *High* for making it with a *Queen!*")

And with much more care and planning than that of the initial wave of masculine vagrants, the queens (prematurely sentenced to a purgatory of half-male, half-female) will begin their fe-male plans, selecting their women's clothes Lovingly. The golden image of at last being Women—for that one glorious day!—of not possibly hassling getting busted (as they were in New York, Los Angeles, Points In Between)—is a fulfilled daydream in which The Newsreel Cameras—The Eyes and Ears of The World—will focus on *them*. Hips siren curved, wrists lily-delicately broken, they will stare in defiant demureness from theater screens and home screens all over the country; and those painted malefaces will challenge—and, Maybe, for an instant, be acknowledged by—the despising, arrogant, apathetic world that produced them and exiled them.

Amid the swishing of taffeta and rayon drag, the queens will now join the Pageant.

Still later, the third and more comfortable wave of this exodus (the tired richmen, the tired richwomen, the not-so-rich but tired men and the not-so-rich but equally tired women—and the other Young men and women—equally curious but not as defiant as the vagrants of the first and second waves) will feel the call of Shrove Tuesday.

And now!

Airplanes will zoom across the heavens. Telegraph wires will buzz for hotel reservations. Into this old, old city, trains will grind past backyards and waiting impatient lines of cars . . . will dash past the awesome scenery of America. In comfortable automobiles, in busloads of carefully chartered tours—along the whooshing winter-purified highways, they will come to join this determined pilgrimage to Frantic Happiness.

Now the exodus will be complete.

With the clamor of this strange invasion, New Orleans will awaken from its feudal memories of Romance to become the center of our desperate Today: a microcosmic arena of the electric nightworld **Aware of the** triumph of loneliness and death.

A religious ritual will take place in this rotting Southern city.

To New Orleans:
Riding on a sea of faces in an army of cars and buses—away from Chicago and the mortally bleeding streets (with stops in St. Louis and Dallas, again—briefly) and hanging in haggard busstations inevitably in the starless dawnhours. . . .

Now at last in New Orleans, in the bright sun of this winterwarm city, I stand outside the Greyhound station where Ive left my bag, and I wonder where to go.

Canal Street lengthens before me—perhaps the widest street I have ever seen. The day was clear. I walked along that wide, store-crowded street, hearing the drawls of the people. The day became slowly grayer—the Southern pall of clouds enshrouding the sky.

I have to find a place to stay—alone—to separate myself when, predictably, the seething world will become intolerable: a place where I can find a lone symbolic Mirror.

I pass through the open door of one of the walls shutting in a courtyard—to ask about a room. The building, constructed like a tenement about the small square yard—which is paradoxically green with plants and trees—is all small balconies, like wooden hammocks sagging resignedly in the middle. The apartments huddle about the garden as if possessively claiming it from the gray streets.

The landlady wasnt in. I knocked at the neighboring door, which was open. A man is painting inside on an enormous canvas: color-smeared, savagely Red, yellow; swatches of black, inkily smeared at the edges, creating tentacles from a solidly dark body—a hungry giant insect groveling on a violent vortex of colors. "Y'ant gonna fine a place now," he tells me. "Too close to Mardi Gras. Shoot, man, rents go up to fifty bucks a day. People sleepin in cars, on the streets. Better fine you someone to shack with," he advises me. Aware that I was staring at the savage painting, he drawled: "This heres a picture of Nawleans." . . . And he slashed at the canvas in a purple, dripping stroke. . . .

Now walking along that punctured area of old New Orleans, I see those famous hints of a world that disappeared long ago: depicted, sheltered like a precious memory, in books: a world that left merely the remnants of what may have been; a city scarred by memories of an elegance and gentility which may never have existed.

A ghost city.

The streets narrow, as if the ocean world of cities has now taken the slower, more sluggish avenues of a crooked river. Attempting futilely to hide beyond the closed doors of courtyards, beyond the grilled ironwork that still surrounds some balconies like rusted spiderwebs, houses drunkenly lopsided (leaning toward the streets as if, given half a chance, in a rubble of wood and stone and oxidated grillwork, they will topple vindictively over those on the other side) hover over the courtyard walls like grotesque, indomitable, painted old women peering into the streets.

Ugly dank places—the ones they call Enchanting in the travel folders; houses tenebrously rising in tiers of shuttered windows above shredded walls; the pallid historical buildings from a timepast of gilded elegance. . . . An almost Biblical feeling of Doom—of the city about to be destroyed, razed, toppled—assaults you. The odor of something stagnant permeates the winter-air of this summercity: not so much an odor that attacks the sense of smell as one that raids the mind. . . . The invitation to dissipate is everywhere. And you wonder how this city has withstood so long the ravenous vermin—the rats, cockroaches which surely hibernate here even in winter. And you wonder how one single match or cigarette has failed to create that holocaust which will consume it to its very gutters. . . .

About Jackson Square, portrait artists line the walks into Pirates Alley, imprisoning on paper the pastel smiles of tourists. General Jackson's stone horse, in the center of the square, seems to balk at the sight.

"Let me draw you, honey," a woman coaxed me. In a whisper she adds: "I'll do it for free"—obviously because all the other portraitmakers are occupied, at $2, $5, and $7 a head, and she feels so Lonesome and Ugly—so lonesome and Unwanted. But I walk instead through the blocks of fish-redolent, color-splashed French Market nearby; along the docks—wondering exactly why I have come to this city.

This decaying city has a hypnotic aspect that leads me through its streets: this city in preparation—I think suddenly (and I stare at St Louis Cathedral, which looms like a gray fortress barricaded for War)—for the confessional ritual before Ash Wednesday.

Before a candy shop in a shabby district, a stuffed black-mammy has a punctured breast revealing very white cotton insides.

An ovaled man has been following me for about a block. I cross quickly, avoiding him. I feel genuinely indifferent to that scene right now. Im churning inside with the implied mysteries of this physically moribund city; and therefore feeling as vitally alive as a child pretending for a moment to be dead, my emotions seesawing from anticipation to revulsion. . . . Seeing that I was about to dodge him, the ovaled man walked faster until he caught up with me. "If yew come to muh house," he says in a thick Southern drawl which I have a feeling he emphasizes purposely, "Ahll make it wuhth yuh while, suguh."

I shrugged, but I went with him to a house on Esplanade. The ovaled man is a parody of The Degenerate Southern Woman. In the apartment, he came on quickly. Just as Im leaving, another youngman comes up the stairs. He appears very distraught when he sees me. He looked masculine, but he acts effeminate. Behind me, I hear him and the ovaled man shouting angrily at each other. The younger one ran back into the street, crying—almost bumped into me. The ovaled one came to where I was standing.

"Thay-at was muh lovuh!" he howls at me. "Ah didn think hed come bayack this aftuhnoon." His hands flutter like an electric fan on "high." "Oh, What Am Ah Going To Dew?— hes gawn—you heah?—he is gaw-on!—an for sure this time! Hes warned me—if Ah bring any tramps up, he'll —. . . Ah don mean tramps, suguh—" mellowing "—Ah only may-ent —well, yew know— . . . Oh, please do come bay-ack into thuh house till Ah can com-*pose* muhself from this Or-*dee*-yall!"

I went back with him largely because he was yelling so loudly and insistently that I was afraid he'd begin to attract attention. Already, a fat woman sweeping the dirty walk before her house was leering at us with a browntoothed, hateful grin.

Back inside, the man whines: "See, suguh, when Ah first met him, he was re-al masculine—then he turns femme on me, jest lak thay-at: ovuhnight. An Ah think: Muh God, Muhciful Jaysus! What am Ah gonna do with a queen on muh hands! Yew know: He turns swish ovuhnight—jest the way yew saw him jest now—swishin like a ballerina. When Ah met him, he was hustlin the Quartuh too—the butchest, straightest numbuh y'evuh laid yuh eyes on, Ah wanna tell yew. Now look at him," he said in abject exasperation, "a walkin camp if th'evuh was one! An, hon, yewve been Around, Ah can tell—an yew know that the lay-ast thing in the world a queen wants is to make it with what turns out to be huh sistuh—why, it is lew-rid and un-nay-tural as well—it's—well, Ah dont care what anybody says: It's exayactly lak bumpin pussies an thay-ats what it is lak—period! . . . So when he turned femme, Ah, nay-turally, yew know, started lookin aroun for othuh butch numbuhs —he was too effeyminate for me now—but Ah don want him to go away—completely. Ah guess Ah kinda got used to havin her around." He stopped sobbing. "In a way, maybe, it's bay-est all aroun—he can fine huhself a husband an let me fine muhself one—an yew know, too, we didn get along— . . ." He started to come on with me again. His teary cheeks are moistening my pants. I put him off.

He says: "Well, yew listen heuh, suguh, now that hes gawn, maybe yewd like to move in with me?" It was certainly, I want to tell you, short-lived remorse over the crushed romance.

"She'll come back," I said absently.

Wrong thing. "Well, yew dont have to rub it in an call her 'she'—Ah mean, call her 'him'—oh, day-am!—whatevuh the hell Ah mean: Ahm so Distracted Ahm outta muh fruit mind!"

"He'll come back," I corrected myself.

Still the wrong thing. He pouted. "Well, Ah jest wanna tell yew, honey, rought this minute, Ah do certainly hope yew are very wrong indeed!"

As I went down the stairs into the street, I saw the masculine-looking, feminine-acting youngman walking sheepishly back toward the ovaled-one's apartment. Then I heard the older one shout melodramatically:

"Honey, Ah jest cay-ant live without yew!"

"Youngman!"

I cant tell where the woman's voice is coming from. Im not even sure Im being addressed.

"Yes, *you!* . . . Youngman. I have an Important Message for you!"

I noticed a door slightly ajar, in a small house with a narrow porch. The door opens. A gaudily braceleted hand summons me to the porch. Swarthy-skinned, about 40, a gypsy woman stood there, a flowered bandanna around her head; dangling gleaming earrings, at least five bracelets tawdrily rainbowing each hand; rings—which she exhibits by holding her fingers open. "Come in." I hesitated. Her eyes are so light they look impossible in the dark skin, as if whoever made her had used too much color on her face and had to compensate with the colorless eyes. "I have an Important Message for you," she persisted.

"Youve got me confused with someone else."

"No. It's for *You*. Come in," she coaxed.

Impulsively I walked into a littered room. Although the day is warm, a fire is burning in a sooty fireplace. The room is excessively hot, closed.

"Just got into town, didn't you, boy?" she asked me.

I nodded.

"See!" she exclaimed proudly. "I *know!*"

There are several couches about the room—all upholstered noticeably amateurishly in bright flowered prints. On the dirty peeling wall was a spiritualist chart—the words LOVE, DEATH, DESIRE, HATE, WEALTH prominent in the beehive map of life. In the center of the room is a table, draped in a screamingly bright serape.

"I been waiting for you," she said mysteriously, pressing her spangled hands to her forehead, posing at intense concentration. Now she takes my hand. I pulled it away instinctively.

"I aint gonna charge you nothin," she says. She reaches again for my hand. "Whatsamatter? Afraid of The Unknown?" She fixes the bizarre eyes on me.

Feeling challenged, I relaxed my hand. Truthfully, she did frighten me, but I watch her coolly as she studies my palm.

"You can get Lost mighty bad," she warned, staring into my hand. "I dont mean lost in the streets or in the Quarter. I mean: Lost deep down. Inside. In your Soul. . . . This is an evil city, boy."

She smells rotten. The heat, the odor of stale food, imprisoned for days in this airless room, the closeness to this filthy woman, nauseate me.

An urchin-boy was standing by the door, picking pecans out of a sticky praline. Now he moves next to me, peering into my palm too. He smells like the woman—his mother, Im convinced: He has the same colorless eyes in the extravagantly brown face. With sugargrimy hands he took my palm. I feel the sticky substance gluing our hands together.

"Evil city, boy," he echoes the woman.

And the woman: "He got Powers too. See, he know!"

"Thanks for warning me," I said, forcing my hand away.

I walked to the door—the rancid air is choking me.

"You wanna stay here?" she asked me. "Lotsa space—see?" She indicates the cluttered room. She can tell Im not interested. "New Orleans is Evil, boy," she warns me again coaxingly.

"I got Powers. They can protect you. You wanna stay here?"

"Im staying with a friend," I lied.

"Your palm says be careful," she insisted, reaching again urgently for my hand. "See?—here it is." With a long-nailed, heavily ringed finger, she outlined a sign on my hand.

The little boy repeats: "Evil city, boy."

"I told you: Im staying with a friend," I said.

"Wont do!" the woman said, shaking her head urgently.

"Ive got to go now," I said.

"Look here," she said, and her voice was no longer sinister; matter-of-fact now, almost business-like now. "I got a real good easy deal for you. Im gonna offer you a job."

"Im not looking for a job," I told her, regretting my words instantly, because shes looking at me knowingly, pegging me.

"Dont have to tell me that," she said. "I know. . . . Im gonna make it easy for you, though. Gonna offer you a good job. . . . Mardi Gras, thats the time to scoop up the money!" She snatched at the table to emphasize the promised ease.

"How?"

"Every way. We decide how. I'll teach you. You grab em!" Thrusting out her hand, she grabbed me by the arm. Now the blank eyes nail me knowingly, and I resented it. "Dont play innocent with me, boy!" she warned, her hand gripping my arm, the long nails almost piercing my flesh. "Save the act for them others," she said contemptuously.

I thrust her arm away angrily.

"Innocence," she whispered. "Innocence may be all right for those that got it. Us that lost it aint never gonna get it back." For a long while she remained silent, staring into my eyes; then, bluntly, she said: "You bring em here. We score—one way or another."

"If I wanted to do that," I said cautiously, trying to keep from showing anger at her sureness, "I'd do it on my own."

"Let me tell you something, smart boy," she said. "I been in the Quarter for years. How long you been here—few hours?"

She threw back her head and laughed raucously. The laughter booms through the room. The earrings glittered crazily in the light from the fireplace, tiny dots stabbing at my eyes in the semidarkness.

"Smart, smart, smart *dumb* boy!" she chortled sinisterly.

I felt angry, but I smiled. "Youve got me all wrong, lady—despite your . . . powers."

"Go ahead—laugh," she said. Then, narrowing the colorless

eyes: almost vindictively, almost as if it were a curse aimed directly at me, she said:

"This is The Message, bright boy: Mardi Gras aint just any old carnival. Them others got it all wrong. Im gonna tell you The Real Truth: People wear masks three hundred and sixty-four days a year. Mardi Gras, they wear their own faces! What you think is masks is really— . . . *Themselves!*" She seemed to be about to spring at me, her face mere inches from mine. "Witches!" she shouted at me. "Devils! Cannibals! Vampires! Clowns—lots of em. . . . And some—" she said, relenting slightly, "just some, mind you: some— . . . *angels! . . .*"

Her strange sudden laughter followed me into the street.

SYLVIA: All My
Saintly Children

1

IN THE MIDST OF THE FRENCH QUARTER, and above the trees
of Jackson Square, the steeples of St Louis Cathedral, threatening Escape into Heaven, thrust crosses bravely into the sky,
the highest a vague icy outline, the frozen ghosts of a cross
from the distance—but slenderly erect overlooking with
heavenly indifference—from that summery winter sky etched
delicately with spider-grilled outlines from the city's balconies
—the sprawling casbah world of the French Quarter.

Even those of us who have just arrived sense it immediately—that invisible boundary enclosing a square area bordered,
arbitrarily, by Canal and Esplanade on parallel sides, Burgun-
dy and Decatur perpendicular to them.

The funereally tolling bells of the Cathedral reverberate insistently into the courtyards and the bars, the coffeehouses
and the restaurants. Like the tolled warning to Judgment
which Miss Destiny had imagined, they summon the in-
habitants of the French Quarter into a constant jolting awareness of their grillcaged world.

Not far from the Cathedral—so that you can almost feel
the vibrations of the pealing bells—there is a bar called The
Rocking Times: a small square bar with two entrances: one
from the street, the other from an alley leading through a
bricked, potted courtyard into a narrow corridor (from which
the head branches off, a dark cave with the ubiquitous sex-
drawings, sexpleadings) and into the bar.

Only minutes earlier, walking through the Quarter in the
yellowing afternoon (after I had luckily found a room at the
Y in this already-jammed city, arriving there at the exact moment when someone was making a hurried, angry exit: a room
to which I will return only periodically when the need to be

292

alone recurs), I had seen a queen enter this bar; and I know it will be a hustling bar.

As my eyes adjusted to the muddy light—a draped door doubly sheltering it from the Outside, the first person I noticed—beyond the cursory recognition of the malehustlers, the queens, the scores—was a blackhaired woman sitting on a stool against the wall of the bar. She leaned toward me, but when I sat near her, wondering if perhaps she had recognized me, she turned her face away from me.

In the right light, she is an attractive woman, somewhere in her 40s. But as she bends toward the lighted bar to bring to her heavily painted mouth the glass shes drinking from, she looks hard, toughened like those women depicted in movies as the hanging-on ex-mistresses of bigtime gangsters.

With an inviting smile which in itself would have indicated that I have come to the right place, the chubby bartender (one of two working the bar this afternoon) set a complimentary Welcoming drink before me. . . . Occasionally, he will talk in confidential tones to the darkhaired woman, and with attempted but unsuccessful subtlety, he indicates by a look or a movement of his head someone in the bar. The woman listens without turning her face. They seem conspiratorially to be keeping track of the people here.

Looking about this bar (the hungry faces of the hunted and the hunting)—as familiar as the others in the nightcities I have left—I feel, recurring, a sense of something hugely ominous, intensified by the interlude earlier with the gypsy woman—then a heavy weariness, quickly replaced by the manic excitement.

Against the whining jukebox near me, a tall pale queen is snapping her long fingers rhythmically to the juke-rocking and twisting. Another queen, with faintly mascaraed eyes in anticipation of the actual day of Mardi Gras when they can legally "masquerade" as women, stormed in and insisted loudly nervously to the finger-snapping queen:

"Mae, youve *got* to come outside with me this *very* minute and help me with Miss Ange! Shes outside pulking her nelly guts out! We *gotta* take her to her pad before the fuzz busts her." In an even more hysterical voice: "Shes *holding*—" (I see the woman sitting next to me straighten up alertly.) "—and I just cant handle her myself, she keeps fighting me off with her *nails!*"

Without interrupting the indifferent snapping of her fingers, the pale queen, flying Sky-High herself, trying for artificial

heaven, hisses: "Am I my sister's keeper or something? . . .
When I needed that nelly bitch once, she didnt know me from
Eve!" Rocking back and forth—sometimes so far back that it
seems she will surely lose her balance—her hands like feather-
less wings over her head—or, more correctly, like swaying
palmtrees in a strong breeze—she calls to the smoky ceiling:
"Im comin, Big Daddy-O!" And she echoes the jukebox:
"Oh, yes, indeedee, babies—let the good times roll!"

As the other queen dashed outside in confused exasperation, the darkhaired woman summoned the chubby bartender
and whispered to him. He left the bar quickly, returning in a
few moments ushering in a tiny queen who looks like a torn
ragdoll: so pale her features seem to have been merely
sketched on her face, all life vampirishly drained from her.

The bartender placed her on one of the small couchlike
benches that outline the bar. Now the blackhaired woman,
crouching before the queen as if to shelter her from foreign,
hostile eyes, holds her own glass to the queen's gurgling mouth,
which insistently rejects the liquid.

I hear the woman say to the sick queen: "Ive warned you
about drinking so much!—honey." The tone of her voice,
which is not Southern, is full of exasperation—but the last
word softens it: It is the tone of a person trying, unsuccessfully, to be angry.

"Not . . . drunk," Miss Ange mutters dazedly. "Pills—
and— . . ."

The woman looked apprehensively about the bar. She rises
from the bench, impatiently; relents, bends down again, insists
curiously: "Ive told you not to *drink* so much."

She whispers again to the bartender, and he begins to frisk
the queen. Finding what hes looking for—pills and joints
buried in the queen's pockets—he disappeared into the head.
The woman goes to the narrow corridor, and I hear her on
the telephone calling a cab. Returning, she paused before the
oblivious queen by the jukebox, as if to reprimand her. Instead,
she merely glared at her and followed the bartender now leading the groggy queen outside. . . . In a few moments, the
bartender and the woman returned to the bar, the woman to
sit again on that same stool against the wall.

Two queens, who look like twins—faces propped on elbows
—keep glancing at me through all this. Simultaneously (when
I catch them looking in my direction), they transformed their
hands—finger-spread—into flirtatious fans behind which they
continued to peer coquettishly like parodies of Grand Spanish

Doñas. Suddenly, the previously fanlike hands droop into two listless pairs of wan broken wrists—as the afternoon light that announces the entrance of someone flashes into the dark bar—and I know that whoever has entered is someone hostile. The woman near me sits up rigidly like someone alerted for battle.

Two tall, burly, suited men had walked in: gangster-types, their faces stamped with the arbitrary arrogance of policemen. Spotting them immediately for what they are—vice cops—just as the others in the bar have already done (the exaggerated poses have eased: even the scores, who are seldom questioned, are feigning indifference, turning their backs pointedly quickly on whatever hustler they may have been speaking to), I looked intently into the glass before me, thinking cornily, but with real apprehension, of a Southern chain-gang of vagrants from The Rocking Times.

The two vice cops are checking identifications at random. From the voices I hear respond, slowly, with emphatic animosity, I can tell that theyre avoiding questioning the queens; concentrating on the malehustlers as if the hustlers' presence somehow threatens them personally.

Obviously I havent been cool enough; the vice cops are already standing behind me. "Where are you staying?" one asked me. I turn to face stone-cold cop-eyes. . . .

Before I could answer, the blackhaired woman said clearly: "Hes staying with me." She adds wryly, addressing the vice cops: "You know where that is, dont you . . . boys?"

The taller of the two smiles at her—but only with his mouth; the irascible meanlook remained on his face, carved there by years of blind hatred. "That house of yours sure must be crowded," he drawled at the woman.

"I got a real large one." Her cold look matches theirs.

They stood momentarily at the draped door, the two cops, looking back into the bar as if to engrave each face here threateningly—indelibly—on their minds: the look of someone who says: "This is only the beginning of the game—a hint; we'll get you eventually; if not here, then somewhere else." . . . Typically cop-swaggering, armed with invisible bullysticks, they walked out. The frozen scenes about me resume, as if a movie film had begun again at the exact point at which it had paused.

The blackhaired woman says to me: "They try to bug everyone before the tourists come in. Mostly the hustlers," she added pointedly. "But after a while, the closer it gets to Mardi Gras, it cools off; they lose control—too many to take care of." Coming from a woman—a woman with whom I havent even spoken —those words, aimed so surely at me, embarrass me curiously. "Where are you really staying?" she asked me.

"At the Y," I told her.

"You sure?" Then: "Look, boy, Im not trying to pry. I know your scene. And I dont give a damn. But if you dont have a pad, theyll bust you for vag. . . . Hey! Desdemona! Drusilla!" she calls out to the two look-alike queens. "Theyre real sisters," she explains to me, "twins: Desdemona and Drusilla Duncan. And theyre cool."

"You callin us, sweetheart?" one queen says, and they both slide off their stools simultaneously and come over demurely.

The woman introduced us.

"Chawmed," says Desdemona Duncan.

"Dee-lighted, Ahm sure," says Drusilla Duncan.

"I really have a place," I said to the woman, realizing why shes asked the two queens over.

The two queens perched on nearby schools. "Too bad," sighed Desdemona and Drusilla Duncan almost at the same time.

The woman shrugged. The bartender refilled her glass— with Seven-Up. "Im Sylvia," the woman introduced herself. "I own this bar."

"And shes a real darling, too," trilled Drusilla Duncan.

Someone entered. Sylvia squinted, leaned forward. Then she turned away.

"I hate the vice cops as much as you do," she told me.

2

Two youngmen near the Bourbon House face each other on the street—one, blackhaired and meanfaced, threatening the other with a large stick; the other, a small blond boy of about 18 (turned-up nose, cleft-chin, blue eyes, masses of blond hair over his forehead—a replica of the current, boyish, blond-faced teenage idols of rock-n-roll), tensely and imminently uncertainly menacing the other with a knife poised gleaming in the blind sun. Behind the dark one hovers a small skinny girl like an anxious vulture. Her painted mouth seems to have been slashed carelessly across her pinched face in a gaping, scarlet gash. The stick and the knife are ready to attack. Eyes starved for violence, the girl shouts malevolently to her dark boyfriend, pushing him forward:

"Go, man! Kill the motherfucker!"

The two poised malebodies hurl themselves against each other, grapple, separate, lock for a long motionless moment as if in passion. The blond boy staggered back, a bloody slit at his temple. The blackhaired youngman stands looking down in bewilderment at his own hand, ripped at the thumb and the finger so that it opened like the webbed foot of a duck.

"Killim!" the girl screamed savagely at the dark one.

Someone from the Bourbon House rushed out shouting: "Police! Police!"

Like a stone scattering birds, that hollered word disbands the group quickly. People dart into doors, cross the street.

"Bring him with you," an older man says peremptorily to me and another youngman who has witnessed the fight, and who, minutes earlier, had been with me and the blond boy at Les Petits bar. We hold the blond boy, the blood from his temple creating a growing dark-crimson flower on his white shirt. As quickly as we can move him—past the startled eyes of tourists as they dodge to one side to avoid Contamination— we turn into Royal, where the man who has asked us to follow him has already called a cab.

Along the trellised balconied houses, the taxi flees from the afternoon, into the protective custody of the approaching night. The youngman holding the blond one, who threatens to pass out at any moment (the older man sits in front, staring straight ahead; the driver is predictably unconcerned), is saying Toughly to me: "That dirty motherin bastard, we gonna come back and git him!"—asking me would we or wouldnt we kill the son of a bitch who had hit our buddy with a stick—although our buddy—the blond boy, whom both of us had met minutes earlier at Les Petits bar (all three of us with the same score), had done nothing but come on to the blackhaired-youngman's girlfriend; and she, sensing the possible conflict (easily brought into play in any hustling bar by the necessity of the hustler to assert his masculinity with a girl— any girl, any woman) and instigating the scene connivingly (by winking at us as the darkhaired youngman embraced her), had told her boyfriend that the blondhaired boy had leaned toward her as if to kiss her. On the street the fight had occurred.

Somewhere beyond the Quarter, the taxi stopped before what looks like a boarded-up store, with black-painted windows. The man pays, we enter the building through an unlocked side door. Inside, the large room is dark, like a cell.

Pushed against the walls are tables, chairs upturned on them.
A couple of booths. Dark, smeared, ugly patches on the wall
behind a bar without stools indicate that several panels of
mirrors have been removed. Only one grayish-amber panel,
smashed in the middle creating a glassy spider web, remained.
A light is on in a room beyond the door.

From the shadows, other faces begin to appear, slowly,
dimly, peering impressionistically out of the darkness. They
seemed to be crawling like giant insects from somewhere out
of the woodwork. Now I can distinguish the faces clearly: three
malehustlers I had seen at The Rocking Times, a bewildered
girl, and a young painted queen.

The man who brought us here disappeared quickly through
the lighted door.

We placed the blond boy, propped, on the seat of a booth.
As if in renewed, dazed surprise, he stared at the blood on his
hand, and he tore at his shirt, holding the piece of cloth to his
wounded temple.

The queen's face hangs like a white, painted mask over him.
"Poor dear," she sighs, "and hes so *cute* too."

Now the shadow of a woman appeared against the light from
the other room, followed by the man who brought us here. As
the woman approached, I recognized her: Sylvia—the woman
at The Rocking Times.

She sat quickly beside the blond boy doubled over in the
booth; she dressed the wound deftly, urgently. Responding to
her authority—and shes in complete command—the two of
us who brought the wounded boy here lift him and follow
Sylvia through the lighted room, which is a kitchen—with a
long table and several chairs, an old coiled refrigerator; through
a corridor; into another room. There are several rollout beds,
couches, mats on the floor; and we laid the blond boy on a bed.

"We gonna git the guy that done this," says the youngman
with me.

Sylvia looked at him uncertainly, as if undecided whether
to chastise or praise him. She merely turned from him, looking down sadly at the wounded boy. "Let him sleep. Hes just
scared," she said with a note of what could be contempt. She
drew a cover over him, at first tenderly. Then she tossed it over
him impatiently. Again, relenting in the impatience, she sighs,
touches him lightly on the bandaged face. Asleep, the boy looks
like a peaceful young kid. . . .

When we returned to the unlighted room with the eyeless
panels of removed mirrors, the man was gone; the youngmen,

the girl, the queen have disappeared, probably to other sections of this strange building. Like the underground stations for Negro fugitives from the South, this place must provide temporary shelter for the Carnival vagrants.

"Are you hungry?" Sylvia asked me and the youngman with me. I said no. The other youngman said yes. She directed him to the kitchen. As he helped himself to food from the old refrigerator, the woman and I sat in one of the booths, facing each other.

With her hand she quickly wiped away a few drops of blood that had dripped onto the table—as if to erase the fact of their existence.

She looked at me questioningly, knotting her eyebrows as if to ask me something, the answer to which, though vastly important, she will nevertheless find perplexing, or even painful. "Why—?" she began. Instead, she shifts the questioning look. Her face had mellowed for a moment. Now the toughness crept back into it. She fixed her eyes stonily on the deserted gray bar. At first, I had thought she hadnt recognized me; now she calls me by my name. "What happened to that kid?" she asked me.

Interrupting my narration of the fight before I could get beyond the girl's goading of her boyfriend, Sylvia shook her head wearily as if she had already heard too much. "I know the girl youre talking about," she said. "Shes always trying to make others prove something—but shes really trying to prove it to herself."

And I think of Barbara, perhaps still somewhere in the maze of downtown Los Angeles. . . .

Sylvia said: "I'll take that knife from that kid, if hes still got it—he probably doesnt even know how to use it." She shook her head again in bewilderment. "You should have taken it from him when you first knew he had it," she said, as if I had failed in some established duty. "All of you—" she started, compelled to approach a certain dangerous subject which, barely neared, must be avoided. She was silent. I felt uncomfortable with her right now—mysteriously guilty, blame-ridden, as if *I* had done something to her.

"Is this your bar too?" I asked her, only to fill the powerful silence.

"Yes," she answered. "It's been closed for quite a while, though—it was too far from the Quarter. I bought that other one instead. The Rocking Times." She added the name with deep sarcasm. "Hell, I couldve sold this place, many times.

But I prefer to keep it—for a while anyway." Like a person prepared to fight even before a hostile situation exists, she added defensively, abruptly belligerently. "Yeah, sure, this was a hustling bar too: hustlers! queens! butch homosexuals! Everything!" She pronounced each word with bravado, like a child who must prove he can use dirty words; and, as with that child, each word had sounded unconvincing. "What else?" she challenged, as if I had been questioning her.

"When those bars swing, they make a lot of money, I guess," I said clumsily, still trying to ease some of the strain I felt with her.

She flashed a ferocious look at me. In the gray darkness, I could almost feel her eyes burning on my face. Predictably, she relented, changing the subject. "Usually, by this time," she was telling me, "Im already at the bar. But what the hell? Everyone whos there now will be there later—or theyll come back."

"You know everyone who goes there?"

"I see everyone," she said. "And I know most of the regulars —the ones who stay here all year. It's mainly during Mardi Gras that the gay scene really changes in this city. . . . I hate that word, 'gay'—'queer' too, even more," she said quickly.

I remember the man on the beach, that afternoon in Santa Monica, with whom I had sat on the sand watching that bird Escape into the sky. He had made much the same protest against the unfairness of the labels thrust at that world—a protest echoed over and over in that life. . . . But this woman? Was her resentment of those labels bred by a consuming guilt for catering in her bar to a world in which, I suspected, she didnt really belong?

While we had been talking, a queen had entered surreptitiously through the side door. She seemed to be hesitating in approaching Sylvia. Suddenly she was there—standing before us.

"Lily, I been looking for you," Sylvia said harshly.

"I *know*, honey," the queen named Lily said querulously. "And—You Believe It Or Not—that is exactly why I have come over looking for you—to clarify certain points of a vicious, untrue, unfounded, utterly fabricated, bitchy story someone has been spreading About Me. . . . I aint been hidin from you or nothing—honestly, honey," she said, oddly prematurely conciliatory. "I want you to know that. You *must* know that," she said like Bette Davis. "It's just that I been—

Really and Truly—I have been Very Busy, what with Mardi
Gras coming up."

"I know," Sylvia said cuttingly.

"Why, Sylvia, honey—it aint at all how you heard it, baby,"
Lily protested, playing nervously with a long strand of beads
about her neck.

"Now how the hell do you know what I heard?"

"Because I been *told!*—by mutual friends." She avoids
looking directly at Sylvia; guiltily studying the strung beads. "I
did *not* clip that drunk sailor," she says, plunging into the
immediate matter. "And I know it was that old queen Whorina
who told you I did. Honey, you know me well enough to
know: that-I-simply-do-not-clip-no-one-that-aint-lookin-to-be-
clipped." She strung out the words, obviously memorized, as
if they constituted what she knew is a ready, forceful defense.
"And that sailor was not! It just so happened I dug him, see,
honey?—and ole Whorina was digging him too (oh, she was
twisted out of her gay mind for him!—she even offered him
money to make it, but he was digging Me)—and, well, Whorina, like the bitchy nelly queen she is, well, she was Bugged—
fit to be tied, I wanna let you know." She swung her beads
in a defiant loop at the thought of Whorina. "Why, I even
heard she— . . ."

"Dont rattle your giddy beads at me, Mary," snapped
Sylvia. "I can tell when youre faking it. I know how you
work with that studhustler—how you pick up someone and
play the helpless, defenseless queen; youll even offer them
money to get them to your pad, and then your studhustler
boyfriend threatens to beat them up unless they hand over
their bread!"

The queen put her hand indignantly to her heart. In
obviously posed amazement, she formed, soundless, the
Astonished word "Me?" and left her mouth gaping in practiced
disbelief.

"I dont give a damn who you clip—as long as it's someone
who knows what hes getting into," Sylvia went on; and I can
feel her begin to relent toward the queen. "But a drunk
sailor—and how many other drunk sailors?" she says in exasperation. "Well, Lily, this isnt the first time Ive told you:
I wont have it. You go find yourself another bar—and thats
that! . . . That sailor was so damn drunk— I saw you with
him—he probably thought you were a girl. Either that or you
offered him trade-sex, or money."

"Well, honey," said the queen, smiling demurely, pleased

at the former, ignoring the latter, "you know yourself how *real* I can look—and that particular night, I had my hair— . . ."

"I told you to stop rattling your beads at me!" Sylvia interrupted her, forcing the queen to retreat a hurried step, her hand anxiously at her throat. "This is the last time I warn you: I wont have anyone in my bar that takes advantage of someone thats not hip enough to know better."

"I am Telling You The God's Truth," Lily protested, hinting, but somehow feebly, at tears—and crossing her heart spiritedly. "It was that washed-out queen Whorina—" She sneered at the name. "—that made up that Utterly Fantastic story—just because, like Im telling you —Cross! My! Heart!—I made it with the sailor she was after. If something happened to his wallet, well, I certainly had nothing to do with that."

I wonder whether Sylvia actually believes the queen's story. Telling it, the queen seems too nervous, too quickly apologetic; I have a strong suspicion that Sylvia doesnt believe it—but, as if it is easier to believe her than face what disbelief will entail, she says to the queen, wearily, "Okay—all right; forget it," like a judge not quite satisfied with the veracity of the defendant's story but considering and bowing to the mitigating circumstances.

"Thank you, honey," sang the queen, enormously relieved. "Introduce me?"

Sylvia introduced us.

"Gotta place to stay, hon?" the queen said to me. "I got an empty bed."

"Yes," I answered. There is something patently lubricous about her manner which turns me off.

"Too bad," she sighed. "That empty bed in my pad just gives me the cold chills."

"What happened to your stud boyfriend?" Sylvia asked cunningly.

Thrown suddenly off balance, the queen blurted: "He split! —with all that money we been making!" And now shes genuinely shaken. Realizing, quickly, that shes trapped herself clearly, she excuses herself with enormous courtesy and slithers into the kitchen. She is now talking to the youngman still eating there.

"Screwed-up world without laws!" Sylvia muttered disgustedly to herself. "Queens, hustlers, fairies—and me!" Suddenly angry, her words accused me harshly: "All of you!—guys like you—and that kid with the gashed head—what the hell are you trying to prove? Why, especially— . . . ?" I was glad she stopped the uncomfortable words—but she had looked at me as if actually expecting an answer to the question that hadnt been asked. Then she reverted to what she had begun to say: "But even in a world without laws—and mostly, hell, we all know it—mostly it's lawless because it's a scene— . . . a scene people shun, are . . . afraid of, dont even want to know exists—even in that kind of world—well, Jesus, Holy, Christ— youve got to have some kind of—hell, yes—decency—some kind of rules. In my bar, *I* make those rules. And I dont give a damn who gets bugged and doesnt come back. Hell, I know everything that goes on. I watch it every day: scores coming in looking for youngmen. Some of them try to impress the hustlers with how Rich they are. So they end up clipped. That doesnt bug me. That kind of score asks for it." She had begun with the familiar bravado, but it had faded quickly, and she dropped her eyes, unable to face me even in the darkness.

"But if a hustler in my bar gets treated decently by a score (and I know most of the scores, too)," she went on, "if he agrees to what hes going to get paid—and exactly for what— and then I hear he clipped the score," she warned, "then, God damn it, hes gonna answer to me or he doesnt come back. The same with the queens and their daddies. . . . Theres *got* to be some kind of morality!" she insisted. "Not the bull they teach you in Sunday-school. I mean; just living in the world you find yourself in—with its own rules, considering everything— yes—but theres *got* to be rules!" She stared into the empty bar, at the shattered mirror.

Yes, it was exactly as if she had been clarifying something, rather unconvincingly, for herself—speaking words shes probably spoken to others many times, memorized now—as if she were torn between a compulsion to understand, to accept—and an innate tendency to reject. . . . And I wonder to what extent she really believes she can impose rules on the flagrant anarchy.

"Why the hell did you come to New Orleans?" she asked me tiredly, as if shes used to getting an inadequate answer.

"For the Carnival," I told her simply.

"And something else," she said to herself. "Beyond the parades and— . . . the rest."

"I guess youre right," I admitted uneasily.

"Theres always something else," she said. "Ive been in New Orleans—oh, several years. I came directly from New York— right after my last divorce," she added pointedly; I had the feeling she was trying to indicate to me that shes been married several times.

"Why did you come here?" I asked her.

She waited a long while before answering. "I came down here— . . . for the Carnival. Like you," she added with bitter sarcasm.

Then she looked at me curiously, as if suddenly I had become a complete stranger with whom she had found herself accidentally speaking intimately. She got up quickly, and she went through the lighted kitchen—to take, I suspected, the knife from the wounded boy. . . .

Sailing in out of the dark in Sylvia's wake, a painted queen stood over me.

"Im Whorina, darling, and I like you," she said.

3

There are of course other bars in the French Quarter where the hunted and the hunting of that world gather.

There was Les Petits, where, nightly, Love Face, a fat Negro woman with bleached hair, made panting, sighing song-love to the mike. And, outside, past the courtyard, was Sandy-Vee's bar—and Sandy-Vee is one of the most flagrant, most famous drag-queens in America. Vaunting her imposed exile, defiantly she dangles his/her orange earring for the curious tourists. (And my first time there, exhibiting herself before the amused tourists—hating them but using them cunningly—as I walked in—she shrieked: "Theres muh new husband!"—and then she said to an ancestrally bored woman sitting with her fat, tired middle-aged companion: "Ahm doin much bettuh than you are, honey!—and theres more where he came from!"—and she underscored the flagrant put-down by squirting seltzer water, fizzing, into a glass and shouting at the woman: "Douche time!")

And there was Cindy's bar, run by a fat, jolly-looking, pursed-mouthed woman who pined after her clients. There was Les Deux Freres. ("Why 'The Two Brothers'?" "Because it's owned by two brothers, and theyre sisters!") And there were the other bars, scattered throughout the Quarter.

But, usually, especially in the moments of needed respite from the compulsive fury of those days, as the city went through that period of initiation before Mardi Gras, I would return to The Rocking Times.

And it was mainly to be with Sylvia that I went there.

In the world of her bar, she treated each member on his own respective level. With the queens, she discussed their drag costumes for Mardi Gras, assuring them that such and such a color would be just right. With the masculine homosexuals —neither scores, hustlers, nor queens—she listened attentively as they confided to her their broken love affairs. With the hustlers, she often spoke roughly, using their own expressions. . . . And on all, at least verbally, she imposed her rigid, though largely unobserved, rules.

Yet there were those other times when she would merely stare gloomily before her, as if she had shut her ears. At such times, within me, she augmented the churning unfocused guilt.

Still, I sought her out. And when she wasnt at the bar— which was rare—I would feel acutely disappointed, personally cheated—almost angry at her as if she had stood me up.

Today shes talking to Sonny—the blond youngman who had been wounded in the fight that afternoon before the Bourbon House. Only minutes earlier, he had walked in Proudly, Cock-ily—like a big-game hunter with a lion's head—with two impressively suited scores.

"Be cool," I heard Sylvia warning him. "Those two are here every year. I see them pick up a green kid like you, each Mardi Gras—" Sonny winced noticeably at her designation of him. "—and they tell him theyre going to take him to Europe, and after Mardi Gras, they split—alone. Youll never see them again."

Sonny nodded impatiently. It is difficult for him to believe that he can be taken. Sylvia watched him with an ambiguous look as he returned to the two well-dressed scores, who have been staring resentfully at Sylvia as if aware that shes been warning Sonny about them.

As usual, Sylvia is drinking Seven-Up. It was all I had ever seen her drink. Occasionally, though, I had noticed her stare longingly at the varicolored bottles of liquor behind the bar, then turn from them as if they threatened her in some powerful way.

The quavering, sensual voice of Elvis Presley is coming from the juke-box in lonesome, sad, sustained, orgasmic moans:

> *The bell-hop's tears keep flowing,*
> *The desk clerk's dressed in black. . . .*

Sylvia studied two youngmen who had just walked into the bar. "Two more new ones," she sighed. "Each year—new

hustlers, new queens, new— . . ." she hesitated, "—new gay
boys just out for kicks—and the ones that keep coming back."
And the juke-box sang lugubriously:

> *Just take a walk down lonely street*
> *To Heartbreak Hotel.* . . .

"Kathy just passed out on the steps of the Maison Blanche!"
a queen blurted at Sylvia.

"Whos with her?" Sylvia asked urgently, shocked out of the
revery the two entering youngmen had smothered her in.

"Whorina is—and, well, I was—but I got so rattled, I didnt
know *what* to do! So I thought I'd better run and tell you."

"You dizzy queen," said Sylvia, "didnt you think to call a
doctor?"

"I just Didnt Know What To Do!—except run to you as fast
as I could!" the queen protested vehemently. "Me and
Whorina—well, we went with Kathy to the Maison Blanche,
to pick up, you know, some drag things for Mardi Gras. . . .
And, oh, we created quite a stir, I want to tell you: All those
tourists just Turning and Looking at Us— . . . Then Kathy,
she just blacks out—" She covered her eyes to indicate the
intensity of the blackness. "—all of a sudden—you know,
Sylvia, like she does—those awful spells she gets! Well, she
just fell back on the escalator, and it hauled her down,
and— . . . Well, I didnt know what to do! Like I say: Me
and Whorina—well, see . . . we had just—well, taken certain
items which didnt *exactly* belong on our persons; and when—
well, see, honey, then I— . . ."

"What about Kathy?" Sylvia said harshly, exasperated.

"Well," the queen says, inflating herself with her importance
as the harbinger of some, to me, obscure doom, "like I say, she
just passed out. Oh, those horrible dizzy spells—"

Sylvia brushed quickly past her, leaving the bar.

When I returned that night—separating at the door from
the man I had just made it with—Sylvia was back too.

"Youre really keeping busy." She smiled a strange smile.

Embarrassed, I didnt answer.

"The first season, it's always great," she said. "Maybe youre
one of those thatll keep coming back each year. Some do."
She studied me for a long moment. "Somehow I doubt that
youll be back," she said flatly.

"What happened to— . . . ?" I asked, to stop her from going
on in that direction.

"Kathy? Shes okay now. They took her home. She gets those spells—more and more often. She hardly ever comes out any more, except during the carnival."

"Has she seen a doctor?"

"Yes. I made her go. I wish I hadnt." And that was all she said; but a dark look had brushed her face like a shadow.

A lighthaired, heavily muscled youngman was standing behind Sylvia, ready to surprise her. He had the kind of goodlooks that is a combination of hinted toughness and the All-American wholesomeness depicted in hundreds of advertisements: the epitomized face of America's young vagrants. But I noticed immediately the telltale brand about his eyes: the eyes of someone who has seen much too much. Suddenly this youngman with the massive arms no longer looked so young. And I remembered Skipper. . . . He placed his hands quickly on Sylvia's shoulders.

"Jocko!" she greeted him warmly.

"Back as usual," he said.

"This is one of the ones I was telling you about—who come back every year," Sylvia told me. "Youre later than usual," she said to him. "How was Miami?"

"I didnt stay there long. I had to split," he said. "I been in St Louis."

Sylvia frowned. Again I get the impression that she doesnt want to know too much. "Well, welcome back—again," she said, looking at him tenderly, almost sadly.

"Always back," he said, moving away.

Staring after Jocko, Sylvia said: "That guy's made it on his muscles long after most of them would be through. He was an acrobat—once. Like everything else, the circus folded. Now he comes here each year to join another kind of circus. . . . He was the best hustler in New Orleans," she said, almost proudly, "and he had iron rules he stuck by—thats why everyone liked him: never clipped anyone, treated everyone straight. . . . Now—well—maybe it's changed." Abruptly, as if to stop the wondering about why Jocko had to leave Miami, she said: "After Mardi Gras, this city clamps up. It dies, as if it's seen too much during the Carnival, and then you can almost feel Lent in the air. You breathe it. It takes over the city. New Orleans goes into mourning. Thats when the plainclothesmen haunt the bars again for vagrants," she warned. "And thats when Jocko leaves—at midnight. The next Mardi Gras, hes back. . . . And yet, each year since Ive been here, I wonder if that will be the last one—if he'll never show up again. . . ."

As if now on an invisible trapeze, I thought suddenly.

"In a few years he'll be old," Sylvia said, "and hes the kind that should stay Young. No brains. Just goodlooks—and an instinctive understanding of so many things. I guess no one can blame him for anything," she said, as if to herself. "Something—something tossed him out!" she said fiercely. An intense silence. Then: "Maybe it would have been better for him if he'd fallen off the damn trapeze," she said brutally.

I looked at her, at the harsh, saddened face, and I realized how violently, at that moment, she hated the world of this bar she owned.

As if she had materialized from the very smoke that clouded the bar, the most beautiful queen I have ever seen appeared. If it hadnt been for her clothes—maleclothes worn to imitate a woman's—I would have thought her a real woman; and as a woman, she would have been one of the most beautiful, too. In her 20s, with a pale perfectly featured face—the face any woman would have envied on another—she had dark-lidded eyes and long, blond, almost-golden hair, which now is tightly bunched in back to conceal its length. She is lithe, slender. There is a ghostquality about her, perhaps because of the way even the feeble light plays on her hair, so that, appearing almost translucent, she seems incandescent.

She surveyed the bar slowly, as if for the first time, with a smile which is unbearably, wistfully sad. In this bar of very real faces—the studied toughness of the malehustlers, the sedulous (but largely unsuccessful to practiced eyes) madeup attempts at femininity of the queens—this youngman, this queen, standing in the midst of it, appears as unreal as an angel: a monument to the utter perversity of her violated sex.

She glides through the bar now, easily, past the bunched groups; nodding to the others—not aloofly, but, rather, as if she herself is aware of the unreality of her person; and they stare at her in a kind of bewildered awe. She moves like fog, as if some invisible wind is carrying her along toward Sylvia. Now, closely, I can see the queen's haunting green eyes. And I feel a great sadness because of the doom so inexorably stamped on that beautiful face.

"How do you feel now, Kathy?" Sylvia asked her softly.

"Oh, Im always all right," Kathy answered. Even her voice has a quality of unreality. "Im fine. . . . Sylvia, what time is it, honey?"

Without looking at her watch, Sylvia said: "It's five o'clock." But I knew it was much later.

"I dont mean what time. Did I say that? I mean what *day?*"
Sylvia answered. She reached out to touch the queen, but
she brought her hand quickly back.

"That late in the week?" Kathy sighs.

"That early," Sylvia laughed unconvincingly.

"Oh, well," Kathy said indifferently. The smile hasnt left
her face. "Youre new in the Quarter, arent you, baby?" she
asked me. "I dont come out very often any more." She
seemed to be looking through me, as if everyone within the
span of her vision is as unreal as she herself. "New people all
the time, some come back, some never do." She asked Sylvia,
"Is Jocko back in town yet?"

"Yes. He was here earlier."

"Good," said Kathy. "I like him. . . . What time did you say
it is?" she asked again, vaguely.

Sylvia answered, this time correctly. But Kathy seemed not
to have noticed the difference.

"Excuse me," she breathed—and she disappeared as unreally as she had appeared.

"Shes beautiful," I said.

Illogically, as if mysteriously it explained the queen's beauty,
Sylvia said: "Her family threw her out, years ago; they even
offered to pay her to stay away." She added proudly: "But
Kathy wouldnt take their money. Shes lived in a little hell-
hole in the Quarter ever since then—on her own. . . . Those
blackouts she has— . . . Shes dying," she said abruptly.

A subtle odor—Kathy's perfume—lingered long after she
was gone. Like the memory of someone's death.

Like flotsam from the world's seas, the vagrants of America's blackcities are washed into New Orleans. And Sylvia
scrutinized each new face of the invading waves as if all—or
perhaps one miraculous one among them—would bring her
the answer to an obsessive question—would . . . perhaps . . .
redeem her for the very fact of her own bar.

She had just warned me that there was a man in the bar
who might be a vice cop playing a score, and she was maneuvering to get a young boy away from him. In the process of
catching the kid's attention, she saw a youngman in a suit
walking into the bar from the courtyard: a goodlooking youngman, evidently not a hustler, probably a masculine homosexual, neither out to score nor to be scored from; looking
for a mutual partner.

Sylvia followed him intently with her eyes as he stops to

talk to another youngman, also in a suit, also obviously neither hustler nor score. Sylvia remained as if bound to the barstool; but her body became tense, as if, of its own volition, beyond her conscious control, it might spring toward the youngman. Together, the two youngmen approached us, standing only a few feet away. Seeing the first one clearly at last, Sylvia turned from him—as she had turned from me that first day—and she sighed in frustrated expectation.

Moments later, without a word, she walked outside into the street.

Through the open door, the curtain pushed back to welcome the street crowds, I saw her standing on the sidewalk, looking in all directions as if undecided which one to take, or as if it made no difference.

She brought her hand to her forehead in a tight fist.

Then she squared her shoulders and walked away.

And at that moment I knew with certainty what I must have suspected from the very first—and I realized why it was that I returned to her constantly.

4

"Fucking queers!" the drunk man roared as two queens swished by him gayly into the head of The Rocking Times.

"What the hell are you doing here if you dont like it?" Sylvia was standing before him like a black panther.

"Hell," the man said, "I dont need em. Im married, got a wife—kids."

"Not much of a wife," Sylvia lashed, "if you have to come here to feel youre a man." Her voice was controlled, but her face blanched.

"If I had a queer in my family, I'd kill him!" the man spat venemously.

Sylvia grabbed him by the shoulders. "Get out of here!" she commanded, pushing him out.

And then, instantly, shockingly, it began.

Like someone yearning for water—deprived of it for long hot smoldering days, Sylvia brushed past the bartender behind the bar, and she reached for a bottle of bourbon, and she poured out a glass. I could see the taut veins on her neck as she leaned her head back, welcoming the stinging amber liquid. Her hands, which had been trembling as she stared at the drunk man stumbling anxiously out of the bar, relaxed. She gulped another drink in one long thirsty swallow.

The bartender is looking at her in helpless pity as if he knew what would happen now; as if perhaps he had witnessed it before.

Released, Sylvia turned to face the jammed bar. Her eyes had misted, whether from the harshness of the burning liquor or from something else.

And she held the glass out—high—in a toast to everyone here.

I left the bar quickly, infinitely depressed. But in the other crowded bars, or on the streets, or walking through Jackson Square, I was obsessed by Sylvia's face. And I went back to The Rocking Times.

Intermittently, she was surrounded by the people she knew, the people whom, I was certain now, she had needfully searched out. She was laughing raucously; but her face was marked clearly by the impact of the liquor and the years-long, clawing desire to understand what everything in her, ancestrally, demanded she hate. Occasionally, someone would place a hand on her shoulder, cautioning her about the fervid, sudden drinking; someone else would coax her to let him take her home. But she pushed the hand away, rejected each suggestion that she should leave.

"No!" she said harshly. "This is it!" Her face clouded, as if she were still sober enough not to be certain whether she wanted to go on. To indicate her instant decision, she gulped another drink. "Gonna sell this bar!" she shouted. "Leave New Orleans—never, never, never come back."

"Not even to see Us?" said Desdemona Duncan sadly.

Sylvia raised a wrenched face toward her, touched the queen's cheek tenderly, and began to cry in drunken, convulsed sobs. She slid off the stool and rushed out into the courtyard.

I found her there, hidden in the shadows, sitting on the steps outside leading to the upper part of the building. Jocko sat next to her. The chilly night wind had dried her tears, and her face is glazed and unreal, as if a mask, worn successfully for years, had been washed away. The toughness is all gone, drained by the liquor and the tears. She covered her face, as if to shut out the vision of the bar, her bar. The cold wind brushed past us like the wing of a huge bird.

About us in the courtyard, people milled in the light-speckled shadows.

And we sat there on the steps with Sylvia—Jocko and I, silently.

"Let me take you home, baby," Jocko said.

"Not yet," she said. "Just stay here—both of you—just for a few minutes—with me."

Now she faced the courtyard, staring, listening raptly to the jumbled conversations, the shrieking of the queens rising above the sounds of the others. . . .

And then Kathy was standing before us, looking down sadly at Sylvia. Sylvia reached for her hand; and Kathy said, "How are you feeling, honey?"

"Kathy," Sylvia stuttered drunkenly, "Kathy—honey—Im sorry."

"Dont be sorry," Kathy said—and she waited. And I will wonder later if she knew it had to be to her that Sylvia must speak the words she will soon say.

"You dont understand," Sylvia insisted.

"I do," Kathy said.

"No, you *cant* understand!" Sylvia said. "Because— . . . because I did to him . . . what they did to you." And she blurted at last: *"I threw my own son out!"*

I felt a sudden cold sadness pass over me at her words.

Jocko sighed.

"I do understand, honey," Kathy said, and she held Sylvia's hand more tightly.

"No," Sylvia sighed. "No one knows. . . ." She looked at Jocko, then at me, again at Kathy. "He could be . . . you . . . or you . . . or any of these other . . . youngmen!" she said. "Your age—their age. Theres just two ages anyway: youngman and oldman." As if an inner echo had accused her—had been accusing her silently for years—she protested haltingly: "It's just—just not possible—to love too much. Too little—okay: The whole screwing world loves too little. But too much?" She paused, as if thoughts, long submerged, had begun to gnaw into the present of her mind. "But maybe it is possible—to love too much—and too blindly—and maybe I did," she muttered, looking at me.

The ferocious love of my mother from which I had fled leapt on my consciousness like a dark animal.

"My only son . . ." Sylvia sighed. "A stranger to me; a stranger to his long . . . long string of fathers," she accused herself.

Jocko straightened up, as if her words had reminded him of something. Whatever he remembered, he seemed to have been carried into a past which had determined his own vagrant future.

"Yeah," Sylvia said, "I did love him too much—except—
. . . except when he needed me. . . . Kathy," she said, as if she
must explain it to her, be vindicated by her, "he came to me,
he started telling me— . . . I made him stop. I said, 'Shut up!'
And he tried to go on, trying to tell me— . . . And he was
crying . . . crying. And I said, 'Dont you dare go on!' I
shouted, *'What youre trying to tell me isnt true!'* "

She put her hands to her ears, drowning out the sounds
from the bar, the courtyard; trying unsuccessfully to drown
other louder, more insistent sounds from the ravenous past.
When she removed her hands, tiredly, from her ears as if
surrendering to this courtyard, we heard, shatteringly clearly,
the high-pitched shrieking voice of a queen saying to another:

"Sweetie, I dont give a damn what nelly queen Lily says
about me. After all!—she dont pay my gay rent!"

Sylvia laughed, hearing that: laughed in pain. And then,
waving her hand in a sweeping gesture that included this
courtyard and the bar, she sighed:

"All—all, all . . . all . . . my . . . saintly . . . children. All
flung out by something—or someone!—to a city like New
Orleans—to a bar—like mine. Flung out guiltily. Guiltily,"
she echoed herself. . . . Then entreatingly, to explain, to
confess: "And, that day, when he wouldnt stop, I shouted to
him, 'Get out! Dont come back!' . . ." She covered her eyes.
"And the memory of his face, that last time—his face smeared
with tears as I yelled after him: 'Youre a *man,* God damn it!
Youre a . . . man.' " This time she whispered the last word
as if it had lost all its meaning. "And you know why? You
know why I couldnt face what he was trying to tell me?"
she asked Kathy. "Because— . . ." She stopped. Then she
finished harshly: "Because I felt— . . . guilty! Crushingly,
crushingly guilty—as if—as if he were accusing *me* in making
this confession to me. . . . And I—didnt—understand— . . ."

"But you understand now," Kathy said.

Sylvia looked up at her, studying the beautiful woman's
face. "Understand?" she said, as if perplexed by the word itself. She shook her head. "No. Ive *tried.* . . . But I'll never . . .
understand." She seemed suddenly to be searching the courtyard, her eyes wide—wide with the hatred which in some
strange way, through pain, had been forced to turn into something else—at least the attempt to understand.

Kathy bent down and kissed Sylvia on the forehead, like a
child kissing her mother at bedtime, forgiving her.

And Sylvia raised her glazed unmasked face to the dark sky, and she said:

"God damn it— I dont give a damn! Either in makeup, either like a queen—in the highest, brightest screaming drag —with sequins and beads— . . . Either like that—or hustling a score, trying to prove with another man, because of my . . . words still ringing in his ears—trying that way to prove that I was right, that he *is* a man. . . . Even— . . . even if he has to prove it by finding another man who will pay him for his . . . masculinity— . . . Even with a bloody gash on his head, proving it with violence. That way . . . or with another youngman, his— . . . lover— . . . Any way! Any shape! I dont give a damn! . . . It's just that—*God damn it!*— I want to see him—if only once more—just once—to tell him— . . ." and her voice trailed off into a barely audible whimper: "— to tell him Im sorry."

CITY OF NIGHT

THOSE DAYS. . . .

Those New Orleans carnival days, divided for me not by clock-hours but by the many, many faces. Vicissitude of sex-locked rooms.

Those face-crammed days in which time existed in the one dimension of Now, immediately. In which I took pills indiscriminately to keep me awake—pills passed from one person to another with more abandon than a cigarette is offered. In which I made it several times a day, often only pretending to come. In which I rushed through the barcrowds crushed like communal massed lovers—as the fugitive armies, expelled shortly from the other nightcities, came daily in restless tides to join that procession before Ash Wednesday.

And occasionally I will remember—during those teeming French Quarter days, like a startlingly recalled dream of long ago—things forgotten for long returning as phantom-memories—and suddenly I'll remember the processions in El Paso when the people marched chanting to the top of the mountain where the statue of Christ looked down, pityingly, arms outstretched—but instead of devout-faced men and women chanting prayers, instead of the priests in bright robes, there will be, now, in New Orleans, soon, only days away, on Shrove Tuesday, the masked clowns, the twisting snakedancing revelers. . . . The seminude sweating bodies writhing along the streets.

The parades. . . .

In one moment of sharing (as on that night, sitting with Sylvia on the steps of the courtyard of her bar: with Jocko and Kathy), the hint of a miracle can occur. But even vague miracles fade, turn inside out. Momentarily, the knowledge of Sylvia's pain, when it had become a spoken thing, had fused with our own knowledge of ourselves, and from that knowledge of guilt, in that courtyard, we had attempted

315

mutually to vindicate each other. But a kind of closeness that joins people too suddenly can be a fleeting thing. Accumulated for years, finally released by liquor, confessions flow out like a flood-swollen river. Then, calmed, the waters seek to return to their source, to retreat; but the memory of the turmoil, of the flooding, remains, scarring the land it washed.

And so it was now with Sylvia. For a whole day she had stayed away from The Rocking Times. When she returned, it with again the Sylvia I had first known: sitting at the bar, drinking Seven-Up. Waiting. But now, although she spoke to me much as before, I could sense that she preferred to avoid me.

As with Pete, those many faces away, when his discovered knowledge of himself had threatened me and we had chosen to pass like strangers on the street, the face which Sylvia turned to me now was the face of someone who, clearly, in the deep night, wishes passionately—because of that fear of vulnerability in a world in which you have to pretend at toughness—that he could erase from another's mind the shared remembrances of what has passed between them.

But, once, for a moment, we had been Close, and perhaps in that remembered closeness, the real miracle might occur, waiting in a chamber of the mind which could open now more readily, with others.

Thursday.
The Parade of the Krewe of the Knights of Momus—the mocking spirit expelled from Olympus—will invade New Orleans tonight, four days before Mardi Gras inflames the city at midnight. Floats will sweep the dirty streets trailing gauze like ghost-wings; silverleafed reflecting the choked lights along Canal Straeet under the winter stars. . . .

Waking up wherever that may be, invariably I'll feel a sudden apprehension, because now I will have to face the Mirror, which will stare at me lividly—and I'll look for Someone; but I wont see whom I want to see, but see, instead, in that morning hour (the hour of waking, whether afternoon or night) a strange accusing face: . . . Myself. With knowing eyes that somehow dont belong: a face violent in its Knowingness, if only so to me.

Scrutinizing that stranger's face, of Myself in the Mirror, I hear the voice of the man Im with, saving: "Dont stare so hard; youre still a boy"—as if understanding from the searching looks that Im hunting Someone, urgently—that someone unfound in the dim past, in the parks, the moviebalconies, the bars, the streets, the sexrooms; that someone perhaps lost or evaded somewhere in the labyrinthine memories leading back to a serene window. . . . But despite that man's words, of course I know—and the face knows—that I am no longer a "boy." I appear Young, yes—but, inside, it's as if miles of years have stretched since I left that window in El Paso.

Turning away from the Mirror, I feel stabbingly guilty. But guilty of what? Perhaps my guilt is a wayward apology for living in a world for which I dont feel responsible.

I walk out of that room, and the sun claws savagely at my eyes.

It means a day has gone by.

But what good is a day going by so easily when, suddenly, there is the devouring sun and another day, another empty stretch of time before you can hide again?—another day standing before me at attention like a private waiting to be told what to do, sir. . . . It's better to wake up nights so you dont have to screw your eyes up and your Dark self adjusting to the sun.

Reluctantly I join the hordes of other nightpeople, stark in the reality of Morning, their features as if erased by the sun from the bloodless faces, more stark in juxtaposition with the sleepfed faces of the others, the morningpeople: the many, infinitely many, varieties of "tourists."

And in that sun, it will begin again, trying to fill the nothing with something —*with anything!*—which this time is God Damn It this:

Sonny said: "See, you go and tell him—over there, see (and, man, I seen his wallet and that score is loaded!)—and tell him Sandy-Vee wants to see him, and when he comes outside, you come with him and shove him toward the stairs and me and my buddy'll grab his ass, and if he dont come across nice, we'll take it and break the bread in three." His childface looks pervertedly demonic—like a fallen angel's—as he whispers the plotted violence—his look reflected by the darkhaired youngman beside him who, that other violent afternoon, had taken Sonny with me to Sylvia's boarded-up bar.

The score was drunk, sitting at Les Petits bar; and responding to the howling anarchy, and challenged by the world implied by Sonny's plotting words, I said to the score: "Sandy-Vee, outside, she wants to talk to you," and he got up smiling and looked blearily through the door of the bar, past Angel Face making starved mouth-love to the mike; and the drunk

score looked into the courtyard leading past the shadowed
steps of balconies to Sandy-Vee's bar, and he started to come
outside with me, placing his arm around my shoulder warmly
as if we were two sudden comrades; and he saw the two moving out and looked at me sadly and sighed and understood
sadly through the liquor and said: "You run along yourself,
son, and you tell Sandy-Vee I'll see her later, hear?"

And I sighed too in relief, as the two outside prowled
waiting.

Friday.
The Parade of Hermes . . . patron of wanderers ruling over
the restless flocks, over the travelers from America's grinding
cities; nightmessenger bringing the news of the approaching
Tuesday. . . .

Although my wallet was loaded, I knew suddenly I had to
clip someone again as urgently as some men need to come
sometimes—for nothing better to do, the way old women knit.
The jaded man from Houston in the tawdry pink Cadillac
(with the jaded younger man with the face like a blubbery
mask—rather, like a fish long out of water—and the tall lanky
dancer, just as male-jaded) said: "Join us for breakfast?"

And we did go to the Bourbon House, but it was jammed—
and so we went, instead, directly to the motel, and I had expected money, but no one said anything, so I used this as my
excuse.

We drank and drank on the bed—and I still felt sober—
still deadly Sober even when the three jaded figures seemed to
swirl in one enormous, composite, gobbling mouth about me.

All three exhausted from the liquor, out—I went through
fishface's pockets first, and counting the money carefully, I
took only half—then the others, and I took just half. Then I
lay down on the floor—because I didnt want to be near them
—and almost-slept and woke up and woke them, in the
diamond-clear afternoon.

Then!

Laughing, Smiling, Being Happy, they rode me into town
through the coldblazing sun and the knowledge of myself, with
the clipped money in the pocket of my levis; and fishface
looked through his wallet and said, "I been robbed." And I
said: "Youve got to be awful careful of that during the carnival, theres lots of thieves around."

I got off at the Y. And I saw the statue of General Lee
surveying Lee Circle, arms crossed, disapproving.

I saluted him.

And I thought he must still be looking at me reprimandingly through the window of the Y as the hot-water steam mushroomed about me, protecting.

Saturday.
The Parade of Iris. . . . Rainbow floats weirdly illuminated, passing in papier-mâchéd splendor. . . .

And still I was sober—despite the maryjane, the pills, the beer, the whiskey; still alertly conscious, feeling at times a parodoxically turbulent calmness, perhaps like the stillness of a stormcloud waiting for a bolt of lightning to release the pent-up rain. Torrents of expectation and alarm rage inside me at the prospect of Mardi Gras, now only two days away.

The queens would be bitchy like petulant children to each other that day in the bars because the vice patrol had made them cut their hair, they looked so much like women and thats against the law If Youre Not—and so, Dejectedly, with short hair, they must face The World; and feeling their female stances somewhat compromised—unfairly—by that short, short hair, theyre arguing rhetorically over which queen would have which of us at her pad that night.

Betti (who was Benny in Nebraska) said I was her new husband, and Vicki and Salli (Victor and Steve, respectively, in Atlanta(grabbed Sonny and Jocko and said: "Well, honey, these are *our* husbands."

And as the queens began to dish each other, myself and the two other "husbands" felt ourselves so Goddamned absurdly Masculine—because, remember, queens always say they want Men—and we kept on studiedly digging a cute young girl nearby—because youre supposed to want real girls only . . . for "love." But, oh, oh, soon Sonny has drifted away, looking for the two momentarily lost scores hes been going around with; and Jocko left—and Im standing outside on the street.

I saw a tiny rag-doll Miss Ange waving at me asking was I looking for A Pad To Sleep?

She had short hair.

And I began to laugh so uncontrollably, right there on the street, that she swished away in understandable indignation.

Suddenly I felt vastly repentant—and very, very sad.

Very sad, sitting in the Coffee House at the French Market, sitting thinking strangely obsessively of the lady-tourists dragging their husbands depressingly along Royal Street (Roo Rowyall), hunting for gay antiques and pralines that are Clean, and feeling, myself, Hugely Bitter that they wouldnt give a royal damn if they knew that only minutes earlier the plainclothes had warned me—as they were warning all the others on the streets (the jails being crowded)—if I was still in town, theyd bust me for novisiblelegalmeansofsupport.

Sunday. The parades canceled.
It snowed today in New Orleans for the first time in more than 20 years, I wrote my mother.
A little boy—his features Youngly real in the icy white glare—rushed excitedly into the street from somewhere to gather the mysterious snow, his face turned questioningly to the Sky.
And the snow fell in white plumes.
Like a million tiny diamonds it covered the cemetery in back of the Church of Our Lady of Guadalupe.
And everyone, even Us, looked pink and real in the white light.
And if it had snowed longer, it might have killed some of the cockroaches. For a few hours, this rotten city was purified.
Someone even threw a snowball!
The snow melted in quilted brown patches, it rained, there was slush. The sun came out with renewed cold fury.

Monday.
The Parade of Proteus, who can assume any shape, any form, will pass tonight in a flaming snake of torches. White-robed mummers, ghosts of ghosts. . . . And at midnight, Mardi Gras begins. . . .
Negro children somersault along the street for Tips. Stray Dixieland bands become more numerous. Spasm bands sprout. . . . And this birthplace of Jazz is now shaking and rolling, twisting, to the new sounds of our ravenous time.
Through the open doors of the welcoming nightclubs on Bourbon (aggressive hawkers like recruiting sergeants luring the tourists with unfulfilled promises), you hear the drum-dominated, subterranean sounds of take-it-off music from the vast neighborhood of sexless sex.
In the cramped rooms, the smoke-choked apartments, the old, old houses, into the patios, the parties are impromptu and laughter reigns tover the city like a reckless deity.
And the afternoon has already aged into grayish yellow, the shadows are lengthening to pull down the night. And soon even that fading light wearies. Stars appear cautiously in the wings

of dark. The gray darkness reaches insidiously soothingly for
its anxious children.

In the swelling cankerous crowds, men and women in the
streets drink out of giant hurricane glasses from O'Malley's
bar, tilting the glasses to capture each drop, seemingly toasting
the faint moon which has already appeared in her own sequined drag. . . . And the cops continue intrepidly, pointlessly,
vengefully to scour the city, nailing the youngmen who look
like vagrants—and who, as the cops stop to interrogate someone else, can dart into the crowded streets, escaping before
their absence is discovered.

Past the Cathedral, obliviously, swelling groups snakedance
dizzily through the weird streets and alleys. And in the rushing
night, the Cathedral—its nebulous spires trying more urgently
to fade into Heaven—girds itself stonily for the masked revelers who will soon appear. . . . And gray, as if preparatory to
mourning, donning the night's dark shroud, it waits—frozen,
austere, ashen—for its own redemptive day:

Ash Wednesday.

Near the French Market is an enormous chicken and rooster
coop. Earlier, I had stood before the wire, watching in fascination as the roosters sliced frantically at the air, feathers like
sparks of many-colored fire. . . . Suddenly, one jumped above
the others, clawing directly before me, urgently at the wired
cage.

Remembering that now as if I were standing before that
cage again, one thought thundered in my mind:

*I'll go to the airport right now, I'll get a plane, I'll fly out
of this city!*

But already, night has inundated New Orleans.

The mob frenzy is like an epidemic out of control, claiming
more victims each darkening moment. I squeeze through the
revelers, and I feel myself once again exploding with excitement. I move from bar to bar, from drink to drink, from person to person—pushed along by that excitement which I know
is suspended precariously over a threatening chasm of despair.
But if I can go on!—hectically!—if I can retain my equilibrium
on this level of excitement, of liquored sobriety!—then the
swallowing void, though already yawning, can be avoided.

Night races toward midnight.

"Let's ball!" A woman's arm curls tightly about my waist,
whirls me around. . . . Someone blows a shrill whistle at me,
its paper body unfurling suddenly like a rigid-spined worm,

tipped with tiny fluttering feathers quivering tensely, mockingly before my face.

Rattles shake like at a children's party out of control. Noises blast their way into silence, into a blare outlasting sound. Drums, voices, laughter! A raging hurricane lashing at the city. A symphony gone made.

Stray costumes appear.

A band of red-dressed men and women in black-tentacled masks dance prematurely in the maddened street—red like flashing rubies crushed together, angry flames burning insanely bright before turning into smoke. Redly. . . . Roses pressed against each other in screaming shapes of red, red shrieking red. And like a flock of startled red-winged bats, the group disbands in separate scarlet bodies caraçoling along the streets to join other screaming groups.

Confetti like colored snow pours from the balconies, quickly stirred by shifting, stamping feet. . . . Streamers float, curl gracefully, are carried aloft by the winter night-breeze—suspire in the air as if reluctant to be trampled on along the littered streets.

Midnight!

The revelers sweep into the streets like tumblers into an arena.

Mardi Gras!

CHI-CHI: Hey, World!

1

As if the door—the only door—to an insane asylum had suddenly been thrust open, the crowds rocketed along the streets, flowed in currents, chose sides; howled the purple laughter; pushed, screamed, shouted, shrieked, roared—crushed against each other in a jigsaw puzzle of unfitting colored pieces.

Whistles, horns!

A churning, violently tossing ocean of angry cacophonous sounds. Multikeyed laughter erupting in unison like a fire-bursting sky rocket scattering a diffusion of burning sparks into the streets. Over the broken noises, momentarily the scream of a woman threatens hysteria, reaches its strident plateau, breaks, veers from its panicked course, becomes a longly sustained joyous laughing, reverting jarringly into an ear-knifing sirenshriek. Floating to the surface of that raging storm of erratic sounds, the beat of bongos underscores the streetmadness as if somewhere a spontaneous parade has begun.

Having waited in their rooms for this magic witching hour to convert them into women to the full extent of drag, the queens are the first to appear in costume. Most of the others will wait until the morning. But the queens have already come out anxiously like prisoners fleeing a jail.

Through the crowds, I spot Miss Ange—self-conscious about her short, short hair, which undauntedly she has arranged in minuscule ringlets over her forehead. In a green-flowered hoop skirt and a wide yellow straw hat—her dress so wide that she shrieks in annoyance when someone threatens to crush it—which keeps her screaming over and over—today she is Scarlett O'Hara. . . . Desdemona and Drusilla Duncan, standing under the yellowish umbrella of a streetlight, For The Whole World To See, are in twin outfits of the fast, vampish 20s—their hair, too, in helpless ringlets—and they carry

323

cigarette holders pointed carefully into the air in order to avoid poking some sympathetic someone. . . . Shimmying recklessly on the street, legs thrashing, looking like an alarm clock jangling insistently out of control, Whorina is a Woman of the Night—in a studded shiny red dress: a vision, at last, of her stifled impossible dreams from the graveyard hours when she knows, inside, that she was meant to be, every bit, a Woman. . . . And Sandy-Vee, in mesh stockings, bustle like a pinned rose—a chorus girl—has left her bar to display herself as A Celebrity. A handsome youngman in tuxedo and cummerbund escorts her Proudly. . . . Another queen, Cinderella, shakes a long metallic wand—gold streamers attached—at the tourists, as if to banish them from her sight forever.

Now, during Mardi Gras, when the barcrowds flow from one place to another—a mob thirsty for the momentary liquid gayety of the carnival—from the blue-shifting, pink lights of the burlesque halls to the offbeat, side-street bars—there will be, too, in overwhelming abundance, the curious and the largely unaware, both men and women.

For this one day, those two worlds will collide—the night-world and the touristworld—on the twisting, grinding, clamoring stage of Carnival, New Orleans.

Even in the melee of queenfaces, painted eyes, bodies in drag—even then, she stood out from all the others at The Rocking Times: a queen perched on a stool like a startled white owl: a man with bleached, burned-out hair and a painted face dominated to the point of absolute impossibility by the largest, widest, darkest eyes I have ever seen, painted into two enormous tadpoles, slanting to the very edges of her temples. The frizzled quality of the bleached curled hair and the devouring wideness of the eyes gave her the appearance of a demented Cassandra whose futile, unattended knowledge makes her burn, inside, with a fire that consumes only herself, while others refuse to heed the prophecy shining from her face.

She wore a lace dress, a ruffle about her shoulders: a misty lavender which nevertheless drained—as any other color would have done—her flour-white face, the skin covered with some kind of cement-like powder. As if aware of the precariousness of the improvised harsh makeup, which may crack suddenly, she holds her face stiffly. Two round smears of rouge burn on her cheeks as if she had been slapped over and over, cheeks painted red like the bright rounded smears on a clown.

She wore bracelets—cheapglass-beaded. Rings. Sequins

sprinkled in her hair. Tiny glittering dots pasted over her blue eyelids. A long, long necklace which wound about her neck at least five times dangled in a pendant where her clumsily stuffed false breasts rounden rather than protrude. Occasionally, she pulled tightly on the strand of the neckbeads—as if to choke herself. Her dress, short, reaches her knees, the legs crossed so that the purple spikeheeled shoes, coming to a long point like those of a witch, protrude on either side of the stool: one foot swinging back and forth impatiently, recklessly, constantly, like a pendulum.

And this man—this queen—holds a foot-long frailly thin silver-beaded cigarette holder—glossy ebony—the beads buried in it teasingly like tiny, winking, alive eyes. She held the cigarette holder tightly—curiously tightly—from a clenched, angry, potentially menacing fist—and she blew the smoke out constantly, her head turning in abrupt snakehead movements, as if expecting to be assaulted from the rear and trying to obviate the surprise attack by diligent alertness.

A queen.

A flamboyant, flagrant, flashy queen. A queen in absurdly grotesque, clumsy drag.

But there was something else.

There is something else that accosts you immediately about this flaming, reckless, gaudy queen contemptuously puffing out smoke as if it were something burning fiercely from Within that will force you to acknowledge her blazing anger:

When she slides off the stool momentarily—and nervously, uncertainly, often—to straighten the lavender folds of the lace dress, you will see that she is enormous, this queen: over six feet tall. And if youre a man and you stand near her—near that painted man, that demented-eyed queen like a startled white owl—you will surely be envious of his/her shoulders: which are immensely, improbably wide.

And youll notice, beyond the lace drag, the idealized body of a powerful man. Her arms, beneath the delicate lace ruffles which dance up and down in curves, are bulgingly muscled, deeply vein-rooted. Her legs, supported precariously on the wobbly high-heeled witchshoes when she stands, reveal themselves strong and firm, molded solidly, massively, as if by years of physical labor or exercise which necessitates sustained straining.

Yet this body and this voice (the husky voice too: as she turns, camping, to speak to me, the Cassandra owleyes becoming momentarily demure, the look of a man patently un-

successfully mimicking a flirt woman), which should belong
to that idealization of a man, are vitiated by the lavender dragclothes. The gestures that were meant to match that man's
body have wilted. . . . Occasionally, as if by an impulse not
quite drowned, not quite smothered by the perfumed femininity, she straightened up very much like a man. Then, as if
realizing what shes done, her body relaxes, melts, curves
effeminately, as if to compensate guiltily for the sudden flash
of masculinity.

An incredible gigantic white owl, I thought—as I leaned
against the bar near her to allow the mashing tides of people
to pass in their fervid display of restlessness (as I lean against
the bar, too, in order to avoid facing Sylvia, whom I can see
sitting at the other end, closely surveying the constantly
changing panorama of her bar). And through pill-clouded
thoughts, I imagine this queen next to me as though she had
descended from the sky through the ceiling, perching owl-like
on that stool—defiantly, to bring her unheard prophecy to
doomed ears.

Through the open door, near which she sat, facing it, the
man-and-woman crowds, howling outside in the compulsive
happiness which may be Terror, are visible like writhing worms
gnawing at each other. And the blond-owl queen in lace drag
turns toward the door, slowly as if to perform a ritual:

With the cigarette holder clenched between her second and
fourth fingers—the third finger, erect, supporting the holder—
she aimed an unequivocal fuck-you symbol at the world Outside—and she rasps loudly:

"Hey, world!"

Then the curious curse of contempt was followed by un-
intelligible grumbling. And now loudly: "Why doesnt somebody close the fuckin doors? You wanna contaminate the Pure
air in Here?" as, at each tossed-out word, she "purifies" the air
with puffs of gray smoke, to create a smokescreen that will
shelter her within the wombgrayness of this bar. She scowled
meanly at the door. Open, it threatens her world.

"Chi-Chi! Chi-Chi honey!" Miss Ange (Scarlett O' Hara)
gushed at her, over somebody's shoulder, unable to advance
any closer through the deadlocking crowd, "you look simply
Fabulous, honey! No, no, you dont look Fabulous—you look
Real! . . . And who made your gorgeous gown?—Im green with
envy," she says, unsuccessfully hiding her astonishment at the
clumsy dress draping the huge body.

"I made it myself," the blond-owl queen, drag-named Chi-Chi, snorted.

"When did you get back into town?" Miss Ange asked, wresting her arm free from between two people pulling her along. "I thought youd decided Not To Come Back. How was Boston, baby?"

"Lousy," Chi-Chi answered. "I kept getting busted. Father-fucking cops! wont leave me! alone!" she called loudly as if addressing a proclamation at every hostile person in this bar.

Farther and farther away, surrendering now to being carried along by the shifting crowd, Miss Ange shouts: "But youre making it All Right?"

"Yeah—yeah, still living off the lean of the land," said Chi-Chi sourly.

"See you later, sweetie!" Miss Ange called, all but swallowed by the other bodies as she adjusts her beribboned straw hat; raising her skirt over her head to make her dizzying way through the crowd. "Y'all stop crushing muh skirt!" she pleads plaintively.

Mostly sporting New-Year's-type hats, the tourists—intrigued, revealing auspicious Interest—eye the queens; and Chi-Chi eyes them back coldly, challenging them.

As I lean against the bar—for protection from the crushing mobs—leaning there next to Chi-Chi until the strategic time when I can move away—another queen, tossed out of the main current of the struggling bodies, spots Chi-Chi incredulously; but toning down the incredulity, she welcomed her to the queen sorority of the French Quarter.

"Im—whew!—Echoes and Encores," she says to the blond owl. "I never—whew!—seen you in the Quarter, but then—whew!— I just got here myself—and, well, I think We Girls —whew!—have got to stick together—or—whew!—we are Lost! . . . Oh, damn this maddening crowd anyway. Why dont they go home!" she shouted.

She squeezed in next to me, smiling at me—Bewitchingly, she thinks—and lets her hand drop casually so that it floated tenuously over my groin. "Dont I know you from the 1-2-3 in L.A., doll?" she asked me. The floating hand finally cupped my crotch. I said maybe. "Well, it's closed now, you know—so is Ji-Ji's—the heat is on in downtown L.A. something fierce." She emphasized the ferocity of heat-heavy Los Angeles with an intimate press of her searching hand. . . . She turns to the owlqueen Chi-Chi: "What is your name, sweetie?" she asks her.

The owlqueen answered: "Chi-Chi. . . . And where did you get such a crazy handle like Echoes and Encores?"

Holding herself as if a hundred cameras are focusing on her nonexistent beauty to record this revelatory moment, Echoes and Encores answers: *"Well!* . . . My Life Has Been Just That: a long, long series of echoes and encores. . . . Oh, Chi-Chi, honey," she said dramatically as her hand more openly and with assurance now explores my thighs since I havent knocked it off, "I just *got* to tell you about a positively shattering experience I had just a while ago." Suddenly she develops a thick, inconsistent Southern accent: "Ahm still shakin from it." She held out her free hand—gloved (shes an elegant lady)— to prove it. "Ah saw this cute butch numbuh—and Ah wouldda swore hes a hustluh—and Ah thought: Well, your mothuh's gonna go aftuh that one! . . Well, honey, that butch numbuh turns out to be a les-bay-an—the butchest dam diesel dike y'evuh haid yuh gay eyes on!" Now she grinds her squirming butt against my pelvis and goes on: "I wanna tell you, Miss Chi-Chi: that dike was so dam butch if Ah wahnt such a lady muhself, why, I wouldda turned *straight* for huh. . . . Why, they are gettin butchuh and butchuh each yeah— those dam bulldikes. And Ah don mine tellin you Ah personally think it is ob-see-an: girls dressed like men!"

"Dikes gotta live too," Chi-Chi growled hostilely at Echoes and Encores.

"But, oh, me-oh-my!" shrieks Echoes and Encores, reaching out delightedly to touch Chi-Chi's massively muscled arm. "Nevuh you mine about *girls!* . . . Ah just wanna ask *you,* Chi-Chi: Where did *you* get those Shoulders? And those Muscles— I swan! Rippling—thats what they are! . . . Honey, you just take off that dress and that paint and I'll marry you!"

"Cut the low camp, bitch!" Chi-Chi barked furiously at Echoes and Encores, shoving the queen's hand roughly away from her shoulder. "Im as much of a Lady as you are—and dont you forget it . . . Now swish your goddam nelly ass away and leave us alone!" To me, as if to reassure me that she *is* a queen: "Stick around till this mob clears, babe; I'll party you like you never been partied before."

At the top of her voice—in order to be heard over the paroxysmal roar of the crowd—and safely away from Chi-Chi, who, because of her enormous size, would have had to struggle for minutes through the crowd to reach her— a startled Echoes and Encores confided to another queen: "That big queen over there—I swear, she must be a Mr America in drag!"

"I saw her!" said the other, hollering too. "She might be the vice squad—you never know what those bastards will pull."

"Do you know?" hollers Echoes and Encores, forgetting about Chi-Chi. "Those tourists over there thought I was A Real Woman!"

"Thats nothing, honey," said the other. "I was sitting in a car the other day with a daddy whod left his ole tired wife at the Roosevelt Hotel to be With Me—and we were necking up a storm—and a vice cop saw us and he says—guess what he says to your sister—he says: 'A Pretty Young Lady like yourself ought to be at home this late in the evening, Miss!' "

Seizing advantage of a break in the mob, I wrested myself from the bar. At the door, I saw Chi-Chi aim the fuck-you cigarette holder once more at the crowds outside, and I heard her roar loudly:

"Hey, world!"

2

Outside in the chilly air, I felt suddenly whirlingly dizzy. Two hands of darkness threaten to enfold me. But I tell myself Im still completely sober—still not even nearly high enough. The moment of panic is followed by renewed dazzlement.

I toss myself into the thickening crowds.

Bodies are passed out in Jackson Square as if on a battlefield before the mop-up, empty hurricane glasses like mock tombs beside them. Occasionally one of the bodies will rouse itself to blow a horn or shout into the night, which is calm and still—a sky like dark ice—and the world so turbulent.

A flurry of tourists like a band of wide-eyed children in the midst of this flowing river of drowning faces passes gleefully blowing horns, and I think: We're trying to swim in a river made for drowning. And I feel harrowingly sober.

At Les Petits, equally crushed: A queen in wilting drag, in withering eye makeup, was singing raucously: "Howre you gonna keep them down on the fawm—after theyve seen a New Wor-lee-eens queen?" . . . The same jangling, jangled crowds. Angel Face—wide livermouthed—is singing a blue jazzsong.

With great difficulty, advancing two steps, being pushed back one—feeling the ubiquitous hands on my legs—I worked my way to the back of the bar, where a glass was suddenly thrust into my hand by someone I know from the dozens of score-faces here. Liberatingly, outside, I stood in the courtyard, and I gulped the drink in a hurried swallow.

The crowd was not so thick in this courtyard. Male-and-female couples, male-and-male partners cling in loveshadows against the wall.

In the center of the courtyard three queens were posing for a man in a small party of tourists. The camera bulb flashed harshly expelling the gray darkness momentarily. The queens, feeling acknowledged as Women, struck impossible languid poses. One bends down, raises her skirt to reveal her man's knee, invitingly. Miss Ange, in Scarlett-O'Hara plantation tones, says to the man taking the pictures: "Now me! Take *My* picture!" . . . Muttering "bitch," the other queens glared at Miss Ange as she poses in her billowing ballgown—as if she has just returned, Triumphantly, to Tara. The flashbulb clicked on the smug at-last womanface of Miss Ange.

I sit exhausted on the steps leading to the balcony over the bar. I breathe in the air, deeply, scanning the crowds—which are slowly thinning in respite for the renewed burst of merriment which will precede and follow the morning parade when the fever will rage uncontrolled, twisting across the city like a tornado, when the invasion of costumed revelers will raid the streets.

In the shadows of the courtyards, Chi-Chi stood against the wall, her head cocked quizzically to one side as if she cant really understand what is going on about her. The breeze had tossed her frizzled hair recklessly, the lace dangles over one massive shoulder. She leaned artlessly, ungracefully against the wall like some kind of lavender vine.

As the flashbulbs popped around her, chasing away the returning yellowish islands created by the lights strung along the balconies, the lights from inside Les Petits and Sandy-Vee's— she looked even more incredible. Like a football tackle in drag. Some careless foot must have ripped her lace dress, it dangles in a long tail. Feeling it on her legs, she tore off the piece of lavender cloth, held it now like a delicate lace handkerchief. With the other hand, she grips the cigarette holder in that still-ominous fist.

I raised myself higher on the steps, sat looking down on the scene, feeling a sense of almost-heavenly safety to be watching the crowds from this distance—remotely.

The man taking the photographs spots Chi-Chi—delightedly like an archeologist finding a rare treasure. He wears an absurd peaked hat, striped red and silver; photographic paraphernalia draped over his shoulders make him look like a futuristic decoration. His wife or companion—but she looks too much like him not to be his wife—his wife is a sadly puffed-up middle-aged woman in a starkly masculine-tailored suit.

The man with the camera approaches Chi-Chi, while his wife, looking on incredulously at the sight of her, muttered in amazement: "My God!—look at the shoulders on that fairy!"

Quickly, the two close in on Chi-Chi in visible fascination, followed by the others in their group—two men and two women—each face stamped with that contemptuous, incredulous smile. As if she were an animal which may escape, they pin Chi-Chi against the wall—like hunters, the man's camera a gun.

Adjusting the camera, the man said loudly to Chi-Chi:

"Okay, sweetheart: Now you. I want to show your picture back home."

"Otherwise theyll never believe it," laughed his wife, her laughter echoed by the others.

"I mean," said the man—and he grins with all the contempt of his ancestry, "I mean that I wanna show everyone back home what a real big fairy looks like."

Chi-Chi shook her head in bewilderment, as if dazed.

The man's wife rocks with bitter laughter, as if Chi-Chi's humiliation will vindicate something inside herself, or perhaps erase something lurking uncomfortably. She stretched the rubber-smile to the point where it seemed her mouth would snap.

Looking into the camera as he inches closer to her, the man addresses Chi-Chi:

"Come on, sweetheart, you go ahead and give us a real big fairy pose!"

"And dont forget to say 'cheethe,' " his wife lisped poisonously.

Instantly!—as if a wire had been uncoiled—Chi-Chi sprang away from the supporting wall toward the man with the camera. She didnt even bother to adjust the lace dress; it clung carelessly to one leg, over the knee, revealing the powerful leg. She glared at the man for long seconds, with a hatred greater than she could possibly have felt toward one individual; and she gnashes suddenly at him: "*You* come on, father-fucker!" And she advanced toward him, toward the encircling group, advanced within that small clearing of grinning, hating faces which is like a symbol of her isolation.

"Whats the matter?" says the rubbermouthed woman viciously. "Arent you a real lady?"

Unflinchingly, Chi-Chi aimed her gaze very surely at the

woman. Her terrifying owleyes rake the woman's body sig-
nificantly—the masculine-suited, frigid body. And Chi-Chi
smiled as if at a private secret, just discovered, between her
and the woman, who looks quickly away.

Then the smile disappeared, and Chi-Chi turns again to the
man with the camera, still unclicked as if the finger is frozen.

"Come on!" Chi-Chi repeats. The cigarette holder fell to
the ground, her hands tightened into enormous manfists. The
paint on her face seemed suddenly to be disappearing—the
calcimine powder stripping itself from the skin as if of some
inner volition. The false breasts dangled absurdly.

As I watch from the steps—aroused by the prospect of what
may happen and wanting it to happen—Chi-Chi's face, contorted angrily, seems painfully aware of the crushing fate of
her tattered lace dress. And I will think later that in that
moment she must have felt the paint like pain on her face. In
a moment of recognition—recognizing herself in the eyes of
the other world, in the eyes of those leering men and women,
in the harsh waiting eye of the camera, recognizing herself
prematurely in the picture which would be laughed at, dis-
believed—as she stands there like an animal who may or may
not be trapped by the hunters, and, if trapped, is determined
to wound back savagely—in that moment, she may perhaps
have faced that image of herself: because her whole massive
body seems to be struggling against something—perhaps that
absurd fate—against the shackles of that dress, those rings,
beads, sequins.

And I will wonder later if Chi-Chi was seeing, then, smothered in youthworlds of humiliation and derision, the youngman—*himself!*—crushed by that something too overwhelm-
ingly unfair to define.

If she didnt see that, I will remember it in her; and the
memory of Miss Destiny, planning her impossible Wedding—
the memory, too, of Trudi, resigned to The Beads—the thought
of Kathy—will fuse with that remembered sight of Chi-Chi—
and I will wonder if Miss Destiny's evil angel had not, that
once, relented—was perhaps even smiling graciously, if only
for a few moments, over Chi-Chi.

Because Chi-Chi still stands menacingly before that man,
those other people. And the man doesn't move, as if the queen-
eyes from a strange, forbidden world are not only making it
difficult for his finger to click the shutter but are warning him
in other, reverberating ways. Chi-Chi is unmistakably a man
as he faces that entrapping group and yells: "Father-fuckers!

I'll take you on together or alone! Prove to *Me* what big men *you* are! Whos first?—whos first? All of you? Come on!" And the fists wait.

Like moths attracted to this blazing inner light emanating from Chi-Chi, the other queens, silent and tense, watched as if seeing a part of themselves, long ago throttled, stunningly revealed in this wide-eyed Cassandra.

And still, no one moves toward Chi-Chi to answer his challenge.

And as the man makes a sudden nervous motion as if to take the picture, Chi-Chi lunges at him like a grotesque jack-in-the-box. The enormous fist crashes into his face.

The camera falls to the ground, the bulb smashes.

The man staggered, reeled against another man, and fell, sprawled on the ground, dazed, at his wife's feet.

Chi-Chi's manfists are still clenched like a champion boxer's, ready for the others.

But no one moved.

And was it only the sudden, ramming violence, the sudden smashing fist prepared to crush again and again, the sudden threatening image of this queen? Or was it, instead—or at least partly—Chi-Chi's shouting for an instant acknowledgment of dignity? Or was it a swift glimpse, by that man now cringing stonecold-afraid beside his wife, of himself in Chi-Chi, not of the woman in himself, but of the hopelessness of his own sad fate, mirrored in his wife's tired face, the frigid body —whatever shape that fate may have assumed for him, whatever destiny hovering over him—over us—like a dreadful cloud?

What is it that makes that man, his face imprinted with the terrible impact of Chi-Chi's giant fist, what is it that makes him turn to his wife and to the others with him, away from this menacing-eyed Cassandra whose message of doom, through violence, has finally flashed out—and, after looking at Chi-Chi in amazement and, now, with only the barest, flimsiest imitation of derision—that derision so carefully taught and practiced, seeded, cultivated, nurtured—what is it that makes that man, rising from the ground, retreat and say to his wife, as he covers his face where the blood is now coming—what is it—really—that makes him say—almost sadly:

"Lets get away from here and leave them alone."

Oh, soon. . . .

Very soon now it will be just another of many incidents quickly to be forgotten by those who have witnessed it *(but remembered, perhaps—perhaps remembered, unmentioned, unacknowledged but festering in the cobweb-infested shadows of their minds—by that fleeting man, that woman).*

Already the cleared space about Chi-Chi is being filled. Already the crowds are milling, the horns are blaring again, the streamers floating, the confetti falling, the couples making love. . . . Already the queens are squealing. . . . And already, Whorina, fluttering a huge ostrich fan, is saying in a husky siren voice: "Never, never, *never* try to dish a queen, babies— thats the moral of *this* story!"

And now!

Now—that mere interlude of his life over—Chi-Chi again leaned languidly, calmly, demurely against the wall, adjusting her dress with auspicious care, arranging the false breasts. Missing her cigarette holder, she spotted it on the ground; and in a composed queenvoice, softly, she says to a man standing next to her:

"Baby—sweetheart—would you mind retrieving her fairy-wand . . . please . . . for a Lady?" But despite the composure, there is a note of frightened, melancholy pleading in her voice.

A noble cavalier, the man bends, picks up the cigarette holder, and presents it to Chi-Chi with a deep, deep acknowledging bow. . . .

Smiling gratefully at him, Chi-Chi clenched the retrieved cigarette holder between those second and fourth fingers. She puffs a long billowing stream of smoke into the air. Then gazing savage-eyed at the hectic crowds, she defied the world in a loud, clear voice:

"*Hey, world!*" she shouted.

And she punctured the dark air sharply with the beaded cigarette holder.

CITY OF NIGHT

PHANTOM CLOUDS SEARCH THE DAWNING SKY.

Like a spurned persistent lover, the night tries possessively to hug the city—but vainly, sensing the approaching dusk, which already imbues the streets with grayish haze.

The morning will come mossily in tatters.

The crowds, which had thinned immediately before dusk— the city holding its breath momentarily—erupt as if hurled from a volcano igniting the streets. As the supernal light claims the sky more surely, the city will be overrun by waves of costumed revelers.

Clowns! Gypsies! Pirates!

Emancipated of their restrictive sex for the length of this one liberating day, women like scavengers will prowl the streets, in and out of the shadows, into the fading yellow-winged streetlights: their bodies flung, given easily; mouths welcoming other mouths glued for long locked moments; and hula skirts will shimmy, unheeding the cool air; anxious thighs revealed beneath diaphanous dresses; waiting bodies displayed in flesh-colored tights covered sparsely with leaves from a violated Garden of Eden: imitation motions of sex while hands easily explore their bodies—bodies passing to other hands, hands to other bodies. . . .

Spanish gauchos, squaws, Arab princes!

Ballerinas, circus strongmen!

Mermaids!

Along the scabrous balconies, people lean like spectators to a Roman circus, encouraging the frenzy with shouted commands. . . . A dark cluster of young Negroes, gathered like purple grapes, make jazzsounds on washboards, tin cans.

Gladiators!

Marie Antoinette dancing with Robin Hood. . . .

And I go from bar to bar, reaching for drinks which sometimes are and sometimes arent for me. Hands which can belong to anyone in the surrounding crowds grope intimately, anonymously, like predatory birds.

At the head in Cindy's bar, malebodies were clamped to each other, kissing, sexhuddling. Standing at the crowded urinal next to me, a man reaches for me mutely, automatically; the unconcerned, mechanical gesture of someone picking up something from the sidewalk. *I could be anyone!* . . .

And in that public head, I see a crewcut man going down on a youngman, and I recognize that crewcut man: the man on the beach who had fled from me that lonely night in Santa Monica—and suddenly I feel like crying because it's true that people dont have wings. . . . But I merely lean with my arm against the scribble-blackened wall, while the man groping me goes on inevitably and the others obliviously continue their own respective lonely games. . . .

Outside again!

Werewolves! . . . *A creature draped in weeping seaweed, dead seahorses glued to the legs.* . . . *Bats!*

Medusa!

Men and women in skin-clinging, purposely revealing tights; in bathing suits of the 20s; in plumage-decorated bikinis . . . *naked peacocks.* . . .

"I been clipped!" a man shouted, staring after a youngman winding along the streets. "They oughtta cut their filthy hands off—like they did in England!" he bellows to the uncaring sky.

He probably asked for it, I tell myself defensively, as if the man had been accusing me. . . .

Improvised costumes: Capes spread like devilwings ready to soar. Masks elaborately protruding in tinseled whiskers from the eyes. Someone covered with playing cards, another with dominoes. . . .

A queen is talking to two men. "My name," shes telling them, "is Miss Ogynyst. And I specialize in group parties—If You Know What I Mean."

A Vampire woman stalking the streets, fangs over her lower lip . . . *craving blood* . . . *craving life.*

Grinding against her from the rear, a sailor pressed himself against the wiggling butt of a young calicoed girl holding hands with another man, who giggles uncontrollably as he crushes eagerly into her from the front. As I pass, the girl turns her face sideways to me, inviting me, and we kiss.

Moving away, I begin to laugh, and I stop laughing and become strangely paranoically angry when a ratty old man out of nowhere says to me: "Wanna go with me, boy? For just a few minutes." And in graphic terms he describes exactly what he wants to do.

"You cant afford me," I said, hugely pleased to put him down this way for taking my mask for granted.

"Who you fooling? Ive seen you every day in the bars." He looked at me with contempt. "Another one with delusions of grandeur," he smirked, which oddly made me start laughing again.

More clown faces, grotesquely paint-tattooed.

At The Rocking Times a youngman I know wants me to help him "finish a rumble with some bad cats from Gretna."

"Hell, man, I dont want to fight anyone. Im not mad at anybody—nobody! Im happy!" I said crazily. At the same time, I feel depression and loneliness hammering at my senses.

"Whats the matter?" he asks me, squint-eyed, "you too chicken to fight?"

"Yes," I said, "too chicken—and too happy—and too tired." feeling my stomach toss, my head throb vengefully.

Grimacing masks, leering masks, laughing masks, weeping masks. . . .

I see Sylvia at the bar. Her face too is a mask.

In a corner a man was glued to a woman in a bathing suit. "Disgusting!" a queen sneered, turning away from The Heterosexual Spectacle and bumping into a lesbian dressed like a male Apache dancer. "Excuse me, sir," the queen said

Tall ears wire-erect, a man beside me in a bunny suit removed the rabbit mask. "Wish fulfillment—thats what theyd call *this* costume!" he laughed merrily, although the wish-fulfillment costume, like the wish itself, was about to come apart; he hangs on to the bob-tailed pants with one hand.

The Tin Man from Oz!

Two youngmen who look like college students have been flirting with two queens in high drag. "You wanna drink?" one asks the queens, who nod demurely. The other youngman said: "Hell, let em get their own." "But theyre ladies," the first one protested. "The crazy-fuck they are!" said the second, staggering away.

"Here we are! Just in from Los gay Angeles!" Arms eagle-spread, there stands Lola, Miss Destiny's ugly queenfriend from downtown Los Angeles. And with her is Pauline, whos already spotted me.

"*Baby!*" she gushes at me. "How *good* to see a *familiar* face —From *Home!* Oh, I just *knew* youd be in New Orleans. *Why* did you *desert* me!"

Acknowledging Lola's hazy salutation—and promising to see Pauline later—I fled back into the streets.

In the reverberating currents of franticness, I tell myself insistently that Im still too sober.

At midmorning the Parade of Rex, King of Mardi Gras, will begin. After that the streets will be ruled by even greater Madness. The true anarchy will reign under the contemptuous Sun.

"I gotta know how big it is before buying," a fairy said to me.

Another one with him lisps: "Mary! He'll think we're *size* queens!"

The other one shrieks: "We are! *Any* size!

From Jackson Square, the steeples of the Cathedral are luminous, uncovered of the night. The Cathedral seems to be expanding as if in preparation for siege. . . . Before it: completely in black, with black angelwings, a longhaired woman stands frozen: a statue who has left its holy sanctuary to mourn over the city.

I avoid looking at Her, turn my attention to an empress gliding along the park, her train held by two candy-striped pages.

Winking, disappearing, someone Ive been with or talked to hands me a pill. Beside me a man holds out a hurricane glass to me. I down the pill with the proffered liquor.

Cannibals! Executioners!

I feel cold but theres no breeze. It will be a warm day. The sun floats on the purplish horizon.

Wrapped around a post near the Bourbon House, a drunk man is proclaiming: "This is my true love!" as he hugs the post passionately. An outraged woman pulls at him insistently. "Get away from me!" he commands her, "I found My True Love!"—as one leg curls about the post like a dog's.

Sorceresses! Wizards!

Crowds whipped up, exacerbated by each fleeing moment.

Alice in Wonderland!—billowing skirt raised obscenely.

Tom Sawyer!—pants open at the rear.

A cruddy-looking youngappearing boy-man, his eyes like black marbles, is talking to me: "I seen you the other day," he said. "You was in a pink Cadillac with some fags. Man, I got contacts you never dreamed of! I connect for guys like you—but I gotta test you out first, myself! . . . I aint queer, myself, dig?—but nacherly I gotta know what youre like."

"Shag, man!" I said belligerently, strangely repelled by him.

The shadows become deeper on the streets, the sky brightens.
A hobo in rainbow patches. . . .
Devils prowling the streets!
"I own a chain of stores," a shabby man is trying to impress me.
I turned away from him.
He tries to dazzle Sonny, nearby. "Shit, man, Im going to Paris," I heard Sonny say to him, turning for affirmation to the two scores hes been with. "Right?" the two scores nodded solemnly, a nod that could have been a permanent farewell.
Seminaked men and women!
For no coherent reason, I thought about Chi-Chi—the cigarette holder in that screw-you symbol of contempt, the mask stripped off for those blazing moments in the courtyard. . . .
And then incongruously, I think. Maybe this will be Jocko's last Mardi Gras. And Kathy's. . . . Not Sylvia's. She'll always be here waiting. The Evil Angel has already passed sentence on her.
A fugitive from some scorched wasteland, his body draped in orange and red crepe paper, howling through the streets in simulated searing pain. . . .
A score at Les Petits says to me and a youngman next to me, "I'll buy one or both of you," and he opened his wallet clumsily, showily. The other snatched it from him, rushed away through the mobs. No one cared. Not even the clipped man. He dug into his pockets, brought out a wad of bills. Laughing, he says to me: "I still got more than enough for you—how about it?" *Hes asking for it!* I snatch the remaining bills from him, all guilt erased by the man's still-unconcerned laughter following me.
Demons!
In flashing waves of bursting colors as they whirl from one to the other, the costumed revelers create patterns like those locked accidentally within the mirror of a child's kaleidoscope, images so easily shattered by a sigh. . . .
Two souls dredged from a netherworld, their bodies draped in ashen mummy-tatters.
Most of the malehustlers are dressed in their ordinary clothes—the studiedly carelessly open shirts, the casual jackets, the levis, the khaki pants. . . . *This is their costume.*
This is our mask!
Heaven, hell, earth have unleashed their restless souls.
Angels!
And lucid suddenly as if I had stepped beyond the world, ı

watch the spectacle, and I remember myself years ago before I left that window through which I had merely watched the world, uninvolved.

Masks!

Masks, masks. . . .

And I think: Beyond all this—beyond that window and this churning world, out of all, all this, something to be found: some undiscovered country within the heart itself. . . .

Suddenly, I feel released—the emotional coil sprung.

But the next moment, I feel horror scratching at my mind. . . . I force myself to think. It's Mardi Gras!—but that thought is followed by another: It's the day before the Ashen mourning.

And to escape that thought, I rush through the streets, fleeing from myself.

Again at The Rocking Times, in the courtyard.

And afterwards—when the vortex of this carnival has become a haunting memory and I recall what occurred then—what Kathy and Jocko, standing in the midst of it, will do in a few moments—I will try to find a clue there for my own subsequent actions, my compulsive attempt to drop my mask, to try, at least, to face myself at last. . . .

In an immaculately white dress of a flimsy material like a veil—shoulders uncovered, smooth and rounded and feminine —Kathy stood gazing into the mashed crowds. Her eyes appear to be fading, as if the color had been washed away by tears. . . . Over her hair, she wore a sequined crown, from which a long white bridal veil flowed over her dress. She shook her hair free of the crown now, and the golden hair came loosely to her shoulders. Even in the midst of the drunken scenes, she commanded awed attention.

Beside her, Jocko is dressed in black circus tights, as if mourning the Lost Trapeze.

Kathy is the bride at that final wedding, and Jocko is her groom.

Moving now, Kathy's gossamer figure reeled. Threatened by that sudden blackout, she staggered a few steps like a puppet tangled on its strings. Jocko held her firmly.

I gravitated through the crowd toward them.

A tourist had made his way eagerly toward Kathy. "Pardon me, buddy," he said to Jocko, "but I gotta say your girlfriend is bee-yoo-tee-ful!"

Jocko looked at him ambiguously. "You want to kiss her?" he asked the man, and Kathy smiled.

"Could I?" the man said enthusiastically.

Kathy turned her smiling face to the man, her parted lips inviting him.

"Yes!" Jocko said, pushing the man savagely toward Kathy. The man kissed Kathy, very long.

And then, suddenly, ferociously, Kathy reaches for his hand, pulling it from where it wound about her back. Leaning slightly back, she plants the man's hand firmly between her thighs. The man's hand explores eagerly. Kathy smiles fiercely. The man pulled his hand away violently, stumbling back in astonishment. Kathy follows him with the fading eyes. Now Jocko smiles too.

I turn away quickly from the sight. I feel gigantically sad for Kathy, for the dropped mask—sad for Jocko—for myself —sad for the man who kissed Kathy and discovered he was kissing a man.

Sad for the whole rotten spectacle of the world wearing cold, cold masks.

And I remember someone's words—from some darkcity: "The ice age of the heart."

Minutes later, my own mask began to crumble.

I was standing drinking at Les Deux Freres with two scores who wanted to make it with me—"before the parade," one said, "weve still got time"—and I had agreed. And as they gulped their drinks hurriedly to leave the bar with me, suddenly something uncontrollable seized me.

Incongruously, like this: out of nowhere, surprising myself by the sounds of my words, I blurted to those two:

"I want to tell you something before we leave. Im not at all the way you think I am. Im not like you want me to be, the way I tried to look and act for you: not unconcerned, nor easygoing—not tough: no, not at all."

And having said that, as if those words had come from someone else—someone else imprisoned inside me, protesting now—I felt as if something had exploded inside me—and exploding at last, I went on, challenging their astonished look: "No, Im not the way I pretended to be for you—and for others. Like you, like everyone else, Im Scared, cold, cold terrified."

Predictably, I became a stranger to them. They had sought something else in me—the opposite from them; and I had acted out a role for them—as I had acted it out for how many, many others?

Almost despising me, I knew, for having duped them—for having exposed my own panic to them when they had sought momentary refuge from theirs in the flaunted, posed lack of it in me—the two moved away, trying perhaps—I think with perverse pleasure—to forget they had ever wanted me. Now theyre talking to a youngman who looks as unconcerned as I had tried to pretend to be with them.

I moved back, against the wall, feeling a wave of depression sweep over me; depression made many times more horrible by the fact that, although unfocused (like the thousand unnamed fears experienced in the dark when you know only that *Something* lurks, waits), it had something to do with vulnerability.

I closed my eyes, right at the point where I will admit: Im going to be drunk.

But I cling to sobriety when I hear someone say: "Youll feel much better if we leave this place." When I opened my eyes, I saw a man standing before me looking at me strangely. "Im staying right around the corner," he said. "Will you come with me?"

Outside, a small stranded hotdog wagon steams ominously like a relic out of hell.

JEREMY: White Sheets

1

PONDEROUSLY EXHAUSTED AFTER THE DETERMINED EJACULA-
TION—which had come, strained up to the actual moment of
discharge, in those doubly orgasmic thrusts as if I had tried
to drain from myself something infinitely more than the mere
sperm—I had lain back in bed and instantly fallen asleep.
Waking up just as suddenly—suddenly alert as if someone had
called me—I saw, still lying on the other side of the bed, looking at me, the man who had talked to me earlier at Les Deux
Freres bar.

Outside, beyond the draped and shuttered windows of this
balconied room on Royal (it's still not time for the Parade, I
notice, looking urgently at my watch), the sounds of the rev-
elry continue, like hundreds of phonographs playing different
but equally blaring records.

Quickly, I sat up on the sheet-rumpled bed and reached for
my clothes—to get out of this room, to hurl myself back into
the streets, to join the summoning anarchy raging outside: as
if I have begun to lag in an important race which I *must* run.

But before I can begin to dress, the man in bed says: "Dont
go yet. Have a cigarette." He holds out the cigarette as if, I
think, it were an indication of truce after the sex act which
has suddenly, for me—now remembered vividly after the
brief, blacked-out period of sleep—made us Strangers.

I take the cigarette from him. He reached for his pants on a
chair next to him and retrieved from a pocket several bills
which he places for me on the table beside the bed. He did this
as if, for him, this is the most insignificant aspect of the scene
we have played out.

Coming here with him—I remember distinctly—I hadnt
mentioned money. There had been nothing about him to suggest he was a score. In the state of pilled and liquored panic
which I had felt threatening to bludgeon my senses at that bar,

343

the evenness of his voice, the calmness, had acted immediately to sap my nerves in that advancing tide of forcedly laughing faces determined above all else to enter an engulfing tide of madness. . . . And so I had merely been grateful to him for the offer of momentary respite from the crowds.

Now, aware acutely of the thriving street, as if its sounds were connected electrically to my senses, and remembering the previous sex scene, during which I had played the unreciprocal role more obsessively than ever before (as if the dropping of the streetpose, in the bar previously with those two scores, had made it necessary for me to prove with greater urgency that I could still wear that mask), I thought of one thing:

Escape from this room!

Escape from the bedcover thrown in a heap on the floor—escape, especially and mysteriously disturbingly, from the rumpled sheets. . . . But I lay back in bed. I would stay only a few more minutes, I told myself, trying momentarily to shut out the hypnotizing, seductively beckoning sounds of the frenzy roaring Outside: beckoning like a ritual prepared especially for me.

"Why is it," this man was saying slowly, almost as if he were seeking an excuse, by talking, in order not to join the streetcrowds—or to keep me from it, "that the moment the orgasm is over—or the moment it's remembered, after sleep," he added, as if understanding very clearly my anxiety to leave —as if, too, he is speaking about me personally, "why is it that people want to leave, as if to forget—with someone else —whats just happened between them—which will happen again and again—and again have to be forgotten?"

The inappropriateness of his searching remarks, while the carnival fury which we have all come to seek—that very cramming of experiences with many, many people—roars outside—the vast inappropriateness of it strikes me immediately. Of course, what he had said was largely true: Afterwards, in those hurried contacts, you want to leave instantly, as if in some kind of shame, or guilt, for something not exchanged.

But I said: "It's just the carnival outside; it's what everyone comes here for."

"Youll see it all," he assured me, indicating that to him it's not important. "It doesnt really begin again until after the morning parade. Ive seen it before. There nothing going on now that wasnt going on when you were down there just a while ago—only more of it." He spoke softly, nevertheless compelling conviction.

He was a well-built, masculine man in his early 30s, with uncannily dark eyes, light hair. He is intensely, moodily handsome. . . . Looking at him, I wonder why such a man would pay another male when he could obviously make it easily and mutually in any of the bars, and I wonder if perhaps there is another reason for his having given unasked-for money. It is a sudden feeling, not substantiated by anything that has actually happened. But it is a strong one. The money rests there, something constantly present, but, still, by the fact of my not having yet taken it, unacknowledged.

He was propped against the headrest on the bed, a pillow at his back; covered from his waist down by the sheet. I lie on top of the sheet in order not to feel that Im actually in bed with him.

This room, just around the corner from the bar where I met him, is obviously one of those expensive rooms reserved months in advance of the carnival: their prices determined almost exclusively by their location in the French Quarter, the balcony from which the carnival rites can be viewed. The furniture attempts to suggest the Old New Orleans of novels and movies, romance; but there is an air of emulation—of carnival-masquerade, even about this room.

"Besides," he was saying, "if you rest a while longer, you can take full advantage of it all. . . . Thats what you feel you have to do, isnt it?" he shot at me strangely. Then, quickly, before I could answer his question, as if he had already known the answer: "What is your name?"

Following the rules of that nightworld which tacitly admits guilt while seldom openly acknowledging it, I told him my first name.

He smiled. "My name is Jeremy—Jeremy Adams," he said, announcing his last name pointedly. And, curiously, something which is seldom done in those interludes, he held out his hand for me to shake, and I took it. . . . (I remember Mr King and his resentment of the distrust implicit in merely giving first names. I remember him with a sharp, pungent loneliness, not only for him but for the situation he had resented. . . . "I'll give you ten, and I dont give a damn for you," Mr King had said, and with those words he had verbalized the imposed coldness of the life he lived, of the life I would soon, then, discover.)

I told Jeremy Adams my own last name.

"It's your first Mardi Gras, isnt it?" he asked me.

"Yes." I felt amazingly sober after the short intense sleep. All at once, Im not so anxious to be back on those streets. For a moment, the prospect terrifies me. It's only that Im still tired, I told myself. It has nothing directly to do with this man.

He moved his leg slightly under the sheet, closer to mine. I leaned over as if to retrieve something from my clothes on the floor. Actually I merely wanted to move away from something oddly threatening about him—strangely, the very evenness of his voice now, the certainty of his manner—the moody handsomeness—the ease. Even during the sex, although I had detected no inhibition in him, this ease had manifested itself. There had been none of the hurried hungriness of some of the others.

And then—as I sat up on the bed again, farther from him now—he said this, completely unexpectedly, without hint of its coming, without preparation; bluntly:

"You want, very much, to be loved—but you dont want to love back, even if you have to force yourself not to."

I faced him on the bed. He was looking at me steadily. I grasp defensively for the streetpose that will dismiss his statement. "Oh, man, dig," I said, "I just want to ball while I can."

"I was standing right near you at the bar when you were talking to the two men you were with," he said. "I heard you —everything you said—everything about 'pretending'—about being just as frightened as everyone else."

I felt my face burning with shame. Emotionally, in that bar, for those few moments, I had stripped myself naked; and this man had witnessed it.

"Dont be embarrassed," he said quickly. "I had sensed something like that, even before I heard you in the bar. I'd seen you several times before—the first time was near the French Market. I saw you staring at the cooped-up roosters there, I saw your reaction when they seemed to want to claw their way out of their cage. Do you know that you actually winced? Do you remember?"

Yes, I remembered—and I remember the eery feeling that I had been in that cage.

"I would have talked to you then," Jeremy went on, "but you walked away very quickly. . . . I knew you wouldnt speak to me—it's difficult for some people, and I was sure it was so for you. . . . I was right, wasnt I?—about not wanting to love back; not even wanting to feel anything—for one person."

Curtly, squashing out the cigarette to indicate that the direction of the conversation will push me to leave, I said: "I dcnt even know that I want to be 'loved.' I just know that I want to feel Wanted. I dont even want to feel that I *need* any one person."

"Just many," he said ineluctably. "Im sorry," he apologized. "Dont be . . . 'bugged,'" he laughed.

His use of that word, so obviously for my benefit, made me laugh too.

He seems to realize that Im not so eager now to leave; and he seems to sense, too, my unfocused fears of the streets. Perhaps taking advantage of that, he pursues the subject. "Youve never loved anyone?" he asked me.

I wanted to say something flippant that will make his question seem ridiculous, particularly at this carnival time. Instead, I answered hurriedly. "Not the way you mean."

But I think of my Mother—her love like a stifling perfume. . . . Yes, that was "love"—on both sides—a devouring potentially choking thing—like Sylvia's love for her son—but love nonetheless. . . . The always-scorching memory of my Father, emerging—"loved"—out of the ashes of that early hatred. . . . Yet I know that this is not what Jeremy means.

He had pushed my thoughts into an area I preferred to leave unexplored. I grasped for the least dangerous thought: Could I have really loved Barbara? (The stabbing unhappiness inside me when I saw her that last time—but hadnt we merely used each other, in some kind of mutual fear?) And my mind sprang forward: Dave. . . . (I try to picture his face when I first met him; but the face I remember is another one—the one which had stared at me in disbelief that afternoon when I had walked out, that look branded in my mind, recalled so clearly, so often. . . .) And how much of what I had fled from had been fear for myself?—how much had been fear of hurting him? . . . Lance. . . . Pete: the feeling of hopelessness and pain and embarrassment and isolation that night when he had held my hand for so long in bed. . . . The man on the beach in Santa Monica (and I remember him, instead, as I had seen him earlier here in New Orleans). . . . Mr King's loneliness—shared!—shared and acknowledged; and it had been that very awareness of his pain (as perhaps, too, it had been toward Dave) which had sent me from him. By fleeing impotently, hadnt I manifested what could be, perhaps, a shape of "love"? . . .

"No," I repeated emphatically, "Ive never loved any *one*."

And when I said that, I thought of this: That night in Chicago, walking along the lake, when I felt myself exploding with love—but it was something else, something that was closer to pity (as it had been in my feelings toward Mr King, the others, I now realized).

Outside, there is a sudden change in the noises. Voices are shouting: "Let them go! Let them go!" Soon the shouting becomes a chant, the same three words: "Let! Them! Go!" The clapping of hands in rhythm to the commanding words. The sound of feet stamping.

"The police, probably," said Jeremy. "Probably trying to arrest someone—but that crowd isnt going to let them. It's the crowd's day of complete freedom, if anarchy is complete freedom. The police know it too. Theyre largely powerless—but still they put up a pretense. *Their* masks are the last to come off," he said ambiguously. . . .

After a short pause, he asked me—again bluntly: "Do you always go for money—only?"

"Yes," I lied. How impossibly difficult it seemed to explain to him that it was the mere proffering of the sexmoney that mattered; the unreciprocated sex: the manifestations that I was really Wanted.

"Oh?" he asked, as if something in the way I had reacted so quickly has made him doubt it, perhaps, too—certainly—the fact that I hadnt asked him for money, that he had given it. "Somehow, listening to you with those two in the bar—and having seen you with others—I got the impression that the money they gave you wasnt the important thing—that you were, maybe, compulsively playing a game."

His words annoyed me. Yet I can stop them by merely walking out on him. Nothing keeps me here, I keep insisting to myself. Still, I remain lying on the bed.

There is a new relief in the knowledge that he has overheard me in the bar with those other two—beyond the adopted pose—when I had acknowledged my own terror. Knowing that, he had nevertheless sought me out.

At the same time, my senses seem completely alive, tingling, after the resurrective sleep. What could be false, momentary sobriety—which, if false, could hammer me into drunkenness with just one more drink—makes me feel reckless. It could be, too, the noises outside, the recurrent anticipation—beyond the fears—of rejoining the people sweeping along the streets madly. It could be that like a child before a luscious dessert, Im savoring the anticipation before the actual taste—trying to stretch the time before I'll be in the midst of the steadily growing, thunderous frenzy. . . .

Perhaps this man, Jeremy, senses my doubts as to why I remain in this room with him.

In an almost amused tone, he said: "Did you think that if I knew—since you didnt know that I had overheard you in that bar—that if I knew what you were really like—or might be like—what you were trying to tell those two about yourself —that I'd lose interest in you?"

"It's happened before," I said. "You saw it happen then. People want you for what you 'appear' to be—unconcerned, toughened. You learn that immediately when you hang around the streets."

"Thats where people looking for streetpeople naturally go," he said. "And maybe it's true that for them you become more masculine if you appear 'tough'—or even dumb. Or maybe— as someone once told me—they feel that, although theyve paid you, theyre 'better'—smarter. And it could be also that theyre searching for their seeming opposite: the seemingly insensitive street-youngmen—as they themselves might want to be in order not to get hurt. . . ."

And I remembered the man in Los Angeles who had almost begged me to rob him.

"Im sure, in part, it's all of these—but not exclusively," Jeremy went on. "It sounds too much like a defense. . . . It could be, rather," he continued slowly, "that theyre resigned to finding nothing but a momentary sex experience. Maybe it isnt that they dont want something more; maybe theyve just given up on finding anything beyond sex, and theyre even afraid to ask, 'Can I see you again?' Theyll look for someone else rather than possibly hearing the answer 'No'—an answer just as frightened perhaps as their own question. So they resign themselves to the brief contacts. Now they look for the people who 'dont care'. . . . And the reasons of the people on your side are just as mysterious as those of the ones who pay you . . . like me," he added, and went on: "How much of it, for you, is being a part of this alluring defiant world without really joining it?—so you can say (and Im talking about 'you' only generally—Im actually talking about many people) —so you can say, 'I do it only for the money involved'; or: 'I dont do anything back in bed myself; my masculinity is still intact—and in the meantime I can go with as many men as I— . . . *need* . . . to'?"

Ordinarily, those words would have resounded as the score's

attempt to compensate for his previously indicated desire by questioning the very masculinity which had originally attracted him. Yet, coming from this man—somehow—perhaps because of the fact that hes paid me without that payment having been asked for or agreed upon—his words dont really register as the ordinary put-down after the battlefield of one-sided sex has been cleared by the leveling orgasms. For that reason, those words are doubly disturbing.

And it was what Barbara had implied—and the memory of her saddens me beyond the fact that I had liked her so much: that she had tried to prove with me what she had told herself that I, and others, were trying to prove with her. . . . Yes, it was at least in part a mutual fear that had brought us together.

Once again my thoughts had veered into a dangerous territory. To stop their direction—astonishing myself, yet responding commandingly to the burgeoning rashness, I reached impulsively for Jeremy's hand and placed it on my leg. He left it there, without comment, almost as if he were unaware of my having done it.

Or is he too pretending? Has he understood what my motion with his hand is meant to convey, what I was trying to indicate to him—that, at least in that direction, it was I who could make the rules.

But he *had* understood: Whatever pang of victory I might have felt by executing that gesture, he erased swiftly by saying: "Wouldnt your masculinity be compromised much less if you tested your being 'wanted' with women instead of men?"

"It's easier to hustle men," I defended myself quickly, at the same time trying to put him down—but, although that is true on the streets, it had sounded weak and I knew it. I had merely mouthed one of the many rationalized legends of that world.

"I think it's something else," he went on relentlessly. "Even a wayward revenge on your own sex—your father's sex. . . ."

I winced. He had aimed too cruelly. "You sound like a damn headshrinker," I hit at him. But, automatically, I had begun to twist the ring my father had given me that lost morning; and Im remembering, out of that gray-shaded world of childhood —out of those moments of tattered happiness—the times when he would ask me for "a thousand"—when I would jump on his lap, when he would fondle me intimately—and then give me a penny, a nickel . . . reassuring me, in that strange way—so briefly!—that he did . . . want me.

But . . . somehow . . . that was much too easy.

"I cant blame my father—for anything," I said sharply, sitting up. And having said that, I was amazed by the certainty, the ease, with which I had been able to vindicate my Father.

"Im sorry," Jeremy retreated. And he went on cautiously but again unexpectedly: "Some people tell themselves they want to be . . . wanted . . . when, actually, they wish, very much, they could want someone back. And notice I said 'could.' "

Suddenly I heard myself saying: "If I ever felt that I had begun to need anyone, I would— . . ." I stopped.

"Run away," he finished.

I stood up, walked to the window.

Against the shutters, restlessly moving shadows of people along the balcony seem to grapple, struggle, creating swallowing shapes in outline, as if to invade this room.

I returned to the bed. Not only the fear of facing the streets —or the prolonging of the recurring anticipation—keeps me here, I admit now. It has something to do with Jeremy's words.

"I saw a dragshow in a bar once," he was saying. "A beautiful queen was singing. She didnt do the actual singing, though. She merely mimed the words from a woman's record. The queen looked very much like a sure woman. But when the record ended, and she was deprived of the female voice that had completed her for those moments, she broke down crying—and the sound of her crying was distinctly that of a man."

Wanting to ward off the mysterious implications of the story he had told me (is he referring to the forced stripping of any sustaining pose?), I said defiantly: "Hell, I knew a queen who was so sure she was a woman that she came to the door once, from taking a bath, covering her 'breasts' with a towel; she even pissed sitting down."

I had expected him to be annoyed at this attempt to explode his seriousness. But he laughed. "Is that a joke, or true?"

"True," I said.

Then, in that unexpected way, he said this: "If I told you, right now, that I love you—and you believed it—what would you do?"

I laughed, but Im sure hes aware that it's a forced laugh— much like the laughter outside. . . . I had never stayed around anyone long enough to hear those words, except during the sex-scenes: words spoken over and over by hundreds of people, meaning the same thing each time—nothing. . . . I remembered that night in New York when I had made the decision that it would be with many, many people—through many rooms, through many parks, through many streets and bars—that I would explore that world. And what, really, had prompted that decision? An attempt to shred the falsely lulling, sheltered innocence of my childhood, yes. But had it also been, at least in part, fear?—a corrosive fear of vulnerability with which the world, with its early manifested coldness, had indoctrinated me; imbued in others: a world which you soon come to see as an emotional jungle; in which you learn very early that you are the sum-total of yourself, nothing more.

I laughed again.

"Im not sure what I'd do—if you told me that—and I believed it," I said. "Maybe youre right: Maybe I would run away. . . . I mean: that word— . . . 'love,' " and I had to pause before I could even bring myself to say it, and I smiled in order to emphasize that I wasnt taking the word seriously, "if such a thing exists as other than some sort of way-off thing, Way Out There, somewhere—if it exists more than as merely four letters—like 'fuck,' " I said, trying to destroy the expected gravity of his answering words, to thwart it by anticipating it, "well, I dont really believe it." The fact that with this man I can no longer resort to the street act of unconcern—and the intense sobriety after neardrunkenness—make me speak much more easily than I have before. "I guess the whole screwed-up world would have to change before I could feel that there was such a thing." Laughing purposely now, I said: "And if there is such a thing as what you call 'love,' just the mention of it should send rockets into the sky."

"Be careful," he warned, also laughing. "They may begin to do that outside at any moment. Then where would you be?" He added seriously: "But it doesnt have to be like that. No rockets. Just the absence of loneliness. Thats love enough. In fact, that can be the strongest kind of love. . . . When you dont believe it's even possible, then you substitute sex. Life becomes what you fill in with between orgasms. And how long does an orgasm last? People— . . . people hunting different people every night—even someone they dont really want: They close their eyes, pretend it's someone else. . . . The furtive, anonymous dumbshows in public toilets, in parks. . . ."

(And as I listened, I remembered—and I felt that strange, numb, helpless, cold fear when you realize you cant change the past—the first time someone had gone down on me in a public restroom. It had been on 42nd Street, in one of the all-night moviehouses. A man had stood smoking on the steps leading down to the toilet. Another had stood by the urinal. After I had finished pissing, I remained standing there with my pants still open, and the man near me approached me, reached quickly for me. The man on the stairs moved lower, watching; and I remember his face—the smiling mouth, and head nodding yes as the other knelt before me now. I remember the bursting excitement at the feel of the other's mouth on my groin, an excitement doubled by the blazing look in the second one's eyes; now tripled by the uncaring awareness of the imminent danger of the scene. It was over in a few frantic moments. The man before me stood up. I glance at him. And in that glance I see a look which somehow begs me to say something to him before I leave—something to acknowledge him as other than someone—a nameless anyone—who has merely executed furtively a desperate sexual act in a public toilet. I avoided the look. And he turned away from me quickly and fled. The man on the steps had remained standing there, now resuming his smoking, coldly. . . . I left the theater, I walked the lonely, crowded, electric streets, trying to forget the face which had turned toward me for acknowledgment after the great anonymous intimacy. . . . That had been at the beginning of a period in New York when, for days and nights, I hunted that fleeting contact, over and over, from theater to theater, park to park; rushing from one to another, not even coming, merely adding to the numbers. At the end of that period, I had masturbated . . . feeling completely alone.)

For a long time, Jeremy had remained silent. He seems to know instinctively when to retreat, or, rather, when to stand still: when he may have come too dangerously close, too soon. Now he asked me: "Have you been to New York?"

"Twice," I answered, still thinking of the electric island. "I never learned how to swim, though," I said jokingly, "and each time I realized I was on an island, I panicked."

"Thats were I live," he said. "But that kind of island never bothered me. Just what I felt when I first went there—the feeling of being alone among so many people."

"I dont mind being alone," I challenged him.

"Then youre very rare—maybe very lucky," he said. "Most people cant stand to be alone. Theyll do anything to avoid it."

"And you think I dont know that?" I asked him, resenting what I consider an implied accusation of coldness. In a way, I begin to interpret what is going on as a kind of battle between us—some secret, not-entirely-understood battle—at least, not understood by me, now. I fluctuate in my feelings toward him and his words. At the same time that he seems to be prying, he seems, too, to be reaching for something inside of me which, whether he is right or not, he feels may somehow release or liberate me. In preparation for the streets? For something else?

"Im sure you do know it," he said, "Im sure youve seen it." After a short pause, he added as if to himself: "Yes, Im sure you can feel compassion. But it stops there."

Compassion! Yes, I knew that was true. There were those times when it ripped me, when I had to retreat from people, from their sadness—as I had done how many times? . . . But perhaps thats what he means. . . . As an end within itself, when it became impotent pity, was compassion merely another subterfuge to grasp at, to resort to in guilt when we questioned ourselves?—so that we could move away more easily, telling ourselves we could do nothing else. . . . Beneath it, was there a sheet of ice which forced all feelings to stop there? (What had the Professor called it?—a flicker of compassion rising up to thaw the icy blanket of the heart, and smothered by the very ice it sought to melt.) Beyond those feelings of abstract compassion, have I merely posed at caring? Again out of that inherited fear?

Faces of strangers return like ghosts out of the graveyard of my mind. I had a sudden feeling of having played a game of charades.

And I felt, suddenly, in that keyed-up, manic mood, as if my heart had begun to listen—to something.

For something.

2

"But you do want love," Jeremy said.

This time there was not the slightest note of a question. Hes so composed, so sure.

And I think purposely: Only a short time earlier my legs straddled his shoulders. And at that thought I feel fully armed to cope with his words, aimed, Im sure now, at some kind of revelation of me. It is only their purpose which is to be determined.

"I want to be *wanted*," I corrected.

"Oh, yes, I forgot. . . . Maybe because Ive stopped running away."

His words slapped at me. This time they resounded unequivocally with the petty, malicious put-down of so many of the others—and I slapped back viciously: "Now you run after?"

"In a way," he said, unperturbed by the clearly vicious intent of my words—and I have the feeling that he may have purposely exposed himself to them. "If you mean that what I do now, sexually, I do without inhibitions—that I can talk to the people I want instead of waiting to be spoken to—attaching no great symbolic significance to it, well, then, youre right."

"And you think it has a 'great symbolic significance' for me?" I asked him. I know that possibly, later, I'll regret these words. Now, freed by the dormant effects of the liquor and the pills into heightened lucidity and rashness, I dont care. The feeling may not last. While it does, I must go on.

"Yes," he said, "as sure of it as you are. . . . Im sure youve thought you have a definite advantage of whatever kind over the people youve been with, because theyve wanted *you*, because theyve paid *you*—some sort of victory beyond the sex-experience, beyond the money. (But dont *you* need *them* just as badly?) . . . Anyway," he continued quickly, "I'd say that when you leave, I'll be less lonely than you. No, not because of the role Ive played (that can be infinitely lonely, too—perhaps lonelier—*certainly* lonelier); but merely because of that very rejection of those symbols. And it's not just on your side that the symbols take over and create the elaborate guilt-ridden defenses: The 'scores' who brag about what the hustler did back, about how they screwed him. The hustlers who brag about how the score didnt even get to touch them—they clipped him. All the legendary defenses—to be used against that lonely, lonely feeling of the lack of love—on both sides. . . . An imitation of sharing."

I want to ask him why he paid me—why he went along with the one-sided sex—especially without my having asked for the money, especially because everything about him suggests desirability within that world. I feel certain now that he has purposely emphasized the giving of the money, given perhaps, at least in part, to underscore all these words—which he seems determined to speak, to me.

Yet I can feel the gap between us broadening into a chasm as he attempts to come closer to me. Or is this his purpose?—does he want to broaden this gap?

This scene. . . . This man's words. . . . So completely incongruous before the Parade. . . . Still, I feel glued to this room as if all that is being spoken, while seeming incongruous, is somehow related to the ritual of the Carnival—mysteriously. And yet there are times when I cant tell how serious he is. Sometimes, when he speaks most gravely, he smiles immediately after, as if half-mocking himself, half-mocking me.

"Anyway," Jeremy had gone on, "all I meant when I said that I'd stopped running is that Im no longer afraid to give of myself. . . . On the other hand," he added, looking at me directly, "Ive known people who have retreated into a symbolic mirror—in order to force themselves *not* to give."

The defensive narcissism, I thought, avoiding his look. . . . That self-love that implies a completeness within yourself—and yet implies a huge incompleteness—your devouring need of others to sustain each battered return to the Mirror. . . . *You have Yourself—only!*

He seemed to be waiting for me to say something; and when I didnt—purposely silent—he continued: "I sometimes wonder," and he aimed the words clearly at me, "if it isnt more difficult for some people to believe theyre loved than it is actually to love. . . ."

"Maybe," I said cautiously, "people like that resort to finding in themselves what they cant find in others because they know what it's all about; and when they run away from those who may claim to 'love' them, they do it because maybe theyre afraid of being duped again with another myth—of finding out that, like 'God,' theres no such thing. And is it really so strange," I went on, "when you consider the world? After all, I didnt make it—neither did you. It made us. . . . Sure, as a kid," I continued slowly, wondering if I really want to go on, "as a kid, I wanted to right the messed-up world—or at least try to, somehow. Then, like everyone else, I looked around, I found out. I found out that nothing justifies innocence. I saw that other lives werent much different. Like me, everyone else had been tossed out."

And: *Yes,* I thought, *you become aware of a terrible imposed fate—fate, or whatever else you called it: "the beads" for Trudi—or whether it became an evil angel, as for Miss Destiny. For the Professor, ugliness—and for Skipper, paradoxically, it had been his physical beauty—as it might have been for Robbie. . . . Lance, searching out his guilt shaped by a "ghost"—in turn, himself, possibly haunting Dean. . . . For Sylvia and her son, it had been . . . "love."*

And as I thought that, and as I had been speaking, I knew how wrong I had been in thinking—so often, so many, many times—that *I* had sought out the world which now claimed me.

No. Even outside that sheltered window, even then, that world had been waiting for me, scratching at the windowpanes, summoning me, tempting me by the very fact of its existence, like that tree in God's primal garden.

And I knew, too, why earlier I had been able—so easily, at last—to vindicate my father. . . . I had seen enough in that journey to know with certainty that the roots of rebellion went far, far beyond that. Beyond the father, beyond the mother. Far beyond childhood—and even birth. An alienation that began much earlier. From the very Beginning. . . . Something about the inherited unfairness—that nobody's responsible but we're all guilty. Something that has to do with destiny—and with so many other things: starting out with the legend about a God who cares—and the discovery of a paradise we were deprived of . . . replaced by a prejudiced Heaven. . . . Something about the fact of death—of decay—of swiftly passing Youth: the knowledge that we're sentenced to live out our deaths, slowly, as if on a prepared gallows. . . . And something about the fact that the heart is made to yearn for what the world cant give. . . . Yes, the seeds which were planted in childhood were already here, in the world. . . . It was something in the wind.

"So, very early, I began to hate the world," I went on; "to suspect everything—mainly 'love'—and to try to become," I added bitterly, " 'strong'—and maybe thats what you mean by 'not giving'—by retreating to the Mirror." I had avoided looking at him as I spoke. When I faced him finally, he was staring at me as if he, too, had felt all those futile emotions.

But he said: "It's strange that we should have to force ourselves *not* to love—or *share*, if you dont like that other word—even force ourselves not to acknowledge that love is possible. And so we make the world even more rotten than it was when we discovered its rot; justifying ourselves by saying it's the only way: Get tough. Or be swallowed by it. And we further that original alienation. . . . And by 'rot' I mean only all the things that repress and forbid—the rot created by people in order to keep themselves from facing the real horror—within themselves—the coldness, the lack of understanding— . . ."

"And yet you cant understand rebellion—in disgust?" I interrupted, thinking of Chi-Chi, of Kathy. Skipper, Jocko.

"Rebellion?" he said. "Or is there a point where it becomes surrender to the very rottenness youve rebelled from?"

"Ive never leeched off anyone," I said defensively, again feeling accused by his words. "It was always someone who wanted me. Ive never even spoken to anyone first," I said pointedly. "And Ive never taken anything from anyone who didnt want to be taken from, who didnt already know the score."

"There isnt any difference, really, between the hunter and the hunted. The hunted makes himself available—usually passively, but available, nevertheless. Thats his way of hunting. . . . Im sorry," he said, relenting. "I just wanted to see you defend the very innocence youve probably set out to violate. . . . You see," he said, again smiling so that I cant tell how serious he is, "even the heart rebels—finally against its own anarchy. And thats the most powerful rebellion."

Cataclysmic bursts of sound from the streets draw me to them. I can shatter his sureness by walking out.

"I want to be outside when it's really swinging again," I told him. "Just before the Parade." But by the way hes looking at me, Im sure that he knows Im afraid of returning to the streets, afraid of the Carnival, the beginning all over again: the ritual—and because I am sure that he knows all this, and feeling that recurrent resentment, Im overwhelmed by a sudden compulsion to do what Im doing now: I draw his hand over my body so that it rests this time between my legs.

"All the symbols," he smiled—understanding again clearly, annoying me that nothing can shatter his composure. "No, it doesnt compromise me. Not at all." It's almost as if we're dueling—but for what stakes? I wonder disturbingly. "You remind me of a youngman I loved very much," he said. "He kept telling me he couldnt love me back the way he knew I did him. He told me that ultimately he'd want women only. Unwittingly, I hurt him. I finally believed that he actually wanted, very much, to get out of the life he'd been living with me. So I stopped seeing him. Then he called me up. He asked to come over. In bed, I could sense him becoming purposely cold. It was what he had plotted, to establish that I still wanted him, on his own terms. What he didnt know was that he didnt have to test anything about me. I would easily have told him— and proved to him—that I wanted him back. And all he had done was to compromise his own stance—his professed stance of indifference. . . . We say we hate the world," he went on mockingly, "but we imitate it constantly: Weve got to make ours a battlefield, in which theres always a winner and a loser. But, really, the line isnt that definite. . . . Have you ever thought that in all those fleeting contacts in which you consider yourself the winner—have you ever thought that youre being used too—by those who want you now only for something that doesnt last?"

"No," I answered sharply, wanting to stop the inevitable direction of his words, "Ive never thought that."

But once again I was thinking of Lance and Skipper, of Esmeralda Drake, the Professor, the fatman in that bar on Main Street. . . . "Who was the giver, who the taker?" the Professor had asked—and even as he eulogized them, he had discovered that it had been the voracious angels who had destroyed him. Yet Skipper (drunk somewhere in downtown Los Angeles . . . remembering the deceptive past) had discovered that it was the scores who had swallowed him. . . . "Angel" and score like intimate enemies, each mortally wounded by the other, hating the other, needing the other. . . . Is it possible that there is no real difference in the two roles? Is that something of what Jeremy is trying to point out?—that the common denominator is loneliness. . . . A momentary sharing of sex. And beyond that the infinite separation, the alienation. . . . Both give, both take. . . . All. Or is it, rather, nothing?

"I have a feeling," Jeremy had gone on, slowly at first, as if again to test how far I'll listen, "that sex isnt even sex any more for people like you. That you actually come to loathe it."

"Sure," I aimed at him. "*You* saw it earlier."

"A compulsion to reach orgasm," he accused me, "to get it over with. Not sex. Something else that youve got to cram your life with—some kind of revenge for what youre convinced is the lack of love. . . . But what a short rebellion which relies exclusively on how long you can look young! . . . Afterwards," came the inevitable words, "after the youth is played out—when youre ghosts, with painful memories of being young—when *they* no longer want you—what form will the rebellion take then?"

And he stared at me relentlessly in that way that makes me retreat from him on the bed, turn my face from him; that glaring uncompromising look which makes me think: He knows things Ive never spoken. And his words conjure phantoms of that insidious empty tomorrow; and I think of youth ebbing out, of youth equated with rebellion, rebellion with orgasm. . . .

"Now it's *you* who arent supposed to care," he said. "But, later, theyll be the ones who *wont* care. . . . In a way we're all phonies, pretending sometimes not to care—out of fear; other times pretending to care more than we really do."

"I hate that word 'phony,' " I told him. "After all, we only see what 'appears.' "

"I agree with that—but underneath, we *know*," he said. "Certainly the hustler knows he hasnt created the legend of what he is in our world. Like all other legends, it's already there, made by the world, waiting for him to fit it. And he tries to live up to what hes supposed to be: And, mainly, hes not supposed to care."

"And yet," I said, "those times when you want to be taken as you think you really are, beyond the Mask—like for example earlier, with those two in the bar, before I met you—when you try, then youve exploded *their* dream of you. Youve shot right out of it, by revealing that you, too, are as terrified by the isolation as they are; and what should bring you together pulls you apart. Not even that other sharing can exist then."

Jeremy said: "I know someone who fell very much in love with an awol marine; he worshiped him, did everything for him. One day the man came home to find the marine ironing the man's clothes. The man wanted nothing more to do with the marine—just like those two in the bar when you said what you did to them. . . . I guess you could say they had given up, to indifference—to the emotional masochism of our world, because of the unfair guilt thrust on it. (When I first realized I was homosexual, I prayed to be changed. I felt guilty, as if I had committed a crime—and the only crime had been in making me feel guilty.) . . . But, yes," he went on, "with those two, you left their dream, but you entered your own reality. And that can be much more important."

And as I listened to this man's words over the sounds of the Carnival—the thundering street noises, the steadfast clashing and clamoring—I had a sudden feeling of having been dreaming for very long. Rather, of having been in someone else's dream.

And how many other dreams?

How many of all the people I had known had ever begun to know me? Had even wanted to? Perhaps thats why I listen to Jeremy—to words which would ordinarily have sent me away —because he seems to want to know *me*, because even when the words themselves are cruel, they seem to be spoken in understanding. . . . Of course, I had hidden purposely from the others. Yes, even from Dave, who might eventually have said the same things, who had in a way prepared me so that Im able to listen to Jeremy now. And it had been at that point

—when some of these same words might have been spoken by him—that I had fled from Dave. . . . No, not even the Professor, certainly, whose obsessive wordhunt "for me" had been merely for himself, by himself, of himself, discovering himself in his own "interviews" (as he measured out his life—or more exactly the length of his sustaining hope . . . on a tape-measure): no, he had not even vaguely approached *me*. . . .

The Professor. . . . Out of all those words—that torrential, tortured flow relating the interludes of his life—those few word-jammed "interviews," what had the Professor revealed? A craving for love, of course. Yet . . . and yet he had had it, had it in the malenurse whose name suddenly eluded me. But he had sought out, instead, as if in a dream, the fleeting contacts with the "angels," who couldnt—or wouldnt—love him back—had sought them out knowing that, like a dream, they would fly away from him. And so he, also, had inherited that pervading suspicion; and he had fled toward desire, away from "love." . . .

Invading the dreams of others who search in you not what there really is but what they want to find. . . . Neil . . . the lost searched father trapped in sexual masquerade. . . . And all, all, all the others for whom one exists as an aspect, merely, of those unfulfilled dreams. Their lives—their days-long, years-long, life-long dreaming—continuing long after youve exited into someone else's dream—having witnessed only a bare pinpoint of their lives, which will go on without you: continuing, those dreams, those terribly lonely nightmares, made tolerable, out of despair, only by their very recurrence. . . .

And how will *I* be remembered, if at all, by those hundreds and hundreds of nightpeople in that long goodbye that life turns into?

And when I remember those lives—when I remember with longing and terror—when I wonder, in awe—will there be time enough? When I'll be haunted by memories of those searching faces, will there be time enough for my own reality?

I have merely breezed through other lives (like an emotionally uninvolved tourist! something accuses me as I remember all those I have fled from—but I reject the accusation), avoiding myself behind a mask as real as those which, now, soon, outside, in the streets, I will face.

And is that why I—and others—have come to New Orleans, sensing the masked ritual of Shrove Tuesday?—is

that why I sit here talking to this man, with his words turning
lights into the darkest parts of me? . . . And my own reality?
Behind my mask, the thin mask of compassion, eventually
what?

I felt a strange longing—a violent, unfocused craving, as if
my heart were screaming. . . . What can be the meaning of
this furious unhappiness?

My God but Im lonely!

I thought that suddenly, and I looked startled at this man in
bed with me, and hes staring back as if he had in a secret way
shared in the disturbing revery of other faces; the faces which
we attempt unsuccessfully to erase with new ones: which
continue to haunt us as if in judgment for nothing really
given, nothing really shared. . . . The dark, dark city. . . . The
city of night of the soul.

And in that moment I realized in astonishment that, no, I
was not a part of Jeremy's dream. It was my own reality
which he is bringing out.

Feeling this—and feeling as if I were on trial and must
prove something to him—I was able at last to speak now what
had been lurking in my mind, nebulously, half-formed, as I
had listened to his words:

"Isnt it possible that wanting to be wanted . . . or 'loved'
. . . could be as much an aspect of what you call 'love' as
actually loving back?" I said. "I mean, in choosing someone
to 'love' you—to be loved by—while that other person chooses
you to 'love'—doesnt one complete the need of the other?"
And having said that much, impulsively, not caring to what
extent I will reveal myself now, I went on: "I mean that to
choose someone to be wanted by—loved by—may be one of
the many, many shapes of . . . 'love'—if it exists," I added
guardedly. He was looking at me very curiously as I spoke. "If
each side could be measured in emotional degrees—the one
loving and the other accepting that love," I continued, feeling
suddenly as if I had to speak rapidly in order to be able to
finish, "each side might balance the other. If someone is able
to take 'love'—and take it with intensity—with the full intensity of his ability—and someone else who can give it gives
it to the full intensity of his, then one is hardly different from
the other. Maybe youll say Im just defending an inability to
love back. But if there is such a thing as what you call 'Love,'
its shape must be as unpredictable as the patterns— . . ."
I stopped. And I remembered this:

So long ago! Those few, rare, treasured days! The strange,

unpredictable patterns I had watched in fascination as a child—patterns created by the water as it poured from the aluminum tub in which my mother washed our clothes: the grayish water spilling onto the dry dirt in directions impossible to determine. . . . And I watched those patterns, on those pure, pure afternoons; watching those odd, intriguing shapes. . . . And then suddenly I remembered: the white sheets which my mother would hang up to dry in the Texas sun. And, drying, they flapped cleanly in the wind under the vast miles of equally clean sky.

3

Jeremy had lain there silently, as if this was something of what he had wanted to draw out of me: a multitude of new— or perhaps merely submerged—emotions whirling within me: a vortex of guilt and sadness and excitement, now, and the most harrowing loneliness . . . and something else: the bare acknowledgment that "love" (the mere acceptance of it, but love nonetheless, with intensity) might be possible. He said nothing, as if expecting me to continue.

But I didnt. The words I had spoken had stirred other thoughts which I could not yet verbalize. . . . Looking at Jeremy, I was trying to conjecture a different direction in the journey I have embarked on. If I allowed myself truly to be loved—if I did acknowledge what I had just said—if I acknowledged love by merely accepting it— . . . ? I tried to imagine this: that miraculously I felt loved. And then? If that feeling proved to be false? . . . That question, I knew, was based on that inherited fear—the wind which sweeps through our lives shaping our destinies . . . eroding belief. . . .

If it proved to be false?

I remembered, then, that once as a child I had watched our neighbor kill a chicken. He had severed the head with an axe. For seconds, the chicken's wings had fluttered urgently, the headless body quivering—the motions doubly terrifying in that the protesting sounds that should have accompanied them could no longer come from the lifeless head. The only sound was the desperate flaying of those wings (just as the wings of that rooster had fluttered earlier when I had stood by the French Market mysteriously intrigued: that rooster's wings lashing as if in protest against the impending slaughter). . . . And then, that earlier afternoon, from that chicken with the severed head, the blood had gushed from the neck—spilling

out deep, deep, violently deep red through that opening as if
to seal the wound that was carrying all life out of the convulsed body. . . .

Why, now, had I remembered that beheaded chicken?

Bewildered, I looked at Jeremy. He seemed again to sense
the whirling thoughts, which had carried me too far, too
dangerously, too swiftly. And still resisting those thoughts—
even after my acknowledgment of the bare possibility of
"love"—I grasped for the memory of the earlier moments
of sex with him, as if that memory were an anchor in turbulent
waters. But my mind moves swiftly forward—the anchor
buried in shifting sand; and I think: Now, beyond the spilled
sperm—if nothing more than sex is possible—are we like
enemies in that spent battlefield of fugitive sex—in which
there is every intimacy and no intimacy at all? . . .

My life was crammed with memories of that corpse-strewn
battlefield. Those memories. . . . Mr King—pretending that he
didnt give a damn (like me!—I thought suddenly—*pretending
like me!*); cultivating a veneer of toughness ("I know judo
like the best of them," he had said) to shield the vulnerability
—to hide, in him, the decency in order to cope with the world.
. . . Pete, pursued by nightmares of moviehouse scores. . . .
Miss Destiny, perhaps this very moment plotting a new, impossible drag wedding. . . . Chuck, searching the lost horse.
. . . Jocko, a lost trapeze. . . . Chi-Chi, futilely defying the
world—with a cigarette holder. . . .

I felt, one moment, a necessity to convey so much to
Jeremy—now, immediately—as if he were my judge, as if I
have to explain, to him, before I can free myself. Another
moment, I feel that strong animosity toward him for having
triggered these new, tumultuous thoughts—and the animosity
recurs fiercely, inexplicably, when I hear him say now:

"And so, at last, youve acknowledged that love might be
possible."

I turned away from him, toward the window.

The sounds outside are growing in volume, welling like a
river preparing to flood. The forced merriment. Discordantly,
some voices are singing within that great Outside. All those
sounds are hugely unreal—as if they come from a radio, their
true origin miles and miles away. The insidious, searching
sunlight is seeping through the shutters, spilling on the floor,
summoning both of us into an awareness of that Outside,
where, soon, the Parade will begin. . . . But, inside, this room

includes the World—which right now is my world and Jeremy's

And what *is* his world—his own reality? my mind questions insistently, knowing that the answer may be important if the drawing out of my reality is to be justified. What lies buried beneath the poise; the calm softly modulated knowing words as he digs beneath what he had overheard me say earlier at that bar? What lies beyond the declared lack of inhibitions? Is it all real? Or is it too a mask? Why is he in the carnival arena of New Orleans, during the naked sexual hunt?

I asked him the question which I had withheld so long: "And what about yourself? Where do you fit? If you know all the things youve been saying, why are *you* here, for the Hunt?"

He sighed, as if he had known all along that that would be the inevitable question. He answered slowly: "Because knowing it doesnt keep me from being a part of it—of all of it. It's *because* Im a part of it that I do know it. . . . Yes," he finished, "Im still hunting." For the first time, he seems disturbed, deeply. . . .

"And you see," he continued after a pause, "because Im still hunting, I cant help feeling—or wanting to feel—that theres something in you beyond all the earlier words and rationalizations. I felt it in that bar, when you wanted to strip your own mask. You wanted to be known for something inside of you— beyond the pose, the 'appearing'—the not-caring. You revealed yourself to be just as lonesome— . . . as lonesome . . . as I am. . . . And I sensed it," he went on even more slowly, "when I heard you, just now, at last reaching for your own definition of . . ." and now curiously it was he who paused before he finished: "love."

Now he said quickly: "I'll be leaving New Orleans, right after Mardi Gras. . . . Back to New York. If you want, you can come with me. We can even leave now, before the Carnival is over." He paused very long.

And this then is why the money lies there waiting. This is why with words he has tried to keep me here—successfully— while the Carnival rages outside like fire out of control.

"I'll help you," he went on softly. "I'll help you—in every way. . . . But it will involve giving of yourself. Loving back. . . . No," he said (and was there resignation in the following words?), "maybe only *accepting* love, with the same intensity it's given."

As a child, I was afraid of the dark, terrified the moment

the lights went out. I felt somehow like that now. Afraid of a
type of darkness that would loom, paradoxically, the brighter
the lights were turned on.

Before the impact of his words can throw me off balance, I
challenged him deliberately, like someone who must make a
life-directing choice immediately: "What would keep me from
going with you and walking out right away?"

"If you went with me, I'd take the chance that it wouldnt
happen. I have a feeling I know you that well."

"And the others that Ive always needed—that I might need
again?" I asked.

"I'd count that eventually, with me, you wouldnt need
them," he answered.

"And if it ends?" I asked—and suddenly I regretted that
question, which already I was correcting: "And *when* it ends?"

"It ends," he finished. "It's ended— . . . many times before.
. . . But beyond that theres something else: which makes life
livable: at the very least, the attempt itself—no matter how
often repeated . . . or, even, merely the remembrance of that
attempt to share—*in* sex and *beyond* sex. . . . I think that you
could love me," he said quickly.

I looked at him very long, and Im not sure what I feel:
Resentment at his words? Or a hint of a kind of balm on the
loneliness? . . . A possible substitute for salvation. . . .

I got up from the bed and I walked to the mirror in the
bathroom. (And I remember the times, the many times, when
I had stood before such a mirror, forcing myself to think: I
have only Me!)

I still look Young.

The streets outside. . . . The Carnival. . . .

In this room, the world is flaunting before me what could,
if tested and found false, be its most deadly myth . . . love
. . . love which, even at the beginning, was revealing itself
as partly resignation; perhaps offering only the memory of an
attempt to touch . . . implying hope of a miracle in a world
so sadly devoid of miracles. Surrender to a myth constantly
belied (a myth which could lull you again falsely in order
to seduce you—like that belief in God—into a trap—away
from the only thing which made sense—rebellion—no matter
how futilely rendered by the fact of decay, of death)—belied,
yet sought—sought over and over—as this man himself has
searched from person to person . . . unfound.

I returned to the bed.

"Well?" he asked me.

And I was thinking: It has to happen—I have to be liberated again. No matter what kind of whirling his words have set off within me, I must undo it all.

Yes, I knew suddenly . . . as if it would be the last time . . . that he must want me again, on my own terms—and that, then, his probing words, their impact on me (my own dangerous thoughts, even now, slowly threatening to succumb to what everything in the world indicates is the most murderous of all myths . . . Love)—all will be erased. . . .

I took the money he had placed earlier on the table for me —the money which, I knew clearly now, had rested there as a test, and I put it into the pocket of my pants on the floor. Then I lay beside him. I reached again for his hand, and I placed it again on my body. And this time his hand was very, very, cold. . . .

His hand didnt move. And then I pushed it with mine. He turned sideways, toward me, and our bodies touched closely. . . . For a moment I didnt move—and then I turned away quickly. I leaned back. Now the movements of his hands are his own.

"This is the answer?" he asked, smiling strangely.

"Yes," I said.

And this time, beyond what I was coaxing him to do, it had to be something else. The symbolic significance! I thought —echoing his words and many other words? And so it had to be this: He turned over on his stomach. My body pressed against his, entering him. . . .

Then it was over. The orgasms have made us strangers again. All the words between us are somehow lost, as if, at least for this moment, they have never been spoken.

I washed slowly and dressed. The sound of the anarchy outside is beating on my senses, summoning me.

If only for this dangerous time, something vastly important, for me, had been reestablished, I told myself.

And yet— . . .

Yet, instead of triumph . . . I felt abject, crushing defeat.

I stood over Jeremy still lying in bed. Complete strangers. I looked at the crumpled white sheets.

But was that so? Were we indeed strangers? Or had we, rather, known each other too intimately? Had we searched too hard and found too much of the despised world in each of us?

He was looking at me smiling. Smiling at me, perhaps. Perhaps smiling at himself. Smiling wryly maybe at the whole world which had determined all that had been said in this room—by him, by me. All that had happened.

That wry smile seemed to be a judgment on the world.

I leaned over him and I kissed him on the lips.

And I was thinking: Yes, maybe youre right. Maybe I could love you. But I wont.

The grinding streets awaited me.

CITY OF NIGHT

FROM ST CHARLES AVENUE, THE PARADE of Rex passed in front of the Mayor, who drank champagne, standing on a platform attended by a Negro in white gloves, while the King of the parade smashed his own wine glass into the street and the people screamed with joy, and someone sang, "If I ever cease to love. . . ." The floats passed opening and closing giant mechanical eyes Insanely and the girls with chilled rosy legs twirled their nervous batons and the Air Force marched by in Military Style, playing a march and feeling much a part of Something—The Parade, in Military Style: winding through the staggering crowds threatening to storm the police-cleared street. Somewhere in the distance a shot sounded with a sharp, unreal *crack!*—and someone gasped: "They was fightin ovuh some beads, an he shot him"—because as the parade passes, men in masks mounted on floats throw beads to the crowds—necklaces and bracelets and one-inch elephants and miniature parasols and whistles, and the people jump up to get them as if swatting flies; and since this is Mardi Gras Day —the day before Ash Wednesday—if you havent caught a bracelet or a necklace, youre as frantic as if life had deprived you of even that mere trinket.

From that room with Jeremy, I had emerged mythless to face the world of the masked pageant. Quickly reinforced by liquor—gulped drink after drink at a bar only moments after walking out of that room—and the previously dormant pills tugging at my senses with renewed fury as I watch the parade in the harsh sun (floats passing vividly beyond their bare physical reality)—I feel myself at last on the very threshold of drunkenness, beyond which, I already know, waits a pit of terror.

And the bright sun directly in my eyes erupted violently, the liquor jolted me anew, the pills were like claws ripping mercilessly inside me. I shut my eyes momentarily. And when I opened them:

Suddenly!

The clown on the float became an angel before my exploding eyes, and it raised sun-luminous wings as if to catapult to Heaven . . . leaving me sadly alone. Down here. Alone. I began to follow it, reeling through the crowds blocking my path; and the angel leaned from the float toward me. *And he threw me a silver star!* And I jumped to catch it but someone else did too, and the cheap necklace the clown-angel had thrown spilled on the street, all pink and blue pieces of glass, my silver star.

And already the disdainful angel, only vaguely visible to my shattered eyes, has been replaced by clowns on other passing floats.

An angel. . . .

Miss Destiny's angel!

The angry angel who plays the swinger in the childgame of statues: here to sentence everyone to pass Eternity doing the same things over and over, with our own huge guilty knowledge of things done—*because we had to do them.* Or perhaps, more importantly, of things undone—*because we couldnt do them.* . . . Here to sentence us for living the only way we could. . . .

Caught!—in whatever absurd fate life has apathetically but elaborately chosen to trap us in. . . .

The Negroes in torn muslin tunics over their pants jazzed It with flaming sticks; a white band played *Dixie;* and a southunn laydy said to a southunn genelmun in a southunn voice: "Aint that gorjus now, all them coluhs?"—and a woman: "Y'all come rought on back," to the stray cotton-candied children, "this instant—y'heuh?"

And the Parade like a long column of giant worms passed squirming slowly: dragon heads, clown heads, monster heads: all with enormous rolling eyes: all peopled by sad mad clowns throwing out the glass beads. They flowed mysteriously along the streets like ships sailing on the surface of my mind.

Then I had the feeling that I was in hell. To be swallowed by those monstrous apparitions; but before I can be swallowed, is it Possible that this nightmare city will suddenly flare into flames—set off from one of the torches carried by the contorted dancing snaking bodies? I imagine the floats devoured by flames, the clowns-turned-angels, the clowns-turned-devils sprouting wings to join that vast exodus to heaven . . . or hell . . . or nowhere; and seeing the costumed people determinedly laughing—and the skeletons, the jesters, the cannibals, the vampires, the ragdolls, the witches, the leopard-people—

I imagined the razing fire sweeping this rotten city. People scream! Attempt to Escape! Flee the holocaust! . . . Entrapped! . . . I imagine the rubble of French irongrillwork, the cockroaches of this city scurrying out of their dank places, the balconies toppling—*crash!*—the peeling falling walls of the Cathedral. . . . The purification.

Vengefully, I cling to the vision of that terrible apocalyptic fire.

But the Parade winds on.

Little children in weird hats run like scurrying, lost mice . . . in a maze.

The Parade.

The Caravan.

The dark masked Ritual.

Clowns passing dumbly throwing out glass beads: a pantomime of life itself.

Later, I'll remember. . . .

Along Royal, the redwigged woman in the tight peppermint skirt leaned toward the half-naked blond Indian covered with rouge and whispered, "Screw me please, dear," where the burgeoning Parade-crowds, released for the afternoon, have been heaved into the Quarter; and youngmen prowl Jackson Square restlessly watching the tourists anxious to wait anxiously in line to have coffee and donuts at the French Market, while Marie Antoinette and Robin Hood are being chased into the Cathedral by a band of cannibals that later caught on fire as the beautiful wideboned Tarzana posed for the newsreel cameras with her scarletpainted nails—while dejectedly at Pirates Alley (the saddest single sight I saw), Scarlett O'Hara, Miss Ange, her hooped skirt high up revealing hairy man's legs—drunk, dead drunk—and frantic and lost and lonesome and sad and desperate—wailed to no one:

"Tara *burned!* And I aint got the money to pay the *taxes!*"

And to escape the sad, sad sight, I think: If I take the subway, I'll be on Times Square. . . .

Times Square, Pershing Square, Market Street, the concrete beach in Chicago . . . movie balconies, bars, dark hunting parks: fusing for me into one City. . . . Yes, If I take the subway, I'll be on '42nd Street. Or in Bryant Park, or on the steps of the library, waiting for Mr King. . . . Or in the park in Chicago, also waiting. . . . Or if I hitchhike on this street,

I'll be on Hollywood Boulevard, which will be lighted like a huge electric snake—and there, I'll meet— . . .

And ghostfaces, ghostwords, ghostrooms haunt me: Cities joined together by that emotional emptiness, blending with dark-city into a vastly stretching plain, into the city of night of the soul.

I see—or I imagine I see—Jeremy within the mobs of people. . . .

Jeremy. . . .

The undiscovered country which may not even exist and which I was too frightened even to attempt to discover.

Life conspiring to trap us!

And I feel trapped by the world which I know now has sought me out as ineluctably as a shadow seeks its source in the bright sunlight. . . .

That world which Ive loved and hated, that submerged gray world; this world which is not unlike your own. . . . Out of the darkness and the shadowed loneliness, like you I tried to find a substitute for Salvation. And the loneliness and the panic have something to do with that: with surfeit; something to do with the spectacle of everyone trying to touch and giving up, surrendering, finding those substitutes which are only momentary, in order to justify the meaningless struggle toward death. . . .

Outside the Bourbon House, another blond Indian, much more cunning and much more naked, danced while cameras clicked, flashed and rolled—until the fat bald man whispered in the Indian's ear, would he consider giving a private performance for himself And Friends?

Now at Les Petits, where, on a small crowded platform, to the blaring of a record at full blast, a few couples try to dance, twisting and squirming as if to leave even their own bodies. Among them, Sonny danced with a small blackhaired girl (while the two scores who have promised to take him to Paris wait coldly for him). The girl's hair is long and straight to her waist. As she bent from her knees, arching her thighs toward him, her hair sweeps the floor behind. Sonny twists before her. Male and female untouching, merely going through the distant gyrations of sex, as if to see how close they can come to each other without touching: carried into that limbo where savage music becomes the expression of life.

And Sonny puts his hands in his pockets and arches his back sensually like a cat's—the hair tumbles over his eyes; and he danced with such frenzy, such abandon, that the other couples left the floor, circled him and the girl—and soon even the girl steps aside, superfluous, while Sonny dances on alone as if with an imaginary partner: the world. He seemed suddenly to be all our defiant youth—desperate to spring from the Cage, futilely defying the world in that twisting dance. In the heat of the feverish dancing, he throws open his shirt, removes it —twirls his hand in the air as if he held a rope—"Yahoo!" he shouted—and he dances shirtless, chest gleaming with sweat—and the crowd applauds as he goes through the sex-gyrations. Alone.

Leaving quickly, Im carried by the rivers of people outside. . . . White-robed mummers from the parade. Spears, plumed helmets catch the light. Devils dance with angels. Skirts part, invite. . . . The dusty-yellow wintersky. Tinseled bodies. Sequined faces.

"The City That Care Forgot": New Orleans.

The Parade of Comus. . . . The last parade of Mardi Gras —a gaudy funeral. . . .

And then, it was as if I were imprisoned in a glass room, looking out—isolated from the world, which could see me, which I could see—which couldnt hear me. Locked inside, away from the million people. And each of those million people in turn is separated within his own glass chamber from the others. . . .

Suddenly the Devil leapt toward me!

In red, with long black horns! He opens His arms to embrace me in His batwinged cape! And I lunge toward Him anxious to be claimed, and He encloses the flapping wings about me. . . .

Freed of his embrace, I look at the ghostly steeples of the Cathedral. *I'll climb to that nonexistent Heaven!* . . .

Now at Cindy's bar a man is groping me, and gropes someone else—and all around, hands are searching—while Cindy herself, globs of frantic, shaking flesh, bouncing, moves chaperonely nervously sighing:

"Please, please, *please*, boys! Be Nice!"

Outside again, I recognized the ovaled fairy who had made it with me that first day in New Orleans; he is a freckled schoolboy, with a lollypop. With him is his youngman-lover who had turned femme—and he is, resignedly perhaps, a schoolgirl: bloomers peeking, ruffled, from beneath the starched skirt.

"Tramp!" the ovaled one sneers at me—and he skipped quickly away as if I would menace or contaminate them.

Past the giant burlesque picture of Holly Sand on Bourbon. And I imagine her making quite a breeze, creating quite a storm, fanning waves of flesh-desire (to go all the way), and the poster of Aloha twirled giant mechanical breasts like windmills—*whoosh!* and around; *whoosh!* and around. . . . I look about me searching Burlesque street, L.A. Instead, I see the costumed orgy of Mardi Gras.

"Lover!" A fat woman embraces me tightly. We kiss. Now I turn to a young girl near me, shes dressed in a leopard suit. I kiss her too, pushing my tongue urgently into her mouth, crushing her mouth—as if to erase from my own the stamp of Jeremy's remembered kiss. . . .

The sky has darkened. The streetlights, turned on now, will prolong the naked street merriment to midnight.

Tomorrow, I keep thinking. Tomorrow . . . When Ash Wednesday will hang like a pall over this city.

"Lets make it, man!" Sonny shouted into my ear, his lips so near they brushed my face. Still shirtless, he embraced me drunkenly while the two suited scores bes still with look on disapprovingly.

"Later," I said dazedly, taking the pill he slipped into my hand. "Later. . . ."

The Cathedral is solemn like a tomb.

I think groggily: Dave. . . . The man on the beach, now somewhere in this city. . . . Lance, Pete, Mr King. . . . Miss Destiny. Skipper. . . . Jeremy. Each in his own way. . . . Each in his own way what? And Barbara. And Jocko in his way. . . . *What!* Nothing, I thought. "Nothing!" I said aloud, as face blends with hunting face.

"Honey," said Whorina, "youre twisted out of your swinging mind. Whatve you been taking? Here. I got something thatll straighten you out." She hands me a strange pill which looks like a raisin. She says: "Nothing like it, honey, You Just Wait and See." I pop it into my mouth and hurl myself back into the crowd.

Although the star-tossed sky is clear—as if to reveal the city, Naked, to the sight of Heaven—I hope it will begin to snow suddenly: a sheet of snow covering this city drowning the shrieking colors. . . . The ice age of the heart. . . . But I forget about that quickly, forget about the snow which would purify the city. . . .

In the courtyard of The Rocking Times, moments later, I saw Kathy. Still with Jocko as if he can protect her from something shadowing her, she smiles as she stares at the mobs.

God damn it, I want to shout to her, dont smile, dont laugh! I want to say to her: Cry, Kathy! But the smile is permanent as she seems to loom over the crowd—a luminous apparition: amused perhaps by the cruel knowledge of herself—the knowl‑ edge that shes been twice doomed: by the limbo sex and death lurking prematurely in a threatening black-out which will end, in her very youth, even her defiance of the despising world that tampered with her sex and stamped her face with Im‑ possible beauty. Struggling through the crowd toward her, I said: "Kathy. . . . Kathy."

"Yes, baby?"

"Why are you smiling?"

"Because," she said easily, "Im going to die."

"Babe, I'd like to eat you," said the man in the ballet tights at Les Deux Freres.

"I dare you," I challenged.

"You do?"

"I dare you," I repeated.

"Right here?"

"I dare you—right here," I said, laughing, feeling out of control. He slid on his knees. He opens my fly, begins to go down on me in the thronged bar. And they started daring each other, and a youngman dressed only in a striped bikini pushed his trunks to his knees and stood there waiting, and immediately there was someone pressing behind him and someone squatting in front.

I leaned groggily against the bar looking down at the bob‑ bing head between my legs.

Strangely, illogically—like a shadowy movie cut indis‑ criminately without logical order, I remember living next to the Y in Los Angeles, where I sunbathed on the roof of that apartment building, and by signals from the residents of the Y, I would meet them later on the street. . . . I remember Griffith Park—the hill where you could make it hidden by trees. . . . I remember the police, the many roustings, finger‑ printings, interrogations: the cops, the rival gang—the enemy: the world. . . . Laguna Beach, the sand drifting into the bar. Lance . . . poised on a cliff. . . . *And I remember a Texas sky*. . . . I remember a party where three of us turned on with marijuana in the locked head, and I remember the indiscrim‑ inate partners, later, outside in the yard. . . . Remembering a man on the Boulevard who picked me up, who paid me to tell him what the others I had been with had done; and as he listened, he tried to conceal the fact that he was pulling off. . . . *That sky recalled from a childhood in gray, gray shades.* . . . I remember a steambath and the naked bodies pacing hungrily along the hallways, the sudden entrances and exits into the tiny cubicles; and, in the phosphorescent grayness, like nameless bodies in a morgue. . . . I think of St Louis Cemetery in this city, the stark graves above the Waiting ground. . . . *And the wind had swept that sky, coming in a steelgray cloud.* . . . I think of the beach in Chicago, deserted except for the maleshadows hugging the cold walls. And I remember the FASCINATION sign in New York. . . . In Dallas—remembering—the doors of rooms left open at the Y and the steamy intimacy in the showers. . . . I imagine Miss Destiny storming heaven, protesting to God, shaking her beads. . . . Remembering Sylvia, I think: And she slaughtered her son and he slaughtered her because they each had to. . . . And I remember: *Out of that Window during that windstorm which is now howling again in my mind, I watched a tree bend with the wind.* . . . Something searched, its fulfillment hinted by the fact that the heart craves it—but not to be found. Not found. And the heart weakens and resists even hope. . . . Twas the night before Ash Wednesday and All Through The City— . . . I remembered someone in San Francisco who had followed me and someone else to an apartment, and later I looked out the window and saw the man who had followed us still waiting, looking up forlornly to where we were, his hands in his pockets. . . . *Finally, the wind had lashed furiously at the tree, tearing off the branches, which had hinted of spring.* . . . *And the dust rose, coming from the orange horizon, settling on my mind.*

Dregs of memories churn.

Remembering. . . .

This:

Once, walking along Hollywood Boulevard in the afternoon, I saw a woman coming out of Kress's: a wild gypsy-looking old woman, like a fugitive from a movie-set—she was dark, screamingly painted . . . kaleidoscopic earrings . . . a red and orange scarf about her long black hair . . . wide blue skirt, lowcut blouse—an old frantic woman with demented burning eyes, and as she stepped into the bright Hollywood street, this old flashy woman began a series of the same strange gestures:

her right hand would rise frantically over her eyes, as if to tear some horrible spectacle from her sight. But halfway down, toward her breast, the gesture of her hand mellowed, slowed, lost its franticness. . . . And she seemed now instead to be blessing the terrible spectacle she had first tried to tear from her sight. . . .

Stupidly, now, I raised my hand as if to imitate that woman's benediction.

Then smash!
Smash! Smash! Smash!
The world collapsed.
And it happened exactly like this:
Suddenly, in one moment—*in one single solitary crazy one-unit moment*, I was both drunk and sober: I was two people. And the sober me was looking on at the drunk me, and it's terrifying to see yourself so beaten and scared. Soberly and clearly I saw myself drunk—drunk worth all those days and nights of determined sobriety. And I saw myself folded over vomiting in the head of The Rocking Times; and I knew it was happening, that the nightworld was caving in—because the terror of a lifetime can be contained in one inexplicable moment. And why that moment? I dont know. But it was *then.*

It was then that the ugly tortured world whirled. It was then that a perimeter of black surrounded the area of my sight, closed in swiftly, heavily, darkly.

And it was then that the sober me saw the drunk me reel to the floor and fall. Felt the drunk laughter like cotton in my mouth choking.

It's Ash Wednesday.
Im out on the streets.
There are only a few stray people, some foreheads smeared with ashes. The city is strangely quiet. It's late night.
The demons, the clowns are gone.
After the smothering black-out, I remember—only hazily, as if my mind had been rubbed over with an imperfect eraser —waking up on a cot in a back room of Sylvia's boarded-up bar where we had taken Sonny that afternoon. Others were still passed out about me when I walked out. I remember walking the streets of the Lenten city, away from the Quarter.
Now, too tired to walk any farther, I enter an all-night moviehouse. The air is excessively hot. Derelicts sleep on the

floor. I slump on a wooden seat. A few rows away, I see
Sonny, dejectedly asleep: deserted. The two scores are no
longer with him.

I close my eyes. I try to sleep. But I cant. Because when I
close my eyes, that recurrent nightmare I had had as a very
little boy comes again: And Im being crushed by wooden
stones, over which theres a thin, flimsy veil. I try to push
them away. But even when I open my eyes, the stones keep
crushing me, the veil melting like wax over my face.

Finally it was gone.

Sleep is coming—not that slow entering into a state of momentary beinglessness. No. It was as if for a long, long time
I struggle to open an enormous black door—beyond which I
shut myself at last in sleep.

Wide awake suddenly, I opened my eyes.

I saw three cockroaches crawling on my arm.

And in the flickering light of the movie, I looked down on
a man squatting before me on the floor, his hungry hot hands
on my thighs, his moist lips glued to the opening of my pants.

The first church I telephoned was St Patrick's. "I cant see
you," said the priest, "not until morning, we're closed now."
And he hung up. I called St Louis Cathedral. "I cant see you
—of course not—I get these calls all the time." A third one—
and I said hurriedly: "Dont hang up, Father. Ive got to talk
to someone!" And he listened only a few moments. "You must
be drunk," he said angrily, and he hung up. And I called The
Church of Eternal Succor, and I called other churches—
and they all said: "No." "Go to sleep." "Come tomorrow to
the confessional." (Where life doesnt roar so loudly—in
whispers, it can be listened to. . . .) "Some time else." "When
we are open." One even said: "God bless you," before he hung
up.

And I was experiencing that only Death, which is the
symbolic death of the soul. It's the death of the soul, not of
the body—it's that which creates ghosts, and in those moments
I felt myself becoming a ghost, drained of all that makes this
journey to achieve some kind of salvation bearable under the
universal sentence of death. And the body becomes cold because the heart and the soul, about to give up, are screaming
for sustenance—from any source, even a remote voice on a
telephone—and they drain the body in order to support
themselves for that one last moment before the horror comes
stifling out that already-dying spark.

And I was thinking that although there is no God, never was a God, and never will be One—considering the world He made, it is possible to understand Him—or that part of Him that had forbidden Knowing, because—Christ!—at that moment I longed for innocence more than for anything else, and I would have thrown away all the frantic knowing for a return to a state of Grace—which is only the state of, *idiot-like,* Not Knowing.

I called one more church. St Vincent de Paul.

And a priest who sounded very young answered, and he didnt hang up and he was the one I had tried to reach, I knew, and he spoke to me and spoke—and I can remember only one thing he said—and the rest doesnt matter because all I had wanted was to hear a voice from a childhood in the wind. . . . And what I do remember that priest saying is merely this:

"I know," he said. *"Yes, I know."*

And I returned to El Paso.

Here, by another window, I'll look back on the world and I'll try to understand. . . . But, perhaps, mysteriously, it's all beyond reasons. Perhaps it's as futile as trying to capture the wind.

And it's windy here now.

No matter how you close the windows or pull the curtains or try to hide from it or shelter yourself from it, it's there. It's impossible to escape the Wind. You can still hear it shrieking. You always know it's there. Waiting.

And I know it will wait patiently for me, ineluctably, when inevitably I'll leave this city again.

And what has been found?

Nothing.

A circle which winds around, without beginning, without end.

The clouds are storming angrily across the orange-gray sky. They rush at each other as if to battle. You know how it is in Texas each year before spring. One moment theres the stunning awareness that soon spring is coming, with the yellow-green clusters of leaves budding on the skeleton trees, hinting of a potential revival—soon, soon.

And the next moment the fierce wind comes screaming, whirling the needle-pointed dust, stifling all hope. And you know then that what has not happened will never happen. That hope is an end within itself.

And the fierce wind is an echo of angry childhood and of a very scared boy looking out the window—remembering my dead dog outside by the wounded house as the gray Texas dust gradually covered her up—and thinking:

It isnt fair! *Why cant dogs go to Heaven?*

Selected Fiction
Available from Grove Weidenfeld

___ WHALE	0-8021-1100-9	Abbey, Lloyd THE LAST WHALES	$19.95
___ BLOOD	0-8021-3193-X	Acker, Kathy BLOOD AND GUTS IN HIGH SCHOOL	9.95
___ EMPIR	0-8021-3179-4	Acker, Kathy EMPIRE OF THE SENSELESS	$7.95
___ CHATT	0-8021-0041-4	Ackroyd, Peter CHATTERTON	$17.95
___ FIRLIG	0-8021-1161-0	Ackroyd, Peter FIRST LIGHT	$19.95
___ SKULL	0-8021-1000-2	Aitmatov, Chingiz THE PLACE OF THE SKULL	$20.95
___ FADO	1-55584-343-3	Antunes, Antonio Lobo FADO ALEXANDRINO	$22.50
___ FORSIN	1-55584-318-2	Appelfeld, Aharon FOR EVERY SIN	$15.95
___ ROSA	0-8021-1092-4	Arenas, Reinaldo OLD ROSA	$16.95
___ TWOAGA	1-55584-214-3	Barthelme, Frederick TWO AGAINST ONE	$17.95
___ LOST	0-8021-3092-5	Beckett, Samuel THE LOST ONES	$8.95
___ BECK3	0-8021-5091-8	Beckett, Samuel THREE NOVELS (Molloy; Malone Dies; and The Unnamable)	$9.95
___ DRAMA	0-8021-3122-0	Biely, Andrei THE DRAMATIC SYMPHONY	$7.95
___ STPETE	0-8021-3158-1	Biely, Andrey ST. PETERSBURG	$9.95
___ ONHER	0-8021-1130-0	Bliven, Naomi ON HER OWN	$19.95
___ FICCI	0-8021-3030-5	Borges, Jorge Luis FICCIONES	$6.95
___ PERSO	0-8021-3077-1	Borges, Jorge Luis A PERSONAL ANTHOLOGY	$8.95
___ MASTER	0-8021-3011-9	Bulgakov, Mikhail THE MASTER AND MARGARITA	$7.95
___ NAKED	0-8021-3093-3	Burroughs, William S. NAKED LUNCH	$6.95
___ AGE	1-55584-371-9	Calisher, Hortense AGE	$6.95
___ KISSI	1-55584-194-5	Calisher, Hortense KISSING COUSINS	$14.95
___ PARAD	1-55584-279-8	Castedo, Elena PARADISE	$18.95
___ CLOSE	0-8021-1093-2	Cooper, Dennis CLOSER	$15.95
___ THUS	0-8021-1077-0	De Crescenzo, Luciano THUS SPAKE BELLAVISTA	$17.95
___ SODOM	0-8021-3012-7	De Sade, The Marquis THE 120 DAYS OF SODOM AND OTHER WRITINGS	$16.95
___ 3EXEMP	0-8021-5153-1	De Unamuno, Miguel THREE EXEMPLARY NOVELS	$7.95
___ CURFEW	1-55584-448-0	Donoso, Jose CURFEW	$9.95
___ OURS	1-55584-281-X	Dovlatov, Sergei OURS	$15.95
___ DURAS	0-8021-5111-6	Duras, Marguerite FOUR NOVELS (The Summer Square; 10:30 on a Summer Night; The Afternoon of Mr. Andesmas; Moderato Cantabile)	$10.95
___ HIROS	0-8021-3104-2	Duras, Marguerite HIROSHIMA, MON AMOUR	$7.95
___ CITIZ	0-8021-3064-X	Fast, Howard CITIZEN TOM PAINE	$10.95
___ CAMBO	0-8021-1082-7	Fawcett, Brian CAMBODIA	$16.95
___ MIRAC	0-8021-3088-7	Genet, Jean THE MIRACLE OF THE ROSE	$10.95
___ WHIJAC	1-55584-049-3	Hawkes, John WHISTLEJACKET	$17.95
___ MEXBLU	0-8021-3060-7	Kerouac, Jack MEXICO CITY BLUES	$10.95
___ SUBTER	0-8021-3186-7	Kerouac, Jack THE SUBTERRANEANS	$6.95
___ NOTEB	0-8021-1024-X	Kristof, Agota THE NOTEBOOK	$15.95
___ ARTNO	0-8021-0011-2	Kundera, Milan THE ART OF THE NOVEL	$17.95
___ LADY	0-8021-3068-2	Lawrence, D.H. LADY CHATTERLEY'S LOVER	$3.95
___ EQUAL	1-55584-202-X	Leavitt, David EQUAL AFFECTIONS	$18.95
___ MONK	0-8021-5107-8	Lewis, Matthew THE MONK	$15.95
___ MOON	0-8021-1027-4	Lively, Penelope MOON TIGER	$15.95
___ PACK	0-8021-1156-4	Lively, Penelope PACK OF CARDS	$19.95
___ WILDAM	0-8021-1106-8	Loader, Jayne WILD AMERICA	$17.95
___ CONFE	1-55584-143-0	Lukacs, John CONFESSIONS OF AN ORIGINAL SINNER	$18.95
___ LAZAR	0-394-17068-7	Malraux, Andre LAZARUS	$2.95
___ SPRING	0-8021-3182-4	Miller, Henry BLACK SPRING	$9.95
___ JASMI	0-8021-1032-0	Mukherjee, Bharati JASMINE	$17.95
___ MIDDLE	0-8021-1031-2	Mukherjee, Bharati THE MIDDLEMAN AND OTHER STORIES	$16.95

Selections from Grove Weidenfeld (continued)

___ HOMTHO	0-8021-1035-5	Parks, Tim HOME THOUGHTS	$16.95
___ CITY	0-8021-3083-6	Rechy, John CITY OF NIGHT	$7.95
___ OUTLAW	0-8021-3163-8	Rechy, John THE SEXUAL OUTLAW	$9.95
___ ERASE	0-8021-5086-1	Robbe-Grillet, Alain THE ERASERS	$12.95
___ GHOMIR	0-8021-1036-3	Robbe-Grillet, Alain GHOSTS IN THE MIRROR	$16.95
___ JEALAB	0-8021-5106-X	Robbe-Grillet, Alain TWO NOVELS (Jealousy and In the Labyrinth)	$8.95
___ PEDRO	0-8021-3119-0	Rulfo, Juan PEDRO PARAMO	$4.95
___ STALI	0-8021-0018-X	Ruta, Suzanne STALIN IN THE BRONX AND OTHER STORIES	$16.95
___ PRINC	0-8021-3144-1	Sainz, Gustavo THE PRINCESS OF THE IRON PALACE	$9.95
___ EXIT	0-8021-3137-9	Selby, Hubert LAST EXIT TO BROOKLYN	$9.95
___ PALAC	1-55584-068-X	Shahar, David THE PALACE OF SHATTERED VESSELS	$22.50
___ TEMPL	0-8021-1057-6	Spender, Stephen THE TEMPLE	$15.95
___ POCZA	0-8021-1140-8	Szczypiorski, Andrzej THE BEAUTIFUL MRS. SEIDENMAN	$18.95
___ DUNCE	0-8021-3020-8	Toole, John Kennedy A CONFEDERACY OF DUNCES	$9.95
___ NEON	0-8021-1108-4	Toole, John Kennedy THE NEON BIBLE	$15.95
___ BUSHGH	0-8021-3105-0	Tutuola, Amos MY LIFE IN BUSH OF GHOSTS	$9.95
___ PALM	0-8021-5048-9	Tutuola, Amos THE PALM-WINE DRINKARD	$5.95
___ MONKE	0-8021-3086-0	Waley, Arthur (trans.) MONKEY	$11.95
___ THIS	1-55584-368-9	Williams, Diane THIS IS ABOUT THE BODY, THE MIND, THE SOUL, THE WORLD, TIME, AND FATE	$15.95
___ TERRA	1-55584-165-1	Womack, Jack TERRAPLANE	$16.95

TO ORDER DIRECTLY FROM GROVE WEIDENFELD:

YES! Please send me the books selected above.

Telephone orders—credit card only: 1-800-937-5557.

Mail orders: Please include $1.50 postage and handling, plus $.50 for each additional book, or credit card information requested below.

Send to: Grove Weidenfeld
 IPS
 1113 Heil Quaker Boulevard
 P.O. Box 7001
 La Vergne, TN 37086-7001

☐ I have enclosed $_____ (check or money order only)

☐ Please charge my Visa/MasterCard card account (circle one).

Card Number _____

Expiration Date _____

Signature _____

Name _____

Address _____ Apt. _____

City _____ State _____ Zip _____

Please allow 4–6 weeks for delivery.
Please note that prices are subject to change without notice.
For additional information, catalogues or bulk sales inquiries, please call 1-800-937-5557.   ADCD